WAILING AND GNASHING OF TEETH

RAY GARTON

This book is for two of my dearest friends

Steven Spruill and Karen Leonard

Thank you for everything you've brought to my life.
I love you both dearly.

And as always, this book is for my wife Dawn,
who helped lead me out of the darkness
and keeps me in the light.

Contents

Wailing and Gnashing of Teeth 1

Graven Image 25

God's Work 68

Choices 94

Monsters 121

Sinema 275

Punishments 327

Introduction

Religion is a touchy subject. That's why I have come to avoid it in conversation. When I was growing up, *everybody* avoided religion in conversation. Politics, as well. At some point, though, that changed and suddenly all anyone wants to talk about is the kind of stuff we used to avoid talking about in order to keep some peace. I have gone back to avoiding the subjects, but at times that's difficult to do because some people like to talk about their religion and their politics. A lot. If you've visited the internet lately, you know that many people have come totally unhinged over religion and politics. And if you look at the events of the world in recent decades, a lot of people are willing, even eager, to *kill* for their religion.

But even though I carefully avoid religion as a conversation topic, I have put together a collection of all my religious horror stories. I didn't do it to piss people off, I did it because I realized that over the last thirty years I had written enough horror stories involving religion to fill a book. So, I did. (I've also written enough horror stories involving house pets to fill a book, so that's probably coming next.)

My personal experience with religion has not been pleasant. I was raised a Seventh-day Adventist, a pseudo-Christian cult that condemns the reading of any kind of fiction whatsoever, and I'm a horror novelist. As you can imagine, that's not a good mix. Some but not all of the stories in this collection are set within the Seventh-day Adventist subculture or on its fringes because, having grown up and been educated in it, that is the sect with which I am most familiar.

I do not have a vendetta against the Seventh-day Adventist church, I'm not angry or bitter, and I do not hate Christians or any other people of faith. Those are accusations that were thrown around pretty liberally back when I was more vocal about religion, and especially when *Wailing and Gnashing of Teeth* was first released as a limited-edition hardcover from Cemetery Dance Publications. The Seventh-day Adventist subculture is a tight one, very insular, and I not only grew up in it, I went through the long, unpleasant, and extremely difficult task of removing myself from it, and it from me. Naturally, all of that has had an influence on my writing, just as all life experiences influence the work of any writer. (I've had a lot of house pets over the years, too, which is why they show up in my work. Nobody seems to mind that, though. Except when I kill one of them, of course. Then I get angry letters.)

Wailing and Gnashing of Teeth was published in 2012 as a promotional item for the Cemetery Dance Collectors Club and there were only enough printed for the club members, which came to 773 copies. For the reprint, I've added two stories that were not available to be included in the original edition, "Graven Image" and "God's Work."

These stories go all the way back to 1988 when my novella "Monsters" appeared in *Night Visions 6*, edited by Dean R. Koontz (published as *The Bone Yard* in paperback), and when "Sinema" appeared in David J. Schow's memorable movie-themed anthology *Silver Scream*. "Punishments" was originally published in *Hot Blood: Tales of Provocative Horror* edited by Jeff Gelb and Lonn Friend, the first in a long and popular series of anthologies. "God's Work" and "Choices" debuted in my 1996 collection *Pieces of Hate*. "Graven Image" was published by Cemetery Dance Publications as a hardcover chapbook in 2007. The book kicks off with a brand-new story, "Wailing and Gnashing of Teeth," which appears for the first time anywhere in this collection.

The title is a phrase that pops up now and then in the Bible, usually in reference to the day of judgment when God throws all the bad people into the furnace of eternal punishment. Seventh-day Adventists are big on the last days, the end times, whatever you want to call them. I grew up under the dark shadow of the coming time of trouble that would lead up to the second coming of Jesus Christ. It plays a big part in the Adventist belief system and is described vividly in the church's literature—and to the church's tender-minded little children. I grew up in fear of it. I first heard the phrase "wailing and gnashing of teeth" in that context when I was very small, and, not knowing exactly what "gnashing" meant, I imagined people being so insane with terror that they tore out their own teeth, so that when Jesus took them all up to heaven, nobody would have a tooth in their heads. All those beautiful, shimmering angels floating in the clouds blowing their trumpets of gold, all basking in the blinding light of the throne of God—and here come the toothless earthlings. The phrase has finally bubbled up in my writing.

Whether or not you are a religious believer, I hope you enjoy the stories that follow.

Now, let's open our hymnals and sing together....

Wailing and Gnashing of Teeth

"Train up a child in the way he should go: and when he is old he will not depart from it."

Proverbs 22:6

Margaret Steensma's front yard was immaculately groomed and neat. Shrubs were squarely trimmed, brilliant red and yellow roses flourished, and tall day lilies gleamed a virginal white. The mailbox out front was a miniature red barn with a golden rooster on top, head tipped back as if to crow. Hummingbirds hovered at the feeder that hung at the edge of the small covered porch. The rest of the yards on Train Street were untended and overgrown or dead and empty, the houses dark and run down. But Margaret's Steensma's cream-colored house with yellow trim looked like a cottage in a fairy tale.

As Lauren Sutherland walked up the front steps, Margaret pushed open the squeaky screen door and stepped out onto the porch with a big smile.

1

"You must be Lauren," she said in a high, chirpy voice. She was a small woman, slightly hunched, with full, curly, silver hair fresh from the beauty parlor and a pair of tortoise-shell glasses perched on her little nose. She wore a bright yellow and green dress and looked ready for church, although it was Tuesday. Lauren suspected that her bright smile had never changed over the decades. She would have looked no different had Norman Rockwell painted her.

"Hello, Mrs. Steensma," Lauren said.

"Oh, please, honey, call me Madge. That's what people have been calling me since I was a girl. And that's a long, long time, believe me. Come inside and get out of this heat. I made ice tea and cookies."

Inside, the house smelled of freshly baked cookies and potpourri. The living room was as neat and orderly as the front yard. Over the fireplace hung a painting of a rugged looking Jesus Christ holding a lamb in his arms and stroking it with a nail-scarred hand. There were family photographs everywhere—pictures of Madge and her late husband Wyatt and the subject of Lauren's visit, their only child, Leroy Arthur Steensma.

Lauren had sat alone in her apartment rehearsing the way she would begin her interview with Mrs. Steensma. Knowing it would be a tough subject for the old woman to discuss, she wanted to get the ball rolling in a way that would put her at ease. Madge knew what the focus of the interview would be, but still, Lauren did not want to make it any more difficult than it was already. The poor woman was all alone at 82. It was bad enough that her son had killed her husband, but he had also killed 14 other people, a few of them children. Years had passed, of course, and maybe time really did heal all wounds...but how did someone get over *that*?

2

"Come into the kitchen," Madge said. "It's sunnier in there and I've set out our family albums for you to look through."

It was indeed bright and sunny in the kitchen. A table in the corner stood between two large windows with yellow curtains. A pitcher of iced tea, a plate of cookies, two glasses and some napkins awaited them. One of the three chairs at the table held a stack of photo albums.

"Please take a seat and have some tea," Madge said, going to the table ahead of her. She poured tea into the glasses, then seated herself. Her smile never faltered and she seemed so eager to please that Lauren couldn't help smiling herself. "You're much younger than I expected," Madge said as Lauren sat down. "Do you mind if I ask how old you are?"

"I just turned 25." She slipped the strap of her bag off her shoulder and put it on the floor beside the chair.

"Oh, my. And you're already writing for a national magazine. Your parents must be terribly proud."

They talked for a little while about Lauren's work, her family and childhood. When Lauren mentioned how beautiful Madge's yard was, the old woman explained that her nephew's son, who had a green thumb, came over once a week and tended it. Finally, after about fifteen minutes of small talk, Madge said, "I suppose you're anxious to get to your questions."

"I don't want to rush you, Madge," Lauren said, taking the small digital recorder from her purse and putting it on the table. She took her folder of notes from the bag as well and opened it before her. "We'll do this at your pace. I want to make sure you're comfortable."

"Oh, you don't have to worry about me, dear. At my age, nothing much bothers me anymore. And if something does, I'll tell you. Politely, of course. I may be old, but I still have manners." She winked.

For weeks, Lauren had been carefully researching the case of Leroy Arthur Steensma. She had read every newspaper and magazine story, every police and coroner's report, everything she could find. She had read sensational true crime books that detailed his killings in ways that were almost loving. She had watched half a dozen documentaries and a made-for-TV movie about the case, and even a straight-to-video horror film loosely based on Steensma's killings. Nowhere in any of that material was there an interview with Steensma's mother. It seemed a natural to Lauren and she could not understand why no one had done it. According to her reading on the subject, experts agreed that serial killers were formed very early in life, during childhood. Why wouldn't anyone talk to Steensma's mother to see what he had been like as a boy and find out what events or environmental conditions might have contributed to the monster he became later? Lauren had pitched the idea to her editor and he had given her the green light.

She did not expect any revelations. Madge was not likely to have an objective view of her son's childhood. What parent would? Or could? But Lauren thought there might be some clues as to why Leroy had grown into such a vicious serial killer who had done such awful things to his victims, even if she had to read between the lines to see them.

"You want to talk about my son," Madge said. "I'm ready to do that."

Lauren turned on the recorder. "What was he like as a boy, Madge?"

"Oh, he was such an angel when he was small," she said, taking the top photo album off the stack and putting it on the table. She opened it and looked for a particular page. "I know that's hard to believe now, but when you see him—here he is. Look at him. Such a beautiful little child." She turned the album around so Lauren could see it and pointed at a photo. "There he is with his pet pigeon. It was so funny—that pigeon loved him. Whenever Leroy was in the back yard, the pigeon would come see him and land on his head. Doesn't he look sweet here?"

In the photo, a toddler with shiny blond hair stood in the sun with a gray-and-white pigeon perched on his left arm. The child's arms were spread and his round face was contorted in a look of abject terror. His eyes were sad below eyebrows that knotted in the center and slanted downward on the outsides.

"The following year, that pigeon just stopped showing up," Madge said. "We thought a hawk might have gotten him because we found some feathers in the back yard one day that looked like they might have been his. There were a lot of hawks around in those days. Not so much anymore."

Madge took a sip of tea, then turned the page in the photo album and pointed to another picture. "There he is at the Christmas parade in…oh, I'm not sure what year that was. He must have been about six or seven years old."

Once again, Leroy looked both frightened and sad as he stood beside a little man dressed as an elf. Christmas lights glowed in the background. Leroy looked fleshier than in the previous photograph. His tense eyebrows again slanted downward at the outer ends. The flesh around Leroy's left eye was a little puffy and slightly discolored.

"Did he hurt himself?" Lauren asked.

Madge frowned as she turned the album around then squinted at the picture. "Oh, yes, I guess he has a little bruise." She smiled as she pushed the album back over to Lauren. "Poor Leroy was a terribly clumsy boy. Always falling off of things, tripping over his own feet. I never let him carry around anything breakable because it was a sure bet he'd drop it. He just wasn't very coordinated. He wasn't at all athletic and avoided participating in sports whenever possible. He was even that way as an adult, poor fellow."

Madge turned the page again.

"This is Leroy in a school play. I think he was in the fifth grade at the time. The play was a re-enactment of the bible story of Shadrach, Meshach and Abednego. I don't remember who Leroy played, but he's giving a little monologue here."

Leroy stood center stage in costume, facing the audience. He had put on more weight—his cheeks were rounder, his belly more prominent—but still somehow looked small on that stage. He stood with his mouth open, right arm outstretched to emphasize a point he was making. Even at the distance from which the photograph had been taken, Lauren could see that same sadness and fear in his face.

"I still have that costume," she said. "I've kept everything over the years. Everything. I guess that makes me a pack rat. But I'm a sentimental pack rat." Madge pointed to a picture on the opposite page and said, "Here we are on a camping trip. Wyatt loved to go camping. Leroy wasn't as fond of it as his father, but he tried to go along with it. The woods scared him."

In the photo, Madge and Wyatt stood together in front of a green tent, and in front of them stood Leroy. Madge's blonde hair reached her shoulders, her face free of wrinkles, eyes bright. Lauren had been right about her smile—it had not changed over the decades. Beside her, Wyatt stood unsmiling, his face stern, dark brown hair short and parted on the side, eyes narrowed slightly, chin jutting to one side. Standing before them, Leroy wore that sad expression, eyebrows slanting downward on the outer ends, lips pressed tightly together, shoulders slumped as if in resignation. In his slightly too-wide eyes, there was some fear. His blond hair was combed exactly like his father's. He looked worried and afraid and had grown quite chubby.

"Leroy and his father didn't get along?" Lauren asked.

"Well…" Her smile faded for the first time and she squinted behind her glasses as if gazing back in time. "At the time, it seemed normal to me. You know, a boy pushing against the dominance of his father. We're all rebellious at heart, being born into sin as we are. We resist authority. That's been our problem since the Garden of Eden. Leroy was…" She took a long moment to find the right word. "…*resistant*. Yes, that's the right word. He was resistant to his father. But I didn't see anything unusual in it. He was such a happy boy, I thought that was just a normal…*boy* thing."

Leroy certainly did not look happy in any of the photographs Lauren had seen so far, but photographs could be deceptive in that way. The camera captured a split-second expression that might have passed over one's face in the blink of an eye; it did not necessarily represent the emotional state of the photograph's subject. But so far, Leroy had the same expression in every picture.

"How did your husband feel about it?" Lauren said.

"Wyatt was often frustrated. He worked very hard. He was at the paper mill for many years until he hurt his back and had to have surgery. Then he had to go on disability. While he was working, when he came home from a long day at work, he didn't need more frustration from Leroy. Then, after the surgery, he was home all the time. That alone frustrated him even more and made him more impatient with Leroy. I tried to intervene and take care of Leroy myself so Wyatt wouldn't have to deal with him. He just…" A look of sadness passed over her face. "Wyatt just seemed so…disappointed in him. We named him after our fathers—Leroy was Wyatt's father's name and Arthur was my father's name. Wyatt's dad was such a big bear of a man, so…masculine. He was physically active his whole life, a carpenter, he could build or fix anything. I think Wyatt was hoping that Leroy would be more like his own father. But…he wasn't. Leroy was very quiet and bookish. He kept to himself. Too much, I think. He seemed happiest when left alone with a book or watching TV. I wish we'd never gotten a TV. I think it had far too much influence on Leroy and I think it was the source of all our problems."

"He liked to watch TV?"

"Oh, yes. Much too much. He liked cartoons and anything with puppets, and that wasn't so bad. But he also liked horror movies and science fiction shows. I knew nothing good could come of that, and so did Wyatt. We prohibited it at first." She frowned slightly. "But it seemed to make him so *happy*. Finally, we gave in. We let him watch the shows he wanted to watch, but we always pointed out the dangers in that kind of entertainment. We never failed to remind him that it was not what Christ wanted us to dwell on. I would often ask him, 'Would you be watching that if Jesus were standing here in this room?'"

"What did he say?"

She shrugged. "He just ignored me."

"Did Leroy do well in school?"

Madge nodded. "His grades were very good. We sent him to a Christian school, of course. The new one that started just two years before Leroy was old enough to go to school. We wanted him to be around other Christians and to get a Christian education. We were afraid public school would only confuse him. You know, the drugs, the sex, the secular teachings."

Lauren consulted her notes. "That would be…Lawncrest Christian Academy?"

"Yes."

Frowning down at the pages before her, Lauren said, "There was a scandal at that school, wasn't there? It was years ago, but apparently a teacher had been molesting students."

Madge bowed her head a moment, cleared her throat and sighed. "Yes. All of that came to a head when Leroy was in, um…let's see, I think he was in the third grade. It was…very sad. It's always been such a good school, but that hurt its reputation."

"Was Leroy affected by that in any way?"

"He certainly didn't seem to be. They kept it as quiet as possible. We all figured the less the students knew about it, the better. But the local press got hold of the story, and then there was a brief period when it was reported nationally. Fortunately, it all blew over very quickly. Uh, you asked if Leroy did well in school. Leroy's grades were always excellent, but he had trouble making friends. He was so terribly shy. I think that was the problem. I tried to encourage him to break out of his shell, but…" She frowned and gazed at the plate of cookies for a while.

"What's wrong?" Lauren said.

"Well, I wish Wyatt had been more supportive. He was often quite…critical of Leroy. I think that hurt the boy. But…oh, I shouldn't say anything." She squeezed her eyes shut and shook her head abruptly. "It's wrong of me to speak negatively of Wyatt."

"I don't want you to discuss anything that makes you uncomfortable, but at the same time, Madge, I want you to speak your mind."

Madge sighed. "Wyatt was a bit hard on Leroy at times, that's all. His method of discipline could be a bit…harsh." She winced, as if simply saying the words caused her pain. "There were so many times I wanted to say something, but it just wasn't my place. The bible is very clear on the family order. In the book of Titus, women are told 'to be discreet, chaste, keepers at home, good, obedient to their husbands'—and it would have been wrong of me to step in."

"Was Wyatt…physical with Leroy?"

"At times, yes. Leroy would push him. Intentionally, I think. Sometimes Leroy would become silent and wouldn't say a word, no matter what we said to him. Wyatt would ask him something but he wouldn't respond. Wyatt would repeat his question again and again and he'd get angrier each time Leroy didn't answer."

"Was it a regular thing?"

"Leroy's obstinance? Yes, I'm afraid so."

"No, I mean Wyatt's physical discipline. Was that a regular thing?"

"Oh. Well…he was only doing what the bible instructed. 'He that spareth his rod hateth his son, but he that loveth him chasteneth him betimes.' That's what Proverbs tells us. He didn't want Leroy to become spoiled, that's all. He wanted him to be tough, prepared for the troubles of life. And if he went a little too far sometimes…well, we're all human. We all fall short of the glory of God."

"In what way did he go too far?"

"Oh…" She shrugged one shoulder as she fidgeted slightly in her chair. "Sometimes he would spank him a little too hard, a little too long. Sometimes he used the belt, and he'd get a little carried away. But like I said, Leroy often pushed him. He sometimes brought it on himself. Leroy could be so rebellious and obstinate."

"What would he do that set off your husband?"

"All kinds of things. He was always asking questions, especially when he was younger. We had a family worship every night. We'd read from the Bible and discuss it, and then have prayer. Sometimes, Leroy would keep interrupting with questions."

"What kind of questions?"

"About whatever Bible story we were studying. He was never satisfied with the story as it was told in the Bible. He wanted all the details filled in and all his questions answered or he just wasn't satisfied. It was very frustrating. I remember one time we were going over the story of Lot and his family. You know, the story of Sodom and Gomorrah. When the angry mob of men gathers outside Lot's house and demands that he turn the visiting angels over to them, Lot offers them his daughters instead. That bothered Leroy. He kept insisting that Lot couldn't be a very righteous man if he was willing to hand his daughters over to those bad, angry men. But of course, the Bible *says* that God found Lot to be a righteous man. Leroy wouldn't stop. He just kept interrupting to say that it didn't make any sense. Wyatt told him that this wasn't just any old book off the shelf we were dealing with, it was the *Bible*, the word of *God*, and he told Leroy he was in no position to argue with it. But Leroy wouldn't stop. And after a while, Wyatt got angry. He'd had enough. He punished Leroy."

"Was Leroy always that way when it came to religion?" Lauren asked.

Madge frowned. "He ran hot and cold with religion. He was very active in church. In fact—" She reached over and began turning pages in the open photo album. "—he used to give special music performances for church. He had a beautiful voice when he was a boy. Sang like an angel. In church, at weddings. He was the youngest member of the church choir. Here." She pointed to a picture and said, "There he is singing in church."

Leroy stood on the church dais before a microphone, his mouth open, head tilted back slightly. There was that sad look again—the eyebrows bunched together above the bridge of his nose and tilting downward at the outer ends. He was quite plump in his blue suit, hair neatly combed with a straight part on the left.

11

"How old was he here?" Lauren asked.

"Oh, probably about nine or ten. He was very active in Sunday school and church and sometimes, he seemed to enjoy it very much. But other times...I don't know, it almost seemed to make him...sad. As if it upset him. And he had all those questions, so many questions. When he was small, sometimes it even scared him. But then, nearly everything scared him. For some reason—and I've never quite understood why—he was a frightened child. I think those horror movies he watched on TV caused it."

"Frightened? Of what?"

Madge leaned forward and put her elbows on the table. Her hands fidgeted with each other for a moment, then she took a cookie from the plate and bit into it, then placed it on a napkin. She raised her eyebrows high as she chewed, shrugged her shoulders and said, "Of almost *everything*, it seemed."

"I don't understand."

"Neither did I," she said. "I remember one of our Bible studies here at home. He was pretty little, maybe in the first grade, something like that. We were on the story of Abraham and Isaac. I've always thought it was a beautiful story, a precursor to God sacrificing his own son to save us all from our sins. But Leroy didn't like that story, not at all. God tells Abraham to sacrifice his son Isaac and naturally, Abraham obeys God without question. He takes the boy to the altar, binds him and raises the knife to kill him—and Leroy screamed. Nearly scared both of us to death. He wouldn't stop. Wyatt had to shout at him and shake him a little before he finally quieted down, but he was still crying. He was terribly upset. We asked him why, and he said that Abraham was a bad man for trying to kill his son. Wyatt explained that God had *told* Abraham to sacrifice Isaac but had stopped him at the last moment, that God was just testing his faith and obedience. Leroy shouted, 'Then

God is *mean*!' Oh, that made Wyatt so angry. He did not like any disrespectful use of God's name, but to say that God was *mean*...oh, no, he did not like that one bit. He warned Leroy never to say such a thing. And Leroy said, 'But he *is*! Only a mean person would want that to happen to a little boy!'"

Frowning slightly, Lauren said, "Do you think Leroy identified with Isaac?"

Madge frowned and cocked her head to one side. She thought about that a moment. "Hmm. Maybe he did. That hadn't occurred to me. Whatever the reason, it upset Wyatt a great deal and he punished Leroy."

Lauren wanted to ask *how* Wyatt punished the boy, but Madge kept talking and she did not want to interrupt.

"Leroy was always doing things like that. He always seemed to be testing Wyatt. Daring him to do something. It was very sad to me, the way Leroy just refused to straighten up. We had a long talk with our pastor about it, but he just told us to pray on it and put it in God's hands. That was Pastor Wheland's response to everything. He was near retirement and I think he'd gotten tired of his work. He just didn't seem to have his heart in it."

"Do you think church or church school had any positive effect on Leroy at all?"

Madge took another bite of her cookie and washed it down with some tea. "There were times when I think it did. He might have been much worse if church and school hadn't kept Jesus in his life. But ultimately...the dark side won."

"Do you mind if I just keep paging through this album?" Lauren said.

"Oh, please do. That's why I brought them out. You're welcome to look through all of them."

Lauren's eyes scanned the photos on page after page. Some families took a lot of pictures while others seldom used a camera. Lauren's family had not done a lot of picture-taking when she was growing up. The Steensma's were the opposite. She came to a picture that made her gasp.

"What's wrong?" Madge said.

"Was Leroy *ill*?" Lauren asked.

"Ill? Not especially. The usual cold and flu, a broken arm, but—" She rose from her chair and leaned forward. "What are you looking at?"

Lauren placed her finger on a photograph of a bald Leroy.

"Oh, my," Madge said, lowering herself back into the chair. "I'd forgotten that was in there."

"Why is he bald?"

"Oh, well, that's…a strange story." She reached over and slid the plate of cookies toward Lauren. "You haven't had a cookie yet. Try one. I think they turned out well."

Lauren picked up a cookie and a napkin, took a bite and smiled. "These are delicious," she said. She took a sip of tea, then asked again, "Why is Leroy bald in this picture, Madge?"

The old woman sighed and rolled her eyes. "It was…well, a stupid thing. He did it himself. I tried to stop him, but he locked himself in the bathroom with the electric clippers I used to groom our poodle Collette with. By the time he let me in, all his hair was on the floor around his feet.

"But why did he do it?"

Another sigh, heavier this time, and another bite of the cookie. Finally, she said, "One of the things that Wyatt used to do when he got angry was grab Leroy by the hair. It was just a tug or two most of the time, but then there were times when Leroy's behavior was so…well, *infuriating* that Wyatt got…a little carried away sometimes. Leroy thought if he had no hair, Wyatt wouldn't be able to drag him around by—well, you know, *pull* his hair. So, he shaved his head."

"How did Wyatt react to that?"

14

Madge closed her eyes and tucked her lower lip between her teeth for a moment. "Not…well. It made him very angry. He was…well, he made a point of showing Leroy that he didn't need hair to punish him."

Lauren frowned down at the picture—that same tense, anxious expression with the same sad eyes. "What did Wyatt do?" she said.

Madge closed her eyes again for a moment, fidgeted in her chair, looked all around the kitchen. "Maybe this wasn't such a good idea," she said, just above a whisper. She seemed to be talking to herself.

Lauren looked at her and said, "What do you mean?"

"I…I just don't want to give the wrong impression about Wyatt. He wasn't perfect, of course. Who of us is? But he was a very godly man. He loved Jesus more than any person I've known in my life, he really did. He was a deacon in our church for many years, he regularly led prayer meetings. His faith was the most important thing in the *world* to him, and he wanted it to be important to *us*, too. To Leroy. That's all he wanted. Leroy made that very difficult and it…it frustrated Wyatt. Satan worked so hard on that boy. I could see it in his behavior, the way he dressed, the posters he put on his bedroom wall later, when he was a teenager." Her eyes drifted toward the window behind Lauren as she chuckled. "Those posters. Movie monsters and…terrible things, so dark and disturbing. I don't know where he got them or how he paid for them. I always suspected he stole the money, but he never got caught. He didn't get it from us." She looked at Lauren again, this time almost pleadingly. "If Leroy had just been more understanding, more cooperative…well, he wouldn't have had so much…difficulty. He wouldn't have had so many problems with his father. Wyatt wouldn't have gotten so angry and hit him and pulled his hair, he wouldn't have had to spend so much time locked up, and our pastor never would've had to—"

"Locked up?"

"Oh, er, um...yes. Well, not really *locked up* in the sense that you're probably thinking. There's a rather large walk-in closet in the hallway. When it became apparent that Leroy's interest in such dark movies and TV shows and books was not just a passing phase, Wyatt put a chair and a light in there. When he reached the end of his rope with Leroy, he'd give him a Bible and lock him in that closet. He told him to read and pray and ask the Holy Spirit to enter him and guide him away from the Devil. Sometimes while Leroy was in his closet, Wyatt and I would get on our knees and pray for him."

"How long was Leroy usually locked in the closet?" Lauren asked as she chewed another bite of her cookie.

Madge shrugged and looked past Lauren at the window again. "Oh, well, now, it was...I don't know, really, it was...never that long. Not really. It was Wyatt's idea, but I supported it. I thought it might help Leroy to, you know, focus. To quiet his mind down enough so the Holy Spirit could speak to him, show him the error of his ways. But...well, it didn't seem to work. But we did it because we loved Leroy. We loved him with all our hearts. We thought it was the best thing for him."

"I'm sorry I interrupted you earlier. You were about to say something about your pastor. Were you referring to Pastor Whelan?"

"Oh, no. He retired when Leroy was quite young and we got a new pastor, a younger man, Pastor Crane. He was a fiery preacher. Oh, boy, his sermons were exciting. He had a burden on his heart for the young people in the church. They were leaving the church in large numbers all over the country. We were very impressed with Pastor Crane's efforts to reach them, to make the Bible more accessible to them. He was also concerned about the widespread interest in the occult that he was afraid was leading young people away from Jesus. So, he focused on that a lot. Leroy had changed so much, we decided to talk to Pastor Crane."

"Leroy had *changed*?"

"Oh, yes. Very much. He became…angry. When Wyatt first started putting him in his study closet—that's what Wyatt called the walk-in closet where he'd send Leroy to study when he misbehaved—Leroy would sit in there quietly, he wouldn't make a sound. But later, he would go into a rage in that little room. He'd pound and kick the walls and door and shout and even *scream*. It was terrifying. He would disappear at night. Not when he was a teenager, when that kind of behavior wouldn't be surprising, but *before* his teen years. He had no friends, so we didn't know where he was going or who he was with, if anyone. That would make Wyatt so angry. And when we tried to talk to Leroy about it, he wouldn't say anything, which just made Wyatt angrier, so he'd…well, punish Leroy. We thought perhaps he could help us with all that, and with Leroy's interest in horror films and scary comic books. We talked to him and he asked to meet with Leroy alone."

"Did they talk here or—"

"No, he met with Leroy in his study at the church. I remember it was a summer afternoon and I had some shopping to do, so I dropped Leroy at the church and did what I had to do, then came back and got him in two or three hours. I took Leroy home, and then that evening, Pastor Crane came to the house and talked with Wyatt and me while Leroy was in his room. Pastor Crane had a lot to say that evening."

Madge drank some of her tea, then released a long, heavy sigh.

17

"He was concerned about Leroy's fear," she continued. "The fact that Leroy was afraid of things in the Bible—I mean, literally *terrified* by Bible stories and sometimes the words of God himself, and especially of the end times—"

"The end times?" Lauren said.

"I didn't tell you about that?"

"You said he was afraid of certain Bible stories, like Abraham and Isaac, but you didn't mention the end times."

"Ah. Well. Wyatt talked a lot about the end times. He was convinced, as so many of us are, that we're living in the last days. So much has changed since Wyatt was...well, since he...passed. If he were alive today, he'd see that he was right back then. All the signs in the Bible are coming to pass. So many earthquakes and floods, diseases, homosexuals taking over and being given special treatment, pagan environmentalists worshipping the earth instead of God, and such an increase in knowledge—all this technology, computers, the internet bringing all kinds of pornography and wickedness right into children's bedrooms. It's all around us, happening right now. Jesus will be coming soon, dear, don't think he won't. Wyatt was eager for that to happen, for Jesus to return. He thought it would happen in his lifetime. He talked about it a lot. For many of our family Bible studies, Wyatt read from Revelation and Daniel and other parts of the New Testament that speak of the end times."

"What was it about the last days that frightened Leroy so much?"

"Well, all the signs of the end were scary to him. He became obsessed with them. He was *terrified* of the Antichrist. By the time he was...oh, I don't know, nine years old or so...he would read the newspaper every night after Wyatt was done with it. He'd pore over it, looking for signs that the Antichrist was here, that he was approaching power. He was too young to really understand the news. But any mention of war in the paper or on the TV news would send him into a panic. You know, because of what Jesus said in Matthew. 'And ye shall hear of wars and rumors of wars.' I tried to point out to him that in that same verse, Jesus said, 'see that ye be not troubled.' I tried to tell him that Jesus was going to take care of his people. But he didn't take any comfort in that. He didn't see any of the promises of the Bible, only the bad things. In that same chapter in Matthew, Jesus said, 'Then shall they deliver up to be afflicted and shall kill you, and ye shall be hated of all nations for my name's sake.' He would have nightmares about that. About being persecuted and hunted and killed by the Antichrist and his followers. He'd wake up at night screaming. It worried us at first, but after a while, after we tried to assure him that he was safe because Jesus would protect the righteous, and he didn't listen, didn't calm down or change…well, Wyatt began to fear that the Bible's promises weren't comforting him because inside, Leroy knew he…he *wasn't* one of the righteous, one of Jesus's people."

"What about Pastor Crane, what did he tell you about his talk with Leroy?"

Madge looked down at the table sadly and slowly turned her head back and forth. "He told us exactly what Wyatt had feared. Pastor Crane said that Wyatt's fear of all things godly was due to the fact that Satan was inside him. He was afraid of the last days because he knew they would bring Satan's doom. He determined that Leroy was suffering from possession."

"Demon possession?"

"Oh, yes. Yes. Pastor Crane said it explained Leroy's attraction to dark things like horror movies. It explained all those posters on his walls. It explained his anger and his nightmares. It explained why he was so terribly worried about his teeth, he was *obsessed* with his teeth, and it—"

"Teeth?" Lauren said, flinching. Teeth had played a significant role in Leroy's killings, one that no one had ever been able to explain fully. "What about his teeth?"

"Oh. I didn't already tell you about that?"

"No."

"Well, when Leroy was quite young—he was just a little thing—Wyatt read something in Matthew that really upset Leroy. I think it's in Matthew 13."

The number 13, Lauren thought, reaching into her bag for a pen. She quickly began jotting notes. Leroy had carved the number 13 into chests of all of his victims.

Madge said, "The passage goes, 'So shall it be at the end of the world: The angels shall come forth, and sever the wicked from the just—'"

Lauren quickly wrote and underlined, "Sever?" in her folder. Leroy had severed the limbs and head of each of his victims.

"'—and shall cast them into the furnace of fire. There shall be wailing and gnashing of teeth.'"

"That frightened Leroy?"

"Well, it's a frightening passage. At least, it's frightening for those who refuse to accept Christ Jesus as their savior and will have that fate at the end. But what bothered Leroy so much was the 'gnashing of teeth.' He misunderstood it. He explained to me once—it was several years later—that he thought 'gnashing of teeth' meant that people would be tearing their own teeth out of their heads. That's the image he saw in his head when he first heard that passage read from the Bible. And from then on, he…oh, I know this sounds silly, but it was a very serious issue to Leroy…he equated teeth problems—loose teeth, cavities, anything at all—with damnation. He thought they meant one was doomed to be thrown into that furnace."

"Did you explain it to him so he could understand it?"

"I tried. I told him that 'gnashing of teeth' meant grinding teeth together, that it was something the wicked would do while they were burning for their sins, for their rejection of God. But by then, I think it was too late. That image was burned into Leroy's mind."

"Do you think that had something to do with what he did?" Lauren said.

"You mean...the killings?"

"Well, specifically what he did with the victims' teeth. He removed all their teeth and kept them. Police found a bag of teeth in his apartment after Leroy...um, after he ended his own life. All of them belonged to his victims."

Madge frowned and her eyes widened slightly. "Oh. My. That...hadn't occurred to me. Do you think there was a connection?"

Lauren pressed her lips together. "Mmm. Could be. What was Pastor Crane's conclusion?"

"Oh, well he decided our only option was an exorcism."

"Really? An exorcism?"

"I know it's controversial. Not all Christians subscribe to that sort of thing. But Pastor Crane thought it was essential. Necessary. And we were so desperate that we agreed to it."

"Where did that take place?"

"Here at the house. In Leroy's bedroom. We followed all of Pastor Crane's instructions. He'd done it before, many times, and knew what he was doing. We put a lock on the outside of Leroy's bedroom door so he couldn't get out. Pastor Crane said that confronting the demons in Leroy would anger them and they would become much more dangerous. They would fight hard. We couldn't let Leroy get out."

"What did the exorcism involve? What was done?"

"I wasn't present for most of it. I took food into the room for Wyatt and Pastor Crane. Leroy didn't eat that week, and he lost a lot of weight."

"That *week*?"

"Oh, yes. The exorcism lasted an entire week. I think being outside the room made it worse for me because I didn't know what was happening. All that screaming. Leroy just screamed and screamed. Well…not exactly Leroy. Pastor Crane told me it was the demons that were screaming. They did terrible things to Leroy. The demons, I mean. He was so beaten up. I had to keep going in there to tend to his wounds. The exorcism might have lasted longer, but Leroy lost consciousness and we couldn't revive him. And he was bleeding. In fact, we had to take him to the hospital. Well, Wyatt took him. To the emergency room."

"Was he okay?"

"He was hurt. Badly beaten up by the demons. And he hadn't eaten."

"How did Wyatt explain that at the hospital?"

"I'm not sure. He never told me. He had to lie because they never would have understood at the hospital, he knew that. And lying upset him. Like I said, he was a very godly man. He took the Ten Commandments seriously. It deeply disturbed him to have to lie. But it was necessary. I remember he prayed long and hard that night for Jesus to forgive him. It was necessary, but it was still a sin."

"What happened to Leroy after that?"

"Well, Pastor Crane had warned us from the start. He said an exorcism would force the issue. It would have one of two results. Either the demons would leave Leroy and he would be filled with the spirit of the Lord, or…or…" Her voice thickened with emotion at the memory. "…or the demons would only become more powerful, more entrenched inside Leroy. He said

22

it would all depend on Leroy. Deep down inside, Leroy would make a decision. He would choose a side. He would decide whether to fight the demons and side with God...or give in to Satan and remain possessed." She sniffled, removed her glasses for a moment and wiped her moist eyes with a knuckle. "I think we all know what Leroy's decision was."

"What happened after the exorcism?"

"It took him a while to recover from his injuries. He was quieter after that. *Very* quiet, in fact. He changed. Not for the better. But it took us a while to realize just how *much* it was not for the better."

Lauren frowned as she leaned forward. "Madge, after all of this came out...after Leroy killed his father and then himself and police discovered that he'd been responsible for all those killings...didn't anyone *ever* sit down and talk to you?"

"Oh, yes, the police. Of course, the police talked to me."

"But I mean any reporters? Weren't there journalists like me who wanted to ask you questions like this? Didn't anyone ever try to figure out why Leroy did what he did?"

"The police asked some questions like that. There were all kinds of journalists who wanted to talk to me, but I turned them down. I knew what would happen, how they would make it all look. Christians are despised in this land, just like Jesus said they would be. America has turned on its Christian heritage and on the Christians who live in its borders. I knew what would happen. So, I turned them all down. Until you came along. All these years have passed and I wondered if perhaps it was time to talk to someone. I prayed about it. I prayed a lot. The Lord impressed me that I should talk to you, dear." She reached over and placed her hand on Lauren's. "He told me it would be okay."

When Lauren gathered her things to leave, Madge stepped in front of her and became very serious. She placed a hand on Lauren's shoulder and said, "I've answered all your questions. Will you answer a question for me, dear?"

Lauren smiled. "If I can."

"You have no idea how difficult life has been for me at times since all of this happened. A day doesn't go by when I don't think about all the people Leroy killed. Especially those children. It happens so often that my heart never has time to heal before it breaks again. I've asked myself...so many times...and now, after talking with you for—oh, what's it been, now, three hours? More? I want to ask you."

"Sure, Madge. Go ahead."

A tear trickled down Madge's left cheek and her lips trembled slightly. "Was there something I should have done? Was there something I *shouldn't* have done? Is it possible...somehow...that I am in some way *responsible* for what Leroy...became? For all the horrible things he did? Could *I* be at fault?"

Lauren put her bag down and embraced the small old woman, held her close, and patted her back comfortingly. She said, "You're a godly woman, Madge. Just as your husband was a godly man. You're a good Christian. You obviously love the Lord." She stepped back with her hands on Madge's shoulders and looked into the old woman's eyes. "It's obvious that Satan had his sight set on your son. You did everything right. You did everything you possibly could. And I'm sure the readers of *Christian Life and Times* will agree."

Graven Image

With apologies to Richard Matheson.

"Thou shalt not make unto thee any graven image, or any likeness of any thing that is in heaven above, or that is in the earth beneath, or that is in the water under the earth: Thou shalt not bow down thyself to them, nor serve them: For I the Lord thy God am a jealous God, visiting the iniquity of the fathers upon the children unto the third and fourth generation of them that hate me; and showing mercy unto thousands of them that love Me, and keep My commandments."

Exodus 20: 4 - 6

1.

Hal Dillon could not take his eyes from the large wooden crucifix hanging on the wall. He and his girlfriend Jacquie stood in the rear of Markum's Curios and Antiques with their heads tilted back, staring up at it. It was a steel-gray, rainy Saturday morning in mid-March and Hal could hear the muffled splashes of cars driving back and forth through puddles outside the store. Thunder purred in the distance.

"You're not actually thinking of buying that, are you?" Jacquie said.

"As a matter of fact, I am," he said.

"You're kidding. You mean, you'd put that on your wall?"

"It's not like it wouldn't go with all the other weird art in my house."

"True. You do have some strange stuff. But this? I don't know. Come here, I want to show you this lamp."

She led him to the front of the curio shop and pointed out a tall brass floor lamp. Three upward-glowing lamps branched off from the top.

"I like it," he said.

"Think it would go in my apartment? Say, in the corner by the couch?"

"Sure, why not?"

"I think I'll get it." Jacquie went to the register, behind which stood a round, bespectacled bald man with a graying Van Dyke beard.

Hal returned to the back of the store and stood with hands in the pockets of his black leather jacket, studying the crucifix.

The cross stood about three feet tall, made of dark wood, with a rough, coarse surface. The figure of Christ had been meticulously painted, the body sickly-pale and covered with blood that ran down from the crown of thorns around the head, a stained loincloth around the middle, hands and feet bloodied and torn from the spikes that pierced them and held them to the cross. Christ's body was slender and stringy, with cords of muscles rigid in the neck, arms, and legs. The ribs looked ready to cut through the flesh of his chest and sides like bony razors. The dark nipples stood out like small pencil erasers. Blood ran from a gash in the lower left side of the abdomen where he had been stabbed with a spear. Jesus's head was tilted back, ropes of blood-matted black hair falling around His face. Below his uneven, scraggly, bloody beard, his trachea was a corrugated tube beneath taut flesh.

Hal could not see the face or the eyes from that angle, but he was eager to see what color they were, how lifelike they were. He reached up and touched the outer side of the left thigh. The skin was smooth, and he could feel the muscles, as if they really were there, beneath that perfectly-smooth skin. It bore no resemblance to the rough surface of the dark cross, although both were carved from the same piece of wood.

Hal went to the front counter where Jacquie was still talking to the proprietor.

"Good news," she said. "Markum's delivers! We'd never get that lamp into your Taurus."

"Very good. I've decided for sure, I want the crucifix."

"You want the crucifix?" the bald man said with a smile that twitched and faltered. "Just got it in a couple of months ago. It's created quite a stir among my regulars. I honestly thought I'd never unload the thing. I *still* might not."

"Really? Why not?"

"Well, you, uh," the bald man chuckled coldly without smiling again, "you haven't seen the face." He pointed a finger in the direction of the crucifix. "You see the face, *then* decide if you want to buy it."

"What's wrong with the face? Is it damaged?"

"No, no, it's in perfect condition."

"So, what is it?"

"You'll see." He turned to the phone, picked up the receiver, and punched a couple of numbers. He waited a moment, then said, "Look, Eric, somebody wants to see the crucifix. Could you bring out the ladder and get it down for me?" He nodded once. "Yes, I understand, but—" He closed his eyes a moment and sighed. "Listen, I don't care about that, just *do* it, okay?" He frowned. "It's just a piece of *wood*, Eric, for God's sake, I don't care if you *are* afraid of it, just come out and take it *down*, please." By the time the bald man replaced the receiver, Hal could hear movement in the rear of the store. "Let's go back and have a look, shall we?" the bald man said as he stepped out from behind the counter and led them down an aisle to the back.

Eric looked like a human bulldog. He had massive shoulders, and a wide, deep barrel chest. He wore a white sweatshirt and jeans, gray sneakers. He carried a ladder from a back room. After setting up the ladder, Eric climbed up and removed the heavy crucifix from the wall and slowly lowered it to the floor.

While that was going on, the bald man turned to Hal and extended his hand. "Charles Markum," he said with a pleasant smile, tipping his head forward so his bulbous eyes could look at Hal over the top edge of the spectacles.

Hal shook his hand and smiled and said, "Hal Dillon. And this is Jacquie Smalls."

"Pleasure to meet you both," Markum said as he gently shook Jacquie's hand. "Now, as to that crucifix," he said to Hal. "I'm willing to bet you'll change your mind when you see the face. Three different people have come in and expressed interest in it, but as soon as they saw the face, they, uh, did not linger. They were gone. I wouldn't mind so much, but most of them are in such a hurry after seeing that thing, they leave the store without buying *anything*. I'm afraid Jesus is losing me some business."

"He's that ugly, huh?"

"Well, I'm not sure I'd say he's *ugly*, so to speak," Markum said. "You'll see in just a few seconds. Thank you very much, Eric."

From a distance, Eric looked quite youthful with that muscular, fit body. But up close, it became obvious that he was, like Markum, in his fifties, with fine webworks of wrinkles just below his eyes and crow's feet on the outer corners. He stepped back, put his hands on his narrow hips, and stood there looking at the crucifix. He nodded abruptly, then disappeared through a door in the back wall.

The crucifix stood on the floor leaning up against the wall. Markum went to it and said, "Look here."

Hal looked down at the upturned face of the wooden Christ. A million tiny, icy spiders crawled down his spine.

The lips of the savior's unnaturally large, yawning mouth were peeled back over small teeth that had been filed down to fine points. A wreath of thorns encircled the crown of the head, the thorns deep in the flesh and bleeding copiously. Blood that had spilled down from the wounded brow ran along the edges of the lips and clung to the sharp, slightly protuberant teeth. From that angle—looking straight down at it—Jesus no longer appeared to be at the agonizing precipice of death. The pain and misery the figure seemed to bear when it was up on the wall changed to something else from a higher angle looking down at the crucifix. The flexed muscles made Christ appear to be defiantly struggling against his bondage, trying to escape the cross rather than humbly accepting his fate as the Savior of mankind. The fingers were curled like claws around the heads of the spikes that stuck out from the bloody palms. The dark eyes were wide beneath the hood of a frowning brow and filled with something that hit Hal like a fist to the solar plexus. The eyes bubbled over with hatred and anger and vengeance.

Hal took in a deep breath and sighed, "Well, it's, uh…it's certainly unlike any other crucifix I've ever seen." He reached down and hooked the tip of his index finger under the upper teeth, feeling the sharp tips. They had been filed down to fat, stubby needles. The teeth looked absolutely real. So did the tongue. And the blood. It was a very disturbing piece.

"I like it," Hal said.

"Honey, that is just...well, it's..." Jacquie sighed. "Honey, it's hideous."

"Yes, but I like it. It's one of a kind. This is...I don't know, Jesus the Vengeful. The angry. How often do you see that? By the way—" He turned to Markum. "—does it have a name?"

"No. And I don't have any idea who carved it, either, or when," Markum said. "I must say, the work itself is quite remarkable, but...well...I was raised in the Church of Christ. I'm a secular humanist now, but growing up in the church like that...I don't know, it leaves something behind in you. It left something in me that just can't stomach this piece."

"I understand," Hal said with a nod.

"Where will you put it?" Jacquie said.

"On the wall over the couch in the living room. I'll take down *American Headless*."

American Headless was a print of a painting by Kristin Kingsbury. It was the first entry in a series of paintings called, collectively, *Classic Dreams*. *American Headless* was a replica of Grant Wood's *American Gothic*, in which a farm couple, a man and his older, unmarried daughter, stand before a house, the man holding a pitchfork, tines-up. But in Kingsbury's painting, the woman's head was impaled on the pitchfork, and the woman held the man's severed head cradled in the crook of her right arm. Their necks were blood-spurting stumps, as if they had just been decapitated. Hal had a Kingsbury print in almost every room in his house.

He would replace *American Headless* with his new purchase, the heavy, nightmarish crucifix.

"I think it'll look good there," Hal said. "Don't you?" He looked at Jacquie with raised eyebrows. She gave him a dubious look.

He turned to Markum, who simply smiled and said, "If you say so."

2.

Jacquie took a couple of steps back and cocked her head to one side, her slender arms folded before her. "Well, I'm not going to say it ties the room together, or anything, but...it has...a certain...something. I guess. I think it's fortunate that we can't see the face from here. If the face were pointing forward, I would've advised against putting this thing in your living room. Are you happy with it there?"

"Yes, I am," Hal said.

"Good."

Hal and Jacquie stood and stared at it, his arm around her shoulders, her head leaning against him.

"It's a very strange thing to hang in your living room," Jacquie said.

"No stranger than a painting of two bloody headless people."

"No, but certainly more volatile."

"Who am I going to invite over here who will be offended by it? I don't know any fundamentalist Christians."

"What about your parents?"

Hal chuckled. "My parents have been offended by *everything* I've done in my life ever since they found out I wasn't going to be a Baptist minister. They had their hearts set on it. I'm sure this won't surprise them. Besides, like you said, they can't see the face."

"I'd think you'd be filled with a little more dread at the prospect of their seeing it."

"They hardly ever come over. My mother thinks I'm a slob because I don't vacuum and dust the entire house every day. Dad doesn't like it over here because he knows I won't let him watch any televangelists on my TV."

"I don't think you're being very realistic," Jacquie said with a slight frown. "They're going to completely freak when they see this thing, and you know it. Even though they can't see the face, there's still something...I don't know...something not right about it. Something almost...sinister. Your mother will probably have to be hospitalized."

Hal laughed. "Either that or she'll think I've come back to Jesus and she'll be thrilled."

She put her arms around him and nuzzled his neck. "Fortunately for me, you don't care, because if you did, you might not be with me."

"If I cared what my parents thought, I probably never would have asked you out."

She kissed him, stroked the back of his head with her left hand.

"Your parents really wanted you to be a minister?" Jacquie said.

"They imagined me with my own TV show."

She chuckled.

"I'm serious," he said. "They always imagined me with my own television show, my own singers, somebody on a big organ, and there I'd be in a shiny white suit standing before an auditorium full of people. They wanted me to be Rex Humbard when I grew up. He was their favorite televangelist. But all I ever wanted to be was an artist."

"You're making a *living* at being an artist. You're very lucky."

"Not talented?"

She rolled her eyes. "Of *course,* you're talented. But the world is full of starving talented people, which means you're one of the *lucky* talented people."

He chuckled. "I'm a *commercial* artist at Meany and Bruckner Marketing. It's not quite the same thing as being an *artist.*" Hal also had managed to get some work now and then illustrating limited edition hardcover horror novels for small-press publishers. His dream was to one day have an entire gallery exhibit devoted to his work. But he was not holding his breath.

"Hey, you're still using your talent, you're still doing what you love to do, right?" Jacquie said.

"Oh, I'm not complaining, not at all. You're right, I'm very lucky."

"You still paint, too, and I hope you never stop." Jacquie had four of Hal's paintings hanging in her apartment across town. She was his biggest fan and cheerleader.

"I don't paint as much as I'd like anymore." Hal had converted his once-cluttered, dusty attic into a studio, where he had planned to paint a few nights a week, although it had been more like a couple of nights a month lately.

"Maybe the crucifix will bring you inspiration," Jacquie said.

"Inspiration? I doubt it. Although it might bring me a nightmare or two."

"I'm gonna head over to my place. Eric will be bringing my lamp over soon."

"Let's do something later," Hal said. "Dinner and a movie?"

"Sure. What do you want to see?"

"Let me surprise you."

"No horror movies. Please?"

"No horror movies."

Hal felt something rub against his right calf. He looked down and saw Grey, his long, sleek, part-Persian cat with a lush, shiny coat of steel-gray. Grey looked up at him with that beautiful face and those big green eyes, and he meowed once.

"Grey wants to be fed," Hal said as he walked out to the porch. Jacquie trotted down the front walk to her Jetta, got in, and drove away.

He stood on the porch a moment and breathed in the damp air. It had stopped raining on the drive home and Whintsey Road was wet and spotted with puddles. Now, as Hal stood with his fingers stuffed into the back pockets of his jeans, it began to rain again. Lightly at first, just enough to make the leaves on the oak trees and shrubbery jitter and dance, but it picked up as he turned and went inside, and was soon a low, aggressive roar.

They were having a long winter in northern California. Marin County and the entire bay area had been getting non-stop rain since last month. People were getting tired of it. Irritable, quick to anger. Even Jacquie, who was the most stable person Hal knew, had been tense. In March of last year, she had spent her free time in her sunny garden. This year, with the month half over, she waited impatiently for the rain to stop.

It hurt Hal to see her feeling depressed, because, for one thing, there was nothing he could do about it and it made him feel helpless, and for another, he'd had his share of experience with that particular illness and wished it on no one. He was thrilled that the light worked. When the lack of sunlight was not getting her down, Jacquie was a vibrant, outgoing woman with a laugh that trumpeted through the air like the horn of a playful angel. She was a force of nature—holding hands with her was like holding hands with the wind. Embracing her as she held still was like holding a column of vibrating energy in his arms. This was not to say she was bouncing off the walls all the time

34

or anything—she was a very calm, laid-back person. But it was there, that natural strength, that humming energy. Hal found that he derived strength from it. He had no doubt that Jacquie was the best thing that had ever happened to him. He'd already decided to ask her to move in with him, he simply had not found the right moment, the *perfect* moment. Because when he asked her to move in with him, he was also going to ask her to marry him. He thought it would be wise for them to live together for a little while first, though, just to make sure they were compatible. He'd been carrying her ring around with him for almost a month, just waiting for that right moment. Maybe it would come tonight, over dinner, or after dinner. He was tired of putting it off, so he would be looking for *any* perfect moment, not necessarily *the* perfect moment. Tonight sounded like as good a time as any. To be honest, he was eager to get it over with. He was tired of worrying over how he would react if she said no. In his mind—in his dreams—she'd already turned him down. Several times. Hal usually expected the worst, especially after he'd had plenty of time to worry about something, so by now, he was *expecting* her to say no, and he wanted to get it over with as soon as possible, so yes, he decided it would *definitely* be tonight.

Grey meowed again. Hal bent down and picked him up, carried him to the kitchen, talking to him the whole way.

"You beautiful cat, you, how's my Grey-boy? Huh? How's my Grey-boy doing?"

In the kitchen, he bent down and put Grey on the floor, then opened one of the cupboards over the counter. He removed a flat, round can of cat food—Ocean Whitefish and Shrimp this time—and hooked his finger in the round loop attached to the top of the can, then peeled the lid off. He tossed it in the garbage under the sink. Took a fork from the drawer, bent down, and scooped the cat food into his bowl, which was black and read in silver letters on the side, *Grey*. There was a bowl of water next to the food. Grey's litter box was kept out in the garage, and there was a little cat-door in the bottom of the door in the kitchen that led out to the garage. Grey was devoted to indoor living. Even when he went out to the garage when the big door was wide open, he never left the garage. Instead, he went back into the house when he was done with his business. Hal liked that. Indoor cats lived years longer than outdoor cats. He was very attached to Grey—he'd had the cat since Grey was a kitten—and wanted to have him around as long as possible. Grey's favorite spot was in the living room, curled up in Hal's recliner, from which he frequently watched television. When Hal was sitting there, Grey spent a great deal of time in his lap. Hal liked that, too. Grey's second favorite spot was the bed in Hal's bedroom. Grey slept with him every night, and when Jacquie was there, Grey slept tucked between them, sometimes on his back, his big paws in the air with their tufts of fur growing out between the pads of his feet. Grey entertained himself by tossing a catnip-stuffed mouse-toy into the air with his mouth, then diving after it, picking it up off the floor in his teeth and throwing it again, diving for it again, over and over.

Grey had been in Hal's life longer than Jacquie, so it had been very important to Hal that the two of them get along, because if Hal had to choose between them—*well, that would be unfortunate,* he decided. The first few times Jacquie came to his house, Grey would not come out of the bedroom, where he hid. He was a very skittish cat, quite picky about whom he showered with affection. Finally, when Jacquie kept coming back, Grey became curious. First, he spent a lot of time cautiously sniffing her. The whole time she was there one night, Grey followed her around wherever she went in the house, sniffing her.

"This is kind of giving me the *creeps*, Hal," Jacquie had said.

"Don't worry, it won't go on much longer. He's just processing all of your many and varied odors. Soon as he's done doing that, he'll be fine. Might even jump in your lap. It's just that cats are very particular about whom they accept, whom they show affection to—if you were someone who hated cats, Grey would know, and he'd probably *never* come out of the bedroom while you were here. Obviously, you don't hate cats."

"I love cats," she'd said.

Hal had smiled. "Then you two should get along well."

So far, they had. When Jacquie sat on the couch, Grey liked to climb up and get behind her head and just stretch out over her shoulders with the back of the couch to lean against.

"It's like wearing this big heavy fur," Jacquie had said as she stroked Grey's silky coat. "He's so long and slinky—it's like wearing this really plush kitty stole."

Hal was ecstatic to see them get along so well. It was a big relief. And whenever he looked over and saw Jacquie sitting there with Grey curled up in her lap, her hand gently stroking his coat—the sight of it made him feel *at home*.

3.

Hal put on, for the first time, a charcoal Armani suit he'd purchased a couple months earlier with a surprise royalty check he'd received for a book cover he'd illustrated. He arrived at her place at seven, and when he saw her, he did not want to go out—he wanted to take her straight to bed.

"Uh-uh-uh," she said with a demure smile when he moved in and began nibbling on her neck. "We're saving that for later tonight."

She wore a black-and-red dress with a long skirt, slit up the right side to her hip, showing flashes of her entire long, pale leg. Tiny red gems glimmered in her silver necklace which ended just between the tops of her breasts, and more sparkled in her matching earrings.

He drove them through the rain in his Taurus, out of their small San Francisco suburb and into the City itself, to Chinatown. There and then, he decided as he parked that he would ask her that night. He decided that, because he found a perfect parking space at the curb without having to drive around the block once. The stars were all in proper alignment, and this would be the perfect night to pop the question—well, *questions*, actually.

Hal had called that afternoon and made reservations at Snow Garden, a popular Chinese restaurant. They were seated in a curtained booth in the rear of the restaurant, where they ordered, then leaned close to each other over the square table, all four hands joined.

"The lamp looks perfect in my apartment," Jacquie said.

"It does?"

"Yes. I'm so glad I bought it."

"How do you think it would look in my place?" Hal said with a smile.

Jacquie's smile slowly crumbled and a frown cut vertical razor-slices into her forehead. "What?" she said. "What...I don't under...what do you mean?"

He chuckled and said, "Just what I said—how do you think the lamp would look in *my* place."

"You...you want me to *give* you the lamp? Is that what you're saying?"

Hal laughed and shook his head. "No, no, that's not what I—" He laughed some more. "I was just asking, in a roundabout way, I guess, if you'd like to move in with me."

"Okay, let me make sure I've got this straight—you're *not* going to take my lamp?"

He laughed some more. "No, I'm not going to take your lamp. I just want you to move in with me. I think we should try living together for a while, see if we can get along, see if we're a good fit."

Her frown disappeared and her eyes got a little wider. "You're serious?"

"Yes, I'm very serious. See, I think it's important that a couple live together first."

She frowned again. "You're confusing me. What do you mean, *first*?"

Hal reached into his right suitcoat pocket and removed the black velvet box, put it on the table, and opened it as he said, just above a whisper, "Will you marry me, Jacquie?"

Jacquie's gasp was so loud that people outside their closed booth suddenly turned and stared at the curtains drawn around them. One woman dropped her chopsticks.

Jacquie slapped both hands over her mouth as she let out a yelp, staring at the glimmering ring with eyes bulging.

"Oh. My. *Gawd!*" she finally said. "You just—I can't believe—you just, just, right there, you just *asked* it!"

Unable to hold back his grin, Hal nodded as he reached out and took her hand in his. He pulled it to his mouth and kissed it, and said, "Yes, I did. I said it, and I meant it, Jacquie. I love you." He kissed her hand again, then lowered it to the table, but did not let go of it. "Are you going to answer?"

"Oh, of *course*, of—I mean, yes—I mean, the *answer* is yes. Yes!"

Hal scooted out of his side of the booth and she did the same, and from outside the booth, people saw the curtain flutter and bulge, while inside, they kissed.

4.

They went to the new Bruce Willis movie, a big-budget action flick that made the theater floor grumble with the sounds of its explosions and exaggerated gunfire.

Hal and Jacquie saw none of it. They kissed like a couple of teenagers who thought it was time to make out because the lights went off. He slid his right hand beneath the red coat with the black fur collar and squeezed Jacquie's left breast over the silk of her dress. Their kisses were, on occasion, interrupted by breathy giggles with their mouths together, and when one of them giggled, the other one giggled, until they were giggling into each other's mouths.

Someone said, "Get a room, for cryin' out loud," and Hal lifted his head to see that everyone was leaving the theater. The closing credits were running on the big screen. He sat up, then so did Jacquie.

They cleared their throats as they brushed at their clothes.

Jacquie stood, but Hal tugged on her hand until she sat down beside him again. "What's wrong?"

"I can't stand up yet."

"Why can't you — oh. Okay." She smiled. "We can wait."

So, they waited. The theater emptied, leaving Hal and Jacquie the only two remaining patrons. Pretty soon, someone would come in and tell them they couldn't stay for the next showing unless they paid for it again —

"Okay," Hal said. "I'm fine now."

It was pouring outside, and they ran together to the car. Bolts of lightning lit up the clouds and part of the night and were followed by thunder that rumbled across the sky. Once on the road, windshield wipers sweeping frantically back and forth over the glass, Hal said, "Well, what did you think of the movie?"

They laughed together. "Look, Hal, I want you to promise me something."

"Anything."

"Promise me that no matter how long we're married, we'll always continue to go on dates. Like tonight. A real date, where you ask me, and I check my schedule and say yes, and you take me someplace nice and treat me the way you treated me tonight, like…like I'm a beautiful woman. Promise me we'll always do that."

"No problem at all. Once every month. No matter how long we're married. No matter how many kids we have. One night every month, you and I go on a date."

Smiling, Jacquie leaned over and kissed him on the cheek.

Jacquie laughed. "We're gonna get *married*!"

"How about that?"

Hal left the freeway and went around a few surface corners.

"Look," he said. "All the lights in the neighborhood are out."

"Oh, no."

"Looks like we don't have any power, either," Hal said as he drove up his driveway, which was slanted at a steep angle. He brought the Taurus to a stop and killed the engine, but he left the lights on.

"Oh, no," Jacquie said.

"What's wrong?"

"Something you don't know about me—I'm terrified of thunderstorms, and of the dark."

"Really? Well, tonight should scare the *hell* out of you, then!"

They both laughed, but Jacquie glanced away uncomfortably and her tone became somber.

"I'm serious. I can't sleep in the dark. You'll have to get used to that about me—haven't you ever noticed that I have to have some kind of light on when I sleep? Because if I wake up in total darkness, I'll start screaming."

"Wow, screaming? Really?"

"Yes. It might not sound like much to you, but it's really —
"

"No, don't say that. I think it's a terrible thing. I take it *very* seriously."

"You do?"

"Of course I do. Don't worry, I have lots of kerosene lanterns and plenty of kerosene, and I've got some big Coleman lanterns, too, so we won't be in the dark. And I'm not going to let anything happen to you."

They just sat there for a moment and looked at each other, looked deep into each other's eyes, the way only new lovers can. Finally, their gaze was broken, and Hal said, "You want me to run inside and get you an umbrella?"

"No, don't be silly. I don't mind getting a little wet."

"You hear that? It's *pouring* out there."

"I don't mind. Really."

They hurried from the Taurus to the porch, where Hal quickly unlocked the front door and they rushed inside, both of them with hair soaked flat to their heads, clothes sagging from being so wet. But they laughed as he closed the door, and they sort of collided, and their arms went around each other as they pressed their mouths together.

There were still a few glowing embers in the fireplace, and Hal pulled away and said, "Let me get a fire going in here to warm the place up."

Ten minutes later, a fire crackled in the fireplace and Hal got some kerosene lanterns and lit them up, lit a few candles. Jacquie had stripped down to nothing and put on one of Hal's sweatshirts, which was quite baggy and large even on Hal, so it was even more so on Jacquie. She looked incredible in it—just a plain old grey sweatshirt that swallowed her up and fell just below her crotch, fully revealing her long, shapely legs. He went to her and bent down to cup a hand to the side of her knee, then rose slowly as he slid the hand up her silky leg, getting a chill from its perfect smoothness, its unbelievable power to speed up his heart rate, to engorge his penis with blood.

Jacquie undressed him and kissed him all over as they moved through the dark and headed slowly for Hal's bedroom. His suit ended up scattered all over the living room, and they ended their short journey by falling onto his bed, naked, hands moving all over, feeling each other, gently squeezing, pinching, stroking, lips closing on flesh, teeth nipping at it.

When he entered her, she cried out. It was a pleasant, happy sound, the kind of sound one might make when surprised by an unexpected gift, or an unpredicted kiss.

Then Hal made *his* pleasant sound. They kissed, and as they kissed, they cooed like panting, sweating doves.

5.

Something ripped Hal from his sleep.

He awoke sitting up in bed, listening. All he could hear was the rain still pouring outside.

Jacquie was not in bed with him.

Disturbed by the sudden movement, Grey, who was curled up beside Hal, lifted his head and looked around. He got up on his feet and stretched, then hopped off the side of the bed and wandered out of the room.

One of the kerosene lanterns burned on Hal's dresser, giving the dark room a soft glow and deep shadows. He'd left it burning for Jacquie. Somehow, he'd never noticed before that she always left some light on—in the bathroom, in the hall— when they slept. Now that he thought about it, he knew it was true.

Rain poured outside, and now a wind blew the rain against the glass of the windows in the bedroom. Lightning flickered and lit up the windows intermittently. Thunder growled across the sky.

The covers on Jacquie's side of the bed had been thrown back. He looked through the darkness and across the room at the bathroom doorway — the door was open and the bathroom was empty.

"Jacquie?" he said, his voice hoarse with sleepiness.

No response.

Something had woken him — a sound, something sudden and loud. It was still ringing in his ears, although he still couldn't identify what it had been.

Maybe it had been a nightmare.

A scream in a nightmare? he thought.

Hal scrubbed a hand down his face and threw back his covers, turned and let his legs fall over the side of the bed. When he clicked on the bedside lamp, nothing happened — the power was still out. He took the flashlight from his nightstand and stood. He slipped his feet into his slippers and took his black-and-grey terrycloth robe from a chair by the bed and put it on.

In the bedroom doorway, he shone the light up and down the hall, but saw no sign of Jacquie.

"Jacquie?" he said again, a little louder.

He shuffled down the hall, his slippers whispering against the carpet, and passed through the living room. He swept the light back and forth as he went, looking for some sign of Jacquie. Surely, she wouldn't have gotten up in the middle of the night and gone home, would she? In this downpour?

Light came from the dining room, and that made him feel better. He rounded the corner into the dining room and found a Coleman lantern lit on the table.

"Jacquie?" he said as he turned left and went into the kitchen.

What he saw made him cry out in horror and pain.

At first, he thought maybe she'd spilled something on the floor, then slipped in it and fallen down. But she did not move.

The light from the Coleman lantern on the dining room table cast deep shadows through the kitchen. Hal raised his flashlight and sent the beam moving over the kitchen floor.

The blood was deep-red against the robin's-egg-blue tiles.

The uncurtained window over the sink flickered with lightning and Hal felt the thunder in the floor under his feet when it roared.

Jacquie lay on her right side, one arm stretched out before her. She was naked and sickly pale. Blood had puddled beneath the lower part of her right leg. Hal turned the light on it and saw a hideous gash in her calf—a large section of flesh was missing, revealing only raw, bloody tissue in a half-moon gash that appeared to be the result of a large bite. Her throat had been ripped open and blood had cascaded down her chest and stomach and pooled beneath her upper body on the floor beneath her. Her mouth was open, as were her eyes.

"Jac...quie?" he said again, this time in a hoarse whisper.

He went to her and hunkered down at her side, careful not to step in the blood, but he could not look at her for long. He clenched his eyes shut and let his head fall forward. His hands trembled and his legs felt weak as he stood again.

Suddenly, he could no longer feel the floor beneath his feet. He felt as if his head were turning inside-out, as if his brain were screaming. But it was Hal himself who screamed. The sound seemed to come to him from a great distance at first, then rapidly grew closer and louder until his own screaming voice was deafening. He swallowed the sound and it ended raggedly as he put both hands over his face. His entire body shivered with sudden cold in spite of his heavy robe, a chill that radiated from deep inside his bones out to his flesh.

The police, he thought, *I have to call the police.*

He looked at the phone across the room and decided to use the phone in the living room so he wouldn't risk messing up what was, he reminded himself, a crime scene. He turned to leave the kitchen when he heard a sound.

It was a creaking sound, as if the creaky part of the floor were being stepped on—except it *wasn't* a creaky floor in this case, because Hal knew all the creaks in his floor, and this simply wasn't one of them. It was some *other* wood creaking—once, then again, then a third time. Then—

Something *clumped* in the living room.

Ice water coursed through Hal's veins. His heartbeat was thunder in his ears. His fingertips tingled and his scrotum shrank.

The killer's still in the house, he thought. It was a loud thought—his voice shouted out the words in his mind. Hal *heard* them, as if he had spoken them out loud, but he had not so much as parted his lips. His teeth clenched so hard that his jaws ached.

Another sound—a shapeless, characterless sound, unidentifiable, but unmistakable. Someone was moving around in the darkened house.

Hal chewed hard on his lower lip. He tried to slow down his breathing, tried to get hold of himself.

In the drawer of his nightstand, he kept a loaded .38 revolver. He closed and opened his hands at his sides as he thought about it, lying there waiting to be used—at the other end of the house.

A cry from Grey cut through the night, then the cat hissed viciously and repeatedly. He let out a yelp, and Hal heard him run down the hall.

He heard what sounded like a low, throaty chuckle.

More strange creaking.

Hal listened closely. He listened hard, actually straining his ears, reaching out with his hearing, waiting with dread for that next sound, focusing on that entirely. He was so intensely focused on that, that when he finally heard it—something in the front bathroom shattered—his whole body jerked.

The windows throbbed with silent lightning, and thunder shook Hal's bones.

If he wanted to get to his bedroom, Hal would have to move now, and fast, while the killer was in the front bathroom, preoccupied with something in there. He would have to run— no, jog, try to be as quiet as possible—he would have to *jog* down the hall to his bedroom and go for that gun. If he waited, the killer would leave the bathroom and maybe go down the hall ahead of Hal, ending Hal's chances of getting to the revolver.

So that was what he did.

He turned the flashlight off and jogged through the dark.

He went out of the kitchen and dining room, and through the living room—past the front bathroom—and he nearly tripped over his own feet when he saw it, when it hit him. It closed like a giant, fetid mouth over his face, over his head—it filled his field of vision, as if his eyes had zoomed in on it like a pair of expensive binoculars.

He clicked on the flashlight and lifted the beam, just to make sure he was seeing what he *thought* he was seeing.

He did not understand it yet, had no grasp of what it meant once he'd fully realized what he was seeing. But the realization poured over him like a bucket of ice-cold water that sent gooseflesh down his back.

The cross on the living room wall was empty.

The wooden, bloody, fanged figure of Christ was gone.

47

Something released a pinched, ragged growl in the front bathroom.

Don't think about it, just go! Hal thought.

He abandoned the idea of jogging, and broke into a run.

6.

Hal dove through the open bedroom door, then dove again for the bed and landed on it, face-down. He flailed across the bedspread, slammed open the drawer of his nightstand, and grabbed the gun.

Gun in hand, he rolled over and sat up with the gun aimed directly at the open door, and quickly got off the bed and to his feet.

His chest rose and fell as he panted. He felt his heartbeat all over his body. As he listened for more sounds, he became unpleasantly *aware* of his tongue—it felt bloated and oversized in his mouth, a fat impediment.

He listened, but heard nothing. Only the rain outside, only the thunder. Every now and then, the windows lit up with the silver flash of lightning—it flickered around the edges of shades, curtains, and blinds. There were long vertical eggshell-colored blinds over the big window that looked out on the back yard.

Nothing inside the house made a sound.

Seconds passed, then minutes. How many? Hal was in a heart-pounding daze. The black rectangular face of the digital clock on his nightstand stared at him blindly, offering nothing. But he felt time pass.

And nothing happened. He heard nothing.

You've got to call the police, he told himself.

Are you sure you saw what you thought you saw?

He closed his eyes for a moment, thinking, trying to be *sure*. Finally, he decided to go back to the living room. Just to make sure. But he didn't move, he just sat there on the edge of the bed.

It was dark. He had the flashlight, but that bright beam could have a distorting effect on things, couldn't it? Was it possible that he'd only *thought* he'd seen an empty cross?

What was he talking about here, after all—a wooden Jesus stepping down from its cross and wandering around?

Someone in the bedroom giggled.

Hal was alone in the bedroom, so he came to the conclusion that it was he who had giggled.

He did it again. The more he thought about it, the funnier it was. His giggle turned into an outright laugh. And the laughing continued until it was like a pair of hands closing on his throat. He laughed until his stomach muscles hurt. He bent over and slapped his thigh once. The very idea—a fanged, wooden Jesus a little under two feet tall—coming down from its cross—how could he not laugh at that? It was hilarious. Even more hilarious is how firmly he believed that was what he'd seen—an empty cross. He had to be mistaken, *had* to be. A trick of the darkness, the shadows, the flashlight beam.

Finally, he regained control of himself and managed to stop laughing, but he had to go to the bathroom very badly, so he left the bedroom and went into the hallway bathroom, led by the flashlight beam, and emptied his bladder into the toilet, then flushed.

He looked at his reflection in the big mirror over the sink, saw how distorted it looked in the glow of the flashlight. Depending on where he held the light, he could make himself look older, angry—hell, he could make himself look as scary as a serial killer.

Jacquie is lying dead in the kitchen.

The thought made him flinch, like a slap to the face. He went on down the hall to the living room. He raised the flashlight beam and shone it *near* the cross rather than *on* it.

His mouth fell open.

The cross was, indeed, empty.

"*Hal…*" a voice whispered somewhere in the dark. "*Harold Lawrence Dillon!*" It was a low, guttural whisper, with a bit of a throaty gurgle in it.

Hal found that he could not move. He felt frozen in place, like an ice carving.

Lightning made the living room glow for a heartbeat and a half. Thunder crashed.

"*Hal…Harold…Harold Lawrence Dillon!*"

The bottom seemed to fall out of Hal's stomach.

It knows my name, he thought.

"*I know your sins, Hal,*" the whispering voice said.

It was coming from his right, from behind the recliner.

Hal turned slowly toward the chair, lifting the gun a little from his side. With the other hand, he shone the flashlight down on the floor in front of the recliner, then to the side a little.

There was a rush of movement suddenly and a frantic creaking as something shot through the flashlight beam, but Hal got only a glimpse of it, and then—

—burning, piercing pain exploded in his bare right calf and tore up his leg.

He staggered to his left and swung the light down to the floor beside him.

It was gone.

He tried to put weight on his right leg and went down to the floor, fast and heavy, with a pained grunt through clenched teeth. He lay there a moment, trying to catch his breath. The wound in his right calf throbbed mercilessly. He felt the warm trickle of blood dribble down into the heel of his slipper. He wondered how bad it was. What had the damned thing *done* to him, anyway?

Still lying on the floor, he rolled onto his back. He held perfectly still and listened, tried to hear above the sound of his heartbeat in his ears.

Nothing.

No, not true—something, but…what?

A faint clicking.

Coming closer. But what was it? This clicking—actually, it was more a kind of *snapping*—sounded almost as if some kind of fabric were being—well, no, it wasn't really. It was as if…as if—

As if something is catching and snagging on the carpet as it moves across the floor…getting closer, he thought.

Accompanying that was another sound: the high creaking of wood.

Hal quickly sat up and found his face only inches from something that stood between his legs. All he saw were wide, flashing, terrifying eyes that burned him with their hatred and anger, and teeth, and blood, so much blood. Bloody, sharp-pointed teeth, with bits of meat stuck between some of them.

In that brief moment, it smiled at him.

Hal swung the long, heavy flashlight with his left hand and it connected with the small figure with a heavy, hard *smack* of metal hitting wood. The figure disappeared into the darkness to his right, and collided with what sounded like the wall.

Then he heard it scurrying through the darkness, the sounds of its wooden body creaking, its feet snagging on the carpet, all fading as it scurried away from him.

Making small, grunting sounds of fear, Hal clambered to his feet, and limped back down the hall to his bedroom. His arms swung at his sides, and the flashlight beam slashed up and down, sending wild, twisting shadows over the walls of the hall as he hobbled back to his bedroom, ducked through the door, then turned and slammed it shut. He turned the lock on the doorknob until it clicked into place. He wished he had a deadbolt on the bedroom door, as well. But who would think to put a deadbolt on their bedroom door? It was absurd. Your bedroom was supposed to be a safe and secure place, a comforting place to wake up in from some awful nightmare. It wasn't supposed to be a refuge in which you locked yourself. It wasn't a bunker, for crying out loud.

Hal paced beside his bed for a while. The bed he'd shared with Jacquie just hours earlier. The bedspread and sheets smelled of her body, of the perfume she wore, something very light and musky and titillating called Magnetic.

Jacquie is dead, he thought. He repeated the thought several times. It made his head feel numb.

That thing out there killed her, he thought.

His teeth ground together, popping and rumbling in his head.

He could not let it get away with that.

Call the police, he thought.

Hal went to the phone on his nightstand and took the cordless receiver from its base. He turned it on, checked for the dial tone, then punched 9-1-1.

He heard nothing on the phone but dead silence. It suddenly occurred to him that cordless phones were electric, and would not work during a power outage. He cursed and quickly went to his messy closet, where he used the flashlight to rummage around until he found the old-fashioned corded phone he kept in there for just such emergencies. He unplugged the cordless phone from the jack, plugged in the other, and tried again.

Three rings.

"Nine-one-one, what is your emergency?" a woman said.

When he spoke, it was barely above a whisper—he did not want that thing to hear him—but he spoke clearly, succinctly, a little breathlessly.

"I'm in my house, and I'm hiding from the…well, it's a…" He stopped, closed his eyes as he gulped once, then said, "The Jesus, it's a Jesus that was on my wall, and I'm hiding from it, from the Jesus."

As soon as the words were out of his mouth, he regretted them. They made him sound crazy.

"Sir, do you understand that this is an emergency-only line?" the woman said.

"My fiancée is dead," he said. "Her body is lying in the kitchen. That thing—it killed her."

"Uh…you say you have a dead body there?"

"Yes, that's right, and—"

A sound in the bedroom. At first, it sounded like a series of light clicks, but then he recognized what it was—a dry, whispered cackle coming from the darkness somewhere behind him.

"*Haaaal…Haaarooold,*" the thing whispered, and it creaked with movement.

It was in the bedroom with him.

Something flew out of the deep darkness of Hal's walk-in closet, something long and grey. It so frightened him that he let out a sharp, loud yelp. The object cartwheeled through the air, and Hal had to step aside to avoid being hit, and it slapped against the wall over the bed. It fell to the mattress.

It was Grey. The cat's throat was a bloody yawning maw, and his tongue dangled loosely from his open mouth.

7.

"Sir, do you understand that you can get into big trouble for holding up this line with pranks?"

Staring into the dark, Hal actually shook his head back and forth as he said, "No...no prank, this...isn't a prank."

"You say you have a dead body?"

"Yes, that's right, a dead body, my fiancée is dead. She was killed, the Jesus killed her."

"The Jesus—what's this about *Jesus*?"

"That's what killed her, the Jesus. And now it wants to kill me."

"Speak up, sir, if you're going to—"

"I can't, I *can't*. He's here. In the bedroom with me."

He dropped the receiver, hoping vaguely that the 911 operator was tracing the call. The receiver fell to the bed, and the operator's tiny ant voice continued to speak, a small, pinched sound.

Hal raised the revolver and aimed it into the darkness of his closet as he slowly got off the bed and up on his feet.

He panted as he stood there, both arms out, the gun in his right hand, which rested on his left wrist, the flashlight in his left hand, its trembling beam shining on a wall, its glow casting long, black shadows in the room. His own breaths sounded thunderous in his ears, interrupted by the loud pounding of his heart.

"*Haaaal*," the voice whispered from the depth of the closet. "*Haaa-rooold*! Don't touch yourself like that, Harold Lawrence Dillon, don't *touch* yourself! Do you...touch yourself, Harold? *Do you*?" The voice was hoarse, throaty, and filled with a grin, slightly muffled—because of the teeth, Hal suspected, all those sharp little teeth.

Even though he was not the one backed into his walk-in closet, Hal felt cornered, trapped. He felt small and helpless and he kept remembering—

Jacquie's dead Jacquie's dead Jacquie's dead …

—and the memory continued to sound in his head, the image in his mind of Jacquie splayed on the floor, naked and dead and drained of blood, eyes and mouth and throat open, made him feel even smaller and weaker.

"Do you play with yourself, Harold?" the voice whispered rapidly. Then it giggled—a sinister series of clicking sounds in the throat.

He heard movement in the closet.

It was coming out, closer and closer to the beam of his flashlight, which he'd been unable to shine into the closet. He had tried to, but simply could not do it. Because he knew what the beam would show him, and he was not sure he was ready to see it again.

It was still cackling and creaking, and it was headed toward him.

The gun made tiny clicking sounds because his right hand, no matter how hard he tried to steady it against his left wrist, would not stop shaking.

Hal quickly turned to his left and ran out the bedroom door, into the hall. With the flashlight lighting the way, he ran back to the living room, tossing worried glances over his shoulder. The flashlight beam passed over dark, bloody footprints on the beige carpet.

A sound followed him—the patter of small running feet snagging quietly on the carpet.

As the cackling grew louder, the small running footsteps stopped.

The thing landed on Hal's back, and he felt something break through the flesh of his left shoulder.

He cried out as the Christ figure's fangs tore into the flesh of his shoulder. With its arms wrapped around his chest and its legs around his waist, it gnawed viciously into flesh and bone.

He spun to the right as he dropped the flashlight and gun and closed both hands on the head that was pressed face-down on his shoulder. A high, ragged sound of pain came through Hal's clenched teeth as he curled his fingers and clawed at the Christ figure's head. The flashlight clunked to the floor and rolled back and forth, making shadows slide fluidly and dizzily over the walls, back and forth.

When it ripped away, it took some of Hal's shoulder with it between its fangs, and he cried out again. Warm blood trickled down his back and his chest and the pain was excruciating.

But the thing continued to hold on to him. Laughing and laughing.

He turned and fell backward onto the couch, landing with his back pressed hard to the couch's back cushion.

It made a pathetic sound that was muffled by Hal's back and the cushion. Then it clamped its teeth into his back, tearing into his flesh.

"Yaaah!" Hal shouted in pain as he threw himself forward off the couch. He got to his feet and realized the Christ figure was no longer on his back. He heard quick movement behind him. When he turned around, it was gone. There were blood stains on the back of the couch. Blood ran down Hal's back.

He bent forward and swept up the flashlight. Every movement seemed to stretch open wider the deep wounds on his back and shoulder. The flashlight beam cut through the darkness as he moved it over the floor until it found his gun. He picked it up with his right hand.

Why didn't you shoot earlier? he thought as he aimed the gun in the direction of the flashlight beam, followed the beam with the barrel. Finally, he lifted his left arm and balanced his right hand on the wrist, although raising his arm like that created explosions of pain in his throbbing shoulder.

"Harold Lawrence Dillon, I know what you've been doing in that bathroom, and you should be ashamed of yourself!"

The voice was so like his mother's that it made him gasp a little. But it repeated itself a couple of times, and when he listened closely, he quickly realized it was not. It sounded like a *recording* of his mother's voice played a tiny bit too fast, as if the tape was old and worn with use. But it still sent a shudder through him.

It laughed somewhere in the dark, a throbbing, gutsy laugh that gurgled slightly.

"You're a dirty boy, you are," the voice said, low now, and throaty, a bit grumbling. Then again in the slightly distorted voice of his mother: *"You're a dirty boy and Jesus is going to punish you for it!"*

Hal was losing a lot of blood. He worried that he might lose consciousness soon, and the thought of being out cold and vulnerable while that fanged *thing* was running loose in the house—it froze his blood.

Lightning made shadows dance on the walls and the thunder was God-like laughter rumbling overhead.

Hal marched forward, toward the dining room, to pursue the thing.

He stopped in the arched entryway to the dining room when he heard an awful sound—*sucking*. Loud, sloppy sucking.

He stepped forward, went past the dining table with the Coleman lantern standing on it and glowing. His shadow was thrown across the kitchen floor, over Jacquie's body. There was something on top of Jacquie. Hal raised his flashlight.

The gaunt, pale, stick-like figure of Christ had managed to turn Jacquie over onto her back and now straddled her stomach with its legs. Its face was nuzzled down in the gaping, bloody opening that used to be her throat. It slurped up her blood and sucked on her torn flesh.

Hal's lips pulled back over clenched teeth as nausea filled his stomach, his chest, his throat. He lifted the gun and fired.

Bits of wood shattered from the figure's back, and it dove off Jacquie's corpse as Hal fired two more rounds. Those bullets landed uselessly in Jacquie's belly.

He lifted the flashlight, swept it back and forth in the kitchen, until he found his target.

The gaunt Christ figure, with its bony knees and elbows jutting, clung to the cupboards over the kitchen counter, its back to Hal. It turned its head and looked back over its scrawny shoulder. Blood glistened in the scraggly beard and mustache carved so finally in the wooden face.

Jesus smiled around its fangs and creaked woodenly as it began to crawl along the cupboards like a giant pale spider. It spanned the corner to its left and came down the cupboards straight toward Hal, cackling as it used its painfully skinny, but somehow muscular, limbs, like the legs of a spider, crept closer and closer to Hal, who was frozen in place, unable to move, his mouth hanging open as he watched the bloody Christ draw near.

It reached the end of the cupboards. Lightning flashed in the window over the sink and gave the already pallid figure a corpse-blue tint. It lit up the bloody face with its eyes lost in pits of shadow, deep lines around its mouth, smiling around all those small, white fangs. Its muscles tensed for a moment as it prepared to leap.

The thing came flying out of the darkness, waving it muscular arms, the loincloth clinging to its middle, lips baring the bloody, pointed teeth. As it came, it made a frightening sound: it was first the loud trumpeting of an elephant, then became the shrieks and cries of an angry ape.

Hal aimed the .38 fast and squeezed the trigger.

Its shoulder jerked back as chips of wood shattered from it, then the rest of the body followed, and the thing spun around, then landed hard, face-down.

Hal stepped forward until he was standing over the still form of the Christ figure. He shone the flashlight directly down on the figure's pale, bloody shoulders. The thing's back was covered with deep gashes that crisscrossed each other and gaped open and oozed, all from a horrible, ancient whipping.

The figure did not move.

Hal aimed the revolver straight down at the thing, and fired once, then twice. With each shot, the small, bloody body jerked, and wood chips flew in all directions.

Then the gun clicked three times before he stopped firing and let his arm fall limp at his side, the gun pointing at the floor.

The figure rolled onto its right side, bent at the waist, and reached out both hands. They closed on Hal's ankle and the head thrust forward to close its large, razor-lined mouth on his shin.

Hal released a long, hoarse cry of pain as his head tipped backward and his right hand squeezed the gun at his side and made it click again. Pain radiated up his left leg as those small teeth pierced his skin and gnawed into his bone, grinding against it, digging into it.

For a moment, Hal lost his balance and began to hop backward on his right leg. The moment he regained his balance, he kicked his left foot out hard.

The figure flew from Hal's leg and tumbled across the room, into the dining room. It hit the Coleman lantern on the table and knocked it over. The lantern rolled back and forth on the table, and the shadows around it became a living, writhing nightmare.

The figure of Christ growled in the darkness, and quickly rushed out of the dining room, heading straight for Hal, repeatedly snapping its rows of bloody fangs together.

8.

Hal kicked his foot hard and knocked the thing across the dining room. He turned and ran from the dining room, through the living room, then threw himself into the front bathroom. He spun around, and slammed himself against the door as he tucked the gun between the waist of his pants and his belly—it was warm against his skin, like a living thing—then used his right hand to lock the bathroom door.

He stepped backward until the backs of his legs bumped into the toilet, the flashlight focused on the bottom half of the door. He reached behind him and put the toilet lid down, then lowered himself onto it. The gun poked him in the gut, so he pulled it from his pants and put it on the corner of the counter, by the sink. It would do him no good, anyway. It was empty, and the extra bullets were in the nightstand drawer in his bedroom.

He was in terrific pain. He had never felt such pain as he did now from the bites the thing had given him. They throbbed, deep and brutal. He did not know how he had made it to the bathroom. His jaws never came unclenched and he trembled all over because of the pain. Perspiration prickled his forehead and cheeks, ran down into the wound on his back, and burned like the stinging of wasps.

The sound of his heavy breathing seemed loud in the tiny bathroom.

"What's taking them so long?" he breathed aloud. Shouldn't the police have arrived by now? How long ago had he called? He was losing his sense of time.

He was alone with his dead fiancée, his dead cat, and the thing that kept taking big bites out of him.

Something scratched at the door. Its laughter trickled through the narrow gap at the bottom.

"You playin' with yourself in there, Harold?" the figure asked, and it sounded as if it had been inhaling helium because its voice was high and squeaky.

Hal tilted his head back and sighed. "Oh, God," he whispered hoarsely. "God help me. Please help me."

He waited.

There were no windows in the front bathroom. It was small and he felt closed in, claustrophobic, and the feeling was rapidly growing worse.

He could still hear the rain pouring on the roof. The thunder clapped, but sounded farther away now, as if the storm were moving on.

He waited.

Hal tried to think, but he could not line up his thoughts and put them together in any cogent way. His mind whirled around in rapid circles, like a top spun by an angry child.

He heard something. Pounding. He wondered what the thing was doing out there. More pounding, then he heard a voice. Was it speaking to him again? He listened closely.

Someone shouted.

Hal stood up and went to the door, put his ear to it.

"Sheriff's Department! Open up!"

They're here.

Hal turned the knob slowly, pulled the door open a couple of inches. He put his left eye to the opening and peered down the dark hall to the right, then leaned a bit farther out and looked to the left.

He took up the flashlight in his left hand, pulled the door open halfway, leaned out, and shone the flashlight to his right, then to his left. Nothing. No sight of the wooden figure.

More pounding, then: "Mr. Dillon? Marin County Sheriff's Department, please open the door."

Without even thinking about it, Hal snatched the gun up from the counter before leaving the bathroom. Even though it was empty and useless, he subconsciously felt more secure holding the gun in his hand.

He broke into a run and made his way to the front door fast. He stopped, turned, and looked around, passed the light along the floor of the living room one way, then back the other.

Jesus figure was not there. The ugly wooden cross still hung empty on the wall over the couch.

A fist pounded on the door again.

Hal tucked the flashlight under his right arm, reached out and unlocked the door, turned the knob and pulled it open. The two deputies each held up small black flashlights, and shone them directly in Hal's eyes, and he squinted as he pulled the door open all the way with his left hand, the gun held down at his side in his right.

"Whoa, gun!" a tall, fat, middle-aged deputy shouted as he quickly drew his gun.

The other deputy was short, younger, much thinner, and fumbled with his gun, caught off-guard, but finally aimed it at Hal.

"Drop the gun!" the big deputy shouted.

"*Drop* it, *now!*" the little guy shouted.

Hal immediately released the gun, let it fall to the floor, and raised his hands as if he were being held up. The flashlight dropped from beneath his right arm and hit the floor, but did not go out. "It's not loaded!" he shouted, his voice hoarse, mouth dry. "The gun's empty, *really*."

"Do you have any other weapons on you, sir?" the big cop said.

The deputies kept their guns trained on Hal.

"Nuh-*no*, I was j-just trying to *defend* myself."

They slowly lowered their guns.

"Are you Mr. Dillon?" the little one said. "Harold Dillon?"

"Yes, that's me."

"Is that your blood, sir?" the big guy said.

Hal glanced down at himself and, in the glow of their flashlights, saw the blood on his robe.

"Yes, I'm bleeding," he said. "I've been injured. It killed my fiancée."

"*It?*" the small deputy said. "*What* killed your fiancée?"

"The Jesus."

The deputies glanced at one another.

"The Jesus," the big one said.

"Yes, it, it came down off its cross and—look, I-I know how this sounds, I know it sounds *crazy*, but that's what happened, I'm *telling* you, *please*, you've got to believe me, it—"

"Calm down, sir," the thin deputy said.

The big one wandered off and looked around a little.

"You say your fiance's been killed?" the thin one said.

"Thuh-that's right," Hal said, his voice suddenly trembling. "Shuh-she…she…that…that *thing*, it…it *killed* her. And it's still *loose* in here, so we've *got* to—"

"In here," the large deputy called from the dining room.

Hal and the small deputy hurried to where he stood shining his light down on the kitchen floor.

"Cuff him, Jeff," the big one said.

The deputy named Jeff grabbed Hal's right wrist and twisted his arm behind his back as he reached down to take his handcuffs from his belt.

"Hey!" Hal shouted.

"You have the right to remain silent," Deputy Jeff said.

"No, no, you can't arrest *me*!" Hal cried. "I-I-I didn't, I didn't *do* this!"

"Don't struggle, sir," Deputy Jeff said.

Hal jerked his wrist from the deputy's grasp and twisted away from him, shouting, "I will not let you cuff me! I can explain everything, the blood, i-it's all *mine*! It's not Jacquie's, it's *mine*, I've been badly injured, I'm *bleeding*!"

Deputy Jeff lunged toward him and Hal stumbled backward, just out of his reach.

Hal realized he was shaking all over. It had not occurred to him that this might happen, had not even crossed his mind.

"Howard," Deputy Jeff said. "Looks like we got a fifty-one fifty."

Deputy Howard lumbered into the living room. "You resisting arrest, there, fella?"

Deputy Jeff grabbed Hal's right wrist again, and Deputy Howard grabbed his left.

"*No!*" Hal cried in a broken, dry voice. "I *couldn't* have done that! Didn't you see what it did to her throat, how it tore her throat open? Or the bite on her leg, did you see *that*? I didn't do those! I *couldn't*! It won't match my mouth; the teeth marks will be—"

"That woman was shot in the abdomen," Deputy Howard said as Deputy Jeff tried to hold Hal's wrists together.

Hal managed to jerk away from both of them and turned around. "No, it wasn't *me*, it was that…that *Jesus*. It came down off its cross and it's running around in here somewhere right *now*. You have to find it." He turned and pointed through the darkness at the crucifix on the wall over the couch. "It came down off there."

Deputy Jeff sent his flashlight beam sweeping over the wall until it found the wooden cross.

64

Hal gasped.

"Oh, God," he croaked abruptly.

The whole world seemed to tilt to one side, as if Hal were on a boat that was slowly capsizing. Tears stung his eyes as he stared at the crucifix.

Jesus was once again nailed to the cross, gaunt and stringy and covered with painted blood, its head looking upward as if in great agony. The figure was dry, no real blood on it anywhere. It looked exactly as it hand when Hal had bought it.

"But it came down," Hal said. "It came *down!*"

When Deputy Jeff tried to cuff him again, Hal did not struggle. He allowed the deputy to put the cuffs on behind him.

Mouth hanging open, eyes impossibly wide, Hal looked at the thing on the wall, watched it there on its cross, holding perfectly still, looking like nothing more than a carving in wood, an inanimate object, a strange but perfectly safe piece of art.

With a deputy on each side of him, Hal was pulled toward the front door.

"I'll get him into the car," Deputy Howard said, "you get the M. E. out here. Tell 'em we're bringin' in a fifty-one fifty"

"Nooo!" Hal suddenly screamed. It was a high, shrill scream. He jerked his arms from the deputies' hands and stumbled backward. "No, you can't *do* this, I didn't *do* it, I swear to *God*, it was that *Jesus!*" He spun out of the way as Deputy Jeff lunged for him but stumbled and fell to the floor with a grunt. He quickly got to his feet as Deputy Howard moved in and grabbed Hal in a headlock.

"Now, are you gonna calm down, or do I pepper-spray you, huh?" Deputy Howard said. "You wanna get *tasered*? It'll hurt, I promise. You don't calm down, I'm gonna light you up, you hear me?"

Hal stopped moving. His breaths were ragged and each exhalation was a miserable groan, but he stopped struggling. In a moment, he was standing between them again, being led out of the house.

Deputy Howard took him from Deputy Jeff and dragged him to the back door of the cruiser parked on the curb in front of the house.

Hal began to scream and fight and shake his head back and forth so fast and so hard that he was rapidly making himself sick. He screamed of his innocence, and told them again and again that it was "the Jesus" that had done it.

The rain was cold on Hal's face.

Up and down the street, flashlight beams bobbed up and down in the darkness as people stepped outside to see what was happening.

Deputy Jeff got on the radio as Deputy Howard put his big hand on the top of Hal's head and pushed him down into the backseat of the cruiser.

He sat there, sobbing, as he stared out the window at his house.

It stood silent and dark.

It looks so empty, Hal thought.

He shook his head back and forth, his jaw jutting. "No," he said. "It's not." Then he screamed, "It's not! It's *not* empty!" He lifted his legs and leaned back and kicked the seat in front of him. "It's *not* empty! *He* did it! You hear me? *Heee* did it!"

Deputy Howard opened the door.

"You don't calm down back here, I'm gonna pepper spray you," Deputy Howard said.

Hal took in a deep breath and bellowed, "It was the *Jesus*! It was the *Jeeee-suuuus* that killed her!"

He screamed on as the deputies waited for more people to come, to investigate, to find him guilty.

And Hal screamed on.

God's Work

Pastor Gil Freeman stood near the back of his church's multi-purpose room watching as only a handful of people gathered for the after-service potluck. On any other Sunday, the room would be filled by now, humming with voices and redolent with the smells of casseroles and lasagnas and Swedish meatballs, croissants and pies and cobblers. But now, it looked bare and the few dishes that had been brought were not enough to fill the room with their warm aromas.

There were well over a dozen banquet tables set up with metal folding chairs lined along the sides, but they were empty today. Those who had shown up would barely fill two of them.

Most of the people there were the older members of his congregation, the stooped and wrinkled, with cloudy but still smiling eyes that had weathered years of heartache and yet never darkened. They were the only ones who had tried to make him feel welcome when he had first come to this church nearly two months ago and now they were the only ones keeping him from feeling completely rejected by the congregation. He was grateful to have them there.

The others—the middle-aged and younger—had been suspicious of him. They seemed to think he was too soft, too easy on sin. Freeman was young—he would turn thirty-one in a month—and soft-spoken; his sermons were quiet and calm rather than loud and charismatic. This was an angry congregation. They were angry about how corrupt the world had become, angry at its sins and offenses, and they wanted someone in the pulpit who would share their anger and give it booming voice.

He would expect the older congregants to be the suspicious ones who would want him to be more rigid and serve up hellfire and brimstone in his sermons, the ones to be angry at the world for its wickedness—and plenty of them were. But this smaller group of church members from the ages of sixty and up had seen more of life and knew things moved in cycles, including good times and bad, and many of them had paid much closer attention to the man they all claimed to love and worship and knew what he stood for.

Freeman was not an angry man and he did not deliver fire-and-brimstone sermons, and today, the church members were showing their disappointment in him more openly than they had before. It had been on vivid display first during that morning's sermon, and now they were driving the point home by not coming to the potluck.

Even worse than their absence was where they had gone instead and why. Freeman knew what they were doing, and it was tying his gut into knots.

He did not see his wife Deborah approaching from his right and was startled when she took his hand, but he quickly smiled.

"Nope, that smile doesn't fool me," she whispered.

"What?"

"You look like you're developing an ulcer over here." She squeezed his hand. "You shouldn't let it bother you so much. You're going to wrinkle early if you keep frowning like that."

He sighed. "I know, but I keep thinking I could've said something more, something that would have changed their minds, made them see the mistake they were making. If only I'd said the right thing this morning."

"Honey, your sermon was wonderful. *Powerful*. That may be the best sermon I've heard you deliver. But their minds were set on doing this. They were determined. There was nothing you could do no matter what you said to them."

He shook his head. "What if these are the only people who show up for church next week?"

"What if they are? Remember what the Bible says about where two or more are gathered?"

He nodded slowly.

"Are you going to come join us, Gil?"

"In a minute, sweetheart."

"Well, don't be long. The kids are worried about you. They wanted to know what was wrong with Daddy, why he looked so 'weird.' Their word."

Freeman smiled. "Tell them I'm fine, and I'll be there in a minute."

He was a tall man, so she had to stand on tiptoes to kiss him on the cheek as she rubbed a hand over his back. Then she joined the others across the room.

Freeman paced a bit, then leaned his back against the wall and looked out the window that provided a view of the parking lot. The nearly empty parking lot.

Yes, he knew where they were. He could imagine what they were doing at that very moment. He looked at his watch. They had no doubt gathered and were waiting.

He closed his eyes, rubbed them with thumb and forefinger, and thought about that morning's sermon, wondering if it could have been better, more effective, if there had been any chance at all of stopping what was no doubt going to happen.

The faces that looked up at Freeman as he stood at the pulpit were not pleasant ones. Their jaws were set, their lips were firm. He could find only a couple of smiles among all the stern faces that seemed to want all of this over with so they could get on with their plans for the day.

He knew what those plans were. That was why he had decided this morning's sermon would be unlike all the others, all those quiet, gentle sermons he had given over the previous weeks that this congregation seemed to disapprove of so much.

Placing his Bible on top of the pulpit and a hand on each of the cold wooden edges, he leaned forward and smiled.

"I decided to scrap the sermon I'd planned for this week," he said, quietly as usual. "After I began working on it, I said to myself, 'Gil, this isn't the sermon you need to give. The one you need to give is...a bit harder, with more of an edge.' And that was very true. But I want you to know that I am saying what I'm about to say this morning out of concern, and nothing more. Not out of anger, not with condemnation, but with deep, sincere concern for my church family.

"I know that you have not been too satisfied with me as your pastor. For that I am truly sorry. Honestly, I have done my best and will continue to do so. I hope that you will give me a chance. And I hope that you will keep in mind that I am having to give you a chance as well. Because I know about something you are planning to do. Today, in fact. And it's something of which I do not approve. But my approval means nothing. The important thing is God's approval, and, to tell you the truth, I think God is hanging his head over what you plan to do today."

His mouth was cotton-dry, but he had anticipated that. He reached down to the glass of water he had placed on the shelf beneath the top of the pulpit, took a sip, then a deep breath, returned the glass, and continued.

"I've heard the whispers," he said, his voice a little louder now, more authoritative. "I've heard the talk about what's to happen today, and I've been saddened by the eagerness in your voices and the joy in your eyes.

"I know about the writer, James K. Denmore. I know about his books. In fact, when I heard all the talk going on among you, I went out and bought a few of them. I wonder how many of you have read any of his work. I wonder only because you are apparently so angry about what he writes. If you haven't read his work, then your anger is not righteous indignation, it is the ugliest kind of hypocrisy. But I am giving you the benefit of the doubt and will assume that you have read it and, having read it myself, I understand your disapproval.

"He writes what is known as 'erotic horror' and he uses religion in his fiction in a deliberately blasphemous and provocative way. I found his work distasteful in the extreme. It's obvious to me that Mr. Denmore is a talented writer, but I feel he's selling himself short by using his talents to write such books. And, worse yet—they sell. I also believe Mr. Denmore to be a marketing genius. He deliberately fills his books with things that he knows will upset *you*, and then you go to your blogs and YouTube channels to condemn him, you grab your signs to protest him. And you draw much more attention to his work than it would receive without your help. I hate to say it, but he knows how to manipulate you. And it always works. You've helped sell a lot of books for Mr. Denmore.

"But I don't *know* Mr. Denmore. I've never met him. I don't know what he believes or what experiences his life has given him or how he treats other people or small animals. I don't know why he writes what he writes or what he thinks about or what's important to him. All I know for sure about Mr. Denmore is that he is a human being, and I feel no differently about him, even after reading his work than I do about any of you. He is still, no matter what any of us feels about his work, a child of God. Just like the rest of us. That makes him *one* of us."

There was a bitter murmur somewhere in the crowd, but it was not loud enough to be considered a voice of protest.

Gil shifted his weight from foot to foot as he took another drink of water, put the side of a fist to his mouth and cleared his throat.

"As I said, the man is talented. The Bible tells us that talents are given to us by God. Therefore, Mr. Denmore's considerable writing talent was given to him by God. But God left it up to him to decide how he would use that talent. Because God, from the beginning in the Garden of Eden and onward, has given us the freedom of choice. He values our free will as much as we should because He knows that without it, we are nothing more than slaves. The Bible is full of examples of God giving choices and letting humankind decide. More often than not, they made the wrong choice. But it was *their* choice because he left it up to them.

"Sometimes we forget that. We take it upon ourselves to impose on others what we feel is God's will. And that, my friends…that is terribly wrong."

Freeman's heart pounded nervously against his ribs and he found it difficult to control his breathing because the faces looking up at him were growing darker and colder. They became angrier with each sentence he spoke. He gulped, and after a moment of nervous silence, he finally continued.

———————

Freeman blinked his eyes several times, pulling his head out of his thoughts, and crossed the room to his wife's side. He said, "Deb, honey, I'm going to take off for a little while."

Her smile fell away and she looked suddenly worried. "Why? Where are you going?"

"Down to the bookstore. I just…I want to do what I can."

She sighed and shook her head. "Do you really feel like you have to do this?"

He nodded. "Please tell everyone that I'll be back soon." He leaned down and gave her a kiss, then headed for the exit. Voices called out "You leaving us, Pastor?" and "Where're *you* off to?" and "Aren't you hungry?"

As he slipped on his coat and put a small Bible in his coat pocket, he smiled, waved, and said, "I'll be back in just a little while. Enjoy yourselves."

Outside, he got into his car, started it up, and headed across town for the bookstore, praying silently that he was doing the right thing. And that he had done the right thing on the pulpit instead of just making the situation worse.

———————

"When God put the Tree of Knowledge of Good and Evil in the Garden of Eden, he didn't put it there for aesthetics. It was there to give Adam and Eve a choice. He told them that if they ate of the tree, death would come to them as surely as they breathed. Not right away, necessarily, but it would come eventually. He told them not to eat of it and left it up to them. He didn't have to. He could have *made* them utterly devoted to him if he'd wanted. Like robots. But would that have been the right thing? No. That would have made them nothing more than automatons forced to love and worship him. Their actions would have held no sincerity, no heartfelt love. And if you've ever loved — and I know each of you has — then you know that true love comes only out of free will. It *cannot* be forced. So, he put that tree right there in the garden with them.

"It was *their* choice!" he shouted, startling many of the people in the pews. "God left it up to *them*. He did not force them to do or believe anything. And when they made the wrong choice, as disappointed as he was, he loved them no less. Their exile from the garden was the result of their own actions, but God stayed with them and watched over them. They were still, after all, his children.

"He does the same with us. He wants us to choose the direction our lives take. Those who are saved have chosen salvation of their own free will. Those who are lost have chosen to turn their backs on God for whatever reason. He doesn't force us to do anything."

Freeman took another sip of water. Beads of sweat were beginning to gather above his upper lip and he removed a handkerchief from his pocket to dab them away.

His voice was stern when he said, "Are we wiser than God? Do we know better than he? Did he put us here on this earth to decide what others should and should not do? What they should and should not read or look at or listen to?

"I've learned of the other protests this church was involved in before I came. I know you went to an exhibit of photographs by a controversial artist. I'm familiar with his work and, once again, I understand your disapproval. But I do *not* understand your *anger!*" he shouted, pounding his fist on the pulpit.

He had rehearsed it at home and was afraid he would not be able to pull it off convincingly, but by the time he reached that point in his sermon, he *felt* it. Even more people were jolted by his outburst this time.

"I'm not saying you should *approve* of these things, but your response should be one of sadness, not anger. That's how God responds to *our* bad choices, and always with continuing love and forgiveness. Instead, windows were broken. A door was destroyed. *Arrests* were made. Dear *God*, what kind of behavior is that? Not Christlike behavior, that's for sure."

He used the handkerchief to dab his forehead this time.

"I know about your visit to the Civic Auditorium on the night of a concert given by a particularly offensive rap group about which I'm sure I feel the same as you. But your *behavior*, I just—I don't understand how you can—was *that* the right thing to do? In front of all those TV cameras? In front of so many young people who, now more than ever, need examples of true Christian love?"

A loud mumble rose sharply from the congregation, another muffled voice of dissent that decided, after all, to remain silent.

"I know about your gatherings at one of the local clinics that performs abortions. At one of those gatherings, *garbage* was thrown at the women going into the clinic and they were called murderers. There were more arrests."

He took another sip of water and another deep breath before continuing.

"When your previous pastor died suddenly, Pastor Warrick, I was available and was called in immediately. I was told that this church was conservative. And the sign out front and the cross on the roof identify it as *Christian*. This behavior is neither, in my opinion. It is nothing less than *hateful*.

"Maybe you remember an incident in the Bible in which a group of scribes and Pharisees brought to Jesus a woman who had committed adultery. They asked him what they should do with her, and with all the righteous indignation they could muster, I'm sure, they reminded Jesus that the law instructed that she be stoned to death for her crime. And Jesus said, 'Yes, stone the whore to death.'"

Sharp gasps rose from the congregation like puffs of smoke.

"Is that what he said? No, of course not. He said, 'He that is without sin among you, let him first cast a stone at her.' They thought about that and then they did exactly what they *should* have done: they high-tailed it out of there. Why? Because *they* knew there wasn't a man among them without sin."

He leaned forward over the pulpit and put his mouth close to the microphone. His next shout was the loudest so far: "*What about you?*" He slowly stood upright and ignored the grumbling from the pews, getting louder now. "Are *you* without sin? Are you sinless enough to accuse a young woman on her way to have an abortion—and going through what is probably the toughest, most painful time of her life—of *murder*? I know I'm not." He raised his right hand. "Maybe a show of hands? Any of you? Sinless?" He waited a moment, then: "*No you are not!* And I think you know it. But you not only hurled terrible accusations at these women, some of you threw *garbage* at them. One would think, judging by your behavior, that your own life records are spotless, that you are completely and utterly without sin. But you're *not*. And I'll tell you what else you aren't. You are not a follower of Christ. Your behavior has been a *perversion* of the teachings of Christ. A slap in the face of God. And if Jesus had been present at that clinic, or that concert, or that art gallery, he would have stood between you and those women, and that rap group, and that photography exhibit and shouted, '*Let those of you without sin cast the first piece of trash at her!*' Or call her a murderer. Or vandalize that building. Let the one who's never done anything wrong in his or her life first step into God's shoes and pass holy judgment on a human soul. Because that is *exactly* what you're doing.

"The son of God came to this earth as a man to live a sinless, selfless, and loving life to give us an example to live by. In that life, he passed judgment on no one. In chapter twelve of the Book of John, Jesus says, 'And if any man hear my words, and believe not, I judge him not: for I came not to judge the world, but to save the world.' Why? Because only his father, only *God* can judge anyone. Jesus himself admitted that. He never gave anyone reason to feel guilt or self-hatred. In the case of the adulteress, the sin had been identified by the accusers, and after Jesus had embarrassed them into running away, he specifically told the woman that he did *not* condemn her, and he said, 'Go, and sin no more.' He was as human as you and I and I'm sure there were times he wanted to destroy a few doors and maybe kick the seats of a few pants. But the only time he did anything remotely close to that was when moneychangers used his father's temple to conduct their crooked, corrupt business, and that, as I'm sure you can understand, was just too much. And even then, he hurt no one. He just knocked over a few tables and yelled a lot."

Freeman scratched the back of his neck and sighed.

"His life and death were meant to give us an example, so that we could have someone to turn to and lean on when our lives get tough, so that we'd have someone who could say he knew what it was like and forgive us our mistakes. But you have *stomped all over that life!* With your anger toward those with whom you disagree. Those are the people to whom you *should* be showing the love and acceptance that you *claim* to have at the center of your life by falsely declaring yourselves Christians. And you should be ashamed of yourselves."

He pulled out the handkerchief and swept it over his entire face this time, trying to catch his breath and calm his trembling hands. And then something happened that, in his time as a pastor, he had never experienced before.

The congregation began to stand up and talk back.

———————

Freeman began to sweat in the car as he drove, thinking about his sermon and the chaos it had caused in the church, about which he felt so guilty. It was a sunny spring day, but not warm. Nearing the bookstore, his palms were sweaty against the steering wheel as he grew increasingly anxious. What would he find? How would they react? And most importantly, what would he *do* once he got there?

He had no idea. He only knew that he had to try to do *something*.

The bookstore was on the corner of a busy intersection and parking was difficult to find, but when he drove by, he saw the crowd inside through the large front window and the crowd outside. There were seventy or eighty people taking up a good chunk of the sidewalk lined with small maples. He recognized those from his congregation and saw that people had come from other churches in town, as well.

He found a parking space a block away and walked back to the store. Up ahead, he could hear chattering voices; a small group of the protesters began chanting, "Perversion! Blasphemy! Evil!"

Most of them held hand-written signs that called James K. Denmore a pornographer, a Satanist, a worshiper of demons, among other things. The signs accused him of polluting young minds, promoting violence and perversion, and offending God.

The signs made Freeman's chest ache.

He was disappointed to see that there were no police officers on hand to maintain order. He knew what groups like this could become—he had gotten a small taste of it in church that day—and had hoped there would be someone around to make sure things did not get out of hand. The absence of any security worried him. His chest felt tight with dread as he neared the bookstore, and he silently prayed, *Take my hand here, Lord. I need your help.*

He shouldered his way through the group until a pair of eyes met his and registered first surprise at his arrival, then darkened with hostile determination. It was Deanne Furst, a middle-aged widow with short reddish hair in tight, beauty-parlor curls, whose body was thickening with age. She wore the simplest of clothes and, always, sensible shoes. She held a sign that read:

JAMES K. DENMORE:
PERVERTER OF CHILDREN
DISCIPLE OF SATAN
OFFENDER OF GOD

Freeman flinched when he read the sign and Deanna saw his reaction. She curled one end of her mouth into a little smirk, enjoying his disapproval. She had been one of the loud and vehemently dissenting voices during his sermon that morning, so he was not surprised.

Then others began to notice him and the chatter dropped in volume as eyes turned to him, some widening with surprise.

Fred Granger had obviously gone home from church and changed into what was, for him, a standard uniform: plaid shirt, khaki jacket, jeans, and brown Oxford shoes. A green canvas bag hung heavily from his shoulder and he carried a sign with shaky, hand-painted letters that read:

DENMORE IS EVIL
AND SATANIC

"THOU SHALT NOT SUFFER
A WITCH TO LIVE!"
EXODUS 22:18

Freeman smiled at Granger, but the man's square face maintained the same stern expression it usually held. His wife Patty stood beside him, a frail looking woman in a simple baggy house dress. Her head was bowed and she stared at the concrete, holding a baby in one arm and clutching the hand of the toddler boy; she was enormously pregnant.

Sam Bigelow, a tall, heavy man with a sad face, saw him and looked confused at first, then smiled, perhaps thinking that he had come to join their protest.

David and Karen Potter, an attractive thirtyish couple, glanced at one another when they saw him, then continued to stare at him with expressionless faces as he drew closer.

Marvin Kent did a double-take, then stared in disbelief as Freeman approached. He held a sign that read:

JAMES K DENMORE'S BOOKS
TEACH EVIL, CORRUPTION
AND SEXUAL PROMISCUITY

Kent's face grew cold as Freeman approached.

Marcus Benworth, a single black man who sang in the church choir, held no sign but stared at Freeman as if he were coming up the sidewalk naked.

Sally Morrisey saw him, too, and a gray shadow of guilt passed briefly over her face. She was a young, single woman in her mid-thirties whose face always conveyed warmth and friendship—except for that moment when she saw Freeman and her face fell. She lowered her eyes and turned away to keep him from seeing her sign, which read:

JAMES K. DENMORE'S BOOKS
DESTROY MORALS AND
GIVE SATAN FREE REIGN

Michael Denny, who had been dating Sally for a short while, did not have a sign. When he saw Freeman, his eyebrows rose as if he were asking himself, *And exactly what is* he *doing here?*

Others from the congregation responded to his presence with their eyes, their body language. No one spoke. No one welcomed him. No one, with the possible exception of Sam Bigelow, wanted him there.

The unfamiliar faces from other churches were every bit as angry, their signs just as ugly.

Freeman clenched his teeth nervously as he went to the center of the crowd and removed the small bible from his pocket. He opened it, took a steadying breath, then lifted an arm and said loudly, "Would you all please listen to me for just a moment!"

The volume lowered further and some bitter murmurs passed through the crowd.

"Please, for just a moment," he said, turning around and passing his eyes over all of them, known and unknown, trying to sound pleasant. He looked down at his Bible a moment, then said, "'And why beholdest thou the mote that is in thy brother's eye, but perceivest not the beam that is in thine own eye?' Those are the words of Jesus Christ from the Book of Luke. Do you know what a mote is? It's a tiny speck. You all know what a beam is. A log. I've come here to ask you just one question: What gives you the right to come here and tell this man that he is evil when each and every one of you here is just as human and just as much a sinner as he is. *What gives you the right*?"

The crowd was silent as traffic rushed by.

Finally, Deanna Furst shouted, "He's spreading his sinfulness!"

"He's *selling* it!" Karen Potter shouted. "He's handing it out to people who don't know any better."

"How do you know they don't know better?" Freeman said. "And if they don't, why don't you *show* them by living your beliefs? A Christian is someone who uses Jesus Christ as a life model, not someone who bullies people whose work they don't like. This is *not* your job. It's not what Christ wanted of his followers, it's the very behavior he rejected."

"How do you know?"

He raised the Bible over his head. "Because he *told* us. He was very clear. If you'd read your Bibles once in a while instead of using them as weapons, *you* would know that. All of you should be ashamed of yourselves. *All* of you!"

Freeman was surrounded by angry eyes, and angry voices rose in response to him. They looked enraged, as if he had insulted their families.

"Look, I'm sorry if I sound angry," he said, trying to be heard above their shouting. "Please, listen! I'm sorry, many of you don't even know me. I'm Pastor Gil—"

"We know who you are, Pastor Freeman." It was a deep, unfamiliar voice, rich and full, and the speaker stepped forward, shouldering his way through the crowd. "We've heard all about you."

He was of average height, but still imposing, with a barrel chest and large belly that filled out his dark suit. His graying hair was balding on top and he wore a pair of large-framed tortoise-shell glasses. His eyes were stern and his mouth was a straight line across his broad, fleshy face. A waddle of skin hung beneath his chin and jiggled as he moved. He clutched a bible at his side and did not look pleased.

"I'm Reverend Perry Wickes from the Celebration of Christ Church across town, Pastor Freeman, and I must say, I'm very disappointed in you. I know you're new to this community and aren't familiar with the spiritual climate here, but…this? I could understand some church members not wanting to participate in a protest like this. I always expect a certain number of people to stay away. But you? A pastor? The *leader* of your congregation? I don't understand it, and I think you've failed your church." His eyes glared, jowls trembled. "And your God."

"I'm sorry you think that of me, Reverend. But for me to support this protest, I would have to go against my beliefs. Against what I believe God wants me to do. I have nothing against a peaceful protest. But this isn't a protest, and it certainly *isn't* the behavior of followers of Christ. It's a hostile attack on a single man. The God I worship would not want me to participate."

Reverend Wickes pointed a stiff, meaty finger at Freeman and bellowed, "Then you are *not* a man of God! You are a friend of darkness."

Freeman had to stifle a surprising laugh that bubbled up in response to the reverend's melodramatic accusation. Before he could respond, there was a stir in the crowd. He turned to see everyone looking up the sidewalk to three people who were approaching the bookstore.

The first was a large, muscular man in a dark suit, eyes hidden by black sunglasses. He did not look friendly. Behind him, a beautiful woman with red hair held the hand of a man Freeman recognized immediately from the pictures on his books: James K. Denmore. A man in his forties, he was slender and youthful even though his thick brown hair was rapidly turning white. He had a pale, childlike face and wide, curious eyes, and Freeman thought he looked vulnerable as he approached the angry crowd. He certainly did not appear to be the evil monster Freeman's congregation made him out to be. He even smiled at them.

The protesters lifted their signs and began to shout at him.

"Pornographer!"

"Your books are Satanic!"

"How would you like your child to read what you write?"

Still smiling as his bodyguard made a path through the crowd, Denmore said, "My books aren't *for* children."

"Pervert!"

"Blasphemer!"

"Demon worshiper!"

Denmore's smile did not falter as he followed the large man through the crowd, and his companion did the same, never letting go of his hand.

A white van with the call letters of a local television station painted on the side came to a stop, double-parked in front of the bookstore.

"Oh, no," Freeman breathed, rolling his eyes.

The shouting grew worse as the bodyguard held out an arm and pushed people aside to clear a path to the door.

Freeman could not believe the things he was hearing from members of his congregation—from any of the other protesters, all of whom claimed to be Christians. Worst of all, it was making *him* feel angry. He tried to resist it, gulp it down like a foul-tasting syrup. But he could not.

He raised both of his arms, clutching the small bible in his right hand, and shouted, "Stop! *Stop* this! This is *wrong*! This is—"

Reverend Wickes stepped forward, slapped a hand onto Freeman's chest, and pushed him backward as he growled through clenched teeth, "Stay out of this. You're no part of this. You've got no business here."

"I have a *lot* of business here, and if you touch me again, I'll call the police and have you arrested for assault."

"Some of your people told me about your little show on the pulpit this morning and I think it's shameful. Some of *them* think it's enough to start a campaign to have you ousted from the church. After only two months at the pulpit. No, Pastor Freeman, you have no business here. Even your own people don't want you."

"I don't live my life according to your opinion, Reverend. Or popular opinion. Only God's opinion. You do what you feel is best for your congregation, and I'll do what I feel is best for mine."

He turned his back on Reverend Wickes as the shouting continued around them and addressed the crowd again.

"Stop this!" he shouted. "You have no right to judge this man."

Someone inside the bookstore pushed the door open and held it for Densmore, but he stopped and turned to Freeman, listening as his smile fell away in surprise.

"Even Christ himself said he could not judge others. Only *God* has the right to judge us."

"Thank you," Densmore said, smiling at Freeman. "I appreciate that. Who are you?"

"Pastor Gil Freeman."

Densmore's eyebrows hiked up in surprise. "You're a *pastor*? And you're defending *me*? Why?"

The crowd had become silent by then and waited for Freeman's answer.

"I, uh, I've read your work. It's not a genre I normally read, but—"

Densmore laughed good-naturedly and said, "I bet it's not."

"Well, given my congregation's preoccupation with it, I thought I should sample it. You're an excellent writer, by the way. The fact that I don't, uh, well, like your fiction, mostly for religious reasons, is irrelevant. My beliefs make me no better than you. And I don't think you deserve the treatment you're getting here. I hope you'll forgive these people for their behavior."

Densmore moved forward and reached out his hand. Freeman shook it.

"I appreciate that," the writer said. "You're a good person, Pastor, and it's nice to meet you."

Then Densmore and his companion disappeared into the bookstore and the bodyguard followed.

The crowd erupted in loud accusations and denouncements aimed now at Freeman. He found himself surrounded by angry faces and hate-filled eyes and mouths that worked furiously, flashing teeth and tongues. Their knuckles were white as they clutched their signs, pumping them up and down now as they railed at him.

Reverend Wickes appeared before him, his large, fleshy face swallowing up Freeman's field of vision, pearls of sweat clinging to the red-splotched, trembling cheeks.

"Well?" he said. "Do you still want to stay here? Where you're not wanted? Where you don't *belong*?"

"I'm not going anywhere, Reverend."

Half of the reverend's mouth curled into an unpleasant smile. "Maybe not right now. We'll see come judgment day."

A heavy, bearded man stepped out of the bookstore wearing slacks and a sport coat and raised a hand, shouting, "Please, could you listen a moment, *please!*" When things calmed down a bit, he said, "My name is Ed Bailey, I'm the manager of this store, and I'd like to ask you—no, no, I'm *telling* you that if you do not calm down and clear this doorway *immediately*, I'm calling the police and having you all arrested. Is that understood? *Arrested*."

They were silent.

Bailey nodded. "Thank you. But I won't speak to you a second time. You're welcome to protest, but if you don't keep it peaceful, the police will be here to deal with you." He went back inside.

Freeman wished he would call the police now. Maybe their presence would keep the hostility from escalating, which he feared was a possibility.

"Just spread out for now," Wickes told the crowd, "and hold your signs high."

They watched Freeman with stabbing eyes as they stood or paced with their signs. Seeing those faces took him back once again to that morning's sermon.

"The Bible says to resist sin!" Deanna Furst shouted as she rose from her pew. "It says to *fight* it. It says to 'take up the armor of God' and fight it."

He froze at the pulpit. No member of any congregation had ever stood up and shouted at him during a sermon. He gathered his thoughts quickly and said, "No, no, God means for us to take up his armor and fight *temptation*. The temptation that comes to us all to drag us *into* sin."

"But this man, this *writer*," she spat disdainfully, "is presenting a *temptation* to others. He's making himself a stumbling block, a—"

"No, Deanna, *personal* temptation, the temptations we face individually in our own lives. *That's* what the armor of God is for. We have no right, no moral *room* to worry about the temptations and sins of others. We have too many of our *own*. God did not intend for us to take up his armor simply to *disagree* with people."

Deanna Furst remained standing, lips pressed tightly together, fists clenched at her sides.

Marvin Kent shot to his feet and said, "How can you condone what that man writes?"

"I *don't* condone it. But I'm not going to condemn him for it, either.

"But what he writes is polluting minds," Kent said, his voice getting louder.

"Yes, maybe so, but they are the minds of people who are *choosing* to be polluted. Our job is not to take away their freedom to make that choice but to show them an alternative by living as the examples Christ wanted us to be. We should be *living* our beliefs instead of beating people over the heads with them. If you could get rid of James K. Denmore, there would be another to take his place, and many more after that. Are you going to try to ruin *all* of them?"

"Yes!" someone shouted.

Another voice cried, "Yes!"

Then another, and another.

Anger welled up in Freeman's chest and he gripped the edges of the pulpit tightly. He said, "Matthew 7:1: 'Judge not, that ye be not judged.' In other words, do you want God to judge you as harshly as you are judging James K. Denmore? If he did, how would you hold up? Would you do any better? Frankly, I think that if God judged me that harshly, I would not do well at *all*. I'm glad to know he won't, though, because I refuse to pass judgment on others. It's not my place. And it's not yours."

"That verse means we shouldn't judge other Christians!" a voice shouted from the back.

Freeman's mouth dropped open in genuine shock. "You think it only applies to other *Christians*? Where does it say *that*? Do you really believe God is that narrow-minded?"

"He put us here to fight evil!" someone shouted.

Then everyone started shouting as they stood and began to leave the church.

———————

They were calm for a while as they carried their signs up and down the sidewalk past the bookstore's large display window, where a sign read:

JAMES K. DENMORE IN PERSON!
AUTHOR OF "LUST AND THE DEVIL"
HERE! TODAY!
2:00 p.m. – 4:00 p.m.

They were waiting for their prey—anyone who showed up to have their books autographed by Denmore. There was already a crowd inside, and more were sure to come. He wondered how those people would feel, on their way home with their autographed books, about the "Christians" who had shouted insults and ridicule at them. If he were in their position, Freeman thought it would be difficult to see Christianity as anything more than divisive and ugly.

Voices rose in the crowd and Freeman turned to see two young couples, books tucked under their arms, walking toward the bookstore, the two women in the middle and the men flanking them. They had just rounded the corner when they saw the protesters and signs and slowed their pace. They stopped, conferred for a moment, then continued toward the bookstore.

The protesters shouted as the couples approached, and Freeman shouldered his way to the door and held it open for them. The young people looked nervous, even fearful, as they made their way through the crowd, but they smiled and thanked Freeman as they went inside.

"I'm sorry," he said. "I hope you'll forgive their behavior."

After that, customers came in force, as if a gate had been opened somewhere. He stood holding the door open while people filed in, and he smiled and greeted them as they passed, asking them to forgive the protesters for their behavior.

Outside the door, Freeman's words angered the protesters, who began shouting at him that he had no business apologizing for them.

Then they started going into the bookstore. Just a couple at a time stepped into the foot traffic entering the door. Then they broke off from the others and began to gather near one end of the long table where James K. Denmore sat signing books with his companion seated beside him and the bodyguard standing behind them both, watching the crowd through his sunglasses.

Horrified, Freeman followed them in after several protesters had entered the bookstore. He walked in directly behind Fred Granger, with his wife, baby, and child, and that heavy-hanging canvas shoulder bag.

Freeman hurried around the group of protesters, stepped between them and the table, and said, "Stop this. *Please* stop this. What you're doing is wrong."

"No, no," Fred Granger said, stepping forward, "*you're* doin' wrong, Pastor. Fact, you're not even a pastor, you're a *traitor*. You shouldn't even be here."

"I'm here to remind you of why *you're* here, Fred, and it's not to pass judgment on this man, or anyone else. Have you completely missed Christ's message?"

"His message was that he came here not to send peace but to send a *sword*."

"But did he ever pick up a sword, Fred? Can you think of any time in the gospels when Jesus picked up a sword and started lopping off heads? No, you can't. You know why? Because it never happened. A lot of things in the Bible are meant *figuratively*, not literally, and that's one of them. Jesus never picked up a sword. His message was that we are here to take care of each other, of everyone, even our enemies. His *message* was the sword because it went against the way the world works. It still does. And the world *still* rejects it. You've been fooled into rejecting it, too. Do you understand?"

Granger's lips pressed together hard and curled into a sneer as his face darkened with anger.

"Please, Fred. The others will listen to you. Call this off now."

"Move or I'll move you myself.

"Fred—"

Granger put both hands on Freeman's shoulders and shoved him aside so hard, the pastor fell to the floor.

Freeman looked up to see Granger turning toward the table again. The bodyguard was already coming around the table in his direction. Granger reached into his canvas bag.

Scrambling to get to his feet, Freeman shouted, "Gun!"

The bodyguard reached his right hand beneath his suit coat.

Granger lifted the shotgun to his shoulder as Freeman got to his feet and dove in front of him. At the same moment, the bodyguard drew a handgun from beneath his coat.

Granger fired the sawed-off shotgun a fraction of an instant before the bodyguard fired his gun.

Freeman's midsection erupted as he moved through the air. Granger collapsed to the floor as Freeman's body landed with a wet sound.

Although the gunfire left everyone's ears ringing, it could not drown out the screams.

"Wait, please *wait!*" Freeman shouted from the pulpit as most of the congregation quickly went to the rear of the church and out the doors. "Please, think about what you're doing. How would you feel if someone came into this church and tried to silence me because they disagreed with what *I* had to say?"

They ignored him and left the church early to gather at the bookstore.

Choices

The whole family was up early because it was Friday. Friday was a special day for the Holts and they were all wide awake in spite of the intrusions on their sleep during the night. There had been an explosive summer storm with thunder so loud it shook the house and rattled the windows and woke the whole family. Summer storms were not uncommon, but something about this one was unlike anything the Holts had seen before.

The thunder had been so spectacular it sounded more like bombs dropping nearby, like a war had broken out all around them. And the lightning—it had flashed an electric blue, sending its light through the gaps in closed window curtains and in flickering shards across the floors. At times, just for a heartbeat every now and then, the blinding blue had become a strange reddish-orange. Al and Nita had reassured the children it was just God's own nature reminding them of his strength, protection, and love. But Al was so concerned, he had gotten up and gone to the living room in his pajamas, pulled the curtain aside, and peered out at the storm.

From the north, a silver bolt of lightning cut through the clouds; from the south, a reddish-orange bolt clawed the sky. Al had never seen anything like it before.

A strong wind blew as the lightning changed the night sky from black to blue to a blood-like color and trees were tossed by the strong gusts.

But no rain fell. He found that odd.

Now it was a bright summer morning and the azure sky stretched cloudless in all directions. School had been out for nearly a month. Al was pleased the kids would be able to participate today. It was something they enjoyed every bit as much as a church picnic, so they were especially boisterous this morning, the first ones at the breakfast table.

Al was a little late, though, as was his habit on Friday mornings. After showering and dressing, he spent more time than usual in Bible study and prayer, preparing himself for what was ahead, sitting on the edge of the bed with his back straight, his King James open on his lap. The bedroom door was always closed and locked during this private, quiet time.

When he was finished, he closed his Bible, set it on the nightstand, and knelt beside the bed, back still straight, folded his hands on the bed, bowed his head and closed his eyes. He prayed aloud.

"Dear Lord, thank you for this new day, for my beautiful family, and for showing me—for showing *us*—the truth and wisdom that so many others have chosen to ignore. Be with us today as we go out to do your work. Guide us as we to try to hold back the tides of sin, to prevent sinners from making their condition worse by killing innocent and helpless human beings. Speak through our lips, use our hands as tools, and let our work to make a difference in bringing an end to the holocaust perpetrated by wicked and hateful agents of the Devil. In the name of Jesus Christ, amen."

Then he stood and went to the kitchen, which smelled warmly of eggs, bacon and coffee.

"Morning," he said cheerfully.

Both children, eight-year-old Matthew and ten-year-old Ruth, returned the greeting happily. The food was on the table, their empty plates before them, and they waited patiently. No one ate until Dad had seated himself at the table and thanks had been given to God.

Nita was still in the kitchen, getting the rest of the food. She was nicely dressed and a bit more made up than usual: modest lipstick, a touch of eye shadow and a little mascara. Once she was seated at the table, all of them automatically bowed their heads.

"Dear Lord, we thank you for this food," Al said, "and for our loving Christian home. We ask that you march with us today as we go forth as soldiers for your cause, to stop the murder of unborn babies and expose the worldly, misguided women who kill them to your word and your will. In the name of Jesus—"

They all said "amen" together, raised their heads, then Nita began moving around the table, serving up the food.

Al noticed a folded newspaper on the table beside his plate. "Is this yesterday's? I didn't get a chance to read yesterday's paper."

"That's why I kept it for you. Today's hasn't come yet. It's too early."

"That was some storm last night, huh?" Al said.

Everyone agreed.

"Something odd about it, though. Did you notice, Nita?"

"Just that it was very loud." She scooped scrambled eggs onto his plate.

"A lot of electricity. I mean, even for an electrical storm. Made the hair on the back of my neck stand up. I wonder if there'll be anything about it in today's paper." He opened yesterday's edition and his head nodded up and down as he scanned the headlines and articles. Al enjoyed reading the newspaper. It saddened him to know that newspapers were closing all over the country—another casualty of the internet. It was far from the most serious casualty, though. He allowed the children only one hour a day online, and only if they used the computer in the living room where he or Nita could keep an eye on what they were doing. They had installed the most rigid child protection software they could find to keep the kids from being exposed to the filth and immorality that was now being vomited from computer screens and into people's homes all over the world.

"Well, what do you know," he said, folding the paper over a couple of times so he could hold it in one hand as he read and ate. "They finally executed that killer upstate."

"The one who killed those women?" Nita asked, circling the table again to dole out the bacon strips.

"Uh-huh. The electric chair. It's about time. All those stays of execution...I'm telling you, if it were up to the liberals and lawyers, psychos like that guy would be running in the streets. They should be killed as soon as they're caught."

"Al, please," Nita said quietly. "The children."

"Well, it's true. They should learn early. The Bible says 'Thou shalt not kill,' and 'The wages of sin is death.' Case closed. No left-wing lawyer has any business putting himself before the word of God."

Once she was through, Nita seated herself at the table.

Al munched on a piece of bacon as he read on. He chuckled. "Oh, listen to this. You know what his last words were? 'I'm right with God, and that's all that matters.' Can you believe that? 'I'm right with God!' From the mouth of a brutal murderer. A serial killer."

"Well," Nita said, taking a dainty bite of scrambled eggs, "they say people like that aren't really in control of themselves. That it's a sickness. A mental illness."

"Nita, for crying out loud, you're not starting to think like them, are you? Insanity. Well of course he was insane! Using it as an excuse is like saying—" He made his voice thin and whiny. "—'I didn't mean to.' It's ridiculous, just plain ridiculous. And don't let me hear you saying things like that again, Nita. It makes me nervous, you talking like some Godless liberal reprobate."

"Daddy, what's a rep-ro-bate?" Matthew asked.

"It's someone who is going to burn in hell because he's turned his back on God's truth."

"What's a liberal?" Ruth asked.

"The same thing." He opened the paper again and began paging through it. "You know, it's sad to say, but this paper seems to get more liberal every day. Anybody who says there's no slant to the press is blind as a bat." He scanned the pages and stopped on something. "Well, what do you know. An article about us."

Nita and both children shot their heads up to look at him.

"What?" Nita asked, surprised.

"About the coalition. It says, 'After last week's demonstration in front of the Women's Health Clinic'—health clinic, can you believe that? It's a *butcher shop*!—'police are prepared for any possible violent outbursts that may occur at tomorrow's weekly demonstration by the Coalition for Unborn Life.' What outbursts? It was just one of those guys escorting a woman into the clinic who got carried away, is all. We had to defend ourselves. He grabbed one of the cameras—remember?—threw it to the ground and started jumping up and down on it."

"Oh, yes, I remember," Nita said. "Mr. Stanfield was very upset. He said that Nikon was terribly expensive. And besides, it was a gift."

"I still don't understand what all this 'pro-choice' business is about! What's to choose? They're killing babies! The only choice is either you're a murderer or you're not. Besides, we're pro-life. They should be called what they are—*anti*-life! I mean, how can we be pro-something and they be pro-something at the same time? They're anti-life, and that's all there is to it!" He pounded a fist on the table.

"I understand, Al, but...well, aren't you getting a little angry?"

"Yes, yes, you're right. I'm sorry." He read the paper with a frown and a sigh. "So...the police will be out there with us this morning. Fine, that's just fine. We know whose side *they're* on. And we know who is on *our* side." He shook his head slowly. "If only this country would go back to its roots, back to God and Christianity and the values that made it the strongest, richest, most powerful country in all the world. God and family and the Bible. Look at us now. We've got a socialist president, a liberal media, socialized medicine, General Motors is now *Government* Motors. These days, the only people you can joke about are Christians. God and Jesus Christ are jokes. Family doesn't matter. Children are sex objects. Pornography is everywhere. We've...degraded. Decayed."

"It takes time," Nita said soothingly. "We always knew it would take time. This new administration is a setback, yes, but we've made a *lot* of progress. And things aren't as bleak as you seem to think. Remember that atheist who challenged the mention of God in the Pledge of Allegiance and on our currency? It was rejected by the Supreme Court. Abstinence-only sex education has had the support of the government for years now. We have a lot of devout Christians in office and running for office. It looks like this administration will make such a mess that people will realize what this country really needs, and those candidates are going to do well, you wait and see. In a few years, things will look very different. All it will take is the right candidate in the next election. A true Christian who's willing to go up against the opposition and stick to what's right. I think the time is right for that and the country's hungry for it. It'll happen."

"I hope you're right," Al said. He set the paper aside and dug into his breakfast, anxious to get on with the day's work, to go head to head, once again, with God's enemies…

———————

"You have all the signs?" Al asked.

"They're already in the car," Nita said.

"All the cameras? I've got two."

"So do I."

"Matthew? Ruth? You have your cameras?"

The children nodded. Each had a brightly colored camera on a neck strap; Matthew's was blue and Ruth's was pink. The cameras were easy to use and took much better pictures and video than a cell phone would. They had found that the people going in were more intimidated by cameras than cell phones and hoped it would discourage some from going inside. "And who do you take pictures of?"

"The people going inside," Matthew said.

"And the people taking them in," Ruth said.

"And why?" Al asked.

Together, the children recited, "So they will know that their crimes against God have been recorded."

Al smiled and nodded slowly. "Very good. You'll have extra jewels in your heavenly crowns for this, you know."

The children beamed up at him.

"Okay," he said, clapping his hands together, "let's go. They'll be gathering there by now. We don't want to be too late. I'll go out and fire up the SUV. Everybody make sure we've got everything, then come on out and we'll be off."

Jangling his keys in his right hand, two cameras dangling from around his neck, Al went out the door, down the front walk, crossed the lawn toward the carport and—

—he froze. He looked around, looked up and down the street. Something was...not quite right. But he couldn't put his finger on it. He frowned as he looked the left, then the right.

Had Baxter torn out his hedge recently? It was gone, completely gone. But then, who could tell what Baxter would do next? He was a man of about thirty, an atheist and a liberal—a noxious but unsurprising combination—and a bachelor who paraded different women in and out of his house at night and in the early morning hours. Al had talked with Jerry Baxter a few times, just to be neighborly, and even visited his home once, but only to find that they had nothing in common, nothing to talk about.

Baxter liked to fancy himself a "thinker" and had shelves of books filled with cold and soulless secular humanism. So, if he had taken out the hedge in the last day or so...what of it?

But that big oak tree that used to shade the Genoveses' yard was gone, too; there was not so much as a stump left, nothing but a sunny, empty yard. They were a Catholic family, but good people, with five children who used to swing from the tire that hung from one of the tree's branches. And there was something else . . .

Either he was just noticing it for the first time or all of the houses on the street had been repainted very recently. All of them were a metallic gray trimmed with deep red, almost a blood red.

Only one house on the street was painted a different color, light blue with white trim: his own.

Even more bizarre was the American flag waving in the warm breeze in every single yard but his. There was nothing wrong with flying the flag, of course, but they had not been there yesterday. Rather than flagpoles, these were all flying from—Al squinted and craned his head forward slightly to make sure he was not mistaken—crosses. Al's frown deepened and he muttered, "When did...how long ago did they..."

"It's getting late, honey," Nita called from in the house.

"Yeah, yeah, okay," he muttered, still frowning as he looked around. He started toward the car again when he heard what sounded like a siren, but not the kind of siren he was accustomed to hearing from police cars, ambulances or fire trucks. It was a siren-like sound that played the first seven notes of a very familiar tune over and over again, and it was drawing closer.

The tune was "Jesus Loves Me."

Tires squealed over pavement down at the intersection and a shiny, squat, black car with a disproportionately large, boxy rear-end and white doors that had official-looking markings on them screeched to a halt before his house. There was a spinning red light on the car's roof. It was a police car, but looked like no police car he had ever seen before. Instead of a gold or silver star or police shield on the door, this car had a metallic-grey cross with blood-red stains at the ends of the crossbar and at the bottom. And from the top of the cross flew the American flag, as if in a strong, whipping wind.

Both doors opened and two men who appeared to be officers bolted out of the car in black uniforms. They were unlike any police officers or security guards Al had ever seen before, but that was clearly the impression they intended to give. Each had as a badge a metallic-grey cross pinned over his heart. Large, odd-looking guns were holstered to their belts and they wore shiny black helmets that left only their faces visible. And their faces looked eerily similar to one another: hard, stern, iron-jawed, and unhappy.

One of the men, the driver, unsnapped his holster, drew his gun, and said, "Sorry, sir, but I'm afraid you're under temporary detention until you can explain a few things."

"What's going on here?" Al asked, not sounding very friendly, as he frowned at the two uniformed men and eyed the gun.

"Don't you at least know enough to cross yourself when you see a Deacon, brother?" the second officer barked.

"A *Deacon*? Cross my—what are you talking about?"

The man with the gun smirked. "Well, if I have to tell you, then you're in even more trouble than I thought."

"For one thing," the second man said, waving toward the house, "this paint job is not regulation."

"It's blasphemous. You ought to know that. How long ago did you paint it?"

"I painted this house three years ago," Al said. "Myself! What's wrong with it?"

"You looked around at your neighborhood lately?" the first one asked sarcastically, gesturing with the gun. "Regulation colors."

"Those colors," the other one said, pointing at the bloodstained, metallic-grey cross on the door of the car.

"And where's your crossflag? In fact...now that I notice it, you're not even *wearing* a cross, are you?"

"Wearing a—" Al's voice dropped to a puzzled mutter as his frown deepened. He vacillated between confusion and anger. "Well, I don't normally wear a—"

"Don't normally? Okay, let's see some I.D., brother."

"Well, I-I, uh—" He fumbled for his wallet and held it open so they could see his driver's license.

"What's *that*?" the second one snapped.

"You know what we want to see. Your CA scancard."

"Scan...CA...*scancard*? Look, I don't what you're—"

"Church of America scancard so we can scan your barcode," the gunholder growled impatiently.

Al could only stare at them silently.

"Either you're suffering from some sort of demon-possession or you are a very, very bold Churchstate Sinner."

"I...I'm afraid I don't know what you're...Churchstate?" he squinted at them. Then he set his jaw and snapped, "What is going on here. Is this some kind of *joke*?"

At that moment, the front door opened and the children came out.

"How come you haven't started the car, Daddy?" Ruth called.

"Yeah, Dad, we're gonna be late," Matthew said.

Both officers looked at the children with widening eyes. The second one drew his gun as well.

"These are your children?" the first one asked, shocked.

Before Al could respond, the front door closed and Nita locked it behind her, then came down the steps to join them. As the children stared curiously at the officers, the officers looked at Nita with horror and each quickly made the sign of the cross over himself.

"You're all under arrest!" the first one shouted.

All of them froze.

Al said, "Wait just a second, here, officer—or, well, *whatever* you're supposed to be—I think you could at least tell us—"

"Deacon! You'll address me properly, as *Deacon*, or you'll be in even more trouble."

"Okay, then, *Deacon*," Al said firmly. "If you're arresting us, then what are the char—wait, *arresting* us? Who *are* you? You are *not* police officers, that's obvious.

The two officers looked at one another in disbelief.

"I *said*," Al repeated, clenching his fists at his sides, "who *are* you?" He clenched his fists in an attempt to hide the feeling of alarm that was rising inside him.

"You're under arrest for crimes against the Churchstate," the first one said. "Your house is painted blasphemously, you have no crossflag, and your wife and daughter are dressed and painted like slutty witches!"

Nita's mouth dropped open with a gasp.

The officer turned to his partner and muttered, "Box her."

The officer removed a small black device from the breast pocket of his shirt, touched the barrel of it to Ruth's temple and there was a quick, quiet crackling sound. Ruth fell to the grass in a limp heap.

Nita screamed and ran to her daughter's side.

Al lunged toward his fallen child, but the first officer put the gun in his face. "Don't move."

Matthew hurried to his father's side and Al put an arm around the boy, holding him close.

Nita screamed and cried hysterically as the other officer picked Ruth up under one arm. "My little girl my little girl, what are you doing to my little girl!"

The first officer nodded toward Nita. "Do her too and shut her up!" he growled.

With another zap, Nita collapsed the ground. The officer carried Ruth to the car, opened up the large, boxy rear, threw her inside roughly, then closed it.

"My wife!" Al shouted, holding Matthew tight. "My daughter! Damn you, what are you *doing* with them?"

"Watch your language, you heathen," the officer growled, pressing the gun to Al's cheek.

Tears welled up in Al's eyes as his entire body grew cold. Helplessness coiled around him like an enormous python and began to squeeze. His breath came faster and faster as he gasped, "Whuh-what're you gonna do to them?"

The officer moved close to Al until their faces were about an inch apart. He squinted, cocked his head curiously. "What's *wrong* with you, anyway?"

Al felt anger boiling in his stomach, burning its way up through his chest. His teeth clenched and his lips trembled as he growled, "Wrong with *me?* What's wrong with *you?* Who the devil are you and what gives you the right to—"

The officer punched Al in the gut. The blow knocked the wind out of him and he doubled over, then dropped to his knees.

Holding the gun on the top of Al's head, the officer snapped, "I told you to watch your language! I can shoot you for using Satanic language like that, brother!"

Al grunted, retched and, when his vision cleared again, turned his head toward Nita, who remained motionless on the grass.

"Nita," he rasped as he started toward her, crawling on hands and knees, "Nita, honey, it's gonna be okay, it's gonna—"

The officer pressed a shiny black boot down on him hard. "Stay right where you are. Stay away from her. You too, boy. Don't move. For the time being, she's condemned."

Al turned his head and looked up at the officer. "Con...*demned?* For *what?*"

The officer got down on one knee, close to Al, and when he spoke, there was, for just a moment, some humanity in that square-jawed face, in those steely eyes and that harsh, deep voice.

"You…you really don't know, do you, brother?" the officer whispered.

Al shook his head slowly as a tear ran down his pale cheek. "No. No. I don't. I don't understand anything you're telling me."

The officer frowned at him, not angrily, but curiously, as if there were something about Al's face that disturbed him.

"Your wife will be given the Mark of the Beast on her forehead," he said, speaking slowly, "then sent to a Prayer Camp for such time as decided by one of the High Priests. When she has truly repented of all of her sins—" He studied Al's face as he spoke slowly. "—and has given her soul back to Christ, she'll be released back into society to serve as an example of the fact that the Churchstate can, indeed, overcome sin." He backed away slowly, still frowning. "Tell me, brother…do I know you from someplace?"

Al could not respond. He could only stare at this strange man who had thrown him into such confusion that he could not even think clearly enough to pray silently for God's help.

The officer's face became cold again and he stood, gesturing with the gun to both Al and Matthew. "Okay, on your feet. Both of you. *Now!*"

Al struggled to his feet. The officer holstered his gun and pulled something else from his belt, jerking Al's hands behind his back to cuff them.

Standing behind them, the officer ordered, "To the car. *Now!*"

They headed toward the car slowly, Matthew sticking close to his father. They watched as the other officer picked up Nita, took her to the car and tossed her into the box-like trunk with Ruth.

"Maaaw-meee!" Matthew screamed.

"Shut up, boy!" the officer roared.

"Just be quiet, Matthew," Al said quietly and tremulously. "Just be quiet and do as they say, everything'll be fine, just pray, Matthew, just pray, that's all."

"Pray!" the second officer laughed as he slammed the trunk. "That's a good one, coming from you!"

"That's a nice name…Matthew," the officer behind them said, once again sounding oddly confused. "A good biblical name. One of Christ's disciples."

As they neared the car, the front door of Baxter's house across the street opened and an old man came outside in robe and slippers. Wisps of thin white hair wreathed a bald pate and a paunch protruded beneath his grey robe. He limped across his lawn slowly, frowning over at them. In the center of his forehead, there was a mark of some kind, like a star. He stopped at the edge of the lawn, then hobbled across the street

"Al?" he called. "Al *Holt*? Is that *you*? What're you doing back here?"

Al said nothing, just watched him with wide eyes beneath furrowed brows. It was Baxter's voice, broken and weaker than usual, but his voice. But the man from whom the voice came was far too old to be Baxter. He looked like he was in his late sixties and not terribly healthy.

"Al? They taking you *away*?" Suddenly, he grinned. "Ha!"

The man came out on the sidewalk and Al saw that the mark on his forehead was a pentagram, one of the many occult images commonly used in the music business and found on the covers of horror novels and books about Satanism.

"Oh, that's a good one!" the man shouted, raising his fist in the air. "This is what you *wanted*, Al! And you *got* it! Ha! And *now* look at you! Ha! *Look* at you!"

The man cackled insanely as Al and Matthew were pushed roughly into the back seat of the car. The door slammed and the man's laughter continued, but muffled now outside the car, sounding as if he were under water.

The officers got in, the driver started the car and they made a U-turn, speeding away from the house and the laughing neighbor who sounded so much like Jerry Baxter, but looked so much older.

The back seat was separated from the front by thick, transparent plastic. There was a small black speaker attached to the ceiling from which poured the tinny sounds of a church hymn, "The Old Rugged Cross."

"Daddy?" Matthew whimpered through his tears. "What's gonna happen to us? Where's Mommy? And Ruth? What did they do with Mommy and Ruth?"

Al looked down at his son. The boy's eyes were red and puffy, his cheeks shiny with tears. He tried to respond but could not. His mouth moved, but nothing came out. Words could not get beyond the burning lump of fear and anger that continued to grow in his throat. Finally, he broke and lost control.

He threw himself forward, slamming his head into the transparent shield, screaming, "Damn you! *Damn* you! Who do you think you are? How can you do this?"

The middle section of the transparent divider slid downward and a hand reached through the opening to touch the familiar small black object to Al's temple.

As his skull filled with a moment of bright, painful whiteness, the last thing Al heard was the sound of his son screaming.

———————

He awoke sitting up in a chair with his hands cuffed behind its stiff, straight back. It took a little while for his blurry vision to clear, but when it did, he looked around to see that he was surrounded by men who stood staring at him. All of them wore odd suits with ties, but one — the driver of the car that had taken him away from his home — wore his uniform, without his helmet, and stood straight with his gloved hands joined before him. Al closed his eyes and let his aching head drop forward as he groaned.

"Brother Holt! Will you please raise your head?"

He could not

Suddenly, the officer's face appeared beneath his. "The Elder is speaking to you, Holt. Lift your head. Now." Then, to the others, he said, "I don't think he understands being addressed as 'brother.'"

It was a battle, but he forced his throbbing head up until he faced them again. His eyes were a little clearer now. There were four men in odd suits with the coat lapels and collars turned inward rather than out and with shirts that had no collars at all. The one on his far left was a pudgy young man, perhaps in his mid-twenties, with brown hair and a face that was stern beyond its years. The second was much older, bald except for a few tufts of white hair above his ears and a number of moles on his face and shiny scalp. The third looked terribly normal: a middle-aged man, a bit droopy, with dark hair salted with white and a pair of wire-rimmed glasses on his rather thick nose. The fourth stood behind an enormous desk, tall and very thin, with silver hair combed straight back. His suit was different from the others; he had epaulets on the shoulders and wore a kind of badge where his lapel should have been, but Al could not see it clearly. On the wall behind the desk was a round emblem, not unlike the Presidential Seal, but in the center was the head of a lamb with a single horn jutting from the middle of its head.

Below the emblem was an elaborately framed painting of Jesus Christ.

And then, of course, there was the officer standing just two feet away from Al.

"You are a mystery to us, broth—uh, Mr. Holt," said the man behind the desk. "You have baffled us. Just as we seem to baffle you. But before we go any further, let me introduce everyone." He pointed to the pudgy man at the far left and went down the line. "Deacon Connor, Elder Duvall, Deacon Jenning and, of course—" He waved toward the uniformed officer. "— Deacon Potter. I am Elder Walters. We know that you are Albert Caymon Holt. But you mystify us. For many reasons. Some of which we'll go into later. We'd like to question you in the hope that we will be able to clarify the confusion that you present to us. Do you understand?"

Al looked at him for a long time, then finally shook his head slowly. "Nuh-no, I-I'm sorry, I…no, I don't under-understand."

"When were you born?" Deacon Connor asked immediately, frowning.

"Uh, born? I was born, uh, October eighth, uh, nineteen, uh, nine…teen seventy, um…seven. Nineteen seventy-seven."

Everyone in the room exchanged shocked glances.

"That's not possible," Deacon Jenning said quietly. He stepped forward and raised his voice. "That's not *possible*! You're much too young to have been born in 1977!"

"Deacon Jenning, please," Elder Walters said quietly, holding up a hand. He walked around his desk. "Brother Holt, we are very interested in your background. It seems that you…well, that you genuinely have no idea of the, uh, world in which you live. We are trying to determine whether you should be sent to an anti-possession facility or if, perhaps…you've come to us from…from someplace we do not understand. I'd like you to tell me what year it is, please."

"2011, of course," Al replied, frowning at the man in spite of his pounding headache. "And I am *not*. Poss*essed*. By *demons*! I wish you people would quit saying that!"

Once again, the men exchanged startled glances.

Elder Walters came closer to him, leaned forward and said, "Are you sure you're not just confused because of the shock administered to you by Deacon Potter? Or perhaps because of the headache you are experiencing now as a result?"

Al closed his eyes for a moment, then opened them again. "Yes, something was done...to my head. And yes, I have an incredible headache. But it is 2011. And I and my family have been wrongly arrested...by two men...*claiming* to be some kind of police officers."

The words "police officers" were muttered by the men in the room as if they were strange, nonsensical words.

Elder Walters turned to him again. "Mr. Holt, did you know that your house is in violation of Churchstate law because of the way it's painted?"

"I...I-I don't even know what—that doesn't make any— Churchstate *law*?" he said, only making his head hurt worse. "I've never heard of such a thing, it's ludicrous."

Elder Duvall came toward him, frowning, and pointed a bent, knobby finger at him. "You mean to say that you are completely and totally unaware of the regulations concerning the colors used in house painting?"

"Regulations? For *house* painting? Are...are you *kidding*? No, I am *not* aware of any—in fact that's—well, it's just the most ridiculous I've ever heard. It's *stupid*."

Elder Duvall's old eyes widened as he backed away. "Stupid!" he barked hoarsely.

"Wait, just wait a moment," Elder Walters said, putting a hand on Duvall's shoulder. "Mr. Holt, in what year did you paint your house blue?"

"Three years ago. 2008."

"And on what street do you live?"

"Chestnut Avenue. 1721 Chestnut Avenue."

Once again, the men exchanged looks, but this time, they were slow and thoughtful.

"Tell me, Mr. Holt," Elder Walters said, "do you believe in miracles?"

"God has been performing miracles since the beginning of time," Al said, bowing his head again because it felt so heavy. "And he continues to perform them. Personal miracles. For those who believe in him."

Another exchange of looks between the men.

"Could you please look at us?" Elder Walters asked.

Al slowly lifted his head.

Deacon Jenning asked, "Mr. Holt...what are your feelings toward abortion?"

"Wrong," Al croaked. "It's wrong. In fact, that's what my family and I were going to—"

"Mr. Holt," Deacon Potter interrupted, "what are your feelings toward pornography?"

"Wrong." He slowly turned his head back and forth, even though it hurt. "Wrong, wrong, wrong. It should be stopped. But now that the internet is bringing it into people's homes— well, a lot of people cry censorship, but it's damaging, it's profoundly harmful and a vile sin, and it has nothing to do with freedom. Pornography is evil. Freedom doesn't shelter evil. Our founding fathers never intended anything like that."

The men looked at one another once again, this time with smiles on their faces.

Elder Walters said, with a bit of reverence in his voice, "Then you are Albert Caymon Holt."

Al looked at all of them, one at a time, then said, "Of course I am. What did you think?"

Elder Walters turned to Deacon Potter and said, "Open the door. Tell them to bring in the signs."

Potter went to the door, opened it and muttered something. A man entered the room holding a number of signs under his right arm, flat wooden sticks with sheets of cardboard covered with writing attached to them. He said, "Where would you like them, brother?"

"Just put them on the floor," Walters said. "Right here. Then you can go."

He did as he was told, then left, closing the door behind him.

Elder Walters leaned down and picked one of them up, leaning it against his shoulder with a slight smile. "Do you recognize this, broth—Mr. Holt?"

In letters that Al himself had painted, the sign read:

JESUS SAID:
"SUFFER THE CHILDREN TO COME UNTO ME."
HE DID NOT SAY:
"MURDER THE CHILDREN BEFORE THEY COME UNTO ME."

"Yes, I recognize that sign," Al said, his voice dry and hoarse. "I made it."

"When did you make it?" Elder Walters asked.

"Oh…a week ago. Maybe ten days."

"Why?" Elder Duvall asked abruptly.

"For the gatherings. The coalition gatherings."

"What coalition?" Deacon Jenning asked.

"The Coalition for Unborn Life."

Another long look from one man to another.

"Of which you are a member," Elder Walters said.

"Well, yes, of course."

"Why was your wife wearing makeup on her face?" Deacon Connor asked. "Why was your daughter dressed the way she was?"

"Because…they wanted to look…nice. That's all."

"Do you have any relatives who have the same name as you?" Elder Walters asked.

"Well…no, of course not. I'm the only Albert Holt."

The men exchanged yet another look.

"Would somebody please tell me what's going on?" Al asked. "Because I'm in pain and I've been separated from my family and I'd really like to know why. I could probably have you all arrested for holding me like this, you know."

Elder Walters got down before him on one knee and said, very quietly, "Mr. Holt. This is the year 2042."

Al frowned at him through the pain that throbbed in his head. "What?"

Elder Duvall said softly. "You are in the year 2042…although every piece of identification you have, not to mention your birth date, puts you in the year 2011. It's a miracle. From God. A holy miracle. Because we…we know who you are. And what is most amazing, and most miraculous…is that you exist today, as well."

Al looked around at them, from one face to another, very slowly. Suddenly, the incredible throbbing in his head meant nothing. All that mattered was his family. He suddenly began to struggle with the cuffs, to try to bring his arms around to his sides, growling like an animal all the while.

Elder Walters put his hand on Al's shoulder and said, "Please, please, calm down. For your own good. Just remain calm."

"Remain calm?" Al barked. "You people have taken my family from me, and now you're saying crazy things that don't make a damned bit of—"

"Watch your language!" Deacon Potter interrupted.

"—sense! Laws about house painting and it's the year 2042 and—" He stopped, panting for breath, clenching his eyes, letting his pounding head drop heavily.

Elder Walters said calmly, "Your wife has already been tried. A High Priest of the Churchstate has sentenced her to five years in a prayer camp."

Al lifted his head very slowly and looked at Elder Walters with teary eyes. "Exactly what…are you…*talking* about? Prayer camps? A Churchstate? You're…you're crazy."

Quite unexpectedly, Elder Walters smiled. "I'm talking about something that you helped to create, Brother Holt."

An expression of horror passed over Al's face. "What?"

"You may not understand as yet, but quite frankly, neither do we. By some miracle, you have been brought to us in…well, in an earlier state. As a younger man. For reasons known only to the Lord God, you have been plucked out of an earlier time and brought here to see your own future. Our present. A present in which you had a great hand, Brother Holt. And for that, you should rejoice. Just as we are rejoicing for your presence here." He looked over his shoulder at Deacon Connor and hissed, "Call him. Get him here. *Now!*"

Deacon Connor left the room, slamming the door behind him.

"As I said, Brother Holt, you should rejoice. A miracle has been performed and for some reason, God has brought you here to see your future. The future that you helped to create."

Al's confusion turned to fear. He trembled all over and his teeth clenched so hard, his jaws ached. He wondered if he were dreaming, or hallucinating. Could he possibly have had a stroke? None of this made sense. It was as illogical as a dream, and yet it was real in every way. Frustration rose in him like bile and finally, he shouted, "What the hell do you mean, the future I helped to create?"

Each man in the room crossed himself and bowed his head for a moment.

Voice trembling ever so slightly, Elder Walters said, "I understand your confusion, Brother Holt, really I do. But there are some things that you must understand as well. Back in 2011, Albert Holt was nothing more than an active member in the Coalition for Unborn Life. But that changed very suddenly. When the country finally came under the rule of a president who had been saved, a true Christian who was willing to go up against some godless protest groups, Albert Holt became—that is to say that *you* became quite important."

Al began to cry. Each sob increased the searing pain in his head and quaked his entire body in spite of its restraint. "You're lying to me," he sobbed, tears falling. "This is no miracle, it's some kind of hoax, it's a-a-a *nightmare!*"

"Do you want us to calm you down?" Elder Walters asked. "We have drugs that will quickly—"

"No, no, no, I…I'm just…you're frightening me, and I just need to…to …" He tried to pull himself together, calm down, think clearly. It was a struggle.

Elder Walters stood, joined his hands behind his back and smiled down at Al. "You're a very important man around here now, Brother Holt. In fact, you're now known as Bishop Holt. You, and you alone, created the prayer camps. That was your idea. Using a combination of intensive bible study, prayer and pharmaceuticals, we have been successful in turning around a lot of misguided lives. Those camps have improved our holy society immeasurably. You had a big hand in creating the CRP—the Children Recovery Program that saves young people who have not received a Christian upbringing. Anyone up to the age of 18 who has not been raised in Christ is…corrected.

And all of this came from your deep-seated belief in old-fashioned American family values. You helped bring this country back to God."

His trembling became powerful convulsive shakes as he looked up at Elder Walters. His lips quivered uncontrollably and tears rolled down his puffy cheeks.

"B-but it's...wrong!" he hissed. "Don't you see that it's *wrong*?"

Elder Walters's smile disappeared and he asked. "What did you say? *What's* wrong?"

"What you're doing. That was not our intention, not at all."

"Well, obviously, you're very confused and upset, and that's understandable. But I want you to know that—"

"I'm not confused about *anything*!" Al shouted. "This is some kind of sick joke! A perverted hoax! It's a—"

The door opened and Deacon Connor came back in. Al stopped his shouting, bowed his head again and tried to catch his breath.

"He'll be here soon," Deacon Connor said quietly. "The secretary will let us know."

"What we're trying to tell you, Brother Holt," Elder Walters said, "is that you are a very important person to us. You are revered here."

Al lifted his head slowly and stared at them with his twisted, tear-streaked face. "Then please...give me back my children and my wife. Please."

The door opened and a young woman walked in. "Bishop Holt is here," she said quietly.

Elder Walters turned and said, "Thank you, Sister Ayers."

She held the door open and a tall, thin man walked in wearing a flowing white robe. A large, ruby-studded cross hung from around his neck. He had silver hair, sunken cheeks, and eyes that stared piercingly from deep within their sockets.

His chin jutted slightly and the corners of his thin-lipped mouth turned slightly downward. He was in his seventies but fit, with rigid posture. His eyes locked with Al's the moment he walked into the room. He moved quickly to stand directly in front of Al, looking down at him with deep lines cut into his forehead, eyebrows furrowing together above the bridge of his nose.

"You are Albert Caymon Holt," he said softly.

Al looked up at that disturbingly familiar face and got a sick feeling in his stomach. He felt light-headed, dizzy. He nodded slowly.

"So am I," the tall man said.

They said nothing for a long time, just looked at one another. They looked long and deep. Al looked for some trace of himself in those eyes, some hint of the things he felt and loved, a sign of the things that had always been important to him. He saw nothing he recognized.

"So," the man they called Bishop said, "what do you think?"

It was a long time before Al could answer. His throat was dry and coarse and his voice came out in a rasp.

"It's wrong. All of it. Everything. This is not what we wanted. We had only one thing in mind, stopping the abortions, bringing an end to that slaughter. But now…now I'm beginning to wonder…if even that was right…if I was misguided about…everything."

Bishop Holt's penetrating eyes narrowed.

"We did not intend to take everyone's choices from them," Al said. "Not *all* of their choices. This is…un-American. It's *blasphemous*. Even…even *God* allows the freedom of choice. Who are we to put ourselves before God? Who are we to say that we can make choices for *everyone*?"

Their eyes remained locked for a long, silent time as the other men waited in the room for Bishop Holt's response. He backed away from Al and turned to Elder Walters.

"Execute him. Now."

"But Bishop Holt," Elder Walters said imploringly, "you must understand that he is your—"

Through clenched teeth, he hissed, "You are mistaken, brother. He is a heretic and a madman. Too far gone even for the camp. Kill him at once. And after you've killed him, do the same with his whole family. You've heard me."

He spun around and left the room, slamming the door.

Elder Walters was a little pale when he turned to Al. He tried to smile, but failed.

"I'm afraid we must follow the orders of Bishop Holt, Bish—uh, Broth—erm, Mr. Holt." He turned to the uniformed officer. "Deacon Potter, you heard the order. Here and now."

Without hesitation, Deacon Potter unholstered his gun, came to Al's side and placed it to his temple.

Folding his hands before him, Elder Walters gave a slight smile and said softly, "If it's any consolation, it certainly has been an honor knowing you."

The gun fired and plunged them all into nothingness.

Monsters

1.

The drive from Los Angeles was like sliding naked along the edge of a razor blade. He hadn't stopped once in nine hours. A rusty nail was imbedded deep in the small of his back, he was sitting on crushed glass and somewhere along the way, he'd swallowed a rock. The rock had gotten stuck between his throat and stomach and remained a lump of dull pain in his chest. He didn't always feel the pain—mostly when he heard the wrong song on the radio or began to worry about returning to the Napa Valley.

Which was most of the time.

2.

The Valley was getting ready to change color when Roger arrived late Thursday afternoon. Fall was a footstep away and with it would come the crush, when the entire Valley would smell like a freshly opened bottle of chilled wine. But now the green of the trees had darkened on the verge of brown and the grapevines, full with leaves ready to be pruned, clung to their trellises as if shocked by the changing of their color.

St. Helena remained cradled among the vineyards, a small town that still seemed uncomfortable with blacktop rather than cobblestone streets. It had not changed.

Why would it, asshole? Roger asked himself. *You were only gone six years, and they didn't exactly log your departure in the fucking town records.*

Upon closer inspection, he found that the town had changed in places.

Jim's Country Kitchen, a coffee shop on the south end of town, was now Molly's and looked more like a houseplant boutique than the noisy greasy spoon it had been.

Taylor's Hardware was now a video store.

The biggest disappointment was that Hollywood North was gone. It was a store that sold only Hollywood memorabilia—posters, stills, lobby cards, decorations, greeting cards and toys—and had been run by Josh Draper. Roger had spent many an afternoon sitting behind the counter in Hollywood North with Josh, drinking coffee and talking about movies, trying to stump him with trivia questions. Josh's specialty was horror films; one whole wall of the store had been covered with posters and stills of old Frankenstein and Wolfman movies and nearly all of the Hammer vampire films, some of which were valuable originals that were not for sale. Roger was sorry to see that it had closed and wondered what had become of Josh.

The sidewalks were busy with fashionably dressed shoppers who crossed the narrow Main Street indiscriminately, slowing traffic to an uncertain stutter.

He was glad to see that the most welcomed sight in town had not changed at all: The barber's pole in front of DiMarco's Deli.

He parked his gray Accord behind the deli and went in the back way past the stacked cases of beer and soft drinks and—

—suddenly he felt as if he had just driven over from his house on Sulphur Springs Avenue after spending a few hours at the typewriter.

Suddenly, he had never decided—after finding his mutilated dog hanging over his back porch—to pack up late one night six years ago and drive back to Los Angeles without telling anyone. He had not yet faked his way through a single pitch for a preoccupied producer and hadn't once been told, "It's just not what we're looking for." He'd never had a gun in his mouth and he'd never *heard* of the Sylmar Neuropsychiatric Hospital, let alone seen its sterile white interior.

It was as if he'd never left St. Helena.

The place still looked more like a garage sale than a delicatessen. In the front was the candy counter and register, then the meat counter, shelves of groceries, coolers of drinks, and the sandwich counter. Above it all were shelves and shelves of souvenirs, knickknacks, mementos, photographs, drawings and other objects unidentifiable from any distance. The walls were covered with posters, postcards, letters, photographs and notes. Nothing was arranged in any particular order but somehow did not look sloppy. It looked...right. As if the place could not possibly look any other way.

Roger was halfway to the meat counter when he heard a hoarse shriek.

"Roger Bernard Carlton!"

Betty DiMarco was already rushing toward him when he turned, her arms open wide. She laughed as they embraced, the cigarette between the first two fingers of her right hand trailing a thread of smoke.

"Holy god!" she cried, her voice muffled against his shoulder. "How long has it been?"

"A long time, Betty. How are you?"

"Well, I'm—oh, you know how I—Jesus, but it's good to—let me *look* at you!" She stepped back, a hand on his shoulder.

Betty, a small, spare woman, wore a red plaid shirt and a pair of blue jeans that still looked good on her despite all the gray in her curly auburn hair and the deepening lines around her eyes and mouth.

"Come on in the back," she said, tugging his arm. "Come *on*."

She led him through a door beneath a sign that read THE MUNCH ROOM and seated him at a rustic picnic table. It was the very same table where he used to sit each morning drinking coffee, reading the paper, and writing.

"A sandwich?" Betty asked.

"Yeah, I was just gonna—"

"Let me. The usual?"

"Roast beef and hav—"

"Havarti dill on dark rye, no onions, no sprouts. Right?" She grinned before hurrying out of the room.

The same pictures and posters adorned the walls in the Munch Room: Nixon and Agnew dressed as Batman and Robin, promotions for a local rock group, an art show, a wine tasting, a few old beer logos, and a painting of Betty and Leo. Mickey Mouse ticked away the time on a wall-sized wristwatch.

The far end of the room was partitioned off and held a large metal sink, a cutting board, and shelves of cutlery and containers.

A few hours ago, at lunch time, there wouldn't have been an empty seat in the room. Patrons would have been shouting to be heard above the din of voices and the single restroom would have been free for only seconds at a time.

Roger remembered sitting at the same table one day more than six years ago during just such a busy lunch hour. A young couple walked in, college age, both neatly but plainly dressed. He didn't recognize them, but knew immediately that they were Seventh-day Adventists—no doubt students from the college up the hill, which he had once attended—and looked away from them, went back to his writing.

A moment later, he realized they were standing by his table, facing him. He looked up to see them staring, lips parted, eyes wide below frowning brows, sandwiches held before them on paper plates. He started to ask them what was wrong when the girl spat on him.

The voices in the Munch Room silenced and all eyes turned to Roger and the couple.

"You're the writer," the girl said quietly with a mixture of fear and awe, as if she were standing before a movie star who also happened to be a serial killer. "I caught my brother reading your book once. I burned it." Her voice lowered to a whisper. "You're sick." She turned and walked out, followed by her boyfriend.

The eyes of the other patrons remained on Roger for several silent seconds, then he said, somewhat nervously, "Probably kept the book and underlined the dirty parts."

A brief chorus of laughter broke the uncomfortable silence and the chatter continued. A man asked if Roger was really a writer; when Roger introduced himself, the man said he'd heard of him but had not read his work, although he would start. They talked for a while, had a laugh about religious nuts, and the man even bought Roger lunch.

But, pleasant as the conversation had been, the lunch had not gone down well. In fact, on his way home, Roger was struck by a pain in the lower right side of his abdomen, a pain so severe that he had to pull over to the side of the road and sit a while. It was a dreadful scraping pain, as if a claw were scooping out his insides, tearing at the inner wall of his abdomen. At home that day, he'd vomited his lunch and kept retching until blood splashed red in the toilet.

It was the first sign of an ailment that would elude many doctors. He spent the next three years undergoing test after test, none of which showed the slightest sign of an ulcer or intestinal problem, and all of which inspired the doctors to suggest he see a therapist. Although he would do so later, he wasn't quite ready to go that route when it was initially recommended.

Instead, he would sometimes spend entire days in bed curled into a ball, either waiting for the pain to go away or fearing it would return, all the while imagining it to be an ugly gnarled claw that scraped through his insides, trying to gut him like a fish. ...

Betty hurried back into the room and seated herself across from him, taking his hand.

"The sandwich is coming, now how *are* you? Where have you *been*, what's the—*oh*!" She held up his left hand and examined his fingers. "You're not married?"

"Uh, no." He gently pulled back his hand and drummed his fingers on the tabletop. "That, um...didn't work out."

"Oh. Well. I must admit, I'm glad to hear that."

Roger chuckled. "You should've said something *then*."

"Oh, I did. Plenty. But when you're in love, honey, you'll hear a gnat fart before you'll hear a friend's warnings. You were deaf to 'em. And understandably so. She was a very appealing, very pretty girl."

"She was selfish," Roger said, shaking his head gently. "She was...deceitful...unfaithful..."

"She was a Seventh-day Adventist."

After a pause, Roger said, "That, too."

"That in *particular*."

"Oh, well. That was…Jesus, that was over five years ago." He shook his head again; he hadn't thought of Denise in a while.

Betty asked how long he'd be in town and if he needed a place to stay, and Roger explained that he'd already rented a house on Beakman.

"Have you even seen it yet?" she asked.

"Not lately, but my friend Eric Neibord—remember Eric? The musician who believed in better living through litigation?"

"The one who tried to sue Springsteen and Sting and…somebody else, I don't remember who."

"Yep. Over songs he claimed they'd stolen from him. Never happened, of course. He was a little crazy back then. Anyway, he's lived in this house for the last few years and now he's moving to L.A. I needed to come here, so I grabbed it up."

"Why are you here?"

"I got a teaching job through Napa Community College. Creative writing and a short story class. Night classes here at St. Helena High."

"Well, that's good." She took an uncertain drag on her cigarette, cocking a brow. "Isn't it?"

"Yeah, sure. Sure, it's good." He tried to give her a genuine smile as he thought, *Better than bouncing around a rubber room or using a gun to repaint my bedroom a deep shade of brain matter*. "I've always wanted to try my hand at teaching."

"But you're still writing, aren't you?"

Roger half-shrugged.

"Well, you *are*, aren't you?" Betty was beginning to sound stern and motherly.

Someone came into the Munch Room and placed a sandwich and a Michelob in front of Roger, saving him from having to reply. He looked up to say thank you but could only stare silently for a moment at the beautiful, frightened eyes that briefly met his.

"Thank, um…thank you," he stuttered after a moment.

The girl quickly turned to leave, but Betty waved her back.

"Sondra, Sondra, c'mere."

The girl stopped suddenly, as if disappointed she hadn't escaped, slowly turned and came back to the table.

"Sondra, I want you to meet Roger Carlton, the writer you've heard so much about." She turned to Roger. "I talk about you all the time and I came in here screaming my head off the morning you were on that talk show." To Sondra: "Remember that?"

Roger was touched that she stilled seemed interested in him after he'd made no attempt to stay in touch for so long. But he gave that little thought; he couldn't take his eyes from the girl.

Her hair was the color of creamed coffee and her eyes, which he could not stop watching, were a deep, solid brown that darkened gradually into the black of her pupils.

She leaned over Betty's shoulder, holding out her hand cautiously, as if he might bite her.

"I knew who you were soon as you came in," the girl said, her eyes turned downward to the table. "I didn't see—" Her mouth was dry and she stopped to swallow. "I didn't see you on TV but, but I saw your picture in the paper."

Betty said, "The *Chronicle* ran your picture when they reviewed *Ledges*. It was a terrible picture, Roger. I hope you've had another taken."

Roger figured Sondra was about seventeen or eighteen. She wore no makeup and her skin was unblemished and fair. There was a darkness about her eyes that made eyeshadow unnecessary and somehow made her look worried.

As Roger shook her hand, her eyes met his for just a moment and he saw something in them: Flecks of gold, like minuscule slashes, tiny slits in the brown that opened up on something else.

She pulled her hand away and—Roger wasn't sure, but he *thought* he saw her wipe it on her apron.

"Nice to meet you," she said quickly, then spun around and hurried out.

Roger noticed as she left that she was quite tall, maybe taller than he.

"I just love watching the brains drip out of men's ears when she walks through the room," Betty said, laughing. She put out her cigarette. "Isn't she a stunner?"

"Yeah," Roger breathed. "Is she new?"

"She's been here about six months. That's a long time for the girls who work here. But then, everybody here's new to you. You've been gone too long." She reached over, took his face between her hands and gave him a big kiss. "Glad you're back, kiddo." Standing, she pointed a finger at him and said, "Tonight. Our place. Seven. We've got a lot to talk about. I'll tell Leo you're here."

After Betty went back to the front of the deli, Roger took a back issue of *American Film* from the basket of magazines on the floor and absently thumbed through it as he ate, just scanning pictures and reading captions. He couldn't start an article because each time Sondra whisked in to wash some lettuce in the sink or slice some tomatoes, he had to look up and watch her go by.

She smelled only faintly of a sweet perfume, the kind a teenager would wear, and quickly rushed by him as if he weren't there, as if she were afraid he might speak to her.

The sandwich was delicious, but Roger couldn't finish it.

3.

Ten years before, when Roger was going to the Seventh-day Adventist college on the hill above St. Helena and living in the dormitory, DiMarco's Deli was a refuge, a place that served real meat, played rock and roll music over the rickety old speakers, and where no one damned you for drinking a beer. Of course, if you weren't careful, you might be spotted by one of the school's many narcs who occasionally came into DiMarco's for a vegetarian sandwich and a bottle of fruit juice, and who would immediately report your transgressions to a dean or some other faculty member.

When Roger quit college to write full time and moved down the hill to St. Helena, he frequented DiMarco's even more. It became a second home, or a sort of office, and the DiMarcos became a second family. His own small house was too enclosed and too empty.

He'd moved to St. Helena for two reasons; he loved the town and he wanted to be close to his friends at the college. He'd grown up with most of the students he knew there because he'd gone to Seventh-day Adventist schools since first grade. The Adventists are a close-knit, self-contained group; they have their own schools, their own hospitals, even their own towns. One of those towns was just eight miles north of St. Helena.

Manning is populated almost exclusively by Seventh-day Adventists and closes up from sundown Friday till sundown Saturday—the Sabbath. By the time Roger left college, he considered himself an Adventist by association only and decided it would be a lie to continue living there. He went to movies, bars, smoked and drank, ate meat—and worse, pork and seafood—and he didn't want to live in a community that gossiped about Adventists who did not live their accepted lifestyle.

When he moved to St. Helena, he got a job in a Napa book store and drove there four days a week. The rest of the time he spent writing his book, trying to finish it as quickly as possible, hoping to sell it and raise enough money to quit his job.

He'd told only his two closest friends at the college of the *real* reason he'd quit school—his writing—telling everyone else that he was just taking a break.

There was a reason for his secrecy and it had nothing to do with shame. Rather than flaunt his choice to write fiction—let alone his chosen genre, which would only make matters worse—Roger wanted to keep peace. As far as Seventh-day Adventists are concerned, fiction of any kind is *not* a peace-keeper. In fact, according to the writings of the church's founder Ellen G. White, an alleged prophet of God and still the arbiter of doctrine and biblical interpretation nearly six decades after her death, the writers of fiction of any kind (and she included fairy tales, comic strips, and even history books in the lot) are directly inspired by Satan to teach their unsuspecting readers to properly serve the devil. She even went so far as to write that some people have been stricken with physical paralysis simply from reading too much fiction; the victims, she claimed, were kept in such a state of excitement by their reading material that their brains simply shut down and their bodies ceased to function. Therefore, reading fiction is not an approved activity in Adventist circles; *writing* it is openly condemned. The people of Manning were no exception. So, Roger decided to keep his plans to himself.

But somehow, word got out; then everyone wanted to know *what* he was writing. The book was called *Restraints* and Roger knew it would not be well received by his Adventist friends and acquaintances. There were a couple of friends, of course, who would probably appreciate it, but no more than that.

His novel was an erotic murder mystery that centered around a secret dominant-submissive relationship between a man and woman. When the woman is murdered, her sister, a straight-laced church-goer, is determined to find the killer herself when the police investigation stalls. In the process, she discovers a dark side to her sexuality that she never knew existed.

Roger had hoped to at least keep the book's plot under wraps, but knew that would be impossible, having had firsthand experience with the Adventist grapevine. So, he prepared himself for the criticism.

It started as a quiet murmur on the hill.

What a disappointment Roger had turned out to be.

To think he'd been president of his senior high school class and used to be a member of the choir and sing solos for church services!

What a shame he was using his god-given talent to titillate and disturb rather than uplift and encourage.

When he went on campus to visit friends, he received stares from people he did not know and had never seen before. Roger thought he was imagining it at first until one day, while waiting for a friend in a dorm lobby, he was approached by a young man in a suit who asked hesitantly, "You're the writer, aren't you?"

Startled, Roger nodded. The boy stared at him for a long, uncomfortable moment, then walked away.

He tried to ignore it at first, but when he noticed that his friends were becoming increasingly unavailable—always too busy or too tired to see him—he could ignore it no longer.

Lying in bed one night, he realized he should have known this would happen, that his work, if he chose to continue it, would require him to cut himself off from the church and its people entirely—just as he should have known how difficult that would be. He'd known nothing else his entire life. All he knew were Seventh-day Adventists, from his parents to his friends to his most casual acquaintances.

As a child, Roger was taught, as was every other child he knew, that the Seventh-day Adventist church was the only true church, the "remnant church," and that he was fortunate to have been born into an Adventist home. He was taught to cling to his faith as if for his very life, because some day it *would* be. Someday, he was told by his parents and his friends' parents, his ministers and Sabbath school teachers and school teachers, even his *gym* teacher, the government would band together with America's Christian churches, under the leadership of the Catholic church—which Adventism taught was the Beast of Revelation—and pass a law that would require *everyone* to worship on Sunday. Because Adventists worship on Saturday, the Sabbath sanctified by the fourth of the Ten Commandments, they would be considered criminals. They would have to flee their homes and hide out in forests and caves, living off the land, while their enemies—all the other churches as well as the federal government—hunted them down like animals to be shot and killed on sight. This "time of trouble," as it was called, had been foreseen by Ellen White and written about at length in her many books. It was to take place just before the second coming of Jesus Christ; he would descend from the clouds to save his people—the Adventists, naturally—and punish everyone else by throwing them into the lake of fire.

Ellen White's clumsy, purple prose conjured powerful and frightening images in young minds, images not soon forgotten and difficult to stop believing. As a small boy, Roger had lived in fear of this coming tribulation. He remembered lying awake in his bed at night, praying to God to kill him before it came so he would not have to endure it. He was hounded by nightmares of cowering in reeking garbage dumpsters and dark, filthy, abandoned buildings while the footsteps and gunshots of his hunters sounded all around. The nightmares always ended with him being captured by the enemy. Sometimes he woke up screaming and was unable to go back to sleep. His parents blamed too much TV. Roger was affected by this belief more than most of his friends, but every other child he knew was somehow influenced by these teachings. On the school playground, it wasn't uncommon to hear one child say to another, "I'll be the Adventist and you be the Sunday-keeper and you try to kill me, okay?"

He had another recurring nightmare as a boy. It involved a picture of the U.N. building his parents had hung on his bedroom wall; beside the building stood a giant, ghost-like Christ as tall as the building and wearing a white robe and sandals, his knuckle crooked, preparing to gently knock on the building.

It was very popular with Adventists and could be found in nearly every Adventist home of the time. Posters were issued to Sabbath school rooms and school offices; there was even a wallet-sized picture available in Adventist book stores.

Roger knew the artist had intended the giant Jesus to look gentle and benevolent, but in bad light, it did not.

In shadows, the beatific, bearded face seemed to take on a sneer, a sinister grin held in check. The crooked finger seemed about to crash through a window and drag out anyone unfortunate enough to be too close.

Christ seemed to be about to say, "I'm back, folks...and guess what I'm going to do to you after killing me the *last* time?"

Roger used to dream of waking to a tremendous rumbling and the agonized screams of people outside. A loud, angry voice that seemed to come from everywhere shouted, "Where's Carlton? Where *is* that little shit? I'm here for Roger Carlton because he reads *comic books* that he buys with his Sabbath school offering, and he watches TV on the *Sabbath* when his parents aren't around, and sometimes at night he *plays with himself—DON'T YOU, ROGER?* Where *is* that little shit?"

In the dream, Roger always went to his bedroom window and, with fear-weakened hands, pulled aside the curtain—

—to see two gigantic, ghostly, sandaled feet crushing cars and houses and people. There was a great, bloody hole through the center of each foot. The feet were always headed straight for Roger's house as the voice roared on:

"Where's Carlton? *WHERE IS THAT LITTLE SHIT?*"

It was not easy to get past images that had been so deeply burned into his consciousness at such a young and formative age.

Even now at the age of twenty-eight he sometimes tensed when a television show was interrupted by a special news report, certain that the announcer would say that a national Sunday law had been decreed and those who broke it—"Like you Seventh-day *Ad*-ventists," he might add with a hateful sneer—would be executed. Even though Roger considered himself the farthest thing from an Adventist—he even held a burning *hatred* for them—the thought of such a broadcast chilled something in him, as if, although he'd shed the beliefs the church had instilled in him, he could not rid himself of the fears it had created.

When it came time for him to sever his ties to the church, he was unable to do it at first. It was like trying to stop smoking, which he had also failed to do; just as he needed a cigarette after a meal, he needed the approval of his Adventist friends—as much as he hated to admit it. They were his whole life, the only friends he'd ever had and he'd spent his life chasing their approval like a little child chasing a balloon in a strong wind.

In order to disconnect himself from the church, he would have to disconnect himself from the first twenty years of his life.

Completely.

Roger needed to know that his friends didn't think there was something *wrong* with him, because there wasn't. He was simply doing something he loved, something he did well: telling stories. He was the same person he had always been.

As he continued writing the book, he tried to reassure his friends.

One of his closest and oldest friends was Marjie Shore. She'd been his first kiss in grammar school, his first girlfriend in high school, and his first lover in college. She knew he'd always planned to be a writer and that he wrote erotic mysteries and thrillers. It never seemed to bother her before and he asked her why she was suddenly uncomfortable with it *now*.

"I always thought you'd outgrow it," she said. "I never liked the stuff you wrote. I've always loved your *writing*— you're very good, God has blessed you with a wonderful talent. But I never liked the stories. All the violence and…and sex."

"But look around you. There's violence everywhere, we live in a violent world. Read the paper lately? And sex—well, Marjie, that's a part of *life*! What was it we did, the two of us, when—"

"I know, but it's…*different*. The things you write are wrong. You dwell on them. Wallow in them. And they're…they're *sick*. They're *wrong*."

"I don't *do* the stuff I write about, *you* know that, right? I make it up. They're just *stories*."

"I never understood it. I thought it would go away."

"You *read* them. You seemed to *enjoy* them."

"But I always prayed it would stop. I always prayed you'd grow out of it and move on to something else. But I always loved you, anyway."

Anyway.

Roger felt like putting his face in his hands and bawling then. It was as if his entire relationship with Marjie had been a little play in which she was simply hitting her mark, reciting her lines. She had been waiting for him to turn into another person, someone he was not, and when she realized that wasn't going to happen—when he got serious about his writing and tried to do something with it—she quit waiting.

She wasn't the only one.

That was the night he began to see bridges burning all around him.

All of his friends—some of whom he'd known since he was a toddler—were no longer waiting for Roger to change, to become someone with whom they would prefer being friends. In their eyes, he was hopelessly lost.

His own family showed him some support at first, but even that changed later, when his work began to sell.

It seemed every relationship he'd ever had was never anything more than an illusion.

That was the night the people in his life began to hurt him. Then he sold *Restraints*. That was when they began to terrify him.

4.

Roger spent the evening with Betty and Leo, sitting at the bar in their kitchen and talking over wine.

He had spent a few hours settling into his new house. Most of his things were in storage, so it hadn't taken long.

Leo, an enormous, solid man with a shiny bald head and a fringe of silvering black hair over his ears, pounded a hammer-like fist on the bar after finishing his fourth glass of wine and rumbled, "Read your last book. You know, the one with the, uh—" He snapped his fingers twice in Betty's direction. "What was it?"

"*Ledges*," Betty said.

"Yeah, yeah. God*damn*, son, that was a horny book. Had me jumpin' on this broad every night that week." He laughed as he leaned over to kiss Betty's hand. "But the movie—"

"Oh, please," Roger groaned, "let's not talk about the movie. It never should have been made." He sipped his wine. "Speaking of movies, I noticed Hollywood North is gone."

Betty and Leo exchanged a dark glance and Betty said, "You haven't heard."

"Heard what? Is Josh all right?"

Shaking her head slowly, Betty said, "He's got AIDS."

Something in Roger's chest deflated when he heard that. "How bad is he?"

"Pretty bad. I saw him Sunday. He likes visitors but doesn't get many. Everybody's too scared they're gonna *catch* it," she added with quiet bitterness.

"S'a scary thing," Leo mumbled.

"It doesn't *have* to be," Betty said. "But it's easier to believe rumors than it is to do some reading and *learn* about something."

"Is he still living in St. Helena, Betty?"

"When he's not in the hospital. It won't be long before he'll need constant care. It won't be long *period*, if you know what I mean."

Roger finished his wine with a gulp. He had not been in contact with Josh in six years, but their long visits together were fond memories and he'd always meant to give Josh a call someday.

"*Meant* to," he murmured angrily to himself as he poured another glass.

"What?" Leo said.

138

"I'm just pissed at myself. I kept meaning to write him or call, but…"

"Go see him," Betty said enthusiastically. "He'd love that. He sits in that little house and watches old movies day and night. Pretty soon he won't be able to do *that*. He'd *love* to see you."

"Yeah, I'll do that."

They talked for another hour about other people in town—who had moved, who had married, who had divorced, who had died—then Leo lifted his bulk from the barstool and slurred, "I'm through for the night, kids. See ya tomorrow."

After they heard the bedroom door close, Betty said, "So what's eating you? Why aren't you writing?"

"I didn't say I'm not writing."

"You didn't say you *are*."

"I am, I'm working on a new book, but it's…slow. The teaching job will do me good. I need a break."

"It's been—how long since your last book?"

"Almost two years.

"And the next one?"

"Whenever it's finished."

"Which will be—when?"

"I…don't know. Look, Betty, I need the break, okay? For however long it lasts, I *need* it." He blinked in surprise at his own words; he hadn't meant to sound so harsh. He picked up his crumpled pack of cigarettes, found it empty, took one of Betty's and lit up. "The last couple of years have been pretty…rough."

"Wanna talk about it?"

He thought about that for a few moments. Betty was just about the most understanding person he knew. She had supported him in everything he'd done and had always made him feel like she was on his side. He could not say that about anyone else in his life. But she knew nothing of Sylmar Neuropsychiatric Hospital, or of his reasons for going there.

Sometimes even the most understanding people cocked a brow when they learned a friend, however close, had spent time in a mental hospital.

"No," he said. "Some day, but not yet."

"Whatever you say."

"So. Who's that girl in the deli? What's her name again? Sandra?"

"Sondra. For god's sake, Roger," she said with a laugh, "she's only seventeen."

"No, *that's* not why I'm asking. She's just...interesting, that's all. She seems so afraid, as if she's used to being hit every time she walks into a room, or something. You know much about her?"

"Not much. She's awfully quiet. She's from Berrien Springs, Michigan."

"An Adventist?" Roger said. Berrien Springs was another Adventist stronghold, like Manning or Loma Linda.

"I think so, but I'm not sure. She always wears dresses, never pants, no jeans, no jewelry. She probably is."

"I'm surprised she's allowed to work there."

"I don't think they have much choice."

"Her parents?"

Betty shook her head. "Her parents were killed over a year ago. Maybe two. Some kind of accident, I think. She moved here to live with her cousin."

"Who's her cousin?"

"Her name is Annie. She comes in to get Sondra at the end of the day. Another quiet one, never says anything. I get the impression money's tight. I suspect Sondra never sees much of her paycheck, if any."

"Is her cousin married?"

"Yeah, but the way Sondra talks about him, he's been hurt, or he's crippled, or something. I don't know. Whatever's wrong, he can't work."

Roger thought about Sondra's eyes, how they never met his for more than a second at a time, the golden flecks in them that looked like tiny puncture wounds.

Punctures from the inside, he thought.

Sipping his wine, he muttered, "Poor kid."

5.

When Roger walked through the back door of DiMarco's the next day, someone was screaming. The deli was dead silent except for the radio and the wailing sobs of a girl who was leaning on Leo at the register, her fingers clutching his big shoulders, face pressed to his chest.

Two girls behind the sandwich counter stared at her. Customers stood in the middle of the store gawking at the crying girl.

Someone's died, Roger thought.

Betty hurried by him from behind, patting his shoulder and saying, "In a minute, hon." She went to the girl's side and gently pulled her away from Leo, whispering something in her ear.

Roger stepped out of the way as Betty led the girl back to the Munch Room, whispering, "Just come in the back and sit down till we can reach your parents, okay, honey? Okay?"

The girl had long red hair and a face sprinkled with freckles and streaked with tears.

Roger went to the meat counter where Leo stood beside the slicer shaking his head as he watched Betty lead the girl into the Munch Room.

"What happened?" he whispered.

"Shelly's fiancé was killed," Leo said. "The boy's parents are out of town, Shelly's parents are at work, so they called here to tell her. I went down and...and identified the body." He pulled his palm across his lips, closed his eyes a moment. "Hope I never again have to..." Instead of finishing the sentence, he sighed.

"What happened?"

"They're not sure and they don't want me to talk about it. But—" He dropped his voice to a whisper. "—he was a mess."

A line had formed at the counter. Voices mixed with the radio's music. The deli was back in order.

"Roast beef and Havarti dill?" Leo said.

"Uh, no. I'm just gonna have coffee for now."

A few tables were occupied in the Munch Room. A cup of coffee sat beside the morning paper at Roger's usual spot. As he seated himself, Betty came out of the restroom and joined him.

"Christ, what a horrible thing," she said.

"Is she okay?"

"Oh, it'll be a while before she's okay, I think." She lit a cigarette, took a drag, and blew smoke hard from her lungs. "They were gonna be married here. In the deli. Right up front between the potato chip racks and the cash register. Can you imagine that? They met here, so they wanted to get married here." She laughed humorlessly.

"How long were they engaged?"

"Not long, about three months. Together less than a year. They're just kids. She's—" Betty lowered her voice. "—pregnant. But they say they would've gotten married, anyway. That they loved each other and..." She waved her cigarette before her face as if to say, *You know the rest.* "I never liked the boy. Benny Kent was his name. He was nice enough, I suppose, but didn't seem the marrying kind, didn't seem...well, like he was going to commit to her. He'd come in here wearing his jogging clothes—he always wore jogging clothes, but I don't think he ever jogged—and start flirting with the girls. He especially liked Sondra. Can you imagine someone trying to pick up Sondra? She's so...timid. He asked for her phone number once and I thought she was gonna have a stroke. Scared her silly. I tried to talk to Shelly about him, but—"

"She wouldn't listen."

"Ah, you're familiar with the problem," she said with a smirk. "Well, I better go back and be with her till someone comes. Later."

Betty returned to the restroom. Roger opened the paper before him but could not concentrate on the words. Instead of giving any thought to the girl whose fiancé had been killed, Roger found himself thinking about Sondra.

He wondered what she was so frightened of.

Roger was still in the deli two hours later. He had chatted with a man in the wine business until Shelly's mother arrived wearing a red grocery store apron and name tag, complaining about being pulled away from work. She told Betty, a bit too loudly, "I never could stand that boy, anyway." He finally read the paper and decided to have a sandwich.

When he went out front to order, he spotted Sondra coming in the front entrance.

"You're early," Leo bellowed.

She seemed to wither a bit at the attention Leo's voice drew to her.

"They...they closed school early," she said softly. "When they heard about B-Buh-Buh—the boy."

Roger thought it was odd that she referred to him as "the boy" instead of by name.

As she hurried by him, hugging her school books to her breasts, he noticed there was something different about her. Something...

"Hello, Sondra," he said, smiling.

She turned her head away from him and breathed, "Hi," then went into the Munch Room.

Roger got his sandwich, a beer, and went back to his table.

An old man sat at the back table noisily chewing his sandwich.

Sondra was the only other person in the room. Her books were spread out on a table across from Roger and she sat hunched over them, her long hair hiding her face, index finger tracing sentences as she silently read.

What had he seen about her that was different from yesterday? Was it something about the way she walked? Something about her hair?

Her hair seemed stringier than yesterday, perhaps greasy, unwashed.

"Are you a senior this year?" he asked.

Without looking up, she nodded.

"Are you going to college next year?"

"No."

"Do you plan to go at all?"

Sondra slowly lifted her head a bit and looked at him through strands of her hair. There were blotches of darkness beneath her eyes and her face looked drawn and weary. Her voice was as fragile as a spider's web. "I don't think we'll ever be able to afford it. I...I might take a few classes."

"What would you like to study?" he asked, spreading a napkin over his lap.

She straightened a bit and pulled some of the hair from her eyes. Sondra seemed to puzzle over that question, as if she'd never given it a thought.

"I...I don't really know," she whispered, looking down at her book.

"What are your best subjects?"

"Well..." She frowned. "All of them, I guess."

Roger raised his eyebrows. "Straight-A student?" She seemed too afraid of everything to be as aggressive as most of the straight-A students he had known.

She nodded, looking at her book again.

"Then you'll have a lot of choices," he said. "In a major, I mean."

She said nothing and didn't look up this time.

"Have you ever considered teaching?" he asked.

Sondra shook her head with a jerk, as if startled.

"Neither have I." Roger chuckled. "I *tell* people I have. I mean, that I'm looking forward to teaching. But you know what?"

Roger waited a moment until she finally said, "What?" in a voice as thin as silk.

"I'm scared to death," he said, leaning toward her a bit.

Nothing for a long time. Then she slowly lifted her head and turned her eyes to him. "Really?" she whispered. "You're really scared."

"Sure."

"Why?"

"Well, who am *I* to tell these people whether or not they can write? Just between you and me, most of them probably *can't*, but I had teachers who told *me* I was bad, that I'd never sell a word, so..." He shrugged and realized she was still looking at him, looking him right in the eyes. But it was the way a deer looks into the eye of the hunter it has just noticed on its trail. "Do you know what I mean?"

"Your teachers told you that?"

"Oh, sure."

She shook her head slightly and whispered, "But you went to school up—" She stopped abruptly and looked away.

Roger chuckled. "Up on the hill?"

A faint nod.

"Yeah, and most of my teachers didn't like *what* I wrote any more than *how* I wrote it. Did Betty tell you that?"

No reply.

"Hm?"

He thought he saw her shake her head once.

"How did you know?"

Her book closed with a *smack* and she stood suddenly, scraping her chair over the concrete floor.

"I've gotta get back to work," she said as she hurried out.

He noticed her clothes—a simple brown skirt, maroon sweater and white top—were mussed and in need of a wash, as if they'd been slept in.

She was an Adventist, all right. If Betty hadn't told her he'd gone to school in Manning, then one of *them* probably had. They'd probably been expecting him. Probably already knew he'd arrived. Why had he, for one moment, thought otherwise?"

You're paranoid, he thought.

But it was true. They always seemed to know where he was, where he was going.

They watched him.

In fact, they'd followed him all the way into a breakdown. Now he had a sinking feeling that they were waiting for him, smiling, on the other side.

6.

News of the sale of *Restraints* spread quickly through Manning. The first sign of it was a phone call. It came shortly after midnight. Roger was up working.

"Hello?"

"'Whatever is true, whatever is honorable, whatever is right, whatever is pure...let your mind dwell on these things.' Does *that* sound familiar?"

It was a woman but he did not recognize her voice.

"Who is this?"

"It's the word of *God*, that's who it is! 'Whatever is *true*! Whatever is *pure*!' What you're doing is a *perversion*! It's dangerous and mind-damaging and—"

Roger wanted to hang up but was too shocked and fascinated.

"—God will *damn* you for it! And you were *given* the truth, *raised* in it your whole life, and—and—" She sounded too frustrated to go on. "God *damn* you for it!"

The loud slam that came over the line made Roger jerk the receiver from his ear. When he heard the dial tone, he replaced it in the cradle.

He called Marjie then, mostly out of habit. He hadn't seen her in almost three months but couldn't get out of the comfortable habit of calling her now and then. He knew her schedule enough to know she'd still be up studying. She had no morning classes the next day.

A second after Roger said hello, Marjie hung up the phone.

He stared at the receiver a while, reached down to call her again, but decided against it. Instead, he called Bill Dunning.

He'd known Bill since first grade when they got in trouble for fighting over a crayon. From that point on, they had been best friends, and roommates in boarding academy, where they had raised no end of mischievous hell without getting caught once. They had always been a couple of teachers' pets and no one ever suspected them of the pranks that befell the school during their two years as students.

Bill was now an engineering major. They were still close but conflicts in their schedules and interests had driven a wedge between them. Bill was a motorcycle enthusiast and Roger couldn't stand them; Bill was a sports fan and Roger was not; Bill's politics swung hard to the right and Roger's were slightly left of center; and rather than growing away from the church as Roger had, Bill's devotion to it seemed to be growing.

That night, Bill was working the desk in one of the men's dorms. Roger called him there.

Bill hung up the second he heard Roger's voice.

He did not sleep that night, and sat instead in front of the television staring blankly at the screen.

Two days later, he found the two front tires of his Accord slashed and flattened.

The following week, someone smeared dog shit all over the front seats of his car. He cleaned it off with trembling hands — it took days to get rid of the smell — and drove to DiMarco's.

Betty told him to call the police.

An officer came to the deli and talked with him. He took notes as Roger spoke.

The officer said, "I don't know what to tell you," he said afterward, tapping his pencil on the table. "You really have no proof of—"

"I have two slashed tires and a pile of rags covered with dog shit."

"They won't do us any good. And even if they could, our hands are tied because nothing was actually *done* to you *personally*. It's just vandalism."

"But they slashed my tires and—"

"Again, that's vandalism, not necessarily a personal threat. We don't know why these people—"

"But I *told* you—"

"You can't prove that. You're speculating at best. We don't know *who* did this."

"So…what has to happen before you *can* do something?"

"They have to be caught harming you in some way, or *trying* to harm you. We have to know who it is and they have to at least make an attempt. Proof, not speculation."

He never could prove it, even though it continued to get worse.

A rumor started at the college and then spread throughout Manning that Roger had broken into the biology lab late one night and had stolen a dead cat to use in some kind of satanic sex ritual.

Several nights after he heard about the rumor from an acquaintance, he got a phone call around nine in the evening.

"What're you gonna steal next, devil worshiper?" a breathy male voice asked. "Babies out of the hospital? Or would you rather—"

Roger hung up, got in his car, and drove up the hill to Bill's dorm. He looked at no one as he hurried upstairs, not wanting to see their staring eyes.

Bill's door was open wide and he lay on his bed studying. On the wall above him was a poster of the picture Roger had always hated so much: the giant Jesus about to knock on the U.N. Building.

"Will you tell me what the hell is going on, Bill?" he said, standing in the doorway on trembling legs. For a moment, he couldn't move. He was paralyzed by the alien look in Bill's eyes.

When he lifted his gaze from the book to Roger, Bill's eyes flashed, in rapid succession, three reactions: Surprise, sudden fear, then the dawn of solid assurance, the absolute *conviction*, that he had nothing to fear after all.

"I'd appreciate it if you didn't come in here, Roger," he said, reaching out to swing the door shut.

Roger caught it with his foot, stepped inside, and closed it behind him.

"Bill, why are you *doing* this?" Roger asked, firmly but quietly.

Sitting up on the bed, Bill said, "I'd really rather you go, Roger."

"We used to be so close, you and me. And Marjie? The three of us were—" Roger felt his voice weaken and start to crack. He took a breath, swallowed. "—we were inseparable. Ever since we were *six*, for Christ's sake."

"Don't talk like that in *my* room," Bill snapped, standing.

"*What*?" Roger was genuinely surprised and stared slack-jawed at Bill for a moment. "My swearing's never bothered you before."

Bill frowned and seemed to carefully choose his words as he shuffled his weight from foot to foot.

"I've lost patience with you," he said finally.

"Lost...patience?"

"You were always interested in such...bad things. Fiction, movies, comic books...all things you knew were wrong. You knew it as well as we did, Roger, and you *still* know it. You were raised and taught the same way we were. But you kept rejecting the truth. No matter how much we prayed. You..." He shook his head sadly. "You're our failure."

"Fai...failure?" A moment before, Roger had feared he might cry. Now boiling anger surged through him.

"Maybe you're not a failure as a writer. But you know, Roger...you *know* what you write is wrong."

Roger turned around, leaned forward and pressed his clenched fists to Bill's desktop.

"It's not of God, Roger. And there's only one other source. You *know* that."

On the desk, Roger saw a paperweight he had given Bill in high school. It was a scorpion encased in a clear half-sphere of resin about the size of a man's fist. Roger touched it lightly with his fingertips. It was hard and cool.

"Your work is evil, Roger," Bill said. "Plain and simple. Evil."

Roger's anger grew hotter and made him tremble. Grinding his teeth together, he swept up the paperweight, spun around and threw it blindly. He regretted it even as his arm was slicing through the air.

Bill threw himself on the bed.

The paperweight hit the poster and stuck in the gypsum wall behind it with a loud *thwack,* tearing a gash into Christ's ghostly head.

Roger stared silently at Bill, mouth hanging open. He had shocked himself with his action.

Bill slowly rose from the bed, gawking at the paperweight sticking out of the side of Jesus's head. He turned and looked at Roger as if he had just committed cold-blooded murder. "I'm calling campus security."

"I-I'm sorry, Bill, really, I-I-I'm just so…*frustrated*!"

Bill went to the phone on his dresser, lifted the receiver and began punching the keys angrily with a stiff forefinger.

Roger moved toward him, saying, "Wait, Bill, just listen to me for a—"

"Don't come *near* me!" Bill said, his voice unsteady. He held the receiver to his ear with a white-knuckled hand and looked at Roger with wide, terrified eyes.

"Just tell me who's calling me at night, Bill just tell me—"

"Jesus Lord, protect me now from this evil," Bill whispered, hunching over the phone. "Shield me from whatever demon has—hello, security?"

Roger heard no more. He hurried out of the room and down the hall.

"Stay away from him!" Bill shouted from his doorway.

Doors opened and heads peered out. A young man wearing a bathrobe stopped on the way to his room and stared as Roger passed.

"He's evil!" Bill shouted. "Stay away from him! He tried to kill me!"

Roger resisted the urge to turn around and shout back, even though he had no idea what he would shout. In the stairwell, he could still hear Bill, no matter how hard he tried not to.

"He's evil! Stay away from him! He's evil!"

Roger sometimes heard it still.

7.

Josh looked as if he had died some time ago but stubbornly refused to accept it. He stood in the doorway, pale as fish meat, a skeleton with a thin sheen of human skin stretched over his bones. His brown hair was greasy and flat and seemed much thinner than when Roger last saw him.

His smile came slowly as his drawn, skull-like face craned forward on a wrist-thin neck to peer at Roger.

"Roger? Roger Carlton?"

"Hey, Josh." Roger tried to smile and almost held out his hand to shake, but a sickening image flashed in his mind that held him back: Josh's arm snapping at the elbow with a crisp, hollow crack and breaking off in his hand.

Josh held out his hand anyway, and Roger could not ignore it. It was cold and feather light with almost no grip at all.

Pulling his bathrobe together in front, Josh led Roger into the house where Humphrey Bogart was shouting at Edward G. Robinson on television. Josh walked slowly and carefully, as if his body might, at any moment, crumble into a heap of splintered, broken parts. The temperature in the small house was cloyingly warm and smelled of pungent, stinging medicines. Josh fell into a chair and turned off the television and VCR with the remote.

Roger seated himself on the sofa and looked at Josh, wondering if he should have come. This was not the same man he had known six years ago. He was a withered stalk of flesh and bone. Roger did not have the foggiest idea what to say. *So, how have you been?* was out of the question.

A tune from the seventies ran through Roger's head, but with slightly altered lyrics: *What do you say to a dying man?*

But Josh managed to make him comfortable. Eventually.

"Did you call?" he asked.

"No, I'm sorry, I should have—"

"Oh, no, I was just wondering. I haven't checked the answering machine lately. I sleep a lot. Practicing, I guess." His chuckle sounded like twigs breaking.

Roger winced.

"You should hear my answering machine tape. 'I'm sorry, I can't come to the phone right now. I'm in the bedroom rehearsing my Greta Garbo death cough.'" His laugh was a wheezing rattle in his chest.

The joke made Roger fidget. He couldn't bring himself to laugh.

"You would have laughed at that a few years ago, Roger."

"But you weren't sick then."

"Yes, so it wouldn't even have been funny. But I'm sick now. And if *I* can laugh at it, so can *you*." After a moment, he added, "Please."

153

Their conversation was peppered with Josh's razor-sharp, jet-black jokes about his illness. It wasn't long before Roger was laughing with him. They talked about movies, Roger's work, his teaching job. The topic of Josh's impending death finally moved in like a bank of storm clouds.

"This isn't going to take me," Josh said quietly. "The doctor doesn't give me long, but I think I've got a little longer than he says. I can feel it." He placed a bony hand on his chest. "Inside. But when I do go, it won't be because of this sickness."

"What do you mean?"

"I have a gun. I've never used it before, but I know how. When I feel I don't have much longer, when I *know* I'm going to go die soon but while I'm still able to do it myself, I'm going to disappear and use that gun."

"Where?"

"I'm the only one who needs to know that."

"But…why?"

"I don't want to be found dead here at home, and I sure as hell don't want to die in some hospital." He cocked his head, looking at Roger thoughtfully. "You're the first person I've told. About my plan. Keep it to yourself, okay? As a favor to me?"

"Sure, Josh, but…well, the thought of you—"

"Then don't think about it. I probably shouldn't have told you. But believe me, Roger, the thought of this thing, this sickness, taking me when *it* wants to…" He shook his head. "It has to be *my* decision."

"I understand," Roger said quietly, remembering the sensation of cold gunmetal against the roof of his mouth. "Believe me, Josh, I understand."

8.

Although the police would confirm nothing, word spread that Benny Kent had been shredded like a life-size paper doll and that parts of him had been eaten. The police made only a brief statement, saying that Benny had been attacked by a wild animal while jogging and had bled to death before he was found.

Roger knew the press would stay with the story for weeks to come, ferreting out every rumor and speculation, wringing as much from it as they could. As he read about it in Saturday's paper, Roger kept remembering what Betty had said about Benny Kent:

He always wore jogging clothes, but I don't think he ever really jogged …

The funeral was going to be Tuesday. The high school would be closed for half a day so students could attend.

… I don't think he ever really jogged.

Roger tried to shake it from his mind. He had a habit of turning unanswered questions into quests with which he became obsessed. Sometimes he pursued them at the expense of his work and sometimes they *became* his work. Sometimes they disrupted his sleep as well.

He didn't need that now.

More than anything, he needed sleep.

9.

Roger's last months in St. Helena were like riding a roller coaster that only went down—*straight* down.

The story of his visit to Bill's room was blown out of proportion and distorted, and it spread like a plague. It went like this:

Roger had burst into Bill's room and begun spouting some kind of evil spell in an ancient tongue. A paperweight had flown across the room, untouched and of its own volition, destroying a picture of Jesus Christ. The evil force that, for years, had been so subtlety inspiring Roger's unholy stories of lust and murder was clearly making itself known. The monster inside him was finally coming out. Roger Carlton was *obviously* possessed by Satan.

The late night phone calls doubled.

"Are you keeping the Sabbath, Roger?"

"Do you know you're going to burn, Roger?"

"Take your demons somewhere else, Roger, your evil isn't welcome here."

"The bible says—"

"Sister White says—"

"God says—"

The voices were male and female, sometimes familiar, sometimes not. He had his number changed twice, always unlisted, but the calls continued.

After the girl spit on him in DiMarco's, Roger began to spend more time at home with his dog Larry, a mutt he'd found outside the deli one evening almost a year earlier.

Stories of Roger's "possession" began to spread among the few non-Adventists in St. Helena. While they were not familiar with the church's beliefs and taboos and did not accept the stories as gospel, they still looked askance at Roger, apparently deciding that there must be *something* strange about him to generate so much talk.

Roger began to see Betty and Leo at their home or his; DiMarco's Deli was no longer the refuge it had once been. He began to drink more than he should and write less.

The phone calls did not stop—he kept his phone off the hook most of the time—and the police said there was nothing they could do unless the calls were specifically life-threatening. The phone company said they would put a tap on the line, but if they caught the offending caller (or callers), he would be required to go to court and press charges. He considered it.

His tires were slashed again and one morning, he awoke to find a red cross painted on his front door. Crudely written beneath it was a bible verse: Exodus 22:18. He went to the library to look it up because he no longer owned a bible.

It read, "Thou shalt not suffer a witch to live."

He filed yet another report with the police, but they did not see it as a threat.

That was when he finally began to think it was time to leave in spite of his love for the Napa Valley. He began to think about possible destinations.

Two nights later, feeling restless, he drove to the coffee shop in Calistoga and did some reading over coffee. On his way back, as he drove through Manning, headlights appeared in his rearview mirror. A car parked behind a large tree beside the road pulled out and followed him. The headlights drew close very fast, filling the mirror, and a few hundred yards farther down the road, two gunshots rang out behind him.

The next few minutes became a blur as Roger slammed his foot on the accelerator and doubled the speed limit the rest of the way through Manning, hoping he would attract a patrolman. Rivulets of sweat cut chilly trails down his neck and back as he hunched over the steering wheel, hugging it as if for protection, breathing to himself, "Oh God, oh fuck, oh shit," as he drove. He tensed in anticipation of another gunshot, of the sensation of a chunk of lead tearing through his flesh, nicking his bone—

—but the headlights were growing smaller in the mirror and the sound of the car's roaring engine was fading away.

Roger did not slow down; he went down the hill from Manning to St. Helena, where he parked in front of the police station and ran inside, nearly sick with fear. After a glass of water and a cigarette, he calmed down enough to tell the on-duty officer—a man named Miller with a barrel chest, thick glasses and thin brown hair—what had happened.

Afterward, Miller began asking questions, shaking his head slightly after each reply.

No, Roger could not identify the car or its driver or passengers.

No, he did not see the license plate.

No, he did not actually *see* a gun, but it sure as hell didn't sound like an engine backfiring.

"Look," Roger said, "this has been going on for a while now. Not as bad as this, but—well, I've reported everything."

After checking a file and shuffling some papers, Miller returned to his desk and said, "You sure have." He kept glancing from the papers to Roger and back again, noisily chewing some gum. "You've reported a *lot* of stuff, haven't you?"

"Everything that's happened."

"But you had no proof *then* that these things were being done by Seventh-day Adventists. Right?"

"But the things they say on the phone, the cross and—"

"Those things aren't proof. Listen, I've lived here most of my life, and you can't do that without getting to know a little about the Adventists. They're kinda strange—no movies, no coffee, no jewelry or dancing—but maybe it works, because they're good people far as I can tell. They do a lot for the community. They—"

"Yeah, I know, they collect clothes for the poor and food for the hungry, they help people stop smoking, yeah, they've got *great* PR." Roger stood. "But they're like *spiders*, Officer Miller. They eat their own."

Miller leaned back in his chair and shrugged. "Well, even if the people who shot at you *were* Adventists, you've got no ID on the car or driver, no witnesses. You've got nothing."

Frustrated, Roger started to leave.

"Wait, Mr. Carlton, I'd like to make a suggestion."

Roger stopped and turned wearily.

"Don't take this wrong, now. I'm on your side. I believe that *somebody's* got it in for you and your work. And, hell, I've dealt with enough religious nuts in my time—all kinds of different religions—but you need solid proof. You don't have it. It might be a good idea if you didn't report any more of these things until you *have* that proof. Think about it. Some kid on the hill gets a wild hare up his ass and burns down one of the school buildings." He shrugged one shoulder. "Just an example. We've got no leads, no suspects. But we *do* have a stack of reports filed by some guy who thinks the Adventists are out to get him but can't *prove* it. Turns out *you* were home alone the night of the fire. No witnesses, no alibi. And we *know* you don't like them. Wouldn't be too good for you. That's why I'm telling you. For your own good. Get some proof before you come back. Think about it."

The short drive home was terrifying. Each time he saw headlights in his rearview mirror, Roger's body buzzed with adrenaline.

When he got home, his front door was open a crack. With his heart pumping its way up into his throat, he cautiously entered, turned on the lights and looked around.

The lock had been broken. No one was inside and nothing seemed to be missing.

But he couldn't find Larry.

Not at first, anyway.

Larry was hanging by a rope over the back porch. All four of his legs had been twisted and broken. His abdomen had been cut open down the middle and his insides lay splashed on the concrete.

Roger moved to Los Angeles that night.

10.

Sunday was covered by a shroud of gray clouds.

Around one o'clock, Roger bought a paper and went to DiMarco's. Sunday was always slow. There were a few people in front but the Munch Room was empty except for Sondra, who was seated at a corner table studying and drinking apple juice. She sat straighter than she had the day before. She looked a little healthier, fresher, more rested. Roger got a bowl of minestrone soup and took a seat at the table closest to hers.

"On a break?" he asked.

She nodded without looking up.

"What are you studying?"

"American history," she whispered.

She seemed to have no interest in talking, but Roger did not want to give up while she was on a break. He wanted her to talk, wanted to have a whole conversation with her. He wanted to put her at ease, to calm whatever fears she was harboring.

"Do you go to St. Helena High?" he asked.

She nodded.

"Why not the prep school on the hill?"

She slowly lifted her eyes to him.

"You're a Seventh-day Adventist, aren't you?" he said.

The light from the small lamp on her table glistened in the tiny golden gashes in her brown eyes. "How did you know?"

"Just a guess. I'm familiar with them and…well, a pretty girl like you should be wearing a little makeup. Maybe a nice necklace, or—"

You're making an idiot of yourself, he thought.

"—but you aren't. I thought maybe—"

"You used to be one," she whispered, turning away from him.

"That's right. That's why I used to go to school in Manning. How did you know that, by the way? That I went to school on the hill?"

She suddenly seemed out of breath as she gathered up her things from the table.

"Where did you hear that?" he said.

"Around."

"Is your break over?"

"Uh, no, I just have to...I have to, uh..." She pushed away from the table and started to stand, then stopped. Frowning, she reconsidered and lowered herself back into the chair as she seemed to come to a decision. "No, it's not over."

Roger turned his chair toward her. "Are you afraid of me, Sondra?"

She bowed her head again. "Well...not...not really. But...they say I should be."

"Who?"

"People at church."

He nodded. "Do you believe them?"

"I...don't know." She whispered this secretively, as if afraid of being overheard. "You don't *seem*...um..."

"Evil?"

She nodded.

He waited because she seemed about to ask something. Finally, she looked at him and, like a fearful schoolgirl asking the principal if it was true that he kept a spiked paddle in the bottom drawer of his desk, Sondra said, "Are your books inspired by Satan?"

"No." He smiled gently. "If anything, they're inspired by the news. I write about the things people do to each other, mostly bad things, and about what happens to them afterward."

Here I go again, he thought, *defending myself against their lies.*

"But...if they're bad things...why write about them?"

"Have you ever read the bible?" He chuckled. "That book is full of more bloodshed and gore and kinky sex and —" He was trying to make a joke but failing by the look of her blank stare, so he dropped it. "If we don't look at the bad things we do to each other — write about them and read about them and think about them and why we do them — they'll only get worse. We'll never figure out a way to make them stop if we don't look at them long enough to figure out why they happen. Unfortunately, everyone in the world doesn't do the things Adventists *think* they should do."

Including Adventists, he thought.

"Don't you ever write about...good things?"

"Of course. About good people and bad people. Good things happen in my books, but bad things happen, too, and sometimes to good people. Because that's just the way it is. I'm interested in writing about the way things are, not about the way I wish they were. Think about it, Sondra, have you ever had a single day when only *good* things happened to you?"

As she thought about that, her face slowly changed, softened, and Roger thought he saw a glimpse of something that made him want to smile: Understanding. Something he'd said had cut through probably seventeen years of Adventist indoctrination and had *reached* her.

This must be how a teacher feels sometimes, he thought, still wanting to smile, but he wasn't sure how she would interpret it.

She gathered up her things, stood and said, "Well, I guess I'd...better go." She started to walk away but quickly turned back and, without making eye contact, whispered, "Do...do you really think...I'm...pretty?"

"*Very*," he said, meaning it. Before she could go, he touched her hand, stopping her, and said, "Would you like to read one of my books?"

Her eyes moved downward to his hand and lingered for a long time, so long that Roger thought she was getting angry, thinking that he was making a pass, and he pulled his hand away. But her hand followed his, gently brushing it with her fingertips. Then she jerked it away as if burned. Sondra's entire body jolted once and she stepped back, bumping her chair and pressing her hand to her stomach.

"*Sondra*?" Roger said, alarmed. "Are you—"

"I'm fine," she whispered, backing away, still holding her stomach. "Fine, just...I just...have to..." She bolted for the bathroom and slammed the door behind her.

Something fell to the bathroom floor with a *smack*—

Her books, he thought.

—and muffled retching sounds came from behind the door.

Roger wondered if he'd said something that had upset her? Made her ill? He pushed away his bowl of minestrone; his appetite had abandoned him.

A moment later, Betty called him from the front of the deli. As he left the Munch Room, Leo passed him coming in, grumbling.

"Where the hell are those *boxes*, goddammit?" he snapped as he passed, heading for the restroom. "*Sondra*? Where the hell is Sondra?"

As Roger walked through the doorway, Betty grabbed his arm and led him past the grocery shelves.

"Somebody I want you to meet," she said.

"Betty, Sondra's pretty sick, I think. She just—"

"Oh, it's just—" She leaned close and lowered her voice. "—her period. It always hits her hard, poor kid."

Betty introduced Roger to a customer who was a fan of his books. They chatted at the register for a moment and Roger answered the usual writer questions, then froze when they heard Sondra's scream.

No one moved for a moment, as if paralyzed, until she screamed again:

"*Leooo!*"

Roger dashed back through the Munch Room and spotted Leo's legs sticking out of the bathroom door, jerking.

He was curled on the floor, clutching his chest, pain shattering his red, sweating face with countless lines and wrinkles. He was groaning, writhing miserably, wheezing for air, and as Roger knelt beside him, Leo vomited onto the concrete floor.

Sondra pressed herself into the corner, hugging her books, her face ashen.

"Call an ambulance," Roger said in a thick voice.

She didn't move.

"Go *now!*"

Betty passed her on the way in, crying, "Leo! God, oh, Leo, oh—"

"Betty, see if there's a doctor out front, somebody who knows what to do. I think it's his heart."

Her hoarse cry faded as she hurried out.

Leo's face was darkening as he struggled for air. He vomited again with a long, agonized groan.

Roger had never felt so helpless, so useless. Tears burned his eyes as he watched Leo's body writhe. "Leo, oh, Leo, just…if you could just…" He did not know what to say.

Leo suddenly clutched Roger's shirt with a meaty hand and pulled him closer, sucking air to speak. His words were wet and garbled.

"What…*is*…she?"

"I don't…who?"

"Son…*dra*."

Roger saw more than pain in Leo's face, in the way his mouth stayed open and his tongue darted around, in the way his eyebrows rose high above his bulging eyes. He saw fear. "What…what about Son—" Leo wouldn't let him finish.

"I *saw*…her. I-I-I came in and…and…she was…she was—"

Leo's big body stiffened and he cried out in pain, tearing Roger's shirt with his fingers.

"What…*is* she?" he gasped.

Leo released a long sigh that seemed to come from the deepest part of his body. His hand relaxed against Roger's chest.

The room filled with the smell of bodily waste as Leo's hand slapped to the floor.

11.

Roger got no sleep for the next twenty-four hours.

Betty crumbled when she returned to the restroom and found Leo dead. She was taken to the hospital at the request of her family doctor, who rushed to the deli when he heard.

Roger stayed behind to take care of things at the deli. Fortunately, the girls knew what they were doing and needed little help because he was not up to supervising. He knew Leo kept a bottle of scotch in a box under the back room sink. After things had calmed down a bit, he had a couple of drinks to warm the cold trembling in his limbs.

When he went out front, he found Sondra sitting at the table by the front window, staring out at Main Street. Roger quietly seated himself across from her.

"Would you like to go home, Sondra?"

"My cousin is coming to get me during her next break." She was silently crying.

"Are you okay? Can I get you something?"

"No, I'm okay."

He chewed his lip a moment, debating his next question.

"Tell me, Sondra…what happened in there?"

She took a deep breath and said, "He…he came in and…he grabbed his chest and…fell over and…and…"

"Did something startle him? Were you talking when it happened?"

She stared out the window a long time, then shook her head, wiping away a tear.

What…is she?

Leo was in a lot of pain, he thought. *He was probably hallucinating.*

Another tear tumbled down her cheek as she whispered, "I didn't do anything."

"There was nothing *any* of us could do, Sondra. It was a bad one. It took him—"

Roger stopped when he noticed she was wringing her hands on the table, squeezing until her knuckles paled. Pearls of sweat clung to her forehead and her lips were a tense, straight line.

She had not meant that she was sorry she didn't do anything to save Leo from his heart attack—she was denying that she had done anything to *cause* it. And she was making the denial for no good reason that Roger could see.

What…is she?

"Well," he said, looking at her differently now, curious about the guilt she was failing to hide, "remember what I said about bad things happening to good people? This is one of them. But Leo wouldn't want us to spend too much time crying over him." Roger stood. "He'd want us to keep the boxes stacked and the slicer clean."

And he'd want us to get good and drunk, he thought.

The bell over the door sounded and a small, weary-looking woman came in wearing a white rectangular name tag on her pink-and-white striped smock. She smelled slightly of medicine and disinfectant, like a doctor's office. Her brown hair was pulled back snugly into a ponytail. Large brown eyes were set deep beneath a worried brow. Her cheekbones were like blades beneath her pale skin. She clutched her purse before her in both hands.

"Ready to go, Sondra?" she asked in a small voice, ignoring Roger.

He saw in Annie the same fear he saw in Sondra and found it fascinating.

Sondra left the table and went to the door. Roger was not sure if he'd heard her whisper "Goodbye" or if it was just a soft exhalation.

"Sorry about your loss," Annie muttered, leaving with Sondra.

Roger watched them through the window for a moment. Sondra's shoulders were tense and a bit hunched, as if she were about to close in on herself.

Roger thought, *What could she have done in that bathroom?*

In the following days, Roger helped Betty arrange for Leo's cremation. She refused to hold any kind of ceremony, claiming that Leo would hate to be the reason for any man to have to put on a suit and tie. Instead, she held an informal gathering at her house the following Tuesday.

DiMarco's Deli had been opened in St. Helena by Leo's grandfather seventy-five years ago. The DiMarcos were a prominent family in the area and Betty received visitors from all over the Valley.

Roger spent that day at the deli. Debi, the cashier, showed him how to clean the new slicer and change the filter on the new coffee maker. They were new to him, anyway.

Sondra came in late that day and said little. Whenever Roger spoke to her, she acted as if she did not hear him and hurried away.

Betty had given him the key to lock up at the end of the day, but after everyone had gone, Roger sat in the Munch Room listening to the radio, sipping scotch and smoking while he stared at his blank-paged notebook.

An hour later, Betty came in the back door and walked unsteadily to his table, smiling.

"Jesus, I've never had so many people in that house at one time," she said, slurring her words.

"Did it go well?"

She lit a cigarette and nodded. "Everybody seemed…comfortable. You know? Leo would have liked it. Everybody was…well, *drunk* is what everybody was. Me, too, I guess." Her smile turned downward and tears began to fall. "Roger, I don't know what I'm gonna do. I think I…want to stay this way for a while. Drunk. You know? I was wondering if you'd mind…well, kinda taking care of things here for a few days? Or…weeks. I don't know how long. Just for a while, Roger, I promise."

"Sure, Betty. I don't know if I'll be any *good* at it, but I'll do my best."

"Oh, you'll be fine. I don't know about *me*." She laughed as she cried, putting out her cigarette and standing.

"Can I drive you home?"

"No, I'd like to walk. Or stagger, as the case may be."

Roger imagined Benny Kent's torn and bloody body lying in a cold, muddy ditch—

I don't think he ever really jogged.

—and became uncomfortable with the idea of Betty walking alone after dark.

He drove her home.

12.

Roger had met Denise in Los Angeles.

When he arrived there, he moved into an apartment with Tony Gavin, an ex-Adventist he had known for years. Tony constructed sets for movies and television shows and shared Roger's feelings about the Seventh-day Adventist church.

The week Roger moved in, Denise Long moved in two doors down. She was a speech therapist from Colorado. And a Seventh-day Adventist. Roger didn't discover that until their third date. By then, it was too late. They got serious fast and on that night, when Denise made a joke about her Adventist upbringing while they were lying tangled half-naked on the sofa, it did not seem very important. She knew about his writing. He decided if it disturbed her, she would have mentioned it already. She was probably a lax, back-slidden Adventist.

He was right. She rarely went to church, was extremely liberal in her observation of the sabbath, and she ate pork, seafood, wore jewelry, danced, and went to movies. And she had nothing against living together before marriage, a topic she brought up very early.

169

Three months after they moved in together, Roger announced their engagement to his parents and sister, as well as to Betty and Leo. Shortly after that, Denise read his book in progress in bed one night. She did not talk about it until a week later.

During that week, something changed between them. Denise seemed preoccupied and frowned a lot. Sometimes Roger would find her staring at him as if he were a total stranger. He thought little of it. He was happy for the first time in a long while. He was in love and his writing was going beautifully. The pain that had made him so miserable for a while had not reared its ugly head in months. He decided Denise was just buried in her work, maybe not getting enough sleep. The possibility of it all going sour seemed so remote that it did not cross his mind.

Until he came into the bedroom one night to find Denise reading a volume of *Testimonies* by Ellen White.

"Roger, why do you write what you write?" she asked.

He took his time replying, trying to give her a clear explanation for his interests in crime and the macabre. When he was done answering her question, he said, "Why?"

She hesitantly told him that his novel had disturbed her deeply, that she had shared her feelings about it with a friend.

"A...pastor," she said. "From Glendale. He's heard of you. *Lots* of people have heard of you, it seems. And none of what they've heard is good."

As Roger tried to decide where to begin his explanation of his reputation, she asked, "Are you *always* going to write this kind of stuff?"

His stomach sank as he looked at her. He saw no point in responding.

"Because if you are," she said, "I can't stay with you."

They did not go to bed that night. They stayed up talking, even though he knew, deep down inside, that it was pointless. Their conversation went in circles as they moved from the bedroom to the kitchen to the living room and back to the bedroom, Denise saying that, even in her disinterested, back-slidden spiritual state, she could not justify his work, could not understand how a person with his upbringing could use a God-given gift toward such dark and unpleasant ends.

It was the same thing he'd heard from Marjie and Bill, and finally, he reached a point in the conversation when he knew he couldn't fight it. He was Sisyphus and the boulder was...everyone he knew. He stopped arguing and started packing. His things were back in Tony's apartment the next day.

But it wasn't that easy. She only lived two doors down. He knew when she walked by the door because he recognized her footsteps in the tile corridor. He saw her car in the parking lot. Sometimes he thought he could smell a faint whiff of her perfume.

Roger began to look for another place to live. He couldn't really afford it, but he had a royalty check coming. He found an apartment in North Hollywood. On the evening he was moving his last few boxes of things out of Tony's apartment, he got a phone call.

"We wanted to wish you luck in your new apartment," a man said.

"Who is this?"

"Because you're gonna need it...devil worshiper."

Although his new number was unlisted, Roger began receiving the calls at his apartment after he moved in.

His tires were slashed again, all four this time. The following week, someone painted a red cross on the hood of his car.

171

He decided not to get a pet.

Roger drove nightly to Tiny Naylor's in Studio city where he spent hours writing over coffee, sometimes with an omelet or a grilled cheese sandwich. He couldn't spend much time in his apartment; the clamber from Tiny's kitchen and the chatter of the patrons and waitresses were comforting and preferable to the confinement of his apartment.

He got to know several other writers who frequented the coffee shop for the same reasons. One was a screenwriter who interested Roger in writing for the movies and even arranged a couple of meetings so Roger could pitch some ideas. Neither meeting was successful, but it was good experience and gave Roger the feeling that he was *doing* something.

The pain returned with a vengeance and brought with it horrifying nightmares. Roger remembered little of what happened in them except for two things: Looking at his hands and seeing, instead, hideous blood-soaked claws, and the burning sensation of his skin changing its texture as it moved over his muscles and bones.

He began to renew his relationship with alcohol, which he had neglected during his months with Denise.

When the calls increased in spite of the fact that he had changed his number, he spent more and more time at Tiny's, never looking forward to going home.

One morning, Roger awoke to find his apartment door open a crack. The lock had been broken during the night and the contents of his open closet were scattered on the floor. With his head pounding from a hangover, Roger went to the closet and fell against the wall suddenly, afraid he would be sick.

His clothes were splattered with blood—clots of it clung to shirt sleeves and had dribbled into small puddles on the floor.

But it was not blood. It was red paint.

All but the dirty clothes in the hamper were ruined.

As he stared in disbelief at the mess, the phone rang.

"Most people have *skeletons* in their closet," a man said. "You've got *blood* in yours. And we want *you* to know…that *we* know."

Roger hung up.

Later that day, he bought new locks and an answering machine.

From then on, he went out only to buy groceries or go to the post office. Even then, he tried to make his errands as brief as possible. Sometimes he got the unshakable feeling that people were staring at him, maybe even whispering about him as he passed. The pain in his gut became a companion that clawed his insides at the most unexpected moments, doubling him over, sometimes sending him retching to the nearest bathroom. Sometimes he lay in bed waiting for the pain, afraid of it.

Tony came over one afternoon and pounded relentlessly on the door until Roger let him in. Tony looked around the messy apartment and stared at Roger like a stranger, muttering, "Shit, man, what's wrong?"

Roger tried to smile. "Caught me on a bad day, I guess."

"Bad day my ass. You need help."

Tony insisted that Roger see a therapist and, reluctantly, Roger agreed.

Her name was Dr. Yee—"But please call me Laurie."—a soft-spoken Asian woman in her thirties whose interest turned to confused shock as Roger told her of the harassment and threats he'd been receiving.

Shortly before the end of their first session, she frowned and said, "Tell me more about the pain in your abdomen."

173

"Well, it has no pattern that I can see, it's not brought on by any food or—"

"Stress? Anxiety?"

"Maybe, but I'm not sure."

"Tell me again what it feels like."

"Like...like a claw scraping me inside."

"Picture the claw in your mind and describe it to me."

"It...it has long, bony fingers...knobby joints...coarse, leathery skin and...and..." He stopped, afraid that talking about it would stir it up, bring it to life. "Razor-sharp talons are growing out of the ends of its fingers."

"Is it always there?"

"Well, it's like it...curls up in a ball and just...waits."

"For what?"

"I don't know."

"What is it trying to do, Roger?"

"Well, it...Jesus, this sounds crazy."

"Go on. Don't worry about how it sounds."

"Sometimes it feels like it's...trying to get out. Like it wants to tear right through my belly and...get out."

He saw Laurie again that week and she continued asking him about the pain. After searching his face for a long, thoughtful moment, she said, "What is it about yourself that you're afraid of, Roger?"

"I'm sorry?"

"Look at the way you're sitting. Arms folded in your lap, hunched forward, like you're covering something up. Or...holding something in."

"I don't understand."

"What do your Adventist friends think of you now, Roger?"

"They think I'm...evil. That I'm some kind of monster."

"Do you agree?"

"Of course not."

"But Roger, you were raised to believe that all of the things you enjoyed and were interested in were bad. That *you* were bad. You said that whenever visitors came to your house, the first thing your mother did—before she even knew who was at the door—was run to your bedroom and close the door so no one could see the posters on your walls or the books on your shelves. You've been taught that the work you're doing now is wrong. *Very* wrong. All of this was pounded in your head from the time you were a baby. Aren't you just a little afraid that maybe the Adventists are *right*?"

He did not respond.

"I'm not saying they *are*. But you can't just throw away almost two decades of indoctrination, of being taught what *they* say is right and wrong. Especially when you've *still* got people telling you how evil you are. You know what I want to do here, Roger? I want to help convince you that what's inside of you — the *real* Roger Carlton—is *not* an evil, clawed monster. Because I don't think you know that yet."

She assured him he would not see instant results, that it would take some time, and that he should be patient and realistic. But patience did not come easily for Roger. He wanted whatever was wrong with him to go away immediately so he could be the person he had always wanted to be right away. That person continued to remain out of reach. Roger was not even sure who knew who that person was.

When that did not happen—when the pain grew worse and the calls continued to come and he drank more and more to numb the fear and pain, and when someone left a large dead rat at his door—Roger bought a gun.

He told himself he was just buying it for protection, but when the man in the store told him he could not have it for two weeks, he suddenly knew the truth about his motives.

"Why two weeks?" Roger asked.

The broad black man behind the counter flashed two rows of bright teeth and said, "California law. We call it a cooling off period. Say you get really pissed at the wife, decide to blow her head off, and you buy a gun. Two weeks later, maybe you'll be cooled off. But then again," he shrugged, "maybe not."

"Two weeks," Roger said, thinking, *That'll give me plenty of time to make arrangements and to decide where to do it.*

Two weeks later, Roger knelt over his bathtub and eased the trembling barrel of the .25 caliber automatic pistol into his mouth as rain thrashed against the windows.

He stayed that way for a long time, feeling disoriented, wincing at the jagged fragments of thoughts that cut through his mind.

The phone rang three times—three long meandering rings—and the answering machine picked up. It was Barry Leese, one of his writer acquaintances from Tiny's.

"Hey, Rog," he said, "if you wanna try your hand at screenwriting, I think I can get you something. It's just a cheap-shit horror flick, but maybe it'll get you out of your cave. Give me a call tonight, let's get together."

All Roger heard was, "Maybe it'll get you out of your cave." He heard it over and over as his sweaty palm slid against the butt of the gun.

Something about the call jarred him and he sat up and pulled the gun away. His stomach hurt and he realized he had shit his pants.

He called Laurie's number and told her answering service that he had an emergency and needed to talk to Dr. Yee. When he finally heard her voice on the line, he began to cry. It was embarrassing but uncontrollable. He couldn't fight it.

They talked for almost an hour. He told her what was happening, what he was feeling and doing. She got him to promise her that he would not hurt himself until after he had spoken to her the next day. When he saw her the following morning, she told him what she thought he should do. It was ultimately up to him, if course, but she thought her advice would be productive.

By early afternoon that day, Roger admitted himself to Sylmar Neuropsychiatric Hospital.

"I really think it's the best thing for you now, Roger," Laurie told him. "You can't be alone like this, and you know it. It's entirely voluntary, so you can spend the night and if you don't think you'll benefit from a stay there, you can leave. Anytime you want. I promise."

Laurie was unable to keep her promise. She was called out of town shortly after Roger was admitted. "A personal emergency," her service said. "She's turned her caseload over to Dr. Henry Stanwick until she returns next month."

Next month?

Roger repeated those words to himself as he waited to see the chief of staff, Dr. Lyle Abbott, who said, "A voluntary admission means nothing if you're still suicidal, Mr. Carlton. And I'm not so sure you've passed that stage yet."

He repeated them as he waited to see Dr. Stanwick, a short, stern gray-haired woman who told him, "You've only been here two days, Mr. Carlton, and I sense no sign of improvement over the symptoms described in these records."

He repeated them silently to himself as he was questioned by Dr. Abbott:

"What do you think of when you see the color black?

"What does 'a rolling stone gathers no moss' mean?

"Do people talk about you behind your back?"

Next month, next month, next month, he thought.

He had a double room all to himself for the first week until he was assigned a roommate, a zombie-like young man named Doug who did not speak, barely opened his eyes and spent most of his time lying in bed. Roger was seldom in his room. He spent most of his time in the TV room reading, watching TV, or chatting with other patients. When it was discovered that Doug had a case of the crabs, Roger was quarantined in his room and had to take a long shower with special soap while an attendant watched.

Next month, next month, next month …

He attended group therapy, took an arts and crafts class (he was surprised to learn that basket weaving in mental hospitals was not just an old joke), and twice a day, he accepted the little paper cup of pills handed out to all the patients. He hated the way the drugs made him feel, the way they seemed to slow time down to a tedious crawl.

Next month, next month, next month …

Most of the patients in Roger's ward of the hospital were women who had suffered a great deal of abuse and had either tried to hurt themselves or someone else. One night, a movie aired about a woman who burned her abusive husband alive in his bed. As the movie played out, the women in the TV room became more and more agitated, some of them pacing with increasing speed. By the end, the room—the entire ward— resonated with their sobs and wails.

It reminded Roger of the last day of every Week of Prayer ever held at the Adventist schools he had attended. By the end of the guest speaker's highly emotional altar call, at least half the girls would be worked into a state of sobbing; it was such a regular occurrence that faculty members were always on hand with boxes of tissue to pass around to the emotional, spiritually moved girls. But Roger had always known the girls would recover and come to their senses—he was not that confident about the poor women in the hospital that night.

Next month, next month, next month …

Laurie returned three weeks later. Roger was polite and reserved when she came to see him. He smiled a lot and answered all of her questions positively, hating her all the while. Pleased with his disposition, Laurie authorized his release. He made an appointment to see her later that week at her request, but he only did that to avoid questions from her and had no intention of keeping it. He returned none of her calls and could not even bear to listen to her messages on the answering machine. Her voice was no longer pleasant and sincere; now it was the very sound of deceit and betrayal. It was the voice of a used car salesman, a carnival barker, a politician during election season. Because he had once trusted it, he could no longer listen to it.

As before, he spent most of his time alone in his apartment trying to write, drinking, and thinking a lot about that gun in the closet.

13.

Leo had been dead for more than a week and Betty still had not come into the deli. She slept until one or two in the afternoon and drank until she went back to bed.

"Should I be worried about you?" Roger asked her one evening.

"Probably. But don't be. Give me just a little more time."

Each night, Roger went to the deli after watching Johnny Carson. There he would write, listen to the radio and sometimes sip scotch. He found it easier to work at his table in the Munch Room, even at night when the place was quiet and dark except for his small lamp. The novel was beginning to unfold and draw Roger into its pages. It was called *Personal Sacrifices* and was about a frustrated young man who, in order to spend more time with a woman he's interested in and also as an act of rebellion against his strict religious upbringing, joins a Satanic cult, never for a moment taking it seriously. The cult members, however, are *very* serious, and he is drawn into an underworld of human sacrifice and ritualistic abuse.

One afternoon, Roger took a break from the deli and drove to the book store in Napa where he used to work. There he picked up eight books on devil worship and Satanism, hoping to give his book as much authenticity as possible

He immersed himself in his work each night and usually lost track of time, sometimes looking up to find that it was four a.m. when just a moment ago it hadn't even been one. He usually left the deli at about the time Sidney, the bread man, delivered the day's supply from the bakery in Rutherford. Sidney let himself into the storeroom in back, usually whistling a tune, and greeted Roger as he left the deli with, "Hey-hey, still at it, huh?" Roger would get a few hours of sleep, then shower and go back to the deli.

Although he was not accustomed to a nine-to-five routine, he did not mind getting up in time to open the deli. He tried to tell himself that he even looked forward to it; secretly, he knew that what he looked forward to was seeing Sondra.

Roger found her very attractive, but knew better than to pursue that because it would be…ridiculous. Still, there were times while they talked quietly at a table in the Munch Room when he had to clench a fist to keep his hand from touching her face, her hair, her slender neck.

For god's sake, Roger, he remembered Betty saying, *She's only seventeen.*

While she still seemed guarded, Sondra had relaxed somewhat over the past week. Her smile came easier, she held her head a bit higher, and she made eye contact when they talked. More than once, she quickly turned away when Roger caught her staring at him from across the deli.

They talked during her breaks. She asked questions about his writing, his experiences in Adventist schools, and he ended up doing most of the talking. He was unsuccessful in his attempts to get her to talk about herself. She no longer seemed afraid or guilty when he asked questions about her but remained closed to him.

But something was bubbling inside her and he wondered when it might come to the surface. There was a chance he was imagining it, but he sensed that she was developing trust in him, that soon she would take him into her confidence. He did not know if that was a good idea, but against his better judgment—which, in this case, was speaking in a hushed voice—he welcomed it. He wanted to get to know her. Spending time with Sondra was not unlike spending time with himself as he'd been ten years earlier. It was like having a conversation with his own past.

Except Sondra, of course, was much prettier.

When she asked about his background in the church, her interest was tempered with caution. She seemed especially curious about his initial feelings of doubt about the church and his abandonment of it altogether. He wondered if Sondra were beginning to ask herself some of the same questions he had once asked:

If there are so many different Christian denominations, how could only one be the true church?

What kind of God would slaughter everyone except the members of one little group?

What kind of God would slaughter any of his "children?"

How could the bloodthirsty, monstrous God of the bible be called loving and merciful?

Why is the fiction I write so wicked when the bible—supposedly God's infallible revealed word—condones child abuse, slavery, rape, incest, murder and genocide?

If this is what God wants me to believe, then why did he bother giving me a functioning brain that sees it all as contradictory, nonsensical bullshit?

He *hoped* she was asking herself those questions, because they were the only thing that could save her from a life of confusing guilt, suppressed desires, and endless self-loathing.

It wasn't until halfway through the second week after Leo's death that his suspicions were confirmed.

Roger and Sondra sat in the Munch Room during her break on a slow Wednesday afternoon. She had asked him about his two years at the Adventist boarding academy in Healdsburg and he was telling her about the time he and a friend played on AC/DC tape over the chapel P.A. system during services, when she interrupted him.

"Did you ever think there was something…wrong with you back then?" she asked. The fingers of both her hands were tangling nervously on the table and she sounded near tears.

"Sure," he said, puzzled by the sudden change in her behavior. "All the time. I didn't fit there. I used to think it was my fault, that there was something wrong with me. But I eventually realized the only thing wrong was that I didn't fit. And the only thing wrong with *that* was that I was pretending I *did*."

For a moment, Sondra's big eyes darted all over the room as if searching for words, and her mouth worked to find a voice, but she said nothing. She finally nodded, as if in agreement.

Roger leaned toward her and whispered, "Are you pretending you fit, Sondra?"

Her nostrils flared and tears glistened in her eyes as she nodded. Through her tears, the golden flecks in her eyes seemed to grow a bit larger, as if they were opening to reveal what lay beyond.

"I know how that feels," he assured her. "I went through it and it hurts. Deeply."

She shifted in her chair, turning away from him, and wiped her face with a palm, trying to compose herself.

Roger ached for her then; he ached with sympathy and, he was half-ashamed to admit, desire. He wanted to hold her, tell her she was going to be okay in a few years, maybe in a couple of decades, *if* she could get out from under whatever cloud the church had put over her.

"Look, Sondra, I want you to know that whenever things get tough and you need someone to talk to—" He reached over and took her hand.

She pulled away and hissed, "Stay away from me."

Roger flinched, shocked.

"I'm sorry, but…you really should. Stay away from me. I'm bad. For you. For everybody." She rushed out of the Munch Room and went back to work.

Sondra did not speak to him again all day.

14.

Roger taught his first class that night. It was small—only nine people—but after twenty minutes of talking about writing with his students, Roger decided they were all genuinely interested and not just taking creative writing to avoid a standard English class.

Then Marjie walked in.

Roger felt a surge of vertigo and had to check his surroundings to make sure he wasn't back in high school or college.

She stood in the doorway a moment, wearing a rust-colored skirt and brown sweater, a notebook tucked under her arm, a denim bag slung over one shoulder. Her hair was longer now, but otherwise she looked exactly as she had the last time he had seen her. When a breeze whispered through the open door behind her, he realized she even wore the same perfume.

Her smile seemed big enough to swallow her whole head as she stepped inside and said, "Sorry I'm late, but I was held up at work and…"

They stared silently at one another long enough to make the students fidget uncomfortably in their seats.

Marjie finally seated herself and Roger spent a few minutes stammering through the course outline, then dismissed the class early for the first of its three hourly ten minute breaks.

The students headed for the restrooms and smoking areas except for Marjie, who remained in her seat smiling at Roger.

"I can't believe you're taking this class," he said, sitting on the edge of his desk. He did not return her smile.

"Oh, it's not for the grade, or anything. I've always wanted to take a shot at writing." She stood. "But mostly…I wanted to see you." Moving toward him, she said, "Don't I get a hug?"

"No."

Her smile went away.

"I can't believe you're doing this, Marjie."

"Doing what?"

"Acting like…like nothing happened. Like you're glad to see me, like we're old friends."

"I *am* glad. And we *are* old friends."

"We *were*."

"Please, Roger," she said softly, her eyes becoming sadly apologetic. "That was a long time ago."

"Six years is not my idea of a *long time*. But even if it were *twenty*-six years, this would be a surprise. Your…*convictions*—" He spat the word. "—seemed pretty firm back then."

"Oh, you know how it is, Roger, you've been through it. They hold a Week of Prayer on campus, get some loud, charismatic guest speaker to give two sermons a day and work everybody into a religious frenzy, get them to burn their novels and rock albums and get re-baptized, and by the altar call at the end, you're practically glowing with Christian love and enthusiasm. On fire for the lord. You try to clean up your life, read the bible every day, it's like...I don't know, like *brainwashing*."

"You think?"

"But it doesn't last. It fades."

"There was no Week of Prayer then, Marjie. You worked *yourself* into a religious frenzy."

"I know, but...well, it's the same principle. I was going through one of those stages."

"Did you chase off any *other* friends during that stage?"

Marjie sighed and moved closer to him. "I tried to find you, Roger. I called your parents, but they wouldn't tell me anything. I wrote a letter to your publisher, but I never heard anything. You just disappeared."

"You expected me to hang *around*? I *had* to disappear, and don't act like you don't know why."

"I know, there were some people who...overreacted."

"*Overreacted*? Jesus, I'm glad they didn't get *pissed off*, they probably would've burned my house down with me *in* it!"

"A lot of people were...disappointed in you, Roger. I don't condone what they did, but they just didn't know how to handle it."

"Handle *what*?"

"The way you disappointed them."

"*Disappointed* them? It's not my job to fulfill their expectations with my life, Marjie. And don't try to pretend that they were the only ones who *overreacted*. You were doing plenty of overreacting yourself. And by the way, they *kept* overreacting because they followed me all the way to L.A."

"I'm sorry," she whispered, lowering her gaze for a moment. "I promise you, I had nothing to do with any of that. I...I've missed you."

When she was finally close enough to put her arms around him, Roger could not resist. Six years quickly melted away as he held her, smelled her, heard her sigh against his ear.

"I've...missed you, too, Marjie," he said, startled by how good it felt to say her name aloud again. He whispered, "But you really hurt me."

She said, "I always prayed—"

... it would go away ...

"—I'd get to apologize to you for that." She pulled back and placed a hand to his cheek. "You're—"

... sick ...

"—still very important to me. Hey, you're—"

... sick sick sicksicksick ...

"—my childhood sweetheart. You don't just *forget* your childhood sweetheart, you know."

Roger's back stiffened when he heard the old echo of her words and remembered how much they had hurt. He gently pulled away from her. Suddenly, he could not even bear to look at her and he felt a twinge of that old pain in the side of his abdomen.

No, no, he thought, *not now, please, not now.*

He put a hand over his stomach, preparing to double over, waiting for the claw inside him to emerge from its sleep and tear at his organs. It never came.

The students began to file back into the room and Roger tried to continue his class without looking at Marjie.

At the next break, she approached him again and put her denim bag on his desk, removing a hardcover and paperback copy of each of his books. With a grin, she asked, "How about signing them?"

———————

Roger told himself he would not see Marjie outside of class. He did not give her his phone number or address and asked her no personal questions, hoping she would do likewise. The very thought of renewing a friendship with Marjie made that claw stir ever so slightly in his gut.

But he had to admit, it sure was good to see her again.

15.

Sondra called in sick the next day. Roger was considering calling her to see what was wrong when Marjie breezed into the deli and kissed him on the cheek.

"It's my day off," she said. "I thought I'd come for lunch and see if you still hang out here."

"I work here now."

"I heard about Leo. I'm sorry. I know you were friends."

Over lunch, Marjie told him she was now living in Napa, working at a property management firm where she was quickly climbing the ladder.

As Roger listened, thinking, *I'm doing exactly what I told myself I wouldn't do,* he noticed tiny studs glistening in Marjie's earlobes.

"What's this," he said, touching one of her ears.

"Oh, yeah," she chuckled, covering her ears with her hair, "guess I'm gonna go for a swim in the lake of fire, huh?" She blushed like a child caught smoking. "I even have a sip of wine now and then. I'm a big girl. I'm thinking of getting some tattoos." She laughed.

But Roger noticed that she was not such a big girl that she did not keep toying with her hair self-consciously to make sure her pierced ears were covered.

She gave Roger her number on a napkin, saying she wanted to get together for dinner soon. Before she left, Marjie glanced around the Munch Room bashfully, then leaned forward and gave Roger a long kiss on the mouth. He neither responded nor resisted.

"I *really* want to see you," she whispered, touching his neck.

After she left, Roger realized she was going through the opposite of what he had experienced. Just as he tried for so long to fit into Adventist circles, she was now trying to fit in with her coworkers by wearing jewelry and having "a sip of wine now and then." Judging by her self-conscious behavior, she was not succeeding.

Fine, Roger thought with a touch of gleeful venom. *See how* she *likes it.*

He tossed her phone number into the trash.

16.

Shortly after four in the morning, Roger sat in the Munch Room squinting at the notebook before him. The radio was playing and the deli was dark except for the pool of light shed by the small lamp on the table and the single overhead light near the back door. His writing was getting sloppy and the scribbled words were doubling before his bleary eyes. He had been drinking more than his usual occasional sip and it had gotten the best of him.

Roger decided to quit for the night but, before he could close his notebook, someone banged on the back door.

He found Sondra shivering in the misty alley.

"Sondra, what's wrong?" he asked, closing the door when she came in.

She stumbled past him, crying and out of breath, and fell into a chair in the Munch Room. Her tall, shapely body was swallowed by a huge wool coat and she sat forward with her arms over her stomach as if in pain.

"Are you all right?" Roger said, sitting across from her.

"I'm scared."

"Of what? What happened?"

"Something's wrong with me. Something *horrible*." Sondra shook with sobs and rested her forehead on the table.

Roger figured it was probably finally hitting her. She was beginning to realize all the things she could never do or be if she remained entombed in her faith. She had begun to question the logic and fairness of such a senselessly restricting lifestyle and now, because of her doubts, she probably thought there was something wrong with *her*.

That's how it works, he thought. *That's how they* want *it to* work.

He poured a couple of swallows of scotch into his glass and put it in front of her.

"Drink this," he said.

"No, I really shouldn't."

"It'll calm you down. Come on, drink it."

She took a sip and coughed a few times.

"How did you get here?" Roger asked.

"My bike."

"Does anyone know?"

"They were asleep when I left." With less reluctance than before, Sondra tipped the glass and finished the scotch. She was still sniffling but her sobs had calmed.

"Now, will you tell me what you think is wrong with you?"

Her face twisted as she whispered, "I don't know." Then she pounded a fist on the table, crying, "I don't *know*, I don't *know*."

"Hey, whoa." He poured another shot of scotch and she drank it with a scowl that slowly relaxed. "Take off your coat."

"I can't. I'm…I didn't change. I'm still in my nightgown."

"Okay. If you'll tell me what's wrong, Sondra, maybe I can help."

"I don't even know what it is, I don't understand it. But I know it's not gonna go away. It just keeps coming back again and again."

"Have you talked to your cousin?"

"She won't do anything."

"What *could* she do?"

"Take me to…a doctor."

"You're *sick*?" He remembered the sound of her vomiting in the restroom the day Leo died and noticed she was still holding her stomach. He wondered if it was something more serious than just a strong period, as Betty had thought.

She nodded, pouring a bit more scotch.

"Hey, maybe you should go easy on that stuff," he said.

"Just a little more, please." Her hand shook as she drank and a small tremor passed through body her afterward.

"Sondra, if you're sick, you should go to a doctor as soon as possible. Right away. I can take you to—"

"*No.*"

"But don't you want to—"

"No, I *can't*. I shouldn't even be telling you any of this."

"You haven't told me anything yet."

She started crying again. "You'll…you'll have me…put away."

That scared Roger. He suddenly realized this was more than just a physical illness or a self-image problem. This was serious.

"Why would I do that?" he asked.

"Because I'm dangerous."

"Why do you think that?"

"I *know* it. So does Annie. But she doesn't talk about it. Neither does Bill."

"Her husband?"

She nodded. "They're scared of me. They *hate* me."

As she began to cry again, Roger wondered if he really wanted to hear any of this. He had planned to keep a low profile in the Valley this time and not get involved with Adventists in any way. But Sondra looked so lost and afraid, so hopeless. Her tear-filled eyes had heavy lids from the scotch and she rested her head in her palm. Roger did not think he could turn his back on her.

"Why are they scared of you?" he asked.

She scrubbed her face with her hands, then she reached for the bottle again.

"That'll make you sick if you're not used to—"

"I've drank before. A little," she said—but not without guilt—then took another swallow.

"But you're underage and I don't want to—" He stopped talking and thought, *At this point, what difference does it make?* "Okay. If you say so."

She sucked in a deep breath, as if for courage, and began:

"When I was a little girl, I wanted to be a dancer. I had this friend, see, a neighbor girl named Rosa who wasn't an Adventist. She was a little older than me and so pretty. I worshipped her. She took ballet classes and every week after her lesson, we'd go into her garage and she'd teach me what she'd learned. Her mom—she was such a nice lady—bought me a pair of ballet slippers and some leotards. I had to leave them at Rosa's house so my parents wouldn't find out. I was so scared they'd discover I was learning to dance.

"Well, they *did*. Mom came to the house one day while I was in the garage with Rosa. The look on her face when she saw me dancing...I thought she was gonna hit me. 'You're lucky *Jesus* didn't come while you were prancing around in there!' she said when we got home. 'You looked like some kind of a...a *pagan* doing that! A little pagan *prostitute!*' The thing is—" She stopped to swallow some tears. "—I thought I was doing so *well*. I was getting *good*. Even Rosa's mother said so. And I loved it. So much.

"Mom and Dad wouldn't let me leave the house for weeks after that, except for school. They stood in my room each night to make sure I studied my Sabbath school lesson and bible, to make sure I said my prayers. They...they took my bedroom door off so they'd be able to see if I danced in my room at night.

"I hated them for that. And I hated the church for making them that way, for saying that dancing was wrong. And I hated Mrs. White for writing all those awful books and...and most of all, I hated myself for feeling so much hate. I prayed to God to take away my love for dancing, but the more I bottled it up inside, the more I wanted to do it.

"Then I got sick. My stomach started hurting once in a while. Not my stomach, really. It was more in my side, the side of my abdomen. I'd get such terrible pains, sometimes I couldn't even *walk*. A few times, I even threw up and...and there was blood in it."

Roger chilled, feeling the fear he could see so clearly in her eyes as she spoke.

It's something else, he thought. *She has to be talking about something else. It* can't *be the same thing.*

"The doctors couldn't find anything," she went on. "They said it was all in my head. Mom and Dad said it was a punishment from God because I was so preoccupied with worldly things. Like dancing.

"The worse it got, the more they ignored it. Sometimes I'd be sitting at the dinner table saying grace and it would hit me so hard I'd fall right out of my chair and run to the bathroom and throw up. After a while, I figured they must be right—that I was being punished. I still wanted to be a dancer. I read books about it, I dreamed about it. No matter how hard I tried to change, I couldn't.

"The pain—" She held her stomach, eyes tensing as she talked about it. "—was like – it still *is* – like something's inside me. Moving. Cutting me."

Something with a claw, trying to get out, he thought, vividly remembering the claw he had imagined, so many times, to be ripping through his insides.

"It kept getting worse and worse until...about three years ago..." She poured another drink and took a couple of swallows.

Instead of protesting, Roger poured more for himself. When she did not continue, he said, "Three years ago what?"

"It got out."

He frowned. "Got...out?"

"I had a pony," she went on. "Three years ago, almost four now, it was killed. I had this nightmare, see, this horrible, bloody nightmare. It didn't make any sense at all, but when I woke up—" Her face lost its color and her voice cracked. She seemed about to be sick as she gulped air a few times. "I was covered with blood," she said, her voice a faint breath. "In my hair, in my mouth. My nightgown was torn up on the floor. And I could...smell...my pony.

"I cleaned up and threw everything in the wash before Mom and Dad woke up. That morning, Dad found my pony in pieces, partially eaten. They said a wild animal had done it." She stared into her drink with distant eyes. The flecks of gold among the brown seemed larger now, and on fire. "A wild animal."

When Roger found his voice, he said, "What—"

What...is she?

"—are you telling me, Sondra?"

She shrugged. "I *said* I don't understand it."

"Well, I'm sure you had nothing to do with the pony," he said, certain of nothing.

"Or the neighborhood dogs?" she asked, looking at him now. "Or the little boy down the street who was always offering me his allowance if I'd show him my coochie?"

Roger could not reply.

"After every one, I woke up the same way, from an awful dream. Covered with blood. When my mother found one of the pillowcases, I think they started to suspect. They became afraid of me. I think they thought I was possessed. You know, by…the devil. When they died, I knew." She squirmed in her chair, clutching her stomach hard with one hand, in pain. "I'd hear them whispering when they thought I wasn't around, talking about how maybe I should be exorcised, or anointed by the pastor, or something. Then they found my dancing books. They went crazy. Mom started screaming at me for bringing the devil into their house, Dad started praying, and all of a sudden the pain hit me like a train and I passed out. Sort of. I…I remember hearing screams. Seeing lots of blood. Then…then when I came to…they were all over the walls…on the floor in pieces…and there were police at the door."

Roger felt light-headed. He tipped the bottle to his lips and took a couple of gulps.

Some kind of accident, I think, Betty had said of the death of Sondra's parents.

"There have been other times," Sondra said. "Each one's worse than the last. And now they're not just worse, they're…different."

Roger's fingers toyed with the bottle and scotch burned in his gut as his mouth worked to ask her *how* it was different. His throat felt tight and the question came out with effort.

"It used to happen just when I was angry," she replied. "But now…well…remember the day Leo died?" Her voice caught

194

and she paused for a moment. "I...I was talking to you in here and...you told me I was pretty and you took my hand and...I wanted so much to touch you," she whispered. "I *wanted* you. But then it started and I ran to the bathroom. I was so sick I forgot to lock the door and...I was on the floor and it was happening to me, the change, and I was fighting it...when Leo walked in. And saw me. And...and he..."

Sondra started to cry again and Roger wanted to comfort her but could not. He could only stare at her, wondering if he should help her because she was crazy or fear her because she was telling the truth.

"Sondra, have you talked to anyone about this?"

"Only you. I thought...well, after all you've said...about thinking there was something wrong with you...I thought you'd understand."

Roger pressed a hand to his stomach, thinking of the horrible pain, the claw, the blood he used to spit into his toilet, the awful nightmares...the gory, sickening nightmares.

"You need help," he said. "You know that."

"Who's going to help me? I'm...I don't know *what* I am. What could anyone do?"

"What do *you* think you are?"

"A...a monster. Like Mom and Dad said. Maybe I *am* evil. Possessed. Maybe when I kept wanting to dance so much, maybe God just...turned his back on me. Maybe..." She couldn't continue.

Roger took her hand as she cried, quickly checking his watch. Sidney would be delivering the bread in about twenty minutes or so. It would not look good for him to find Roger alone with Sondra at that hour, and with a three-quarters-empty bottle of scotch on the table, particularly if Sondra's problem, whether real or imagined, later came to light. He felt he should call someone but knew of no one but Betty. As much as he hated to wake her at such an hour, he decided he had no choice.

"You sit right here, Sondra, okay? I'll be back in a minute."

He went to the phone behind the register and called Betty. It rang a dozen times before she answered.

"Betty? This is Roger. Sorry to wake you, but I've got a—"

She made a deep, gargled noise into the phone.

"Betty?"

"Whum?"

"Betty, this is Roger. *Please* wake up."

"Rah? Whum."

"Listen, Betty, I'm at the deli and Sondra's here with me. Betty?"

She had hung up.

Roger dialed again, certain she had been drinking all day and had no idea what she was doing.

"Betty, *don't hang up!*" he shouted. "Listen to me. Sondra is here with me and—"

"Hoozis?"

"It's *Roger*. Look, can you get up and—"

She hung up again.

"God*damn*."

As he made the call again, he felt two arms slide around his waist and firm breasts press to his back.

"Don't call anybody," Sondra whispered huskily.

Her breath smelled heavily of scotch and her words were slurred. When he turned around, he looked into her big, heavy brown eyes and knew she had finished the bottle

"Sondra…"

"C'mon back to the Munch Room."

She took his hand and led him back through the deli. He followed without protest partly because he knew he would never get through to Betty and partly for reasons he did not want to think about.

Her coat lay over the back of the chair and she wore only a small dark purple nightshirt that didn't quite reach her knees and was slit up to her waist on each side.

Before he could take a seat, her arms were around him and she was trying to kiss him.

"Hey-hey, Sondra, *wait*—"

"It's okay," she said, her voice thick as honey. "I've seen the way you look at me. I *know*."

"Uh, uh, no, just—"

Her mouth was on his and his eyes, wide with surprise, slowly closed as her tongue moved over his closed lips and—

It feels sooo good …

—it was only seconds before his tongue met hers—

It's been sooo long …

—and his arms slid around her, his hands moving over her back. Sondra's mouth opened and closed over his, drew his tongue in and sucked on it hungrily. One hand clutched his neck and the other squeezed his ass, pressing his hardening crotch to her. Their breathing grew frantic as they bumped the table.

Roger gently pushed her away but she moved forward again, kissing his throat and face, mumbling, "Don't you like it? Huh? Don't you?"

"Look, Sondra, we can't do this."

"Why not?"

"We…we *shouldn't*. We've both had too much to drink and—"

"Not *too* much. Is there any more?"

"Sondra, *stop*."

He firmly held her at arm's length as he tried to regain his composure.

197

"You *do* like it," she purred drunkenly, closing her hand over the bulge in his jeans. She stroked it as she kicked a chair aside and sat on the table, hugging one knee to her chest and gathering the nightshirt up around her waist.

"Sondra..." Roger's voice lost some of its forcefulness as his eyes traveled up her long, smooth legs, over her thighs to the small thatch of sunset-colored hair that glistened with moisture. "Put your coat back on," he whispered.

She leaned back and tried to pull his head down between her legs.

"*No,*" he said.

"Do you want me to suck this then?" She squeezed his erection. "That's what Benny wanted."

"Buh...Benny?" Roger stuttered, his mouth dry.

...I don't think he ever really jogged...

"You were with Benny?" Roger whispered.

"Just once." She leaned her head back and slid her fingers through her long, full hair.

He especially liked Sondra...

"Just...once..." She frowned and gently rubbed her hand in circles over her stomach. Her face suddenly had less color.

Roger knew he had to get her out of there and back home to bed, but did not know how to do it without getting himself into trouble. He cursed himself for giving her the scotch.

"Come on, Sondra. I'm taking you home."

She turned desperate eyes to him and gripped his collar. "No, please don't do that. Fuck me. Right here. Nobody'll know."

"I can't do that."

"Why? You *want* to." There was a desperate pleading in her voice and her eyes welled with tears. "Is there something wrong with me?"

What...is she?

"You said, you said—" Sobs interrupted her. "—that I was *pretty*, you *said* that!"

"You *are*, Sondra, but I can't—"

"*Please!*" she shouted, clutching his shirt. "I want to so *bad*—"

With her other hand, she unbuckled his belt—

"—so *bad*, I *need* to—"

—unbuttoned his pants—

"—please, let me know what it feels like—"

—and reached underneath to touch him.

"—before it happens, *please*, before it happens *again!*"

"Before *what* happens?" he gasped as she closed her fingers around his cock, pulled it from his pants, and began stroking it frantically.

Instead of replying, she gasped and sobbed.

Roger gently pushed her arm away and said, "No, Sondra."

She began touching herself as she reached for him again, whimpering between words as she said, "Please put it in me, puh-*please*, before it's...before it's—"

Her body stiffened. She bucked a couple of times. Roger thought she was making herself come, but then she made a sound that changed his mind.

She slapped a hand over her stomach and let out a long, wretched groan, turned over on her side and vomited onto the table, knocking over the small lamp and tossing the light over the walls like dancing ghosts.

Blood speckled her nightshirt and was smeared over her lips and Roger panicked, reached out to support her so she wouldn't fall off the table, but she faced him as her eyes rolled back in her head and her body curled into a ball as if cramped, and she grunted, "Too late."

The lamp rolled back and forth over the table making light dance wildly on the walls and ceiling.

Sondra's head craned back and her throat worked, making dry clicking sounds, as her tongue began to flap rapidly in and out of her mouth. Strands of blond hair writhed like tentacles as her head thrashed from side to side and she began to pull at the collar of her nightshirt as if it were a tightening noose.

Roger leaned over her and shouted, "Sondra, what's *wrong*? What can I *do*?" and her arm sliced the air, hit the side of his head like a club, and knocked him against the wall and to the floor.

Pain throbbed in his skull like a drumbeat and he lay face-down for a moment, blinking his eyes and trying to see clearly again.

Sondra made the ragged, throaty sounds of an animal in pain as Roger raised himself to his hands and knees. He heard the nightshirt rip as he got to his feet.

His first thought was to go to the phone and call an ambulance, but Sondra fell from the table and landed in a crouch between him and the door and Roger stumbled backward in horror.

Sondra's teeth—now jagged and tapering to deadly points—protruded from her mouth, pushing her lips outward into a kind of snout. Bloody saliva dribbled from her mouth, glistening in the still-shifting light. Her nightshirt hung from her bare body in tatters; her knees jutted upward on each side of her body and her hands scraped the concrete floor between her sneakers, making a harsh sound.

Something was wrong with her fingers.

They were longer now, knobby, as if arthritic, and a curved, razor-sharp claw protruded from the tip of each finger.

Claws ...

As her claws scraped over the concrete, sparks flashed and died in the shadows.

Sondra sounded as if she were strangulating, her chin jutting forward, eyes clenched in pain. Her lips writhed over her hideous fangs, her tongue squirmed in her mouth like a pink dying worm—

—and she seemed to be trying to say his name.

"Raaaw…Raaaw…juuhhh…"

Roger could not speak, felt cold and paralyzed with fear, numb. He groped for something to hold on to as Sondra moved backward into the funnel of light that spilled from the toppled lamp.

Her skin was horribly mangled now, as if burned, and tufts of thin hair had appeared in patches over her body. Her breasts were withered tubes of useless flesh that dangled between her arms as her tortured body quaked.

What…is she?

When he was finally able to move, Roger stepped backward, knocking over a chair as he babbled, trying to find his voice. There was no other way out of the Munch Room and he could not bear to get closer to Sondra.

Or what had once been Sondra.

He thought of the knives lined up in cutlery boards by the sink and tripped around a table to get them, afraid to take his eyes off the creature that was now on all fours before him.

He was turning toward the sink when a distant sound froze him in place and made him sob with a combination of relief and dread.

Whistling.

The door to the storeroom in back clattered open and Roger could hear the engine of Sidney's bread truck idling.

"Oh, God," Roger groaned, "oh, God, *Sidney!*"

The whistling stopped.

"Sidney! Get help!"

"Mr. Carlton? That you?"

"Get help! Call the police!"

"What? Can't hear you. Where are you?" His voice was closer, inside the deli now.

Roger screamed the words again so loudly that his chest hurt.

The beam of Sidney's flashlight cut through the darkness beyond the Munch Room doorway and his feet scraped heavily over the floor.

Sondra's eyes opened then and she was suddenly alert. The golden flecks had spread like fire through her eyes and glowed hungrily in the darkness.

"Don't come in here!" Roger shouted, his knees weakening. "Get *help*, Sidney, don't come—"

Sidney stepped into the Munch Room, sweeping his flashlight in an arc before him, holding it on Sondra, who turned toward him with a throaty growl.

"What in the fuh—"

She was on him.

Sidney's screams were high and piercing, but they did not last long.

Warm blood spattered Roger's face and his legs gave way. He leaned against the wall, swallowing his gorge as bones snapped and gristle tore.

The wet smacking of Sondra's lips was the last sound he heard before fainting.

———————

He returned to consciousness slowly with a horrible odor in his nostrils. He lifted his head and looked around.

Roger never knew that blood had such an overpowering smell. He had never been around so much of it. It was splashed in deadly Rorschach designs all over the wall above the quivering, dying man—

Jesus Christ, Roger thought, hugging himself in the corner, *he's still alive, his chest is open, oh fuck, how can he STILL BE ALIVE?*

—and dribbled to the floor in long, thin, black-red streaks. Dark strands of it shot from the man's chest and tattered throat in rhythmic but gradually weakening spurts. His blood-gloved hands slapped the concrete floor, leaving smeared handprints, and the heels of his boots thunked together spastically.

The alcohol in Roger's stomach burned as it tried to come back up and his own babbling voice sounded unfamiliar to his ears. He was babbling not only because of the bloodshed before him, but because of the cause of it all.

The creature that hunkered over Sidney's dying body was only vaguely human in shape. Its patches of mangy hair were clotted with blood. Bits of flesh clung to its jagged teeth like chives. Tremors of pleasure passed over its leathery skin as it plunged a clawed hand into the man's chest and tore something out with a moist ripping sound.

When Sondra began to eat, Roger lost consciousness again.

17.

He heard Sondra crying before he opened his eyes.

Roger had no idea how long he had been unconscious and, for a moment, wasn't even sure what had happened. Warm moisture clung to his face and hands. Trembling, he struggled to his feet and limped to the light switch, his shoes slopping over the wet floor.

When the fluorescent lights flickered on, Roger wanted to scream but could only whimper like a frightened child.

Pieces of Sidney lay scattered about the floor. Patches of tattered skin were indistinguishable from the shreds of his blood-soaked clothes. One limb—Roger wasn't sure if it was an arm or a leg—remained attached to the torso, which lay open like a huge misshapen melon. Sidney's head was propped against the wall two feet away from the body, the face a mask of blood, mouth yawning, only one eye remaining, wide and glazed.

Roger took a long, deep breath, fighting to hold on to his consciousness as he thought to himself, *It's not a person anymore, it's not a person, not a person ...*

It did not help.

Sondra was huddled, naked, bloody, and shaking, beneath a table, hugging herself and rocking, sobbing and then laughing in turns.

Blood dribbled down the face of the Mickey Mouse clock on the wall, which read three minutes to five.

The bread truck idled faithfully in the alley outside.

The room reeked of blood and excrement.

Sondra's huge eyes were frightened and strangely innocent in spite of the tears of blood that trickled over her now smooth cheeks. The flecks of gold were invisible from where Roger stood and her eyes were once again a deep brown. Although she was staring at him, Roger knew she was not seeing him.

"Sondra?" he said hoarsely. "Are you hurt? Sondra?"

She whispered something unintelligible, something that was not directed at Roger.

He moved closer and realized she was singing softly to herself. It was a song he remembered singing as a child in Sabbath school.

"Jesus loves me...this I know..."

Careful not to step on anything, Roger went to the table, bent down, and cautiously reached for her.

"…for the bible tells me so…"

He took her arm and gently tugged.

"…little ones to him belong…"

"C'mon, Sondra," he whispered, and she let him pull her out, but kept whispering the song.

"…they are weak…but he is strong…"

He seated her in a chair and told her to stay put, although he knew she was not hearing him.

"…yes, Jeee-zus loves meee…yes, Jeee-zus loves meee…"

Roger surveyed the bloody mess again, then looked at Sondra, who rocked in the chair like a retarded child, and knew he had to help her. For her sake as well as his own.

"…yes, Jeee-zus loves meee…"

He began to look for cleaning supplies and garbage bags as the bread truck continued to idle outside.

"…the bible tells me soooo."

18.

By the time the girls began to arrive at the deli to prepare for another day of work. Roger was exhausted but practically vibrating with adrenaline.

His fear that he had overlooked something that one of them might notice was so great he was barely able to speak when they greeted him.

"Hey, Roger," Michelle called as she came out of the Munch Room tying her apron, "what happened to the Batman and Robin poster?"

"What?" He felt his heart moving up his throat.

"It's gone. The Batman and Robin poster. You know, Nixon and Agnew. Did you take it down?"

"Oh, that. Yeah. Betty wants to start replacing all that stuff in there." He'd had to throw it away. It was the only wall hanging that had been irreparably bloodied.

"She's gonna remodel the Munch Room?"

"Guess so." Somehow, he would have to cover for that lie. Among others.

After a few minutes of agonizing over where to start, Roger had filled a garbage bag with the remains of Sidney the bread man and stuffed it into a bin at the south end of the back alley. He made sure Sidney had delivered the day's bread in the storeroom, then, wearing Playtex gloves, he drove the bread truck to the north end of the alley, the direction in which it had been headed, and killed the engine. He wanted to give the impression that Sidney had simply left his truck and decided he might be more successful if he did not leave the keys. He dropped them into his coat pocket.

Once Sondra was coherent, Roger led her to the big sink in back, took a cloth soaked in warm soapy water, and gently began to clean her up. He slowly moved the cloth around her neck, over her face, across her breasts and belly, speaking soothingly to her, trying to hide the horror and disgust he felt at the sight of her beautiful young body covered with blood and strips of human flesh. When he had her rinse her mouth with water, she gagged and spit up a hunk of Sidney's scalp and hair.

After using cold water to remove the few streaks of blood on her wool coat, Roger put her bike in the backseat of his car and drove her home, following as many back roads as possible. He stopped the car half a block from her house to drop her off.

"Now, you're sure you're okay?" he said.

She nodded and when she spoke, her voice was hoarse and strained. "I may not come to work today."

"Sondra, you *have* to come to work. *And* go to school. Do *nothing* unusual, do you understand?"

"But I'll be so tired." Her casual, weary tone suggested this had happened before and she had simply walked away from it, just as she had explained earlier that morning. It gave Roger a deep, profound chill, as if he had stepped through a door and suddenly found himself standing on the edge of the Grand Canyon, naked and cold in the middle of the night. He heard no regret in her voice, not even a hint of understanding of what she had done.

"I promise you, Sondra, you won't have to do much. Just look busy, that's all."

Roger watched her walk the bike down the sidewalk until she turned in at the drive, then he returned to the deli where he spent the next few hours vigorously scrubbing the Munch Room.

When he was finished and everything was put away, he stood in the middle of the room and scanned the walls and floor, searching for the slightest telltale sign.

Then he went to the bathroom, knelt at the toilet and threw up until he could hardly breathe.

Now, as he sipped his coffee, having gone home for a shower and a change of clothes, he thought about everything he had done and the fear began to eat into his bones like termites into wood.

The keys to Sidney's truck were in the back corner of his bottom dresser drawer, about a dozen of them splayed from their ring like the stiff, barbed legs of a metal spider waiting to pounce on the next person to open the drawer.

Roger knew that, had he called the police, there would have been no way to explain the killing. They would not have believed the truth—*Roger* still did not believe it—and he had the feeling that the blame would somehow fall on him.

But there was another reason he helped her, one he could not pinpoint. It seemed to hover on the edge of his thoughts, unwilling to be discovered. It had something to do with the claws that Sondra's hands had become, with the talons that had grown from her fingers.

He had seen them before in his imagination, watched them, with his mind's eye, tearing through his insides as he lay curled in his bed, clutching his abdomen in agony.

It had something to do with the fear he had felt as Sondra spoke of her mysterious illness, described the painful symptoms and the equally painful circumstances under which they'd arisen.

He had felt an unsettling bond with Sondra when he saw her huddled beneath that table splattered with blood, a sort of empathy, as if he had been in the same situation himself once.

That, of course, was ridiculous.

But when he thought of those claws and of the pain that used to cut through him until he bled inside, when he thought of the way he used to dream of changing, his skin burning as it writhed and squirmed into something that was not human, he wondered if he had been close—perhaps *very* close—to experiencing the same transformation.

19.

Late that morning, a man from the Rutherford Bakehouse called to ask if Sidney Nelson had made his delivery. When Roger said that he had, trying to hide the dryness in his throat, the man said Sidney had not yet returned. He was going to call the police and they might come by and ask Roger a few questions. He said that was fine, hung up, then went to the back and quickly drank a glass of wine to calm his tattered nerves.

A police officer did indeed come in that afternoon—officer Chuck Niles, a boyish freckled man—and asked if Roger had spoken to Sidney, if the delivery man's behavior was in any way unusual, if he'd been angry or mentioned quitting his job, if he'd been alone.

Roger answered the questions calmly and with assurance, saying that Sidney had simply come in, said hello, made his delivery, then left.

When the officer left, Roger had more wine, only because there was no more scotch.

Sondra came in a few minutes late looking weary and pale, just as she had the day Benny Kent's body had been discovered. The confidence she had developed over the past weeks, however small, was gone. She would not look at Roger.

Although he had not slept, Roger was not tired. Instead, he was jumpy and irritable and could not think straight. He dropped things and bumped into things and once looked up at the sign over the Munch Room doorway and began to giggle uncontrollably —remembering the sound of Sondra's wet, sloppy chewing early that morning gave new meaning to the Munch Room sign and he found it horribly funny.

Shortly before closing time that evening, Roger spotted Sondra going into the bathroom with a broom and followed her.

"Did you get caught this morning?" he asked quietly, half-closing the door.

"No. They were asleep."

"How do you feel?"

"The way I always feel afterward. Tired. Shaky." Her eyes never met his.

"How many times has this happened?"

"I don't know."

"What brings it on?"

"*I don't know,*" she hissed.

"You killed Benny Kent, didn't you?"

After a long moment, she nodded and began sweeping as if he were not there.

"What happened?"

"He wanted to…to…be with me. We met that night by the footpath. Between here and Manning? And we started to…you know…"

"Did you want to?"

"*Yes*, I wanted to. Just like with you. But when we started…I…like always, it happened."

"Sondra, you've got to do something about this. I know you're scared, but you've got to see someone or—"

"Forget it."

"What? What do you mean, forg—"

"Thank you for helping me, but…you have to forget it because…I'll be looking for a new job now."

"What? Why?" He was speaking in urgent whispers now, fists clenched at his sides.

"They don't want me to work here anymore."

"They? Annie?"

"And Bill. I shouldn't even be talking to you like this. She could come in any minute and—"

"Because of me? They want you to quit because of *me*?"

She started for the door but Roger stepped in front of her.

"What do they know about me?" he asked.

"I have to go, let me *go*," she snapped, moving around him and leaving the bathroom.

210

Roger followed her into the Munch Room where he froze when a familiar voice said, "Sondra? You ready?"

Bill Dunning stood before them leaning on a cane.

A silence as solid and cold as stone filled the room.

Sondra stopped, folded her arms protectively over her breasts and stared at her shoes.

A second, minute, or hour could have passed as Roger stood in the doorway, eyes locked with Bill's—he was not sure and did not care.

Bill's face was solid now, the boyish roundness it had in college replaced by a stern, jaw-clenched look of bitterness. It might have been because he was looking at Roger, but Roger didn't think so. It was not a passing look; it was chiseled into the bones beneath his skin, carved into his jaw. He was thicker and stubble sprinkled the lower half of his face. His right leg was gone. The leg of his black pants was filled out but stiff, and when he shifted his weight once, the leg clicked noisily. It was a prosthesis.

"Come on, Sondra," Bill said, his voice low and level, his eyes still on Roger. "Let's go. Annie's waiting."

Sondra was hurrying for the door before Bill was finished.

Bill remained for a moment, eyeing Roger warily.

Swallowing a clot of felt in his throat, Roger tried hard to smile, to sound congenial when he stepped forward and said, "Well, hey, Bill, it's been—"

"Sondra won't be working here anymore," Bill said. "Thought I'd let you know." As he turned and walked out, leaning heavily on his cane, Bill's right leg clicked with each step and he muttered, "Getting a job someplace else."

Roger listened until he heard the bell out front jangle over the closing door. Then he sent the others home and closed up for the night.

20.

A thin mist crept into the Valley that night and spread itself through the vineyards like a blanket of cobwebs. The stars were hidden by gathering clouds and the air had fangs of ice.

When he turned down his street, he noticed a car pulling up in front of his house.

Roger felt sick.

It was not a police car, but it was unfamiliar.

As Roger pulled into his drive, the driver's door of the car opened and a woman got out. Marjie.

"*There* you are," she called happily as he got out of his car. "I was afraid I'd come up here for nothing. Hope you haven't eaten yet." She lifted two grocery bags from her car.

Hiding his annoyance, and the fact that eating was the *last* thing on his mind, He took one of the bags and they went inside.

"Spaghetti sound good?" Marjie asked as she emptied the bags on the kitchen counter.

"Sure, Marjie, but I really don't—"

She held up a bottle of wine. "Do you want this before, during or after dinner?"

"Right now, please." Roger sighed as he sat at the table. "How did you find me?"

"I've got a friend in payroll at Napa College. She looked up your address for me. Why, did I come at a bad time? You look terrible. Are you sick?"

"No, just tired." He yawned.

She opened the wine and poured two glasses, then busied herself with the groceries, preparing dinner.

It was not until he had finished his first glass of wine that Roger realized how beautiful Marjie looked.

She wore a tight black skirt, a red-and-black top with a scooped neckline, and a dark gray blazer. Her hair was up in the back and gently curling strands of it fell to the sides of her face.

"You look nice," he said, pouring more wine. "What are you all dressed up for?"

"For *you*," she said, sounding disappointed that he would think otherwise.

As she darted around the kitchen, chatting about work and her two cats, Roger watched her and realized this was not just a friendly visit—this was a *very* friendly visit. Marjie meant to start something. Roger thought it might be nice to spend the night in her arms—*God, it's been a long time,* he thought—and forget about everything else for a while. But he could not do that and knew he shouldn't even be having dinner with her. He could not very well tell her to take her spaghetti dinner and go home.

Things had happened between them that no amount of explaining or apologizing could erase and, knowing that the average back-slidden Adventist could undergo a spiritual about-face at any time, he did not want to open himself up to more of the same. He knew Marjie would be more of the same.

Over dinner, she brought him up to date on some of their former schoolmates.

Clearing his throat, Roger asked, "Whatever happened to Bill?"

"Dunning? Oh, what a sad story *that* is. He's married now, you know. Married some girl from Michigan just out of college. Annie something. A little wallflower. He got *really* religious and was planning to go right back to school—the seminary—and become a minister. Then he had an accident on his motorcycle. Lost his right leg. Couldn't work. Annie works at the hospital. And if Bill was religious *before*…well, he and God are best buds now. The accident…I don't know, I think it made him go a little, you know, wiggy. Annie's cousin from Michigan is living with

213

them now. She's got a job somewhere in St. Helena and helps pay some of the bills."

"Not anymore."

"Oh?"

Roger told her about Bill's visit to the deli that day.

"Then you know the girl," she said.

"Not very well." He began to feel uncomfortable with the subject.

"I met her once. I hear she's a real troublemaker."

Roger swallowed a black, morbid chuckle.

"A horny little devil, from what I've heard."

"I...wouldn't know."

There was a pause filled with the clatter of forks against plates, then Roger asked, "Are you sure Bill lost his leg in a motorcycle accident?"

"Yeah. I mean, there aren't too many ways to lose a whole leg, you know? Why?"

He shrugged. "Just wondering."

"No, really, tell me why you asked. You seem...I don't know, troubled. Did Bill say something today that—"

"Never mind, Marjie, I really don't want to talk about it."

After dinner, they had ice cream and Marjie turned on the television and cuddled up beside Roger on the sofa after opening another bottle of wine.

Roger stiffened, forcing himself not to respond.

"What?" Marjie said, puzzled. "What's wrong?"

"I...don't think it's such a good idea, Marjie."

She pulled away from him, smiling, and removed a baggie and a small pipe from her purse on the floor. "You just need to relax, that's all," she said, waving a lump of marijuana under his nose.

Roger had tried to get her to smoke pot with him the summer of their senior year in high school, but she'd refused politely, saying she had no intention of ever trying it.

"Like I said before, Roger, I'm a big girl now," she whispered conspiratorially, as if reading his thoughts.

They each took a few hits and began laughing at some vapid sitcom on TV until Marjie spilled some wine on herself.

She stood, giggling. "Shit, oh shit," she said as she brushed at the spreading stain. "Do you have a robe, or—"

"Sure." Roger went to his room.

"Where's your washer?" she called. "Do you have one?"

"In the garage. Through the kitchen."

Roger returned to the living room with his bathrobe and was about to sit down again when he remembered his blood-spattered clothes stacked on the washer and he bolted through the house after her.

"Roger, what *happened*?" she asked as he stepped down into the garage. She was holding up the shirt splashed with Sidney Nelson's blood.

"Oh, that," he said, trying to calm himself as his mind raced. "I, uh, I hit a, um, deer. Last night. With my car. I had to, you know, move it out of the road. It was…messy." His hands trembled and he began to perspire as he took the shirt from her and tossed it aside along with the pants.

When Marjie had her shirt off, Roger handed her the robe and quickly started the wash, then led her back into the house.

"That must've been awful," she said. "Hitting a deer. I did that once and thought I'd never stop crying."

On the sofa once again, Roger suddenly felt giddy at having succeeded with his lie.

They smoked some more, drank some more, and kept laughing at the TV show. But now Roger's laughter was deep and heartfelt and he was relaxed beside Marjie. They leaned on one another as they guffawed with the laugh track, her arm around his shoulders, his arm resting across her thighs.

Then they were kissing.

Minutes later, they were in bed.

Laughter continued from the television set, blending with their sighs and whispers, and with the sound of the rain that had begun to fall gently outside.

When Roger closed his eyes, thrusting his hips, moving inside her, it was not Marjie who filled his mind.

It was Sondra.

21.

Roger woke the next morning to find Marjie gone. She had left a note: "It's still as good as before! Soon, M."

Over coffee in the deli, Roger searched the paper for any mention of Sidney Nelson. A small article said only that the delivery man's truck had been abandoned in an alley. A tiny smear of blood hinted at foul play.

Roger grew faint for a moment, but was relieved to read that the police suspected Sidney had been attacked and robbed and was perhaps wandering around, injured, lost, and confused. The search was ongoing.

Roger called Betty, woke her, and told her Sondra had quit and she would need to hire a new girl. He was not familiar with the procedure and said he would be more comfortable if she came in and did it herself.

"Oh, sure, honey," she said groggily. "You've been awfully good to me. I should've come back before this. I'll be in this afternoon. Why don't you go home and relax?"

He did. He watched a Godzilla movie on television that afternoon, munching on pretzels. He read through some of the books on Satanism he had bought and leisurely wrote pages of helpful notes. He finished a chapter that had been stumping him for days.

Marjie called him from work and said she wanted to see him again that night.

By the time she arrived, Roger had set up a tray of take-out Chinese food in the bedroom. The focus of their attention alternated between the food and each other's bodies.

The next week was smooth as glass, and so were the days that followed. Roger enjoyed teaching his classes. He had regained an old friendship—and then some. He thought hardly at all of Sondra. He was able to enter the Munch Room without seeing Sidney the bread man scattered over the floor and walls. He began to feel as if it had never happened.

For the first time in years, Roger's life was good. He would even go so far as to say he was happy.

That worried him.

It had been so long since Roger had felt anything like happiness that he began to wonder what would happen to end it. Surely it could not last long.

It did not.

22.

Roger tore himself from a nightmare—

Sondra was peeling a bloody sheet of skin from the back of Sidney the bread man, who was convulsing on the Munch Room floor, and who, for some reason, had an enormous set of antlers growing from his skull.

I hit a deer last night...

—and sat up in bed gasping in the dark.

"What is it?" Marjie pressed warmly against his back and her breath was hot on his neck.

"Night. Mare." He was out of breath.

"Get you something?"

"No." He lay back down and Marjie curled up beside him, kissed him, and whispered, "Be right back."

She went into the bathroom and he heard her urinate, flush, wash, then go to the kitchen for a drink.

After a few moments of silence, Roger started to doze.

"Roger, what are these books?"

He opened his eyes and saw her standing in the rectangle of soft light spilling in through the door, holding a book in each hand.

"*The Satanic Bible*?" she said in a tiny voice. "*Satanic Invocations*? Roger, what are you—"

"Research." He rolled over.

"Roger," she whispered, "this is…these are…I can't believe you—"

"C'mon, Marjie, it's just research for the book I'm writing. That's all."

"But why so many? You've got *more* out there. What are you *writing*?"

"Another thriller," he mumbled into his pillow. When she did not return to bed for a while, he sat up and saw her still standing in the doorway looking at the books. "Marjie, it's just *research*. What's the problem?"

Still, she did not move for a while. Then she put the books on his dresser, turned off the hall light and slowly returned to bed. They were silent for a while, then, voice cautious and just a little afraid, touched with a nervous chuckle, she asked, "Roger, that…that blood on your shirt the other night…"

But Roger was asleep.

23.

At noon the next day, Roger was hunched over his notebook in the Munch Room when some of the high school students began to crowd into the deli for lunch. The noise level rose as they filled the tables around him, laughing, and constantly smoking.

Roger hardly looked up from his work, leaned back in his chair with a sigh and chewed on the end of his pen. His eyes fell on Sondra at a table on the other side of the room. She saw him at that moment, too, as she half-smiled at something said by someone at her table. When their eyes met, her smile crumbled until it was gone.

She looked tired. Her beautiful bright eyes seemed dimmed and had puffy half-moons beneath them. She looked just like she had the day Benny Kent had been discovered.

Their eyes remained locked like the bumpers of two cars that had collided and Roger became deaf to the voices in the room. He was suddenly afraid that if he were to look around him, he would see Sidney's blood splashed on the walls and pieces of him scattered over the floor and he would have to clean it up all over again. He tried to keep those images out of his mind, but it wasn't easy. He had not seen Sondra—had hardly even thought of her—for nearly two wonderfully comfortable, content weeks that had passed mercifully slowly. Seeing her now brought it back, reminded him how she had touched him that night...how her breasts had felt beneath his hands as he washed the blood from them...how much he had wanted her.

Movement twitched on her face, as if searching for a hold, then her lips curled upward at the ends. The smile warmed slowly, grew, and for a moment, Roger thought she was going to cry.

Sondra stood and quickly left.

24.

His writing did not take off again that day. He pieced together a few more paragraphs, then gave up.

When he got home, the red light on his answering machine was winking lecherously and he played his messages.

There were three hang-ups.

He called Marjie at her office and invited her out to dinner that night.

"Um, I don't think so, Roger," she said. "I'm kind of, you know, um, tired."

"We have been pretty active the last few nights, haven't we?" He laughed, but she didn't respond. Silence hissed over the line. "Is anything wrong?"

"Things are kind of hectic here today, really busy, you know? I'll probably have to work late and…"

She left the sentence suspended in the air.

"Well, if you change your mind," he said, "give me a call."

"Yeah, sure, that's a good idea. I'll call you. If not tonight, then…well, maybe tomorrow. But…things look pretty thick here for the whole week. I don't know…"

"I'll see you in class tomorrow night, though, right?"

"Yeah, sure."

He stood by the phone for a while after hanging up, puzzled. Marjie sounded as if something were definitely wrong.

The phone rang and Roger picked it up immediately.

"Hello?"

"Leave the Valley."

It was unfamiliar, a low male voice, so low it was almost a growl.

"You didn't learn your lesson the first time, demon-lover. Don't make us teach you another one."

The voice hung up.

Roger slowly replaced the receiver. He turned on the stereo, found a San Francisco station that played hard rock and roll—none of that middle-of-the-road cotton candy—turned it up loud and started doing some housework.

He did not let himself think about the phone call. He did not let himself wonder if it had anything to do with Marjie's odd behavior, if the three hang-ups had been the caller waiting for Roger to answer. Each time he started to think, *It's happening again,* he stopped himself by singing loudly with the radio or dancing hard to the beat as he vacuumed.

He decided he would ignore it.

He would ignore it if it killed him.

25.

The phone did not ring again until shortly before two o'clock the next morning while Roger was typing.

He had spent the entire evening cleaning and the house was immaculate. After a couple of hours of TV watching, he had gone back to work, having pushed the phone call far into the back of his mind, deciding it was an isolated incident.

Before the third ring, he had gone through all the possible reasons someone might be calling him at such an hour and decided to let the machine get it. Just in case.

By the fifth ring, it occurred to him that he had not turned the answering machine back on.

By the ninth ring, he decided perhaps it was important and answered it.

"Your lights are on. Don't you ever sleep? Or *can* you sleep?"

Roger slammed the receiver down so hard, the phone gave a startled little *ding!* sound, then he went to the front window and pulled the curtain aside, peering out at the early morning darkness.

The street lamp across from his house was out and he could see nothing.

He turned off his porch light, went out front and walked down the drive, shivering in the cold. The street was silent and lifeless.

Roger tried to remember if he had heard a car drive by earlier, but could not.

When he got back inside, he was still shivering. But not from the cold.

26.

Roger held up his class for five minutes waiting for Marjie to arrive. When she did not, he clumsily began the first hour's discussion on characterization, glancing now and then at the door, hoping to see her sheepishly peering through the window.

He ended up letting the class go early, unable to shake the feeling, the *fear*, that something was wrong. He suspected that it had been more than an unusually busy day or a flat tire that had kept Marjie from the class. After her behavior on the phone yesterday, he would not be too surprised to find that she had dropped the class.

As he pulled into his drive and his headlights passed over the front of his house, he saw what looked like a small sack on the porch with two short sticks protruding from the top.

He got out of the car and headed up the walk, his pace slowing as he neared the object. In the glaring yellow glow of his porch light, there seemed to be two glistening marbles stuck to the object's sides and something dark and wet was puddled around the bottom of what Roger no longer believed to be a sack.

The puddle dribbled over the edge of the top step and onto the next.

Roger moved closer, squinting in the poor light, and when he was certain what it was, small clicking noises sounded in his throat as he swallowed dryly again and again. He gingerly touched the toe of his shoe to the severed goat's head and it fell heavily to one side, the freshly hacked neck pulling away from the concrete with a gentle, moist sound.

Light glinted off the yellowed teeth revealed by the curled back lips and the eyes were comically wide and bulging, a morbid caricature.

Roger stepped over the head, avoiding the blood, sucking the cold air deep into his lungs. He turned his back on the front door and kicked the head onto the front lawn. It hit with a heavy thunk and rolled over the grass.

Inside, he poured himself a drink and finished it in a couple of gulps, then poured another. He leaned on the kitchen counter, waiting for the liquor to calm his trembling.

"No," he said quietly, flatly, as the pain in his side returned for a moment, just an instant, then disappeared. He took another drink, then spit it into the sink, crying out like a child when the pain hit again, the worst since his stay in Sylmar, chewing through his insides like a ravenous demon, silently screaming at him in a mocking, nails-on-a-chalkboard voice:
I'm baaaack, you jelly-assed motherfuckerrrr, I'm back and it's been TOOOO LOOOONG!

27.

When Roger shuffled into the deli the next day, exhausted from lack of sleep, Betty stared at him open-mouthed for a moment, took his hand, led him into the Munch Room, and sat him down. He fidgeted as she watched him, chewing her lip.

"What's wrong, honey?" she asked.

"I didn't sleep well last night. I was working on—"

"Don't jerk me around. What's wrong?"

Roger tried to look puzzled, but when he saw she wasn't buying it, he slumped in the chair. "Just tired, Betty. Really."

"Roger, you look like *hell*. You're pale, you're...you're..." She chewed a thumbnail nervously. "A police officer was here this morning. It wasn't Chucky, it was someone I don't know. He was asking...questions about you."

Roger's stomach twisted.

"I'm not sure," she went on, "but I think it has something to do with Sidney."

"Well, that makes sense. Apparently, I was the last one to see him."

She shook her head. "It sounds like more than that, Roger. Please. Tell me. Just between us. Did something happen here? Is there something I should know? Do they...*suspect* you of something?"

"Jesus, Betty," he laughed, "what *is* this? The guy came in, said hi, delivered the bread and *left*. That's it."

She tugged at her lower lip, searching his face.

"Betty, I'm telling you, there's nothing to—"

Glass shattered out front and someone screamed.

"*Jesus!*" Roger blurted as he dashed out of the room, Betty close behind.

There was a jagged hole in the window facing Main Street. Michelle stood frozen behind the register, both hands over her mouth. Broken glass was scattered over the floor and on the front table, which was fortunately unoccupied.

A brick lay among the pieces of glass. Attached to it with a rubber band was a crumpled piece of paper.

"Is everyone okay?" Betty asked.

No one was hurt.

Roger felt a needle-like twinge in his side as he stared at the brick, afraid to pick it up.

Betty bent down, grabbed the brick, and took the paper from it. Her eyes scanned it, then looked at Roger.

"What is it?" he asked.

She handed it to him.

In crude block letters, the note read: "ROGER CARLTON IS EVIL. HE BROUGHT DEATH HERE.

He could not bear to look at Betty, at *anyone*. He wadded the note in his fist, spun around and went back to the Munch room. He gathered up his things, feeling sick.

Betty followed him, calling his name. In the Munch Room, she said, "Roger, we'll call the police."

"No."

"Where are you going? We should report this to—"

"I'm going home. Don't report it to anyone. I'll pay for the window."

"Roger, *wait!*"

He did not wait. He had to get out. The pain was coming.

28.

When he got home, he began to drink, pacing the house like an expectant father, chain smoking and muttering to himself under his breath.

What had happened to bring it all back? Everything had been going so well.

He wondered what the police had asked about him, what they knew, what they had found. He could not have felt more confined, more enclosed, if he were hunkering in his closet.

The liquor hit and he began crying like a barfly, sitting on the sofa, elbows on his knees, hands hanging between his thighs. He quickly tired of his own company. He took a long shower, first hot then cold, guzzled some coffee, and drove to Josh's house.

The cold day smelled sweet, which made the odor of death in Josh's house even more overwhelming.

Roger had spoken with him on the phone twice since their last visit, but the dying man's voice, although weaker and more hollow, could not have prepared him for the visible progression of Josh's illness.

His face seemed to be collapsing, his skull deflating like a balloon with a slow leak. He walked with two canes now. When he walked.

The shock Roger felt showed on his face and Josh chuckled—it sounded like someone slowly crumpling a sheet of wax paper—and said in his trembling, pencil-thin voice, "I'm dying, for Christ's sake, what'd you expect, the cover of *GQ*?"

Josh nearly fell in the living room and Roger quickly reached out for him, felt the skeleton beneath the robe, the ribs and fragile joints, the sticks that would serve as limbs for only a short while longer.

Later, Roger would remember the clothes—a long-sleeved shirt, pants, a heavy sweater, and an overcoat—neatly laid out on the sofa. He would even remember seeing Josh's car keys on the coffee table. But his eyes passed distractedly over them now, his head too crowded with his own problems for him to realize their significance.

"Did Betty get my flowers?" Josh asked.

"Yes. She wanted to thank you, but—"

Josh held up a twig-fingered hand. "I understand. So. What brings you here?"

"Haven't seen you in a couple of weeks. I thought I'd drop by."

"And I appreciate that. But what's *wrong*?"

Roger laughed and said, "Am I that transparent?" An instant later, he had his face in his hands and was bawling like a frightened toddler.

Roger had never discussed his problems with Josh. Their conversations had always been limited to movie and show business trivia, Hollywood gossip, talk that Roger had been unable to get from his other friends and which—having been a movie fan long before he ever mustered the courage to risk his soul to the Lake of Fire by entering a movie theater—he craved. Roger had always talked to Josh to forget his problems, not stir them up or work them out, so Josh knew nothing of his ordeal with the church.

Roger told him everything up to the time he'd left Sylmar.

"After that, I did some screen work, sold *Ledges,* and wrote a draft of the screenplay. I kept busy and made quite a bit of money, but...nothing changed. It went on. Phone calls, occasional vandalism. Finally, I just sort of disappeared for a year. I drove. That's all I did. All over the country." He sighed. "Didn't even go home for Christmas. I spent New Year's Eve watching Dick Clark on a black-and-white television in some roach-eaten motel outside Kansas City. I told no one where I was. I wanted to be unreachable. To be honest, it kind of felt good. I got no more threatening phone calls because I had no phone. I found no surprises in my closet because I had no closet. Just suitcases. I drove and stopped and wrote and ate and slept and drove. It was nice. A relief. For a while, anyway."

"After all that happened," Josh said, "why the hell did you come back here?"

"I love it here. I missed the Valley. It made me angry that I'd allowed myself to be chased out of a place I loved. And I got sick of being alone. I wanted to prove to myself that it was over. I figured it *had* to be by now. I wanted to see Betty and Leo. You. Sit in the deli and write again. I've missed it."

"Is the pain gone now?"

Roger shook his head. "It's...come back."

"Then it's not over."

After a silent period of thought, Roger decided to tell Josh everything. He knew it would go no further than the room and Josh would take it with him to the grave—probably quite soon.

He told him about Sondra, about her parents and Benny Kent and Leo and Sidney Nelson, and Josh listened silently without moving. When Roger was done, Josh stared at him for a while, then a smile grew slowly on his skull-like face.

"You're afraid I don't believe you," he said.

"What sane person would?"

"Listen to me, Roger. All my life, without even being aware of it, I have lived, thought and acted as if I would never die. As if I would live forever. Well, now I'm sitting here at Death's table, we've finished desert and the place is about to close. I mean, I'm *dying*, here. It's real. And suddenly, a lot of other things are beginning to seem real. Suddenly...flying saucers don't sound so crazy. Bigfoot and the Loch Ness Monster seem possible. Maybe even likely. Things don't seem as...*absolute* as they used to. If *I* can die...well, then I guess *anything* can happen. Knowing the end is coming soon has somehow been liberating to my mind. Does that make sense?"

"Then...you *do* believe me?"

"Go to the bookcase. Third shelf down, far left, the black book."

Roger removed a trade paperback titled, *Lon Chaney, Full Moons and Lycanthropy*. There was a picture of Lon Chaney in full Wolfman makeup on the cover.

"I bought it because I thought it was about the werewolf movies," Josh said. "You know, 'Even a man who is pure of heart and says his prayers by night,' That sort of thing. It is, in a way. But it's more than that. It turned out to be more serious than I expected."

Roger thumbed through it.

"Did I ever tell you I was a Mormon, Roger?"

Sitting down, Roger shook his head.

"Well, I was. A good one, too. I loved my church, grew up in it. My family was devout. We consumed no stimulants, wore our magic underwear. But when I got to junior high…ah, those were hellish years. I knew I was…different than the others. I went to church school so everyone was Mormon and everyone was pretty much alike. Except me.

"When all my friends started noticing girls, I started noticing all my friends." He chuckled. "The *guys*, you know. I got so scared. I didn't understand what was wrong with me, and I didn't dare tell anyone.

"I was taking piano lessons from Mr. Coswell. A kinder, gentler man never lived. He knew something was wrong and started to pry a little. Didn't take him long to figure it out. He was gay, too, it turned out. No one knew. He would've lost his job, been ostracized. We became very good friends. Not lovers, though. No, he was only gay in his head, not in his pants. He was celibate. He could accept that he was gay, but he'd been a Mormon too long to *do* anything about it without being…I don't know, *strangled* by guilt. He helped me understand myself. Accept myself. Yes, he was a good man." Josh's eyes looked past Roger, past the walls of his house, and focused on something far away. Fifteen or twenty seconds later, he came back. "Anyway, Mr. Coswell helped me to believe that there was nothing wrong with me. I wasn't a monster or a pervert. And the…the summer before I went to college…I told my parents." He frowned as he looked at Roger again. "Have you ever heard of the Doctrine of Blood Atonement, Roger?"

"No."

"It's Mormon. A lot of them deny it. Some have left the church because of it and formed little offshoots. Very controversial. Some people take it very seriously.

"It's like this. Some sinners have committed a sin *so* heinous, or have sinned unrepentantly for *so* long, that they cannot be forgiven. Their only hope for salvation is death. Their life must be ended, their blood spilled, in order for them to be accepted into the kingdom.

"I told my parents and I thought they'd take it well. We'd always gotten along. I thought they would accept me unconditionally. But no. My father went insane. Tried to kill me. Chased me out of the house with a knife. Destroyed all my belongings. He even called the college I was planning to attend—a Mormon college, of course—and told them I was a homosexual. Naturally, I was not accepted.

"I lost all of my Mormon friends and the church—the church I loved and had actively contributed to all my life—no longer wanted me." He smiled. "I don't have to tell *you* how that felt, do I?"

Josh carefully shifted in his chair and took a deep, labored breath.

"I was the same person I'd always been," he went on, "but suddenly everyone in my life—including my family—felt differently about me. They rejected me. I was bitter for years. I hated god and Christianity and any organization that vaguely resembled a religion. My life became…it was…oh, well, I don't need to go into that.

"I feel a little better about it all now. Mostly because of that book, silly as it may seem. There's a section in there—you'll know it when you find it—that made me think long and hard about all this, and I found some answers to my *whys*. I'm at peace with them now.

"People like you and me, Roger, we're the lucky ones. We went through hell, and yours isn't over yet, but we're *still* lucky. There aren't many like us."

"I don't understand," Roger said. "Why are we lucky?"

"*They* are being controlled, those people. So, in turn, they try to control others. It's like a sort of pecking order. Ever since their childhood, they were taught to believe in the enormous importance of a list of rules. Some of the rules are contradictory, some are impossible to follow, but they have become all-important to these people, whether they're Adventist rules or Mormon rules or Catholic rules. So, they are under the control of this list and the people who enforce it.

"Then along comes someone like you or me who very innocently breaks one of those rules. You wanted to be a writer, I learned to accept the fact that I'm gay. It doesn't matter how innocently we broke them—we *broke* them. These other people—Adventists, Mormons, whatever—see that we're not following the rules that control *their* lives, so they try to enforce them. They try to scare us, or *hurt* us, into keeping those rules. They try to control us as they are controlled. They do this by convincing us we're sick, evil monsters. Do you know why that so often works, Roger?"

Roger shook his head.

"Because if you tell someone he's a monster long enough, he *becomes* one. If you say it's evil to be gay and enforce that, then gay people have to find their companionship in a dark, secret place, and it *becomes* dirty. Evil. If you tell a writer it's evil to write stories because stories that aren't true make people ill,

231

depress them, whatever—I believe Mrs. White said something along those lines, didn't she?—then harass him and tell him he's going to burn for doing something he loves, well, pretty soon it affects his work. The stories become dark tales. Bleak. Stories of pain and violence. Evil stories, if you want. You see, Roger, their little plan is really quite beautiful. With all those rules, they *create* their own monsters. Otherwise, they would have nothing to fight. No one to control. No one to blame. But," he smiled, "they didn't get me. That's why I'm one of the lucky ones. And they haven't gotten you, Roger, not yet. Even though they're still trying. But this girl, Sondra…"

Josh shook his head and his eyes darkened. His sunken face soured in an expression of bitterness. It was so bitter that Roger asked, "What's wrong? I thought you said you're at peace with them."

"Oh, no, no. I'm at peace with my *whys*. I'll never truly be at peace with the Mormons. Or *any* of them, actually. I hate the fuckers." He paused a while, resting his face against a palm, then said, "My father called about six months ago, when he found out I had AIDS. I hadn't heard his voice since the day he chased me out of the house, but I knew it immediately. He laughed at me and said, 'God always finds a way to spill the blood of the sinners.' See…*that's* what bothers me the most. He thinks I'm being punished for my wicked life. *I* don't think that. I just happened to be one of the unlucky ones who got this horrible sickness that gave me a death sentence. But after I'm dead, he'll smile, and all his friends will smile, and all the people who used to be *my* friends…and they'll think that they are right. That they are victorious. I'm at peace with myself in spite of how they tried to make me feel. The truth is, *I'm* right. They're wrong. But there are only a few like me. Like you. Most people are controlled and are in turn controlling others. The only truth to them is that list of rules. What bothers me most is...in the end, they always win. People like you and me, Roger...we're outnumbered. In the end...*they* always win."

Roger sat in confused, overwhelmed silence for a while, drained by what Josh had said. He thumbed through the book, glancing at the stills from old werewolf movies, the sketchy illustrations of bodies writhing through hideous transformations.

Josh said, "Take it."

"I'll bring it back."

Josh laughed dryly. "Keep it, Roger. I have no use for it." He stood with effort, as if his frail body were several times its actual weight. "I think there are some things in that book that you'll find interesting. I wish I could be of more help."

"You listened."

"Happy to."

"Sorry to dump on you like—"

"Hush." He struggled away from the chair. "I don't mean to be rude, Roger, but why don't you take off now. I'm very tired."

Roger closed the book and said, "Sure, Josh. You gonna be okay?" He realized even as he was speaking how stupid the words were.

"No." Josh laughed.

"Jesus, I didn't mean—"

"Don't *worry* about it." He hobbled toward Roger, his bony shoulders rising and falling slowly above his stiff arms like the pistons of a dying engine. He stopped, lifted his arms with the canes dangling from his hands, swayed slightly, and embraced Roger as he said, "Thank you for coming by. You take care of yourself, Roger."

He cautiously returned Josh's hug, afraid the man might break, and said, "I'll come back in a couple of days and let you know what I think of the book."

Josh smirked as he pulled away. "You do that."

It was the last time Roger would ever see him.

29.

Roger went home, made some coffee, and sat down to read the book.

It was poorly written and not even bound very well, but once Roger skimmed through the first three chapters, all of which dealt with the Hollywoodized myth of lycanthropy, he began to find passages that rang chillingly true.

There were several different theories behind the physical transformation that allegedly plagued victims of lycanthropy. Some attributed it to supernatural curses: A gypsy's hex, a witch's spell. Others claimed it was a rare disease that caused hair to grow over its victim's body at regular intervals, made him unable to walk upright, and caused him to crave raw meat. It was a subheading in bold print near the end of the chapter that fully captured Roger's attention: LYCANTHROPY AND RELIGION. He read the section slowly, then read it again.

A psychiatrist in Boston had linked religious repression to a mental and physical aberration that resembled lycanthropy.

"Often, one who is raised in the confines of a fundamentalist faith," Dr. Regis Maine said at a 1978 psychiatric conference in Washington, D.C., "will, at some point, begin to doubt or reject the doctrines of his church. This independent thinking is inevitably met with severe negative reinforcement from family and friends within the religion who try, through various means of exclusion and harassment, to convince the subject that the fault is with *him* rather than the church."

"No shit," Roger muttered as he read.

Dr. Maine claimed to have several patients who, after extensive counseling, admitted that they were "monsters" and were physically transformed with increasing regularity—some at times of anger, others with feeling of sexual arousal or even simple happiness and contentment. He even claimed to have *witnessed* one of these transformations.

"While the physical alterations were nothing like those seen in films or on television, they were, without doubt, complete and inhuman, animal-like, and the patient became extremely violent and exhibited a drastic increase in physical strength."

With continued therapy, Dr. Maine learned that each patient, all of whom were raised in very conservative fundamentalist homes, had been the subject of what he called "intense reconversion or ostracization campaigns" designed either to woo the backslidden, wayward patient back into the fold or shame or even frighten him into rededicating himself to Christ. During this process, the patients became convinced that they were in some way monstrous or even possessed, that they were indeed evil and deserved the treatment shown them. It was during this time that they began to experience mysterious physical ailments—particularly severe abdominal pains—all of which escaped the diagnosis of doctors, even after extensive tests. These eventually developed into the physical metamorphosis which Dr. Maine suggested had, for centuries, been identified by the superstitious and fanatically religious as a demonic curse that turned its victims into ravenous wolves.

"It was not a curse at all," Maine said, "but quite likely a severe mental *and* physical condition imposed upon its victim by the very people who feared it most."

Dr. Maine proposed a treatment. If the patient were convinced that the desires and aspirations considered to be so evil and monstrous by the religious oppressors—sexual longings, artistic goals, alternate lifestyles—were perfectly natural and healthy, and if those things were encouraged and ultimately acted upon, the patient would come to accept and love himself and learn to reject the harmful accusations and teachings of the religious zealots surrounding him.

No one took Dr. Maine seriously. According to the book, by the time Dr. Maine went public with his theory, he was exhibiting some rather bizarre behavior himself. He had just lost a great deal of weight, his hands shook as he stammered through his address, and his fellow psychiatrists speculated that Dr. Maine was nearing a breakdown.

They were right.

Only two weeks after the 1978 conference where Main shocked his colleagues into an embarrassed silence with his "findings," he was forcibly admitted to a mental institution, hysterical and violent, after being found running naked down a city street babbling wildly about monsters, "horrible flesh-eating monsters."

30.

Dr. Maine was a small man with wiry hair the color of a silent film and, because it seemed appropriate to Roger's subconscious, he spoke with a stereotypical German accent. He sat facing Roger in a Naugahyde chair, hugging himself in a straitjacket and clamping a sweet-smelling pipe between his teeth. A strip of perspiration glistened like jewels above his wide, darting eyes.

"Sumzink is vorryink you, no?" the doctor asked through clenched teeth, puffing smoke. "Ze monster, perhaps?"

"Yes."

"Yours or hers?"

"I'm sorry?"

"*Your* monster or *Zondra's* monster?"

"I don't understand."

"Vell, zat *is* ze problem, no?"

236

"The problem?"

Dr. Maine began rocking in his chair. "You und ze girl, you are zo much alike, no? Und your zymptoms are zo much alike, no? You *vant* her, und yet you *fear* her. She brings you too close to *zem*. You fear zat, had you not fought zem, *fled* zem, und continued to exorzize your demons on paper mit your writing, ze pain vould have continued. Vould have come *out*. Like *hers*. No?"

"Come out?"

"Like *zat*," Dr. Maine laughed, nodding toward Roger's stomach.

Roger looked down to find that he was naked and his belly was bulging as something pressed at the flesh from the inside, tore at it, cut it, sliced through it, until a hideously gnarled claw ripped its way out of him, dangling bracelets of viscera.

When he woke from the nightmare, he was sitting up, holding his belly and grunting. The pain was snacking on his guts again.

Roger had reread the section titled LYCANTHROPY AND RELIGION until he almost knew it by heart. That section of the book could have been written specifically for him, *meant* to be read by him.

Meant to *frighten* him.

And frighten him it did.

He tried to go back to sleep and did drop off a couple of times, but his sleep was shallow and diseased with nightmares he had thought long gone.

He heard the thunderous footsteps of a giant raging Jesus destroying the neighborhood as he bellowed, "Where's Carlton? Where *is* that little shit?"

He hid in black filthy corners—a child again, weak and terrified—as the Sunday-keepers stormed around him with bright flashlights and powerful guns, shouting, "There's one over there!" and, "Hah! I got another one!"

He writhed in bed as he dreamed that his skin was moving over his body, changing, twisting.

And the claw. He saw it when the pain came in his sleep, its curved talons dark with blood.

He finally gave up and sat at his bedroom window with a drink, watching as the sun rose behind the thick veil of raining clouds that glowed a dull steel gray. As he watched the day begin, he imagined Sondra waking, showering, eating breakfast as Bill limped silently around the house on his clicking leg. She would go to school, go from class to class, eat lunch with friends, acting like just another high school senior, a shy and silent teenager...acting as if she had never hurt a soul, ended a life, tasted blood, or eaten human flesh. Until it happened again.

And when will that be? he wondered.

Roger decided he had to talk with Sondra soon.

Today.

31.

Roger parked outside the high school and waited for thirty minutes. Shortly before three o'clock, students began to spill down the front steps and scatter in the parking lot to board buses and speed away in cars. When he spotted Sondra, he honked his horn and called to her out the window.

She approached the car warily.

"We have to talk," he said.

"I can't. I've gotta work."

"I'll drive you. Get in."

"Roger, I'm not even supposed to *see* you, and if I—"

"Get. In."

Once she was in the car, he turned to her and asked how she felt.

"I'm...fine, I guess."

"You look tired."

She shrugged.

"Has it happened again?"

"Roger, I told you to forget it."

"I *can't*. And neither can you. It's only going to get worse unless you try to do something about it. Look, I think I know what's wrong, what's causing it. It's not your fault, Sondra, it's—"

"I have to go to work." She opened her door and Roger reached across and pulled it shut, then started the car.

"Where?"

"Vintage Video."

Jesus, he thought, *first they let her work in a deli serving food they'd never let her eat, now they let her work in a store that rents movies they'd probably never let her watch. They may say I'm evil, but at least I'm consistent.*

As he drove, he told her what Niles had said about Sidney.

"They know something," he said. "I'm afraid maybe they've found him."

She seemed not to hear him.

He parked the car in front of the video store, getting angry.

"Goddammit, Sondra, quit acting like nothing's wrong, like nothing's happened!" he snapped. "I think I can help you. I need to know if Bill knows about—"

Sondra gasped, looking out her window.

Bill stood on the sidewalk in front of the video store glaring at them.

"Oh, no," she breathed, closing her eyes, "oh, no, no, no..."

"Jesus," Roger hissed. The dread in Sondra's face made him ache for her. He reached over and squeezed her hand as Bill began to hobble toward them. "Listen, Sondra, *listen* to me, you can get my number from Betty and call me, I want to help you. We *have* to talk. Is there anything you should tell me?"

She looked at him with terrified eyes and whispered, "You should be very careful. Be careful of—"

Bill opened the door.

"C'mon," he said, his voice low and ominous.

Sondra quickly got out and Bill leaned into the car.

"I *had* to talk to her, Bill," Roger said quickly, "please believe me, I had to—"

"You've got nothing to say to her."

"Bill, we've got to talk, you and me, it's important, *very* important, it's about Sondra, and I'm afraid that—"

"You've got nothing to say to me, either. And if I ever...*ever*...see you with Sondra again..." His lips trembled with quiet rage.

"Listen, Bill, we *have* to put our differences aside and talk about—"

"Don't let it happen again." Bill stared at Roger with stony eyes a moment, then shook his head and said, "You were stupid to come back here." He slammed the door so hard the car shook.

As he drove home, Roger pounded the wheel with his fist, furiously cursing God, the church, and Bill Dunning.

32.

When Roger got home, he was useless. He was angry and afraid and exhausted. He couldn't think or relax or sit still. He searched his bedroom, hoping to find a little pot to calm him down. He finally found some old stuff in a baggy with a pipe tucked away in his closet—

—along with his gun.

It was in its box, wrapped in red cloth, where it had been since he had moved from North Hollywood. He stared up at the closet shelf where it lay under a stack of books and, a few moments later, took it into the living room.

As he filled the pipe, Roger stared at the gun lying on his coffee table. He took a couple of hits, then picked up the gun and hefted it. The phone rang and he had the urge to aim the gun and stop the noise with one shot, but the gun was empty.

The answering machine picked up.

A dial tone hummed into the recorder.

It would be nice to end his problems with a single gunshot, but shooting the phone wouldn't do it. They would find another way to contact him, harass him. He could shoot *them* until his trigger finger fell off, but there would always be more to replace them.

There was only one person he could shoot to end all of his problems.

God always finds a way to spill the blood of the sinners …

He returned to his closet and found a box of ammunition, then sat down and loaded the gun. Before he could finish, he heard someone crying outside his door. The bell rang and he recognized Sondra's voice calling his name. He hurried to the door, pulling his robe closed and tying it.

She was covered with blood and her left eye was nearly swollen shut. Her clothes hung in tatters on her otherwise naked body and she was hugging herself, her whole body violently shaking. She looked much the same as she had looked after killing Sidney Nelson, and Roger wondered who had died tonight.

"I'm cuh-cuh-cold," she whimpered, falling into his arms.

The blood was cold and sticky and clung to Roger's bare chest when his robe fell open. He kicked the door shut and carried her into the bathroom. The remnants of her clothes peeled from her body easily, like tender meat from the bone, and he tossed them into the bathtub.

"What happened?" he asked, holding a washcloth under hot water.

"I-I-I'm not sure."

"Are you hurt?"

She nodded.

"Did Bill hurt you?"

"He buh-beat me. But I'm cut, too."

"Cut?"

"I think."

"Is all this blood yours?"

She shook her head.

The dirty copper smell of blood turned Roger's stomach and he flipped on the fan, then began to gently dab the blood away with the cloth.

"Does he hit you often?" he asked.

"Never this bad." She flicked her tongue over a loose tooth and muttered, "Think I'm gonna lose that one."

"And all this blood? Where did it come from?"

"Some…man, I think. Out in the woods."

"Where?"

"Off Silverado Trail."

"Jesus Christ."

Once her face was clean, Roger hunkered down in front of her, took her bloody hands in his and spoke softly.

"You've gotta let me try to help you, Sondra. You can't keep doing this. And it'll *never* stop on its own. You have to at least let me *try*."

With a slight shake of her head, she said, "That's why Bill beat me. Because he found me with you."

"Why was he waiting for you at work?"

"To catch me doing something wrong. Anything at all." She pushed a blood-caked strand of her hair from her eyes. "He was afraid you'd try to see me because...well, he's been worried about you."

"About *me*? Why?"

She looked away from him. "I want to wash."

Roger let it pass. He handed her the washcloth, pulled back the curtain and removed her torn, bloody clothes from the tub. He tossed them into the hamper, then turned on the tub's faucet. He said, "I'll leave you alone. Is there anything I can—"

"Don't leave me alone," she whispered, standing and pressing herself against him, crying softly. "Please don't."

Roger helped her into the tub, sat on the edge, and began passing the cloth over her back.

"Why is Bill so concerned about me?" he asked.

"He has been ever since you came."

"I didn't tell anyone I was coming. How did he know?"

She shrugged, then reclined in the tub, wetting her hair. The water quickly turned an ugly brown from all the blood.

The same way somebody always managed to learn my phone number even when it was unlisted, Roger thought, *and the same way they always knew where I lived no matter where I went.*

He handed her a clean washcloth and she dipped it in the water, rubbed it with a bar of soap from the dish beside the tub and lathered it up. She ran the soapy washcloth over her body slowly, wincing at times.

Roger looked at the cuts and scratches on Sondra's arms and shoulders. "How did you get those?" he asked.

"In the woods. I think. It happens."

His eyes settled on her breasts as her nipples broke the surface of the water. The marijuana had made him just loose enough for the sight of Sondra's wet and soapy body to make him forget all his problems. He felt himself becoming erect. He took a bottle of shampoo from the shelf on the wall and began to wash her hair.

"I'm not going back," she whispered. "I won't live with them anymore. With *him*."

"Where will you go? What will you do?"

"I don't know, but I can't live like that anymore." After a long silence, she said, "Can I...could I stay with you?"

He wanted to say yes immediately, without a second thought. But he could not."

"How about if we go see Bill together and I'll talk with him."

"Oh, God, no," she gasped. "No, he'd...he'd...no, you can't do that. You can't." She turned to face him, head crowned with bloody suds. "They've been talking about you. A lot. Bill and some of the men from the church. Elders and deacons. Especially lately."

"Why lately?"

"Marjie's been coming over."

"*Who?*"

"Marjie Shore. She told him...she said you had some books."

He remembered Marjie's reaction to his research books. That was when things had changed between them, when she found those books on Satanism. He silently cursed his stupidity.

"She said you had some bloody clothes, too, and...well...they all figured you were...you know...doing it again."

"Doing *what* again?"

"The rituals. Worshiping Satan."

"Jesus H. *Christ*, Sondra, I've *never* worshipped—"

"I know that. But they're convinced. That's why Bill was so upset with me for being with you. See, my whole family...all of them…have always thought there was something wrong with me, that I was evil, 'cause I've always been such a…a…" She bowed her head, shrugged once. "Such a black sheep. Then, when *this* started…you know, this…*change* in me…they figured I was possessed, like I told you before." She laughed bitterly. "And now they figure you and I are gonna get together, y'know? Have demon parties and maybe give birth to the antichrist, or something." Another laugh.

Roger found it difficult to follow what she was saying. He was still shocked about Marjie. If she really thought he was serious about Satanism, why didn't she *say* so? Why didn't she confront him with it directly so he could defend himself instead of going to Bill—especially after talking about Bill as if he were crazy and she had written him off—and stirring up more ridiculous stories that weren't true?

You asshole, Roger thought, *you knew the risks, you knew what might happen if you got involved with her again, you* knew, *goddammit!*

"Do you love her?" Sondra asked.

Roger blinked rapidly, shaking off his thoughts. "Marjie? Uh, no. We used to be…close. But…" He did not finish. He kept thinking, *How could she? How could she when things were going so well?*

He stood and said, "I'll get you a towel."

———————————

Roger put her in his bed.

"Do they know where you are?" he asked, pulling the covers up around her.

"No."

"Should I call them? Let them know you're all right?"

She gave him a worried look. "You're not very smart, are you?"

He blinked.

"That would be a really bad idea," she said.

"Okay, okay. We'll wait until morning." He went to the door and turned out the light. "If you need anything, just call.

"Roger?"

"Hm?"

She threw the covers back. "Please…come stay with me."

He sighed at the temptation, turned it over in his mind. He decided he had already made too many mistakes.

"Get some sleep," he whispered, pulling the door closed.

33.

Roger made himself a drink, sat down in front of the television, and chewed on what Sondra had told him about Marjie until his feeling of betrayal had become a smoldering anger.

Two drinks later, the doorbell rang and Roger somehow knew that it was Marjie.

"Is she here?" she asked when he opened the door.

"Who?"

"Please, Roger, don't play with me. If she's here, let me take her home. If you know where she is, *tell* me. Please."

"I don't understand why it's any of your business, Marjie."

"I'm doing this for your own good, Roger."

"Oh? Running to Bill and telling him I'm worshiping *Satan*, for Christ's sake? Was *that* for my own good, too?"

With a frustrated sigh, Marjie bowed her head and said, "Bill told me what happened today, and I thought—" Her words caught in her throat and she gasped, "Oh, my God!"

There were blood stains on the cream-colored carpet.

"What have you done?" she breathed.

"Nothing. It was—it's just—she—"

"Sondra?" she called, scared now.

"She's *fine*, Marjie, she's sleeping."

"Get her." She was trembling, apparently from anger as well as fear.

"I'm going to take her home in the morning, don't worry. I'm going to talk to Bill about—"

"You *can't* take her home in the morning, Roger, *dammit*, will you listen! Right now, Bill is getting some men together to come over here looking for Sondra and if they find her with you…please, won't you just let me take her home. It'll save a lot of trouble."

Roger was livid. "They're coming over *here*? Jesus, like some kind of fucking holy posse? And what will they do, lynch me? Stone me to death, maybe?" His voice was raising to the level of a shout. "Very Christian of them, and certainly in keeping with everything else they've been doing, like the goat's head on my porch and the brick through DiMarco's window. Were you in on that, too, Marjie? Did you play along, huh? Maybe the goat's head was *your* idea. Inspired by the books you found, were you?"

"I had nothing to do with that. I didn't even know about it."

"Uh-huh. Sure." He stepped toward her and she moved back flinchingly, frightened. "I don't suppose you mentioned to Bill that you've been fucking the neighborhood Satanist, did you? Because if you did, the son of a bitch'd probably be throwing things through *your* window, too, you ever think of *that*? Huh? Did it occur to you that you're dealing with a very sick person?"

"Roger, h-he's a f-friend," she said, trying to hold in her tears. "We…*all* of us used to be f-friends."

"And what brought *that* to a screeching halt? I never had any friends, Marjie. For the first twenty years of my life, I never *had* any friends. Jesus, and to think I trusted you and...and...it's happened all over again, I let you..." Anger constricted his throat and he could say no more. He kicked the ottoman and it slid over the carpet and slammed into the coffee table, knocking off a full ash tray. "Get out of here."

Moving back toward the door, Marjie shook her head and said, "No, Roger, I'm not going to—"

"Get the fuck out of here!"

Wringing her hands, she tried to sound calm and reasonable. "I am not leaving without—" She looked past him. "Sondra!"

Roger spun around to see Sondra standing in the hall holding his robe before her.

"Sondra," Marjie pleaded, *"please* come with me. Bill is furious."

She stepped backward into the shadows, shaking her head.

"Sondra, *please!"* She turned to Roger, her face red with anger. "She's only seventeen, for crying out loud, how could you—how *could* you?"

"How could I *what*? You think I'm fucking her? Well, I'm not. I'm trying to help her. No one else will. Maybe you've heard of it, it's called *decency.* You could use some." He turned toward the hall. "Go back to bed, Sondra." Stepping past Marjie to open the door, he said, "And you. Go."

"I will not."

He grabbed her elbow and steered her roughly to the door, but she pulled away, screaming, "Let *go* of me. What's wrong with you, Roger, don't you see I'm trying to help you? I'm thinking of *you*." Her face twisted and tears rolled from her eyes as she massaged her elbow. "You act like I hate you, or something, but I duh-*don't*." Her words garbled by sobs, she lowered her voice to a raspy whisper. "I've never for a second stopped loving you. And *admiring* you. You weren't afraid to do what you wanted to do even though everyone was telling you it was wrong. I...I never had that kind of strength. I'm a...conformist. That's me, Roger. A weak, spineless conformist. I've always admired your independence. I never believed all that Satanist stuff, not...not *really*. Not back then. But I was...concerned about you. I was different back then, I bought it all, the whole idea of going to heaven and...*all* that. And because you were breaking the rules...I wanted to *save* you. I'm not that way anymore. Well...not quite. But when I saw those books here...I looked through them and they're *awful*. I got scared. I thought maybe...maybe it *was* true. And those bloody clothes out in the garage...it made sense, sort of. I started to worry again and I talked to Bill. You say he's crazy...and he *does* have problems, I know...but he is a sincere Christian, a good Adventist, he means well, and...I thought he could help, could tell me what to do. I was worried about you, Roger, that's all."

"Worried? That I was committing some great sin? Breaking a few commandments? Not following all of good old Sister White's rules? Is that what you were worried about while you were sipping wine like a *big girl*?" He spit the words mockingly, hurtfully, and Marjie's pain bled from her eyes. He enjoyed it. "Were you worried about that while you were smoking pot? Or sucking my *cock* out of wedlock?"

She pressed a fist to her chest and tried to stifle a sob.

"*You* were worried about *me*, Marjie?"

"I was wrong," she cried. "I was truh-trying to, to *fit*, Roger, I *told* you, I'm *spineless*. I had the same upbringing as you, I didn't know anything else, and I've just been trying to fit into an environment that's still new to me. Wine, pot, all that—what do *I* know? But no, I don't...I don't really *believe* in that kind of life, I just didn't know how else to fit."

"What *do* you believe in?"

249

She tugged on her hair nervously as she sobbed again. "I don't know. I'm always trying so duh-desperately to fit. I-I don't *know* what I believe in!"

"You fucking hypocrite," Roger growled through clenched teeth just an instant before the pain tore through his guts. He doubled over, fell, tried to get up, but fell again, groaning as it wrenched his insides.

"Ruh-Roger?" Marjie sputtered.

He rolled over the floor, retching.

"Roger, what's wrong? Roger!"

"Go," he grunted. "Get out."

"Roger, what…what should I do? What's *wrong*?" Her tears were subsiding and the pain in her voice was replaced by urgency.

"Go…away." He tried to sit up but curled into a ball instead, releasing a high-pitched wail of misery.

It had never hit him so hard, had never been so intense. The pain exploded in his abdomen, sending shrapnel upward into his throat and downward into his testicles, down his arms to the very tips of his fingers. He screamed a shrill, jagged scream, opening his eyes to see Marjie and Sondra standing over him, their mouths working soundlessly, and he realized he could no longer hear them, could not even hear himself. Just a bone-deep throbbing in his ears, a powerful liquid rush that threatened to send his eyes shooting from their sockets.

He tried to speak, to plead for help, but he had no control over his tongue. It was a thick, numb chunk of meat and his teeth were gritty pieces of stone that sliced at his lips like razors and his hands—

Oh my God oh Jesus my haaaands, his mind screamed.

—were cracking open, the fingertips splitting to make way for deadly, hook-like claws.

When he looked up, Sondra was smiling as if she had found a long-lost friend, smiling and crying at once, and Marjie was pressing her fists to her mouth, shaking her head as she stumbled backward.

As the pain reached a crescendo, Roger felt a hatred for Marjie, a hatred so heavy and thick that he felt he could vomit it up like a steaming lump of half-digested food, and he swung his arm through the air, clutching at Marjie's leg.

She turned to run but her foot struck the ottoman and she fell, arms and legs splayed as she hit the floor.

A thin veil of red covered Roger's vision as he crawled on all fours toward Marjie, the throbbing growing louder in his skull, the pain in his center turning into a deep, engulfing hunger. The red darkened to a rust...

...then to a brown...

...then black.

34.

Laughter.

High, musical, crystal-clear laughter.

Roger's vision returned slowly, rising from a dark sludge to a soft glow, from blurred light and colors to a slowly growing clarity. The drumming pain in his head began to subside as physical sensations returned.

The floor beneath his back...

The carpet strangely wet and warm...

And something else...something wonderful.

Roger moaned and slowly lifted his hips from the floor —

What's happened?

— sliding his cock deeper into the warm sucking mouth that held it.

Hands on his body, nails scratching, clutching...too hard...cutting ...

Why am I here? On the floor? Doing this?

The sensation stopped, the laughter rang out again, then the sucking continued, the mouth panting, grunting. The mouth pulled away briefly, breath hot against him as a voice said, "You're like me. We're the same."

He tried to lift his head but was too weak, drained, empty.

"We're alike, Roger."

It was Sondra.

Her nails scraped over his chest and stomach, digging as she crawled up his body and moaned, still panting. Her hand clutched his cock, then she slid down on it, moaning again.

He tried to speak but only made a hoarse, clogged sound in his throat—

—and tasted blood.

It slicked the inside of his mouth like oil and he coughed, retched, turned his head and spit as she moved on him, continued clawing him, scratching him.

"Aaahhh, just like meeee," she panted.

She leaned forward and lay on top of him, their naked bodies rubbing together, slick with something warm and wet. She put her mouth over his and sucked.

He opened his eyes wider. There were spots on the ceiling, dark red spots that had not been there before, but he noticed them only peripherally because of the powerful warmth growing between his legs, throbbing.

Must be drunk, he thought, because he remembered nothing and did not know how this had started. But he did not care.

She sat up again, reached behind her and cupped his testicles as she moved on him, faster now.

He found the strength to lift his head just enough to see her towering over him, grinding herself against him, her body covered with dark red smears...blood...and scratches...and cuts ...

One hand stroked her breast. A left hand...on her right arm. It made no sense.

Roger squeezed his eyes shut tightly, opened them, blinked several times.

Sondra held a left arm in her right hand. It had been torn off at the elbow, the skin pale, the fingers splayed and slightly bent just enough to cup her breast, lift it, press it hard against her ribs.

Roger croaked, "What...what's...what're you..."

"We're the same," she breathed through a dreamy smile, eyes half-closed, hair draped over her shoulders.

Roger turned his head to the right, groaning when he saw the splash of blood on the side of the recliner.

The other arm was beneath the coffee table. The leg not far from that, a lump of bone protruding from the tattered gob of black-red meat above the thigh.

And the head...

Marjie's head rested on its side, mouth open in a scream, tongue hanging from the corner.

Roger screamed as he came, but it was not a scream of pleasure.

35.

Sondra slid off of him and curled up on the bloody carpet, nuzzling his neck, purring like a kitten.

The scratches her nails had left on his bloody skin burned.

"No, no, no," Roger hissed, rolling over and getting on his knees, looking around at the scattered, gory mess that used to be Marjie Shore, his first kiss, his first date, his first girlfriend. "I...I...*did* this?" he cried. "Did *I* do this?"

Sondra embraced him from behind, her breasts pressing hard against his back. "Mmm-hmmm. You're like me, Roger. I'm like you."

"No," he croaked, stumbling to his feet. "No, I couldn't have." But he knew he had. Marjie's blood was in his mouth, bits of skin and hair were stuck beneath his fingernails. If he thought about it, if he were to close his eyes and concentrate on it, he knew he would remember doing it in the same murky way he might remember a bad dream.

He limped into the bathroom and splashed cold water on his face, then began to clean himself off so he could decide what to do next.

36.

"We have to clean this up," he said, his voice unsteady, standing in the hall and facing the mess.

Sondra stood at the window staring at the night, twisting a strand of hair around her finger.

"They'll be coming soon," she muttered.

A burst of adrenaline surged through Roger because he knew she was right, and he clapped his hands together sharply and said, "C'mon, *c'mon*, get cleaned up, let's go."

He looked out the window and saw Marjie's car parked on the street in front of his house. He paced as Sondra slowly made her way down the hall.

This would be a lot more difficult than cleaning up after Sidney the bread man.

The phone rang and Roger ignored it. The answering machine picked up.

"Roger?" It was Betty and she sound upset. "Roger, if you're there, *please*—"

He picked up the phone. "Betty?"

"Oh, Roger, Roger—" Her words smeared together drunkenly. "—it's the police! They're *everywhere*! Running around with their chemicals and little brushes and—"

"Betty, what are you talking about?"

"The police! They're here at the deli going over *everything*. They called me, got me out of bed, said they had a search warrant and that they, they've brought some men in from San Francisco, *lab* men, they said. It sounds like they're looking for blood," she hissed, lowering her voice. "They're in the Munch Room talking, whispering to each other, and Roger, they keep talking about *you*, they keep saying your *name*. I'm scared, Roger, what's going on? What have you *done*?"

Roger clutched the receiver so hard, his knuckles ached and he was struck with the urge to laugh, to throw back his head and guffaw. It was so absurd, all of it.

"Look, Betty, just...just, uh..."

"You're keeping something from me, Roger," she said. "What is it? Does it have something to do with the brick through the window? What *is* it?"

"No, no, that's something...that's a...oh, Jesus." He did laugh, then, a giggle at first that built to a deep belly laugh, and he had to sit down, holding his sides with one arm, his eyes filling with tears as Betty spoke his name again and again.

Then he heard voices.

There were several of them outside, all male. First one spoke, then another, then several at once, as if in disagreement.

Then silence.

Footsteps.

Roger stopped laughing in time to hear one of them say, "I still think we should call the police."

Another said, "As long as you don't *use* that gun, we'll be okay."

Gun?

"Betty," Roger whispered, "hang on a sec." He put down the receiver with Betty's pinched, insect-like voice still coming from the earpiece. Pulling the curtain aside slightly, Roger peered out the front window and saw five men coming across the lawn toward the house. Bill was leading them with a shotgun cradled in one arm. "Christ," Roger hissed, returning to the phone. "I'm sorry, Betty, but I've gotta go."

"You *can't*! Roger, I don't know what's—"

"I'm sorry," he said again before hanging up and rushing to the bathroom. Sondra stood naked before the mirror brushing her hair, her eyes heavy-lidded and distant as she whistled tunelessly through her teeth. "C'mon, we've gotta go," he said.

"Hm?"

"Get *dressed*, we have to—shit, you don't have any clothes." He led her to his bedroom where he took a pair of sweats from the closet. They were baggy on her, but there was no time to be choosey.

The doorbell rang.

Sondra turned to Roger with panic in her eyes.

Roger put a finger over his lips. "The back door," he whispered.

The bell rang again, three times in rapid, impatient succession

After putting on his coat, Roger went to the living room and got his gun from the coffee table, loaded it, and stuffed it in his pocket. He got his car keys, then led Sondra through the kitchen, out the back door and around to the side of the house. A drizzle was falling and an icy breeze made Sondra's teeth chatter.

As they rounded the front corner of the house and approached the car, Roger could hear Bill's deep, unfriendly voice.

"Roger? Open up. I've come for Sondra."

Sondra took Roger's hand and squeezed fearfully.

He quietly opened the door on the driver's side and waved Sondra in. Behind the wheel, he softly clicked the door shut and slid the key into the ignition.

Someone pounded on the front door and Bill shouted, "Roger? *Sondra!*"

"Let's go, Roger," Sondra whispered frantically, "please, please, *please* hurry, let's *go,* if he takes me home he's gonna be so mad, *so* mad."

Roger started the engine, punched the car in reverse and sped out of the drive.

Even in the car, Roger could hear the burst of voices from the porch. The men turned and jogged to a pickup truck and an old Pinto parked across the street. Bill hobbled behind them on his cane, glaring at Roger as he put the car in gear and drove away.

"He has a gun," Sondra said tremulously. "He means business. We have to go to the police, Roger, we have to—"

"No. Not the police."

"Why *not?*"

"I just killed somebody, remember? And now they think I killed Sidney Nelson, too." He quickly told her about Betty's phone call, glancing in the rearview mirror to see the truck and Pinto coming after him. "If they've got a warrant to search the deli and they've brought a bunch of lab guys in from the city, *they* mean business, too."

"Then…what're we gonna do?"

Roger took a sudden left off Beakman, then another left onto Watson.

"First, we've got to lose them," he said, taking yet another turn, zigzagging past warmly lit houses with smoke rising from the chimneys. "Then we've got to get rid of this car."

Then what? he thought. *Leave town? Hide out? Take a minor across state lines and make things even worse?*

Headlights appeared in the rearview mirror.

"Damn!" Roger barked, hitting the wheel.

"Where are we going?"

He rounded another corner, increasing his speed, making his way toward Silverado Trail. He thought for a moment, going over his options, which did not take long, then said, "To see my friend Josh."

37.

Josh lived in one of a row of small bungalow-like houses on the south side of town, behind which ran a narrow alley.

Roger parked his car in the alley where it would be invisible from the street, went through the gate that opened onto the small rectangle of grass that served as a backyard, and knocked on the back door. When there was no answer, no sound from inside at all, he knocked again and called for Josh.

"Maybe he's gone," Sondra whispered, shivering as she looked around them nervously.

"No, he's very sick." Roger knocked again.

They had managed to stay far enough ahead of Bill and his friends to get to Josh's without being tailed, but now Roger began to think perhaps he had brought them there for nothing.

When he tried the door, it opened.

"Josh?" Roger called, taking Sondra's hand and going inside. He checked all the rooms, but the small house was empty. When he looked out the front window, he muttered, "His car's gone. But where could he—" Then he turned to the sofa where he had seen the neatly placed clothes the day before, and he knew.

I'm going to disappear…

Roger slumped onto the sofa and scrubbed his hands over his face, hating himself for being so blinded by his own problems that he did not see what Josh was about to do—even after Josh had *told* him he was going to do it.

"My…God," Sondra whispered.

Her voice startled Roger. He had forgotten he wasn't alone. She stood across the room looking at a row of pictures on the mantle over the small fireplace.

"What?" he said.

"Him." She pointed at one of the pictures, backing away slowly.

Roger stood and looked over her shoulder at the picture. It was Josh at Disneyland, a healthier Josh but still very thin and quite obviously ailing. He stood between Mickey and Minnie, arm in arm, grinning like a thrilled little boy.

"It was him," she whispered. "The man. In the woods. Tonight. It was him."

38.

Roger stumbled backward and fell onto the sofa again, his arms loose at his sides.

"He's…the one…you killed?" He weakly lifted an arm and pointed at the picture. "That was his blood?"

Four fingertips over her mouth, tears sparkling in her eyes, she nodded. "He looked really sick, but yeah, it was him."

"He was sick," Roger whispered. "He had AIDS."

Sondra turned to him slowly, very slowly, her jaw slack, face blank, eyes disbelieving.

"Whuh…what?" Her head bobbed with a dry gulp as she leaned against the wall. "What did you say?"

Roger repeated himself.

They looked at one another for a long time, their eyes speaking for them, both thinking about the same things: The blood that had covered Sondra when she arrived at Roger's...sex on the floor...the cuts and scratches on both their bodies as they writhed in the blood...

Sondra went to Roger. "I'm sorry," she rasped.

"You couldn't have known."

She took his hands in hers and made a futile attempt to smile.

"We're gonna die, anyway," she said.

"I know."

The gun resting heavily in Roger's coat pocket suddenly felt comforting—not as a means of defense, but of escape.

They held each other for a while until they heard a vehicle slowing outside. Sondra pulled away from him and said, "That's Bill's pickup."

39.

When Roger looked out the window, Bill was limping toward the house. He met Roger's eyes with a smile as cold as a tomb and called, "I figured you'd be here with your fag friend." Bill's voice was padded by distance. He still held the shotgun in his arm but appeared to be alone now.

Roger dropped the curtain and turned to Sondra.

"Let's go." He grabbed her arm and rushed her through the house, out the back door, across the yard and to the car. She got in and slammed her door as Roger hurried around the front of the car—

—and staggered to a halt.

The left front tire had been slashed and was now flat.

So was the right.

And the two in the rear.

"Out, out," he said, waving her from the car, "they've slashed the tires."

"What?" she cried, panicked.

"C'mon." He pulled her out and, clutching her arm, led her toward the north end of the alley—

—where two men were headed toward them taking long rapid steps. One of them carried a baseball bat, the other a flashlight.

Sondra backpedaled, whispering, "No, no, no, no."

"Just give us the girl," one of the men said.

They walked with such purpose, such force, that Roger wanted to cringe, frozen in place, like a frightened animal. Instead, he steeled himself and led Sondra in the opposite direction. His heart battered his ribs as he broke into a jog.

For a terrifying, brain-searing instant, he was a child again, the child of his nightmares, weak-kneed with the debilitating fear of a hunted animal looking for a place to hide.

He reached into his jacket pocket and clutched the cold, heavy gun, holding it like a lover in a last embrace.

Sondra began to cry, coughing sobs that made her stumble against Roger and nearly fall. He held her up and dragged her with him until they reached the cross street.

"This way," he gasped, pulling her to the right—

—and stumbling to a stop when Bill rounded the corner before them.

His stiff leg clicked as he neared them, hefting the shotgun threateningly.

Once again, Roger and Sondra began to walk backwards, clinging closely to one another.

"Sondra!" Bill shouted. "Come here. Now. Annie's worried sick."

Roger said, "Bill...Bill, you've gotta listen to me."

"No. No, I don't." He raised the shotgun, aimed it at Roger.

"You don't want to do that, Bill."

"Maybe it'd be good. You're *both* as evil as the night is dark."

Roger thought with chilling certainty, *He's insane.*

"Listen, Bill, Sondra is *sick*. What you're doing is only making her worse. She needs help. She needs—"

"She needs to get away from you, *that's* what she needs. She's always been a problem, but you've only made it worse. She needs to get down on her knees and plead for God's forgiveness. Isn't that *right*, Sondra?"

Digging her fingers into Roger's arm, groaning miserably, Sondra leaned forward, clutching her stomach. Roger put an arm around her shoulders to support her.

"No, Sondra," he whispered, "hang on, don't let it happen now." He turned to Bill. "We're both sick. It's not our fault, Bill. You've done this to us. To both of us. You and people like you."

Bill laughed, shaking his head.

There were hurried footsteps behind them. The other men were closing in.

Roger remembered the baseball bat and, holding Sondra close to his side, he drew his gun, spun around and leveled it the man who was holding the bat over his head, preparing to strike.

The men froze and their faces registered shock. Both of them were large and cast an imposing shadow in the glow of the single yellow sodium light in the otherwise dark alley.

Roger advanced toward them, aiming the gun as he shouted, "Stay back!"

The bat dropped to the ground as the other man tripped over his own feet and fell over backward.

Sondra struggled in Roger's embrace as he turned toward Bill. She hid her face against his shoulder, her voice a muffled growl as she began to chew on his coat.

"Why have you done this, Bill?" Roger shouted. "Why do you—"

Sharp teeth broke through his coat and pierced his flesh. Sondra writhed in pain against him and Roger felt blood trickling from his new wound, soaking into his shirt. He grunted as he felt her teeth gnaw deeper into his arm. Then he felt something else, a blade-fingered fist of pain closing around his entrails, squeezing, crushing.

No, Roger thought, *no, not now.*

The pain raged and Roger bent forward as hot bile rose in his throat. He swallowed, coughed, and continued.

"Why do you *keep* doing this, Bill? Why don't you leave me alone?"

Bill started toward them as they staggered backward, the shotgun aimed at Roger's midsection. Bill wore an icy smirk, but said nothing.

"It's gone on too long," Roger gasped, trying to talk through the pain. "It's time to stop now, time to…to just…leave me alone."

Still no response.

Roger screamed, "What do you want from me—a fucking apology for being myself?"

A door slammed somewhere on the block and a voice shouted, "Take it home or I'm calling the cops, asshole! People are tryna *sleep!*"

Bill spoke softly. "It's too late for repentance now, Roger. You're too far gone and you've taken too many souls with you." His prosthetic leg clumped as he walked. The rubber end of his cane made sloppy kissing sounds on the wet pavement. "The books you've written, Roger…they're evil. 'Developed by agents of Satan.' Recognize those words, Roger? Know what that makes *you*, Roger? An agent of Satan. Bewitching the minds of your readers 'with theories formed in the synagogue of Satan.' Recognize *those* words, Roger?"

Roger was crying now, overwhelmed by pain as he stumbled off the sidewalk and into the street with Sondra still leaning on him heavily, her cries garbled against him, fingers digging into his chest now, tearing his shirt.

"They were written by Ellen White," Bill went on. "God's prophet. Heaven's scribe. Leader of the remnant church. She used her gifts for *him*, for *his* glory. But you...you've used yours for the prince of darkness. *You* are an agent of Satan. *You* have put his words into every book store and supermarket in the country and you have trampled the truth to do it! You've rejected God's word and his plan for you in favor of leading precious souls to the lake of fire!" His voice was rising, trembling with righteous indignation. "Every person who reads one of your books is a step closer to eternal darkness and *you* are responsible for their loss!" He kept coming steadily: Step...*clump*...step...*clump*... "You're a disease, Roger, and you're spreading, infecting minds, turning thousands, maybe *millions*, away from the plan of salvation by corrupting them with the devil's dictations!"

The man who had fallen into the bushes struggled to his feet and warily approached Bill, saying, "Bill...c'mon now, Bill, that's enough, don't you—"

"Back off, Matt!" Bill snapped. He turned to Roger again, pointed his cane at him, and shouted, "*You have to be stopped!*"

Sondra bit Roger through his clothes again, squirming in agony, but he didn't feel the bite because it was eclipsed by the pain spreading and worsening inside him, digging its way into his testicles and down his arms as it had earlier that night.

Bill dropped his cane and lifted the gun with both arms, put it to his shoulder.

"Run!" Roger cried, pushing Sondra across the alley to the other side and whispered, "Run, just start *running*."

"No, Bill, wait!" one of the men shouted, afraid now, apparently unaware that Bill would go to such an extreme. He rushed Bill and grabbed the shotgun.

Roger ran after Sondra in a half-crouch, the intensity of his pain making him unable to stand upright. He felt spittle dribbling down his chin, felt himself quickly losing control over his own body.

There were shouts and sounds of struggle behind them.

Roger shouted Sondra's name but it came from his mouth a thick and mangled sound: "Shon-daaah!"

The shotgun exploded behind him.

40.

Time slowed to a heavy crawl after the gunshot.

Roger tried to run fast when he heard the shotgun go off, but he was hit. He felt the burning sprinkle of buckshot over his back and legs and he fell, skinning his palms on the ground. His skin felt like fire and his clothes clung to his bloody wounds.

He didn't stop moving. He crawled along the alley, sobbing as he looked down at his hands scrambling over the ground below him and saw the black claws scraping the pavement.

"No," he growled, fighting the pain and the changes that moved through his body. He tried to hold them off by biting his lower lip until he tasted his own blood, trying to use one pain to battle another.

On his left was a tall brick wall and on his right a cyclone fence that separated the row of backyards from the alley. He hooked his clawed fingers into the fence wire and pulled himself up. The fence was crawling with ivy through which webs of soft light from the houses on the other side cut into the murky alley. He pushed away from the fence and staggered after Sondra, who was even farther ahead of him now.

Every few yards, a garbage dumpster hunkered against the wall like a giant metal toad patiently waiting for a passing morsel. A cat dove from the top of one of the dumpsters and shot across the alley in front of Roger.

Up ahead, Sondra careened back and forth down the alley like a pinball, slamming into the fence, then the wall, her arms joined over her abdomen, her miserable cries echoing in the night.

Roger called her name, gaining on her in spite of the flames of pain licking his back and legs.

The sound of a scuffle broke out behind them.

"Go on, then!" Bill shouted. "*Don't* take part in the Lord's work! *Let* evil spread like a—"

"This is not what we came to do, Bill!"

"It's what *I* came to do," Bill growled. "It's what I'm *supposed* to do. It's part of his plan for me."

Roger glanced over his shoulder and saw them some distance back, facing each other, preoccupied.

Sondra collided with a corner of one of the dumpsters, spun like a top, and sprawled onto the ground face down.

Kneeling beside her, Roger rolled her over.

Bits of gravel clung to her forehead and her left eyebrow was bleeding from a deep gash and she was shaking like a junkie in need of a fix.

Her skin moved over her face, shifted into a leathery distortion, then smoothed out again. Her chin jutted as her mouth snapped open and shut repeatedly like a deadly trap, spitting and snarling.

Roger put the gun back in his pocket and helped her up. She could not stand but was able to sit up, leaning against him. Her eyes seemed to notice him for the first time and she clasped his wrists.

"Roger, Roger!" she gasped, speaking as if through a mouthful of barbed wire. "Make it stop, please, make it go away!"

Her fingers tightened painfully on his wrists and her knuckles became knobby and purple before his eyes. At the same time, Roger realized that his hands were once again his own—the claws were gone.

"Please make it stop, Roger. Kill me. Kuh-kill me now before I—" Her head fell back and she gurgled in her throat. Her teeth ground together loudly as they lengthened, sharpened, splitting her gums—then they returned to their normal shape and size. She began to thrash and pummel Roger's chest with her fists—which were once again dainty and pale and smooth-skinned—hissing, "I hate them, I *hate* them, oh God, *howIhatethem!*"

"Stop it, Sondra." He tried to hold her but she was too strong and broke away.

Well behind them in the alley, the men were fighting, a single struggling silhouette against the glow of the yellow light.

"Stand *up*, Sondra!" Roger hissed, pulling her arm, jerking her to her feet. But he knew she would not get far. He glanced back at the men again. The two men fought with Bill and the three of them were paying no attention to Roger and Sondra. He searched frantically for refuge. "Over here," he whispered, dragging her toward one of the dumpsters.

Her knees buckled and she whimpered, "Kill me, please, before he comes."

Roger lifted the lid of the dumpster and leaned it against the fence. With a gush of breath, fighting his own pain, he lifted Sondra into the bin, climbed in after her and pulled the lid down.

The stench of rotten vegetables and cat shit and old cigarette butts and a dozen other reeking odors stung Roger's eyes and nostrils and made him gag.

Sondra immediately tried to climb back out, hacking and gagging, and Roger pulled her back down, slapping a palm over her mouth.

"Don't move, Sondra," he whispered. "Be very quiet."

She mumbled into his hand and he pressed her head to his chest.

The shouting in the alley had stopped.

Distant footsteps clopped over the wet pavement.

Step...*click*...step...*click* ...

"I'm pretty sure he was hit," Bill said. "But not bad enough."

Roger closed his eyes and tried to calm his raspy breathing. Surely someone in the neighborhood had called the police about the gunshot. Roger did not care to see them arrive knowing his own probable fate, but they were preferable to this.

"Did they make it all the way to the street up there?" one of the men said.

Bill said, "Maybe they did. Turn on that flashlight."

There was a thunderous *gong* that bounced the length of the alley, lingering for several seconds.

"You in there?" Bill shouted. After several more footsteps, the gong sounded again, closer now. "Where are you, Roger? You can't hide from God, you know. He'll find you!"

Gaaawng ...

"And so will I!"

Roger realized that bill was hitting the Dumpsters with his cane.

"Come on, Roger!" *Gaaawng...* "Judgment day is here!"

He's gonna find us before the cops get here, Roger thought with sickening dread.

Sondra's hand clutched at his coat. "Please, she said, her voice less than a whisper. "Please kill me. *Please*." She groped for his gun. "Kill me, Roger, please."

She opened her mouth and vomited loudly in the darkness.

Roger's eyes slowly adjusted to the lack of light. He grabbed the back of her head and pulled her face close to his as she writhed, groaning in pain. When her eyes were close, he saw their faint golden gleam. She was changing.

"No, Sondra, don't let it—"

She punched him in the face and knocked his head against the wall of the dumpster. Firecrackers went off inside his skull and voices whispered in his ears. She hit him again, and his head slammed against the wall a second time. Roger felt himself shrinking.

The next echoing gong was not the sound of Bill's cane pounding one of the dumpsters but a huge, monolithic footstep...followed by another...and another...accompanied by an angry, roaring voice that only Roger could hear:

Where's Carlton? Where is that little shit? Where—

"—*are* you, Roger?" Bill shouted.

"Listen to me, Bill," one of the men said quietly. They were close now, several feet from the Dumpster. "Maybe you should give this up, you know? I mean, there's—"

—*one over there!* a loud male voice echoed off the inner walls of Roger's skull.

The pop of a gunshot was followed by laughter.

Got him!

Running feet and panting lungs sounded all around Roger's hiding place.

Another gunshot. *Got another one! Hah! Quick, get—*

"—off my back, Matt," Bill ordered. "I *have* to do this. It's my purpose. It's his will."

Roger squeezed his head between his hands as if trying to put it back together. He opened his throbbing eyes and, as dark as it was, he could see Sondra's claws tearing at her clothes as she gagged and tried to gulp air, growling, "Raaah-juuuh! Kuuuh maaay! *Peeeze!* Kuuuh maaay!"

She slammed her bulging knuckles against the wall of the bin and the metal made a thick wrinkling sound beneath the force of the blow.

"There!" Bill cried. "You hear that?"

Roger clutched the butt of the gun tightly.

Sondra went wild, flailing and hitting and clawing.

She hit Roger in the face again and his head slammed against the wall harder than before—

—and he was on his back on the bloody carpet, naked, with Sondra sliding slowly up and down on his hard cock.

Josh stood over them, healthy again, smiling, arm in arm with Mickey and Minnie. Mickey giggled as he scratched his back with one of Marjie's severed arms.

"What...what is it again?" Roger panted.

Josh said, "Five to seven years. Maybe a little longer. Maybe sooner. Who knows? But think about it. Even if you've got a whole seven years of health left before you get really bad, what kind of years will they be? I mean, *listen* to them!" From somewhere in the distance, Roger could hear Bill shouting his name in a voice filled with hatred.

"And if it's not *that* guy and his friends," Josh said as he and the two big grinning mice slowly began to dissolve, "it'll be others like them. Or the cops. Right? Remember the cops? They want you, too. And they won't believe the truth. Nobody ever believes the truth, Roger."

Yeah, Roger thought, hearing the far-off wail of a siren steadily drawing nearer. *The cops...*

"And what kind of life will *she* have?" Josh said sadly, nodding toward Sondra, who bucked and writhed on top of him, naked, lost in pleasure, her skin shriveling, breasts collapsing like large draining boils, fangs shredding her own lips. "Providing she lives at all, that is." Josh was a faint glow now, fading to a mist. "Remember, Roger...in the end, they always win."

... they always win ...

... always win ...

The echo of his words dwindled as he became little more than a shadow.

Mickey waved goodbye with Marjie's bloody, flopping arm as the three of them disappeared.

The gun.

It was in his hand.

Heavy.

Almost too heavy for his weakened fingers to grasp.

He lifted it—

I'm so sorry.

—and fired.

The sound was deafening in the small space and in the white flash of the gunshot, Roger saw the small hole bloom like a flower in Sondra's left cheek and felt moist warmth spatter his face.

Sondra's body convulsed a couple of times, then fell still.

Through the ringing in his ears, Roger heard Bill cry, "Over here! In this one over here!"

The lid of the bin flew open and hit the fence.

A beam of light flashed in Roger's eyes.

Bill screamed.

The siren grew louder.

In the light, Roger saw his hands—the claws, the patchy hair, the mottled, crusty skin.

Has it happened again? he wondered. He had felt none of the pain, none of the sickness.

"Oh, dear *Lord*!" Bill shrieked. "Oh, father in heaven, Jesus, Jesus!"

Roger glanced down at Sondra. Blood ran down her cheeks like tears. Her face was smooth and unblemished once again.

Lifeless...but beautiful.

The monster was gone.

Roger's eyes filled with tears, his heart with loss, and his gut with a burning hatred. He shot to his feet, slapped a hand onto the side of Bill's head and closed his fist on hair and flesh, digging the claws in deep. He pulled Bill's face close to his own and pressed the gun to Bill's throat.

Forming his words with effort, Roger screamed, *"Look what you've done!"*

The other men stumbled backward.

Bill's pale face quivered like Jell-O, eyes impossibly wide.

A deadly silence fell over the alley, broken only by the approaching siren and by the soft, hissing trickle of Bill's urine spilling down his leg as he pissed his pants.

Roger's voice was a low growl. "Look...what...you've done...to us."

Roger wasn't even sure if they could understand what he was saying because his words were so distorted by the mouthful of deadly shards his teeth had become.

But it did not matter.

In the end, nothing mattered because—

—*they always win.*

Roger stuffed the gun into his own mouth, bit down on the barrel and leaned into Bill's face.

In the half-heartbeat before Roger squeezed the trigger, his mind screamed, *I only wish I could live long enough to see my brains splash all over your fucking head you goddamned worthless hypocritical son of—*

42.

AUTHOR'S PAST REVEALS
SATANIC CULT CONNECTIONS

Napa Police are sorting through the past of bestselling author Roger Carlton, who killed himself, 17-year-old Sondra Nivens, and police suspect at least four other people over the last eighteen months, including Nivens's parents, Paul Nivens, 49, and Georgia Nivens, 40, as well as Sidney Nelson, 50, a bakery delivery man from Rutherford, and Napa resident Marjie Shore, 28.

According to police reports and people close to the author, Carlton, who twice hit the bestseller lists with his novels of murder and sexual obsession, was an active member in a satanic cult. Books on Satanism and the occult were found in his St. Helena home along with keys belonging to one of Carlton's victims.

The FBI took up the case when it was learned that Carlton "just dropped completely out of sight for about 11 months last year, during which time Paul and Georgia Nivens were murdered in Berrian Springs, Michigan," according to Special Agent Garson Petrie.

Although some questions still remain unanswered, investigators believe Carlton met Sondra during those 11 months while she was living with her parents and involved her in his

273

satanic practices. After the death of her parents, Sondra moved in with her cousin, Annie Dunning, and her husband, Bill, in Manning. Investigators believe she participated in the murders that took place shortly after Carlton returned to St. Helena, where he had lived six years earlier.

Bill Dunning, who attended high school and college with Carlton, was the last to see the writer alive and witnessed his suicide. Minutes later, he was found by police, running down an alley in St. Helena. According to attending officer Brian Spottaford, Dunning was screaming, "Jesus help me! Jesus help me! I've seen the face of Satan!" That night, he was admitted to the psychiatric ward of St. Helena Medical Center, where he was released after 24 hours of observation.

After attending a memorial service at the Manning Seventh-day Adventist church, Dunning told a reporter, "We loved each other like brothers once, Roger and I. But he changed. All I can do now is pray for him. And forgive him."

Sinema

Brett Deever had been looking for his dog, Gabby, for nearly half an hour when he found, instead, a hand.

It lay a couple of yards below him at the edge of Vintner Creek, which rushed with muddy waters left over from unexpectedly heavy summer rains. A tangle of tree branches was jammed between two large rocks, resisting the flow, and stuck along with other netted detritus was the hand. From Brett's vantage atop the creek's three-foot-high embankment, it could have been a dark, tattered glove clinging to the branches as if for life.

Brett's typical nine-year-old curiosity took him down the embankment and carefully through the mud until he was within reach of the glove, or doll's hand, or whatever it was.

He stopped when he saw the jut of bone sticking from the purple mush of wrist. It did not look like a doll's hand now.

"Gabby?" he called softly, nervously, backing up the bank. A clump of bushes to his left began to rustle, and when Brett finally turned his head, he saw Gabby's German Shepherd rump sticking out of the brush, tail sweeping back and forth with enthusiasm. The dog grumbled contentedly, making moist chewing sounds. As Brett drew closer, his stomach roiled like a cluster of worms when he caught a whiff of the odor.

Gabby was flat on his belly, eyes bright as he turned his head to smile at Brett around dark, meat-flecked teeth, pink tongue dangling. He had been worrying what looked like the stripped branch of a sapling.

Except it had a foot on the end of it.

There was more, and after a sharp, happy bark, Gabby flopped on his back and rolled in it. Flies took to the air in clouds, like specks of soot on a breeze.

Brett stared.

He knew he should be reacting strongly, somehow, screaming or running or vomiting, something like that. The awful smell made him queasy, of course, but what he could see—some stubby fingers and toes, the swollen, blackened half of the face that was visible—elicited no emotions in him.

The walls were up. He felt numb, detached. He felt nothing.

Just like in church.

In a town as small as Manning, any death, even one by natural causes, remained the topic of conversation for weeks. A murder was talked about for months on end. When it was one in a series of murders, however, as this was, it was not talked about as much as it was *felt*.

But Manning was not just any small town. It was located in California's Napa Valley atop a hill above the town of St. Helena. It was actually a village more than a town, with a population of only 1,750. Most people in the Valley thought of it as neither a town nor a village but a kind of commune.

It was inhabited almost exclusively by Seventh-day Adventists and was the location of one of their major colleges.

It was founded in 1897, when the Seventh-day Adventists, led by their "prophet" and founder, Ellen G. White, settled in the Napa Valley.

Seventh-day Adventists worship on Saturday, the seventh day, rather than Sunday, although they are a Christian sect. As with the Jewish faith, their Sabbath begins at sunset Friday and ends at sunset Saturday. During that time, the only place in Manning that was open was the church. The village had its own little post office, but it was closed on Saturday and weekend mail was delivered on Sunday. Sometimes Delbert Mundy, manager of the Manning Food Market—which sold no alcoholic beverages, no meat, nothing containing caffeine, and no cigarettes, in accordance with the writings of Ellen G. White—could be seen on Saturday evenings standing just inside the market's front doors, keys in hand, staring at his wristwatch, waiting for the sun to go down so he could open up for a few hours.

The thing about Manning that Brett Deever hated most—despised, in fact—was that, unlike its neighboring towns St. Helena and Calistoga, both of which were larger but still quite small, Manning had no movie theater. It would have done him no good if it had, though. Along with drinking alcohol and caffeine, eating pork and seafood, reading fiction, wearing makeup or jewelry, dancing, playing cards, and anything that might run the risk of being pleasurable, the Seventh-day Adventist church's list of condemned activities also included going to movies.

———————

The summer rains that had hit the valley with such a vengeance earlier in the month had caused Vintner Creek to disgorge all kinds of garbage onto its muddy banks, none of which was as horrible as the chewy treat Gabby had discovered.

The police turned the remains found by Gabby and Brett over to lab techs in San Francisco. Despite their decayed condition, the body parts were identified as belonging to Jimmy Greenlaw. He was the third such victim in two years.

All three boys had been approximately the same age. The first had been a resident of St. Helena, and the other two had lived in Manning. All three had been Seventh-day Adventists. The boys had been sodomized, then dismembered, and their remains cast into the waters of Vintner Creek to find their way into the digestive tracts of fish and forest animals. The bone scoring, identical in all the victims, suggested the killer had used a dull implement to sloppily hack the bodies into pieces. Semen tracks in all three victims were identical as well. The police claimed there was other evidence to link the murders to the same killer or killers, but refused to discuss such niceties as chemical proof and tissue damage with the press.

That was just fine with Brett's grandma.

"They'll be back, those reporters," she said a few days after Brett's discovery, seating him at the kitchen table. Grandma was a large, gray woman who dressed colorlessly and seldom smiled. She was especially unsmiling now as she had just chased two more reporters from the front door. As she poured Brett a glass of soy milk, she said sternly, "And you'll not talk to them. Always sticking their microphones into people's faces after something awful's happened. The more awful the *better*, far as they're concerned. That's why I'll not have any newspapers in this house. Rags, all of them." She lowered herself into a chair across from Brett. "No television, either. All those reporters *smiling* while they tell about murders and rapes and homo-seck-shuls spreading the AIDS. Course, the television *shows* are just as bad. Nothing but sex and killing."

Brett sipped the thick milk. He didn't like it, but he had no choice in the matter. He wiped off his creamy white mustache and said, "Larry Jackson says *they* have a TV, but his parents only let him watch *good* shows. He says—"

"I don't care *what* he says. A television is Satan's doorway into the home. I know *some* say they can handle it, but if Sister White were alive today, *she'd* tell them differently. Maybe they're watching good shows now—" She spat the words "good shows" with bitter skepticism. "—but you just *wait*. You watch enough of that stuff and it…it *affects* you." She searched Brett's face for a moment and her eyes clouded with worry. She reached across the table and closed her puffy, liver-spotted hand over Brett's small one. "You haven't been thinking about that boy, have you? About…what you found?"

Brett shook his head, resisting the urge to roll his eyes. "No, Grandma."

"Good. Good. It's not healthy to dwell on that sort of thing. It can…affect you." She watched him a moment longer, as if waiting for a reaction of some kind, then said, "Go study your Sabbath school lesson, Brett, honey. And say a prayer for that poor boy's family. After dinner, you can give me a back rub."

He polished off his milk and Grandma stroked his hair gently, still looking at him with concern.

The policemen had been the same way. All of a sudden, everyone was treating him as if he were breakable just because he had found a dead boy. Brett did not understand what the big deal was. It was not as if Jimmy had been a friend of his. They had a passing acquaintance in Sabbath school, but that was all. Brett had no friends to speak of. Sure, it was a bad thing that had happened and Jimmy's parents were probably crushed, he understood that. But he would not *let* his own feelings get involved.

On his way through the living room, Brett got a glimpse of Grandpa. He seldom got more than a glimpse of him, usually rounding a corner or going through a doorway in his wheelchair, the two stumps of his legs—"Souvenirs from the Big War," he once growled—hidden beneath a brown wool blanket. He had his own bedroom downstairs where he ate all of his meals and spent most of his time listening to gospel music on his old record player. Brett never heard Grandma talking to him and could not remember the last time he had heard Grandpa speak; the only sound he made was the muffled rumble of his chair wheeling over the old wooden floor.

In his room upstairs, Brett locked his door, something Grandma strongly disapproved of, and pulled a fat three-ring binder from under his bed. He flopped onto the mattress and opened the book, searching through the heavy construction paper pages. Pasted to each page were movie advertisements cut out of newspapers. He looked for one in particular, the newest addition to his collection, and when he found it, he folded his arms beneath his chest, tucked the tip of his tongue into the corner of his mouth and stared at it, relished it.

The ad took up a quarter of the page and written at the top in letters that appeared to be carved in flesh was the title:

BEDSIDE MANNERS

Below that:

> **If you sleep in the dark,**
> **he'll find you ...**
> **If you sleep with a light on,**
> **he'll find you FASTER!**

Below the words was a picture of a man's legs from behind in faded blue jeans. A bloodied ax hung at his right side.

Between his spread legs, facing him, a woman lay in bed clutching the blankets to her breasts, mouth open in a horrified scream. The woman was Brett's mother.

The book held nearly sixty ads for all kinds of movies ranging from Oscar winners complete with quotes of praise from critics to grade-Z horror films promising lots of blood; Brett collected them all. Because Grandma would not allow newspapers into the house, Brett had to fish discarded editions from garbage cans and trash bins, always careful that no one was watching. He kept only the entertainment section and tossed the rest back in the garbage. In his room, he subjected the pages to scissors and paste. When he hid the treasured binder, he pushed it far under his bed, all the way over against the wall.

Grandma had a nervous tic that wriggled her lower lip now and then, especially when she was upset. At the very mention of movies or theaters, Grandma's lip began to twitch so fast it seemed about to wriggle off of her face.

"If you ever go into such a place," she would say firmly, "your guardian angel will *not* go in with you. Being in a movie house puts distance between you and the Lord and can be dangerous. Bad things can happen. Your soul is unprotected and if you should die within those walls, you'll be lost forever. It would be no different than committing suicide. You'd have no way to repent. You'd be condemned to the Lake of Fire."

Brett never understood exactly *why* it was wrong to go to movies. He knew that Ellen White had condemned going to theaters in her writing, but at the time, movie theaters had not existed. She had referred to live theater and burlesque. Maybe it was just the theater itself that was wrong, although he failed to see why. There were no rules against having a television or watching movies at home on a VCR, though most Adventists he knew were very cautious about that sort of thing; they claimed to use great discretion in choosing programs and movies, but they still *watched* them. Sometimes the church held a "Family Film Night" where they would show movies like *The Sound of Music* or some dumb Disney movie that was on the Approved List, and they would charge admission to raise money for new carpet in the sanctuary, or to repaint the multi-purpose room, or something. But going to see a movie in a theater was, for some reason, a bad thing and not allowed.

He had been given several explanations for this rule, such as, "In a theater you're with a bad crowd, the wrong element," and, "Movies contain un-Christian and immoral themes and are a powerful negative influence." None of them satisfied him. *Lost forever* seemed a pretty severe price to pay for seeing a movie in a theater, but it did not dampen Brett's desire. He dreamed of going to movies the way most boys his age dreamed of being secret agents or firemen.

He sometimes met other children his age who were not Adventists and asked them what it was like to go to movies. Puzzled by his urgent questioning, they told him of the warm smell of the popcorn in the lobby, the posters on the wall, the coming attractions that ran before the movie. And the *movies*…

He asked them again and again about the movies they saw, wanting to hear every detail from beginning to end.

"How come bad things don't happen to the other kids who go to movies?" he had asked Grandma once.

"They haven't been shown the truth yet. You *have*. They don't know they're doing wrong so the Lord won't hold it against them. But someday, he'll show them. Oh, yes, he'll show *them*."

Brett often envied those children who had not been shown the truth. They seemed so much happier than everyone he knew, certainly happier than Brett himself. It did not make sense that having the truth would make you unhappy, but that was how it looked to Brett. A lot of things did not make sense to him. In the Old Testament, God was angry most of the time and often killed people he did not like, entire civilizations of them. Or worse, he sometimes made them so miserable that they *wished* they were dead, like the Egyptians in the story of Moses. In the New Testament, Jesus was supposed to be the son of God, but he seemed a lot nicer and talked about how everyone should love each other and take care of each other. Jesus and God, he was told, were pretty much the same person. But they sure did not *seem* the same to him.

When he asked questions about these things, though, he was told by his teachers and pastors and especially by Grandma that his doubt was a sign that the devil was working in him, that he was being bad just by...*thinking*. It did not make sense. But everyone *agreed* with it—everyone at church, everyone at school, everyone in the whole town of Manning. So, he figured there was something he was missing, something he was too young or stupid to understand. Maybe it would all become clear to him someday.

But something told him that was not very likely.

Everyone with this truth was so nervous about the fact that God was always watching them and that every bad thing they did, every bad thought they had—and, according to Ellen White, even every good thing they did *not* do—was being written down in a book. A record was being kept and on Judgment Day it would be used against them. They would go to heaven or be thrown into the lake of fire depending on what was in that book. Who could pass such a test? It seemed impossible. And that was why everyone with the Seventh-day Adventist truth was so unhappy, even though they were always smiling and cheerful. Sometimes Brett thought that was the worst part of living in Manning and going to an Adventist school and the Adventist church—all that forced, strained happiness and cheer.

It had been so long since Brett had seen his mother that he had forgotten what her voice sounded like and she seemed to be nothing more than an image in photographs. She called every Christmas and on his birthdays (although she had forgotten his ninth a few months ago), but the calls were brief and her voice sounded pinched over the telephone. He remembered her face only because he had a picture of her tucked in the back of his movie binder with her letters and postcards.

And now he had a new one: *Bedside Manners*.

Four years ago, Mom had left Brett with Grandma and Grandpa so she could go to Hollywood and become an actress. That's what she had been doing before he came along, she had claimed. She had not quite made it, though, so she wanted to give it another try.

Grandma spoke of Mom only when Brett got a phone call from her. After the call, Grandma would hug Brett to her enormous breasts, which always smelled of mothballs and Ben Gay, and mutter, "Imagine your own mother running off like that. And to *that* town to work with those, those *people*. At least she had the good sense to leave you with me so I could raise you in Christ."

Sometimes Brett hated his mother for leaving him with Grandma and Grandpa. He hated Manning, the church, and everything else that made up his life. The sad fact was that there was little *else* in his life. Sometimes it filled him with rage to be trapped there with no options, nowhere else to go, no one to turn to but his grandparents. But Adventism had taught him how to deal with that.

In church and school—he attended the Adventist grammar school in Manning—he was always reminded that he was bad. He was born bad, everyone was—according to them, anyway— and only Jesus could make him good, give him worth.

Everything he liked was bad. He wanted to go to movies, watch television, read comic books—all bad things. He was told that he wanted to do those things because Satan was working hard inside him, and without Jesus, he was helpless, worthless and lost to the devil.

Years ago, Brett had become tired of it all. He had taught himself how to shut down his feelings, to turn himself off, to put up walls and protect himself from the constant negative onslaught.

He did the same thing whenever he felt like hating his mother, whenever he got angry about his situation. He just put up the walls and shut it all out.

He had always hoped his mother would come back for him some day and take him away from Grandma and Manning and the Adventists. And now it was finally going to happen.

Brett took his mother's most recent letter from the back of the binder. He only got her letters during the summer when he was home from school and could get to the mailbox first. Otherwise, Grandma got to them first and burned them.

> Brett honey,
> Got my first movie role! It's a cheapie horror
> flick called "Bedside Manners" and the part
> is small. I play a "victim" in the first 10
> minutes. But they're using me on the poster,
> so it's good exposure…

Brett skipped down to the last paragraph.

> I've got a little money now and hope to
> come up north and get you soon. Would
> you like to live in L.A. with me? There are
> good schools here and lots of things to do…

His chest swelled at the very thought of going away with Mom.

...hope to come up north and get you soon...

...get you soon...

...soon...

He heard Grandma clumping up the stairs. He closed the binder and shoved it under the bed, then quickly unlocked the door before she tried the knob. He lay back on his bed.

Brett was so happy that even the thought of having to give Grandma another of those smelly Ben Gay back rubs after dinner could not depress him.

Mr. Moser was the only person in the Manning Adventist church with whom Brett felt comfortable. The rest of the people there seemed to be stiff, emotionless machines programmed to smile at certain times, frown or look sympathetic at others, set to shed a tear or say, "*Amen!*" during the sermon, and to sing the designated hymn when Miss Potter, the timid church organist, began to play. On Friday afternoons, they washed their cars, cleaned and pressed their finest clothes, and on Saturdays they came to church looking their best. But they seemed to leave their souls at home—if they had souls at all.

As Brett sat with his grandparents (Grandma always parked Grandpa's wheelchair at the end of a pew) and looked at the empty staring faces around him—some nodding off, others watching the droning pastor with half-closed eyes—he felt a sadness that was hard to shake. Church always made him sad, so he did not watch them anymore. He put the walls up and shut them all out until he could no longer hear the whining organ or the pastor's level, reverent voice that went on and on. Once he shut them all out, he felt better, and after the service was over, instead of feeling agitated and depressed as he would otherwise, he felt relaxed, as if he had taken a nap.

He did not have to do that in Sabbath school, though, because his teacher, Mr. Moser, was different than the others. Brett was not the only one fond of him; all the kids liked Mr. Moser. There was nothing forced or artificial or robotic about him. When he laughed, it was real; his round little belly bounced like a ball and his darkly bearded moon face split into a broad grin. When he was concerned, as he was that Sabbath after Brett's discovery, his heavy eyebrows lowered over his eyes and his forehead became creased with lines of genuine worry.

He took Brett aside after Sabbath school, before the church service.

"How are you, Brett?"

"Fine."

"You're sure?"

"Oh. You mean after finding that...boy? Sheesh, everybody's so worried about me now. Nobody *noticed* me before."

"Well, that's a pretty awful thing to find."

Brett shrugged.

"A pretty hard thing to forget, too, I'd think," Mr. Moser added.

"I'm okay. Really."

Mr. Moser studied Brett's face thoughtfully for a moment, then smiled. "How would you like to come out to my place after church, Brett? We could have lunch, then go for a walk and look for lizards."

Brett was thrilled at the opportunity to get out of his grandparents' smothering house for the day, and even happier that he could spend the afternoon with Mr. Moser.

"I'll have to ask Grandma," he said. "She's pretty careful about letting me out of the house because of this…well, you know, the killer."

"I'll talk to her," Mr. Moser said. "She'll let you come. She knows I'm safe. After all, I'm your Sabbath school teacher." He grinned.

———————

Mr. Moser lived at the end of a dirt road about a mile and a half off of Glass Mountain Road. His house was small and homey, nestled in the shade of several tall trees. He had no neighbors within sight of his house and plenty of rocky, hilly land around which to hunt lizards and snakes.

They had a lunch of taco salad and strawberry shortcake for dessert, then went outside for a long walk in the summer sun.

It made Brett feel important to be alone with his teacher; he had Mr. Moser's undivided attention and interest. As they walked, they did not talk about Sabbath school or church—in fact, Brett completely forgot it was the Sabbath, which would have been impossible had he been with Grandma. Mr. Moser wanted only to talk about Brett.

"What would you like to do, Brett, more than anything in the world?"

"Do? What do you mean?"

"Go to Disneyland? Fly a plane? Ride a rocket to the moon?"

They were walking along a dusty trail and Brett began to thoughtfully kick a rock along ahead of him, wondering if he could confide in Mr. Moser. He decided it would be safe to be honest.

"I'd like to go to a movie," he said quietly.

"Pardon?"

"A movie. You know, in a theater."

"Ah, the forbidden fruit." Mr. Moser smiled knowingly.

"Huh?"

"Never been to a movie, huh?"

"I've never even *seen* a movie. Not a *real* one, anyway, like *Raiders of the Lost Ark* or *Alien*. Just those stupid movies they show on Family Nights. And sometimes Grandma won't even let me go to *those*."

Mr. Moser stopped and sat on a fat tree stump, chuckling quietly.

Brett frowned, thinking perhaps he had said something wrong. "What's funny?"

"Well, it's just that...see, I'm chairman of the Entertainment Committee. I'm one of the people who *chooses* those stupid movies."

"Oh." Brett felt his face grow hot with embarrassment. "I'm sorry."

"No, no, don't apologize, Brett," Mr. Moser said with a laugh. "I know most of those movies aren't very good, but we're kind of limited. It *is* a church function, after all. There aren't many good family-oriented films to choose from. We're always looking for new ones to put on the approved list, but the committee's standards are pretty rigid. No swearing, no drinking, no smoking, no dancing. I know what you mean, though. If I have to sit through *Zebra in the Kitchen* one more time, I may be sick." He rubbed his palms up and down the thighs of his blue jeans thoughtfully for a moment, then asked, "If you haven't seen any real movies, then how do you know about *Raiders of the Lost Ark* and *Alien*?"

Hesitantly, Brett told him about his collection of movie ads.

Mr. Moser listened intently, watching Brett with great interest. When he was finished, Mr. Moser said, "Have you ever seen a VCR, Brett?"

"We don't even have a TV."

Mr. Moser winked. "Then let's go back to the house. I've got something to show you."

Back in the house, Mr. Moser opened a tall cabinet in the living room. On the middle shelf was a large television set. Below that was a black machine with the time glowing in green numbers on the side. Rows of what appeared to be books filled the top shelf.

"This is a video cassette recorder," Mr. Moser said, "and these—" He gestured at the book-like objects. "—are video cassettes.

Brett stared into the cabinet with awe, his lips parted.

"When a movie is submitted for approval," Mr. Moser said, "I sometimes invite the committee over here and, if it's available on video cassette, we watch the movie and vote on it."

"So, you get to see *unapproved* movies, too?" Brett whispered. "Not just the kid stuff?"

"Well, it's not likely that anyone is going to submit anything by Martin Scorsese or Woody Allen for approval, but yes, I get to see all the movies."

"Woody who?"

"Never mind."

"Wow," he breathed as he reverently inspected the VCR. "How many videos do you have?"

"About sixty movies or so on tape."

"*Sixty*? Sheesh." Brett stared up at the tapes, imagining what it would be like to sit down and watch all of them back to back, without knowing what movie was coming up next. He glanced at Mr. Moser hopefully, but suspected there was little chance of seeing any of those movies.

But Mr. Moser had a broad grin on his face. "Would you like to see one, Brett?"

"But...it's the Sabbath."

"Would that bother you?"

"Wouldn't it bother *you*?"

"Well...why don't we make it our little secret. Just between the two of us. I won't tell if you won't tell, okay?"

Brett held his breath a moment, expecting him to say he was only joking. It was too much to hope for.

"Okay, Brett?"

Slowly, disbelievingly, Brett nodded, then smiled as he realized Mr. Moser was serious. *Really serious*!

Mr. Moser scanned the tapes and pulled one down, took it from its box, and slipped it into the machine.

"This is a good one to start with," he said. "It's a Disney movie from a few years ago, but a very good one. It's called *Never Cry Wolf*. It wasn't approved because there are some swear words and a shot of Charles Martin Smith in the buff from behind. It's a great movie, though. Sit down. You want some chips?"

Within minutes, Brett was seated wide-eyed in front of the television munching on Doritos and drinking an Orange Crush. For two hours, he was far away from Manning.

Over the next few weeks, Brett spent a good deal of his time at Mr. Moser's house watching one movie after another.

Grandma was pleased because Brett had told her he was working with Mr. Moser on some Sabbath school projects. No further explanation was needed; she was glad to know he was investing his time in wholesome pursuits.

The day after he watched *Never Cry Wolf*, Brett saw *Starman*, a movie that would never even be *considered* for approval. Seventh-day Adventists frowned bitterly on science fiction and fantasy—unless it was written by C.S. Lewis, of course. At the end of the movie, the alien, played by Jeff Bridges, made love with Karen Allen. It was a PG-rated love scene, but it was nevertheless startling to Brett. He had neither seen nor imagined people touching each other the way Jeff Bridges and Karen Allen touched each other on the screen—with their hands *and* their mouths.

He squinted curiously, straightened his posture and said, "What are they *doing*?"

Mr. Moser sniffed and fidgeted on the sofa. "They're, um, making love."

"What?"

"Making love."

"Yeah, but...what's that?"

"Well...when a man and woman care very much for each other, they, um...they share their bodies with each other. They kiss and hold each other. Like that." He gestured toward the screen.

"You mean *sex*?"

Mr. Moser nodded slightly, his eyes on the television; he looked embarrassed and uncomfortable.

So that's what Grandma's always complaining about, Brett thought, turning his attention back to the movie.

Nothing but sex and killing, Grandma often said about TV.

He could see nothing bad about what the man and woman were doing. In fact, it seemed pleasant; *they* certainly seemed to be enjoying themselves. What was bad about that?

As the tape was rewinding, Brett turned to Mr. Moser and said, "That didn't look like a bad thing. The sex, I mean. People are always talking about it like it's a bad thing."

"Well, it can be...misused," Mr. Moser said. "But if it's between people who care about each other, it's perfectly natural and...healthy."

Brett returned the following day for a showing of *The Color Purple.*

"I really wanted this to make the approved list," Mr. Moser said as he put the movie into the VCR, "but it didn't stand a chance."

"How come?"

"Swearing, drinking. But what really did it was the lesbian relationship."

"The *what*?"

"We'll talk about it after the movie."

Brett was surprised by how much the film moved him. By the time it was over, he was embarrassed to find that his eyes were puffy and sticky with tears. He did not want to talk for a while and was silent as the tape rewound.

Mr. Moser watched him, waiting for him to speak.

"So, what's a...a lez-bean?" he finally asked.

"What did you think of the movie?"

"It was good. But I didn't see anything that looked like it might be a lez-bean relationship. Whatever that is. So, what is it?"

"It was subtle. Remember when Shug and Celie went home after the big fight at the bar?"

Brett nodded.

"And they were alone together? And they started...well, touching each other?"

Another nod.

"That's where, um, their lesbian relationship began."

Brett waited for him to go on. When he did not, Brett said, "I still don't know what it is."

"A lesbian is...well, a woman who would rather make love with another woman than with a man."

Brett frowned as he thought that over. "You mean...*sex*? The women do *sex* together?"

Mr. Moser nodded. "Have sex, not do."

Brett pondered this new information, chewing his lip as he tried to fit it into his rapidly growing view of things. "Are there men lesbians, too?" he said.

Mr. Moser nodded as he put the videotape back in its box. "Gay men. Homosexuals."

...and the homo-seck-shuls spreading the AIDS, Grandma often grumbled.

There was another of her mysterious complaints explained. Brett was learning a lot. And it seemed that everything he was learning would be strongly condemned by Grandma and everyone in his Adventist community. And yet it seemed these things were not condemned in the outside world. Apparently, *some* people did not find fault with these things the way Adventists did. In fact, it had to be a *lot* of people if they were making *movies* about these things.

Brett began to get the sense that a vast world existed beyond Manning where everything was very different than it was in his life. He began to get the feeling that he was...locked up. In a box. He almost felt as if he were being held prisoner.

Brett waited for the mail carrier each day, but received no more letters from his mother. After each disappointing delivery, he would play with Gabby until he knew Mr. Moser was home from work. Mr. Moser was an X-ray technician at the Seventh-day Adventist hospital in Deer Park and got off at three p.m. Then Brett would hop on his bike and head for his Sabbath school teacher's house.

A day did not pass without a few warnings from Grandma.

"Don't talk to any strangers," she'd say. "And stay away from those Mexican hitch-hikers, you hear? Probably one of *them* who's killing all those poor little boys. Always drinking their beer and smoking their dope. Course, if you keep saying your prayers, Jesus'll watch over you and nothing bad will ever happen."

In Brett, Mr. Moser had found a protégé; in Mr. Moser, Brett had found a mentor. He watched one movie after another, so many that he would have lost count if he did not list them in a spiral-bound note pad. It was a new kind of scrapbook, a companion to his collection of movie advertisements. Beneath the title of each film, Brett made notes; he learned something new from every movie, whether he liked the movie or not.

Gremlins, The Terminator, Cujo, all three *Star Wars* movies in a row. Of the trilogy, Brett's favorite was the first. He jumped to his feet and cheered during the final scene in which the heroes were rewarded for their valor.

At first, Brett found it a bit disconcerting to be watching unapproved movies with the chairman of the church's entertainment committee. But Mr. Moser reassured him.

"Remember, Brett," he said, "it's our secret. I won't tell if you won't tell."

———————

For three weeks, Brett kept their secret and his list of movies grew a little longer each day. From Mr. Moser, he learned about movies; from the movies, he learned about life and the world.

It was the Friday night of the third week of their secret that things changed.

Friday nights were always gloomy. Grandma never smiled—not that she did much smiling the rest of the week—and was grumpier than usual. The darkness seemed a little darker and the scratchy music from Grandpa's record player seemed more mournful than the rest of the week. Grandpa usually sat in the living room on Friday nights, his grave, shiny-bald head hanging heavily from his neck, for which it seemed much too big. He drummed his thick fingers on the armrests of his wheelchair, eyes blackened by shadow, as Grandma rocked in the squeaky rocking chair, reading Sister White and humming off-key to the music. The summer brought some relief because the oppressive darkness of the night did not settle in until much later.

Brett was more than eager to get out for the evening and rode his bike over to Mr. Moser's well before sundown. He arrived to find Mr. Moser on the phone.

"I'm sorry, Jim," he was saying, "I completely forgot about it. I can be there in five minutes.... No, no, it's fine, I'll be right over."

When he hung up, Mr. Moser paced by the phone for a moment, chewing a thumbnail, almost as if Brett were not there. His eyes finally darted to Brett and his lips curled into a forced smile that was little more than a flash of teeth.

"A Sabbath school committee meeting," he said. "Forgot all about it."

"Oh. Do you want me to go?"

"No, no," he replied quickly, turning fully to Brett, holding out his arms and waggling his hands. "No, sit down, have a soda, put in a movie. I shouldn't be gone more than twenty-thirty minutes. I have—" He lowered his voice secretively and smiled. "—a surprise for you, Brett. It'll just have to wait until I get back, that's all." He took his wallet and keys from the coffee table. "Don't answer the phone, just let the machine get it. Be back in a few."

After he was gone, Brett opened the cabinet and, with the help of a chair from the kitchen, pulled *Ghostbusters* down from the shelf. Mr. Moser had shown him how to operate the VCR, so he turned it on, then turned on the television. But he did not put the tape in yet. Instead, he headed for the bathroom.

Mr. Moser had given Brett a tour of the house during his first visit. Pointing to the door beyond the bathroom, Mr. Moser had said, "That's my bedroom, and that," he had added, pointing across the hall, "is the linen closet. If you ever spend the night, there are extra blankets and pillows in there."

"What's this?" Brett had gone to a closed door at the end of the hall.

"Laundry room." He'd taken Brett's arm then and led him away from the door, saying, "It's a mess."

After he finished in the bathroom, Brett stood at the bedroom door a moment and decided Mr. Moser would not mind if he just took a peek inside to see what his bedroom looked like.

It was dark in the bedroom and Brett reached for a light switch, found it, flipped it up. The first thing he saw was the huge screen across the room. He had heard of big-screen TVs but had never seen one before. He had not known they were *that* big.

He stepped over to the TV and saw that there was another VCR hooked up to it, just like the one in the living room. He brushed his fingertips lightly around the television's labeled controls—ON-OFF, VOLUME, COLOR, TINT...

Watching a movie on that big screen would be almost like watching it in a theater.

Maybe this is the surprise, he thought.

Brett hurried into the living room, got the *Ghostbusters* tape, returned to the bedroom and turned on the big television. When he tried to insert the tape into the VCR, he found another already in the slot. He pushed EJECT and the tape eased out like a tongue from a mouth.

The top of the tape was black as night and the white spools in the casing stared at him like dead eyes.

Looking around, Brett found no box for the tape, but a white label was attached to the tape's edge. In block letters written with a felt-tip marker were the words, WARNER BROS. CARTOONS #2.

He glanced at the clock beside the bed. Mr. Moser had been gone only ten minutes. That left another fifteen at least—he probably would be gone longer than he had said if it was a meeting. Brett had found that adults seldom acted as efficiently as they promised.

Slipping the tape back into the slot, he pressed PLAY and sat on the foot of the bed.

Cheerful music began to play and the words LOONEY TOONS appeared on the large screen.

"Bugs Bunny!" Brett exclaimed happily when the rabbit appeared, munching on a carrot. He had seen pictures of Bugs in a coloring book his mother had sent him once. Grandma had taken the book away from him and, in its place, had given him a book called *Uncle Arthur's Bible Stories*. No rabbits in *that* book.

After the credits, a little bald man appeared holding a rifle. He walked through the woods on tiptoe looking right and left.

"Shhh!" he said to Brett, looking right out of the screen at him. "I'm hunting wabbit. Heh-heh-heh-heh!"

Bugs suddenly poked his head out of a hole in the ground, took a bite of his carrot, smacked his lips a few times and said, "Aaaahhh, what's up, D—"

The cartoon was gone.

The screen danced with black and white speckles. Mr. Moser called them "ant races."

For a moment, Brett chilled with the fear that he had done something wrong, something that had perhaps damaged the VCR.

He sighed with relief when the picture returned. But it was not the cartoon he had been watching a moment ago.

A naked woman filled the screen. She was pale and had waves of cascading blonde hair, bright red lips, and heavily made up eyes. Her breasts were enormous. They bounced and wobbled like great water balloons made of flesh and tied with hard pink knots. They were bouncing because she was rapidly and enthusiastically sliding both fists up and down a large, hard penis. She laughed as she pounded her fists and her breasts flopped and the man thrust his hips upward.

Brett stared with a slack jaw, eyes wide as the camera pulled back to reveal more naked people doing things to each other.

He could not move. For a long moment, he could not even breathe.

The Sabbath school committee meeting, which began and ended with prayer, was over in twenty minutes, just as Mr. Moser had suspected it would be. The entire committee was present—eight people in all—and, as usual, they sat around the conference table and socialized after the official business was out of the way.

Mr. Moser excused himself from the chatter, left the room, and headed down the main corridor of the church toward the front entrance, walking at a brisk pace, thinking of Brett.

"Ed! What's your hurry?"

He jerked to a stop and spun around to see Pastor Alexander coming out of his study.

"Well," he began, pushing a smile onto his face, "I'm, uh...I'm in no hurry, really."

"Then step in here for a minute. I'd like you to meet someone."

Mr. Moser followed the little man with the big walrus mustache into his study where a man, woman, and little boy were seated on a brown vinyl-upholstered sofa facing his desk.

"Ed Moser," Pastor Alexander said formally, "I'd like you to meet the Rileys, Jack, Betty and their son Jason."

Mr. Moser smiled, shook Jack Riley's hand and said, "Pleased to meet you."

"The Rileys have just moved to Manning," the pastor said. "This is going to be their first Sabbath with us."

"Oh. Well. Glad to have you." Still forcing that smile, he glanced at his watch and made a note of the time. He had been gone almost half an hour.

Pastor Alexander moved behind his desk and seated himself in his squeaky chair. "Have a seat, Ed."

Mr. Moser thought of Brett back at the house, sitting in front of the television set watching a movie. What would it be tonight? *Jaws*? *Stripes*? *The Wizard of Oz*? Brett would not be going anywhere. Mr. Moser seated himself in a chair and turned it to so he could face both Pastor Alexander at his desk and the Rileys on the sofa.

"Ed is one of our Sabbath school teachers," Pastor Alexander said. "He works in X-ray at our hospital. Has quite a reputation up there, too. But I'm happy to say he's very generous with his time and he's devoted to our children here at the church." The pastor winked at Jason and said, "You'll be in his class tomorrow, Jason."

The boy smiled hesitantly at Mr. Moser.

"We'll be glad to have you, Jason," Mr. Moser said. "I've got a great bunch of boys and girls in my class."

Jason blushed beneath his freckles and looked away bashfully.

"That's a fine looking boy you have there," Mr. Moser said to the proudly beaming Rileys. "A fine-looking boy.

300

There were several movies on the tape, one after another in a continuous parade of naked bodies, thrusting hips and fondled genitals. Each one ended in explosions of what looked to Brett like thick soy milk.

He hit FAST FORWARD, waited a moment, the pushed PLAY. More of the same. He did it again and found still more. He stopped the tape, then pushed REWIND and sat watching the ant races, thinking.

Did Mr. Moser *watch* these movies? He must, or why else would he have them? Did he ever show them to anyone else? To whom? The movies would probably get him in big trouble with people at the church. Brett had never seen such movies before, but he had a pretty good idea they were *not* on the approved list.

Brett wondered if his Sabbath school teacher had any *more* of these movies.

He dashed down the hall to the living room and looked out the front window. Shadows were lengthening outside as the dark Sabbath approached, but there was no sign of Mr. Moser's car.

He hurried back to the bedroom and began his search.

Being careful not to disturb anything, Brett looked through drawers, under the bed, in the closet. He found nothing but underwear and clothes, shoes and some dusty boxes and books. Disappointed, he sat on the edge of the bed and slowly looked around for a place he might have missed.

To his left, he saw two rectangular sliding doors in the headboard, each with a round brass knob in the center. He reached over and slid one aside, then the other.

Boxed videotapes were neatly stored on the headboard shelf, labels facing out. From left to right were WARNER BROS.

CARTOONS #1 through #7, with #2 missing. There were three more tapes labeled LITTLE RASCALS #1 through #3.

Brett removed the fourth cartoon tape and put it in the VCR.

After about two minutes of Daffy Duck and Bugs Bunny arguing about whether it was duck season or rabbit season, more naked people appeared. Their movements made wet sounds as they gasped and grunted and said words Brett had never heard before. Brett rewound the tape, ejected it, and put it back on the headboard shelf.

Wondering why they were labeled differently, Brett could not resist taking a look at one of the LITTLE RASCALS tapes. He chose #3. Once it was in the VCR, he sat on the bed again.

The film—Our Gang in "The He-Man Woman-Haters Club"—was old with fuzzy black-and-white images and music and voices that seemed to be coming through a wall of gauze.

A fat little boy and a tall skinny one with funny hair entered a makeshift clubhouse The fat one said, "Well, Alfalfa, this is the headquarters of the He-Man Woman-Haters Club."

There were some other boys in the clubhouse and they all waved at Alfalfa, who waved back and said, "Gee, Spanky, I'd sure like to join. What do I have to—"

Ant races.

Then blackness.

Brett slowly realized the blackness was a room, unlit and unoccupied. A light came on with a distant *click,* and Brett saw what looked like a doctor's examination table. It was covered with a sheet of heavy plastic. Tied to the table was a naked little boy. Brett squinted at the boy's still face.

It was Jimmy Greenlaw.

A naked man stepped into the picture, his back to the camera. His skin was white and flabby. When he finally spoke—

"Okay," he breathed with moist anticipation, "*oookay.*"

—Brett recognized the voice.

It belonged to Mr. Moser.

It was only a matter of minutes before Jason Riley lost his bashfulness and was chatting with Mr. Moser as if they were old buddies.

"Do you like bible stories, Jason?" Mr. Moser asked.

"Sure do," the boy said, nodding.

"They're my specialty. Tomorrow I'm telling the story of Daniel in the lion's den."

"Oh, that's his *favorite!*" Mrs. Riley chimed in, putting an arm around her son's shoulders.

Mr. Moser grinned. "Good. It's my favorite story to tell."

Mr. Riley politely said it was time to go home and they all stood at once. Pastor Alexander suggested that he and Mr. Moser walk them to their car and they headed down the corridor at a leisurely pace, Jason walking beside Mr. Moser, who rested his hand on the boy's shoulder.

Mr. Moser said with a smile, "I'm looking forward to having you in my class, Jason."

Brett's fingers dug into the mattress and he felt something uncoil in his gut as he watched.

His back still turned, Mr. Moser ran his hands over Jimmy's small, still body, his breaths heavy and wet and coming steadily faster. He turned so Brett could see him in profile, reached under the table and produced a white bottle. He squeezed something onto his palm and began rubbing it on his rigid penis as he stared open-mouthed down at Jimmy.

Brett closed his eyes. He tried to put the walls up, tried to shut everything off the way he did in church. But it did not work.

When Brett opened his eyes again, his Sabbath school teacher was holding Jimmy's legs up in the air and grunting as his dimpled buttocks made spastic thrusts.

At the Riley's car in the parking lot, Pastor Alexander suggested Mr. Moser say a prayer and the five people joined hands in a small circle.

"Dear heavenly father," he began, "we thank you for bringing these good people to our town and our church. We ask that you watch over them as they settle into their new home...."

Brett sucked in a sharp, sickened breath and diverted his eyes, looking at the room on the screen.

It looked like a garage only smaller, with lots of dusty shelves on the walls. Behind Mr. Moser and Jimmy was a large rusty metal sink; next to that were a washer and dryer. Below the table was a drain centered on the concrete floor surrounded by a large dark stain.

Laundry room...it's a mess...

When Jimmy screamed, Brett clenched his eyes shut for a moment. He opened them again just in time to see Mr. Moser lift a hatchet over his head and bring it down with a heavy, wet *crunch*.

"…We especially ask that you watch over young Jason. Guide him in your way, oh lord, and protect him from the snares and temptations of the evil one…."

———————

Blood shot upward in a crimson spray.
Jimmy's scream ended abruptly in a wet coughing sound.

———————

"…Guide them safely home now, heavenly father, and rest them well so that we can all gather tomorrow in your name. We ask these favors in the name of your son Jesus…amen."

"Amen," they repeated in unison.

Mr. Moser gave Jason a friendly hug and said, "You'll have to come over to my place real soon and we'll go lizard hunting."

"Okay!" Jason said happily. "I'd like that."

Mr. Moser bid them goodnight and walked to his car.

———————

Another chop.

…a mess…

Brett's fists unclenched and the tight knot in his stomach relaxed as he was finally able to put those walls up. Soon he felt numb, detached. He felt nothing.

Just like in church.

———————

Driving down the road in his car, Mr. Moser slipped a cassette into his stereo. It was a tape he often played for his children in Sabbath school, an old album of Anita Bryant singing some children's gospel favorites. The first song began and he sang along.

"Jesus loves the little chiiillldren...all the children of the wooorld..."

He smiled, knowing that in just a few minutes, he would be able to give Brett his surprise.

Brett stopped the tape.

He thought of Mr. Moser teaching Sabbath school, leading them in song, in prayer, acting out bible stories and making them laugh. And he thought of what he had just seen.

I have a surprise for you, Brett....

...a surprise...

Brett stood, left the room, went to the door at the end of the hall and opened it. He was surprised to find it unlocked.

The sink was across the room. The table was covered with canvas and boxes were stacked on it, making it look like a sort of workbench.

The drain in the floor looked clogged with black, soggy lumps.

To the right of the door was a tall wooden cupboard. Brett opened it and stared for a moment at the tripod, the black and gray camera case beneath it.

He hurried down the hall to the front window and looked out again. He still saw no sign of Mr. Moser, but knew he probably had little time left to cover his tracks. It was getting darker.

Back in the bedroom, he felt vaguely ill, like he might throw up. He hummed a church hymn and ignored it. He did not want to make a mess he would not have time to clean up.

He ejected the LITTLE RASCALS tape and returned it to the headboard, then picked up *Ghostbusters* from the floor where he had left it. He wished he had time to see the movie. It would be even better if he could see *Ghostbusters* in a *real* theater on a *real* movie screen.

The idea that came from that thought made his hands tremble.

Hurried by a gnawing feeling of urgency—he *knew* Mr. Moser could not be gone much longer—Brett returned to the living room and put *Ghostbusters* back on the shelf. He found a small brown paper bag in the kitchen, took it to the bedroom and retrieved LITTLE RASCALS #3 from the headboard. He stuffed it into the bag, rushed out of the house and put the bag in the basket between his handlebars.

Only seconds after he turned onto Glass Mountain Road, Brett heard a car up ahead. He drove his bike into a deep ditch, tumbled into the weeds and remained perfectly still, hoping he was out of sight.

The car passed, slowed, then turned into the driveway. It was Mr. Moser.

Brett waited until the crunch of tires on the dirt road began to fade, then pulled his bike onto the pavement again. Before getting back on, he leaned over and vomited into the ditch until his eyes ached.

He wiped his mouth on the back of his hand, then rode home, already thinking about tomorrow morning.

———————

Mr. Moser came to Sabbath school late the following morning. He rushed in looking rumpled and winded; his hair was mussed and his brow glowed with perspiration. The moment he entered, his eyes locked with Brett's and narrowed briefly to dark, bloodless cuts.

He seemed preoccupied as he led the class through a few songs, kept tugging at his tie as he quizzed them on the weekly Sabbath school lesson, and wiped his brow again and again as he stuttered through a retelling of Daniel's stay in the lion's den. He cut the story short and excused himself, asking Mrs. Juarez, the pianist, to take over. Before leaving the room, Mr. Moser looked at Brett and nodded toward the door.

Brett followed him.

In the main corridor, Brett could hear the sanctuary organ played mournfully by Miss Potter in the adult Sabbath school class. Voices sang along glumly, blending and garbling until they seemed to be singing in some old dead language.

Mr. Moser took a handkerchief from his pocket and mopped his face and neck. When he was done, the cloth looked drenched.

"I don't seem to be feeling too well, Brett," he said nervously. "What do you suppose might be wrong?"

"I don't know. The flu, maybe?"

"I don't think so." He dabbed the underside of his chin with the soggy handkerchief. "Enjoy the movie last night?"

"Uh-huh."

"You, uh...you left before I could give you your surprise. That wasn't very nice. I thought maybe—"

"I took it, Mr. Moser."

He froze, still as a snapshot, his eyes searching Brett's face, mouth open slightly, tongue darting around inside.

"Don't worry," Brett whispered. "The tape's in a safe place. And I won't tell anyone. *If...*"

"If?" Mr. Moser breathed. "If *what*?"

"If you do what I ask."

A moment later, Mr. Moser chuckled. His nostrils flared and unspilled tears glistened in his eyes.

"Blackmail," he muttered, shaking his head in wonderment. "I'm being blackmailed."

"If anything happens to me," Brett said, "someone will find the tape. There's a note attached that explains everything." The part about the note was a lie, of course, but Mr. Moser had no way of knowing that.

Mr. Moser wiped an eye with a knuckle, then scrubbed his shiny face with his palm.

"I don't want much," Brett said.

"And what...is that?"

"I want you to take me to the movies. Whenever I want to go."

The music and singing stopped and somewhere in the church, a chorus of voices exclaimed, "Amen!"

The following morning, Brett called Mr. Moser and said he wanted to see the new Clint Eastwood movie. He *really* wanted to see *Bedside Manner* more than anything, but it was only playing in San Francisco, which was too far away. Besides, he wanted to see that movie with Mom; that would make it special. He and Mr. Moser agreed to go to a theater in Santa Rosa so no one they knew would see them.

After hanging up, Brett went to the kitchen and told Grandma he was going for a bike ride and would be back in time for supper.

"You stick close to the house," she ordered. "Don't go riding off someplace where you're all alone. And say your *prayers!*"

On his way through the dark living room—it was dark even on sunny days—Brett saw Grandpa sitting in the far corner by the phone table. His big gnarled hands were joined on what little lap he had and his head turned slowly, following Brett as he passed.

"See you later," he said, his voice sounding like gravel being crushed. Grandpa did something then that Brett had never seen him do before and he did not know quite what to make of it at first. The old man's lips pulled back around his scraggly teeth and the corners of his mouth twitched into slight curls. He was *smiling*! "Have a good time," he said.

In the car, Brett and Mr. Moser were silent for the first half of the drive. Mr. Moser fidgeted at the wheel, drumming his fingers and cracking his knuckles as he drove. He acted as if he were alone in the car.

Brett finally spoke: "Was I going to be next?"

Mr. Moser blinked, wiped his mouth, shifted his buttocks in the seat, but kept his eyes on the road and said nothing.

"That was the surprise, wasn't it?"

No reply.

"Why do you do it?"

Still nothing.

"Because you enjoy it?"

More silence. Brett almost gave up on the idea of getting a response, but then Mr. Moser spoke.

"I can't help it," he said quietly.

"Can't help what?"

"What I do."

Brett frowned. "Sure you can help it. Nobody *has* to do something like that."

"I…I crave it. And the temptation…it's too strong."

"Temptation? You mean, like from Satan?"

"Yes. I'm too weak. I can't fight it. And I give in."

"But why do you kill them?"

Mr. Moser chewed on his lip a moment. "If I don't...they'll tell. I can't let that happen."

"So, you do sex to them because you...you *crave* it. And then you kill them to keep from getting caught."

After a long pause, he nodded.

"Then you were going to kill me."

No reply.

"But it's wrong. Doesn't it *bother* you that it's wrong to kill people?"

Mr. Moser gulped, licked his lips, and said, "Of course it bothers me." His voice was thick. "But I know that Jesus forgives me."

Brett's eyes widened slightly as he thought of what he had seen Mr. Moser do on that videotape. "Even...even for *that*?"

Mr. Moser turned to Brett, frowning intensely. "You *know* he does, Brett. We've discussed this in Sabbath school. Jesus forgives everyone of everything if they ask and are truly sorry. Hebrews tells us that. And it says that once he's forgiven us, he forgets our sins. Remember? 'And their sins and iniquities will I remember no more.'"

"But aren't you supposed to *stop* after you've been forgiven?"

He spoke in little more than a breath. "I...I try. I do, I really try. But...I can't. I *can't*."

"Well, maybe...maybe you should go to someone for help. You know? Maybe you could talk to Pastor Alexander."

"No," Mr. Moser said abruptly, turning his head back and forth. He breathed through his nose for a while as his jaw moved back and forth. He seemed to be choosing his words carefully. "That...doesn't work."

"You've tried it?"

"Not here. At the...place I was before I came here. I was a teacher. A school teacher at the Adventist school where I lived. And I...I weakened. I couldn't fight the temptation. But the boy...he told."

"You got in trouble? With the police?"

"No. They didn't call the police. But I had to meet with several people from the school and church. They put me into a counseling program with the pastor. He prayed with me a lot and we asked Jesus to forgive me. And then they decided I shouldn't teach there anymore. So, I left. And I came here."

Brett thought, *And you make sure nobody tells on you again.*

They said nothing more for the rest of the drive.

The theater they went to had six screens. Brett stood in the lobby, breathed in the smell of popcorn, and looked at the rows of movie posters on the walls. He took in each and every detail around him, even the feeling of the thick carpet beneath his shoes, as if he were in the last hour of his life and wanted to miss nothing.

He looked up at Mr. Moser and said, "I'd like some popcorn."

Without meeting Brett's eyes, Mr. Moser got in line, bought a tub of popcorn with butter, then they went into the auditorium and found seats.

Moments later, the lights dimmed and the screen came alive.

The back of Brett's neck prickled with excitement and he stuffed a fistful of popcorn into his mouth. It was the most delicious popcorn he had ever tasted in his life.

The next two hours were everything Brett had hoped they would be.

Two days later, Brett called Mr. Moser again from the upstairs phone and said he wanted to go see the new James Bond movie. Grandma was gone shopping and Brett wanted to hurry out before she returned; the less explaining he had to do, the better. He raced downstairs and through the living room, stumbling to a halt when he heard his name called.

Grandpa was sitting in the corner again by the phone table. He was holding something out to Brett.

"Here," he said.

Brett stepped forward and saw two one-dollar bills held between Grandpa's beefy, gnarled fingers.

"For Milk Duds," Grandpa whispered conspiratorially with a crooked smile.

Brett chilled for a moment, realizing he had been found out, but Grandpa's smile was reassuring. He seemed to be saying, *Just between us.*

As Brett took the money, Grandpa said, "Have fun."

Riding his bike to Mr. Moser's house, Brett wondered how often Grandpa listened in on telephone conversations, and how much he had heard.

Over the next two weeks, Mr. Moser took Brett to eight movies. One day, they even saw two, back to back.

At first, they said little, but they began to talk a bit more each time, until it seemed they were nothing more than two friends going to the movies together.

They did not mention Jimmy Greenlaw or the tape or Mr. Moser's laundry room.

Sometimes Brett spotted Mr. Moser staring at him, like he used to when Brett watched movies on his VCR. But now he stared with tense eyes and chewed his lip nervously. He always looked away immediately, as soon as Brett spotted him, but Brett always knew—he felt, anyway—that Mr. Moser had been staring at him for a while. Brett tried not to wonder what Mr. Moser thought about while he stared at him because that reminded him of what he had seen on that videotape, and that conjured thoughts too frightening to entertain.

During the first week, Brett worried about Grandpa. How much did he know? Most importantly, would he tell Grandma?

By the second week, Brett felt better. Grandma knew nothing yet, and when they passed in the house, Grandpa always gave him a silent, secret smile and a wink, something he had never done before.

For the time being, he seemed to be safe.

It was turning out to be a fun and exciting summer.

He came home after his eighth movie, a Steve Martin comedy, and found his mother seated on the sofa talking to Grandpa.

When Brett walked in, she dashed across the room and greeted him with a laughing, perfumed embrace. She was beautiful. Her hair fell around her head in a golden mane, tiny stones sparkled in her earlobes—they were actually *stuck through* her earlobes!—and bracelets clicked and rattled on her wrists. She looked like a movie star. She *was* a movie star!

"How *are* you, baby?" she breathed. "*Look* at you, oh, honey, you're such a *big* boy! Oh, give your mom another hug." She covered his face with kisses and ran her fingers through his hair.

Brett could hear Grandma washing dishes and humming a hymn in the kitchen. Naturally, she would not be visiting with

Mom. Grandma had nothing good to say about her daughter, and Brett supposed she had nothing good to say *to* her, either.

"How about an ice cream!" Mom exclaimed. "A big one! Two big scoops—*three* if you want—on a sugar cone. Would you like that?"

He nodded and she kissed him again.

"C'mon, let's go. I've got some surprises for you in the car." She kissed Grandpa's forehead and said, "Be back in a while, Pop."

As Brett followed her out of the house, he heard Grandma's voice behind him.

"*Brett!*" she hissed.

When he turned, she hunkered down in front of him, clutched his shoulders with her hands and whispered, "Now, I don't want you eating *any* of that ice cream stuff, do you hear? Jesus doesn't like you to pour all that bad sugar into your body. It's *his* temple." She tossed a glance over his shoulder in the direction Mom had gone and her face darkened with intense bitterness. "And I don't care *what* your *mother* says. You hear me?"

Brett went out the front door behind Mom, and Grandpa's quiet, throaty laughter faded behind him.

———————————

On the way down the hill to St. Helena, Brett trembled with anticipation, unable to stop smiling. He knew his days in Manning were numbered now and he would be going to live with Mom in Los Angeles soon. He would be able to go to movies and watch TV anytime he wanted without fear of being caught or punished or lost forever. There would be no more dreary Sabbaths, no more long church services to endure among all those long church faces, and, best of *all*, no more Grandma!

"The stuff in the back seat's all yours," Mom said breathlessly. She was bouncing in her seat like a little girl.

Brett turned in his seat and retrieved two boxes from the back. He put them in his lap and opened them. One held shirts and pants, the other held a blazer and tie.

"Brand new, all designer, expensive stuff," Mom said. "See that blazer? Roll up the sleeves a little and you'll look just like Don Johnson on *Miami Vice*."

Brett had never seen *Miami Vice*. She knew that. She *had* to remember what living with Grandma was like. Sure, she did. Grandma was her *mother*.

"You'll be the best dressed guy in church, kiddo!" she said with a laugh.

Church? Brett thought.

"There's more back there, keep looking.

He found a bag full of school supplies—paper, pens and binders with pictures of the Hollywood sign on them—and a drinking mug that read on the side, HOORAY FOR HOLLYWOOD!

"Now you're all set for school in the fall," Mom said.

Something was not right.

Brett said, "But I thought I was gonna—"

"Where shall we go for ice cream?" Mom asked quickly.

Brett felt himself sinking into the seat of the rented car as a great deal of his excitement drifted away like a thin mist on a passing breeze.

———————————

"I thought I was gonna come live with you," Brett said over his banana split.

They sat facing each other in a booth at the Big Dipper ice cream parlor in St. Helena.

She said, "Well, honey...we'll see."

"But you said—"

"I know, and I *meant* it, sweetie. It's just that...well, things are a little different now." She stirred her milkshake thoughtfully, frowning. "I met this man. He's a producer, a very *successful* producer, I should add. Four big hits in two years. He's...I've...well, I moved in with him last week. He's got this *incredible* place, you should see it. His name is Jeff, and he wants to use me."

"Use you?"

"Yes. He thinks I'd be good for a lead. Can you imagine that, baby, a *lead*! A starring role! But...well, for now, there's just no way I could take you back with me. Not now. Maybe later, after I've done a couple of pictures for him. But not now."

Brett suddenly lost all interest in the banana split. His stomach ached and his head felt bloated with thoughts of staying in Manning, trapped in Grandma's house, listening to those skin-crawling hymns on the scratchy record player and having to give Grandma more Ben Gay back rubs.

He had to concentrate hard to steady his voice. "But Mom, you said—"

"I know, honey, but I *can't*. Not *now*. But...that's okay, isn't it? I mean, you're doing well here, aren't you? Grandpa says your grades are good, and he says you've made friends with your Sabbath school teacher. That's *wonderful*. I mean, I'm not much of a Bible reader these days, but I suppose it's good for you. I'm glad you're getting a Christian education. The right morals, and all that. It's good for you. C'mon, sweetie, don't look at me like that. You've waited this long. Can't you wait a little longer?"

He put his spoon down and stared at the table.

"Hey, how about a movie tonight?" Mom said, reaching across the table to take his hand. "I'll go back to my hotel and change and we can go to dinner, then catch a movie. Whatever you want to see. Tonight's your night. Can't be out too late, though. I've got an early plane to catch."

She was leaving *tomorrow*.

Without him.

Panic began to rise in his throat. He wanted to cry, to scream, kick something. He tried to make the walls come up and shut it all out, but he could not. No matter how hard he tried, he could not stop feeling things. It was worse than that, though. Feelings seemed to be rising up in him, flooding him. It felt as if all the hurt and anger and bitterness he had been able to hold off over the years by raising those walls suddenly filled him all at once until he felt that he might burst and splatter black ugliness in every direction.

It took every ounce of strength Brett possessed to hold it all in. He swallowed it in big, thick, throat-clogging lumps. After taking a few deep breaths, he tried to see the bright side. They would go to dinner and a movie that night and maybe he could change her mind. At least he got to pick the movie. And he knew exactly which one he wanted to see.

After he showered and changed, Brett went downstairs to wait for Mom to come back from her hotel and get him. He slumped on the sofa.

Grandpa's chair rumbled into the living room and his gravelly voice said, "You don't look too happy, boy."

Brett didn't reply.

Grandpa stopped in front of him and began drumming his fingers on the wheelchair's armrests.

"Your mom's not gonna take you with her, eh?"

Brett shook his head.

"Well. Guess you'll just have to make the best of things here, eh?"

Brett shrugged.

"Not so bad, is it? You got your friend Mr. Moser to keep you company." He winked and added, "Don't worry, boy, your secret's safe with me. You got Gabby, too. And in her own way, I suppose, you got Grandma. She thinks the world of you." With a frown, he muttered, "Hell of a lot more'n she thinks of me." His eyes suddenly snapped open wide and he looked around cautiously as if he might have been overheard. In a moment, his face relaxed and he smiled as if he had suddenly remembered something. "Grocery shopping, that's right," he mumbled. "She's grocery shopping."

Brett sat up straight, surprised. This was the most Grandpa had ever said to him. It was the most Brett had ever heard him say, *period*.

"Course, now, if I had a pair of those," Grandpa said, pointing at Brett's legs, "you and me, we would have a good old time."

Brett chuckled. "Grandma wouldn't let us."

Grandpa's head fell back and his wheelchair squeaked beneath the weight of his laughter. "I suppose not. Fact, I just might be better off *without her* than I would be *with legs*. But..." He waved a hand with resignation. "You going to the movies with your mom tonight?"

Brett nodded. "Have you ever been to the movies, Grandpa?"

"Used to go a lot. Before I met your grandma. I often wish we had a TV in here so I could watch some of them old movies late at night. Don't sleep like I used to. We got enough money

319

saved up to get a good one, you know. Color. Remote control. I look at 'em in the catalogs sometimes. But..." Another wave.

Brett looked at Grandpa for a long moment, seeing a different person in that wheelchair, much different from the silent, empty old man who wheeled around in the dark. He wondered what it would be like to live there with Grandpa, just the two of them. Maybe they would stay up late at night and watch old movies on their TV. Grandpa could tell him about the movies he had seen when he was a boy, about his days in the Big War, and how it felt to be on the battlefield. And they could listen to *real* music instead of those depressing hymns, music like he heard in the movies.

A car rolled to a stop out front and honked.

"There's your mom," Grandpa said. "You better git. And don't worry. Things won't be so bad."

Brett stood and gave Grandpa a long hug so unexpectedly that it surprised them both. Then he rushed out to meet his mother.

———

Over dinner, Mom said, "So what movie would you like to see?"

Brett smiled with anticipation and said, *"Bedside Manners."*

Mom's fork stopped halfway to her mouth and she slowly lowered it to her plate with a frown.

"Well," she said, drawing the word out to a troubled length. "I don't think so, honey."

Brett's smile disappeared and his spirits dropped even further.

"How *come*?"

"It's not such a good movie. *Really*. I mean, it's low budget and, and…well, there's one scene where you can see the boom hanging about two feet into the frame, and—"

"What's a boom?"

"Never mind. It's just a bad movie, that's all."

"I don't care, Mom. I just wanna see *you* in it."

"Look, sweetie, my part is really small and I'm…well, I get…" She sniffed and straightened her posture. "I just don't think you should see it, that's all. It's not a movie for kids."

"I've seen movies that aren't for kids before."

"Not like this one, honey."

Wanna bet? Brett thought.

"But *Mom*, I wanted to see it with *you*!"

"Lower your voice!" she hissed, glancing around the restaurant to see if anyone had heard. "Now that's *it*, okay? There's a lot of sex and violence in the movie and I don't want you to see it. Maybe when you're older. Now that's *it*." She took a bite of food and chewed for a moment, then said, "Hey, how about the new Benji movie, huh? I hear it's pretty good."

Brett clenched his fist around his fork and turned his eyes away from Mom. He knew he could not conceal his anger and disappointment if he looked at her. The walls were not working. They would not come up. His appetite was gone.

Mom continued eating, apparently unaware of how upset he was.

"Are you really gonna leave tomorrow?" he whispered.

"I have to, honey. Good grief, you sound like you'll never see me again."

"For how long?"

"I don't know. Until…well, for a while. It's not so bad, babe." She reached for his hand, but he pulled it away. "Don't do this now, Brett. Please. You've got friends here."

No, I don't, he thought.

"Grandma takes good care of you."

No, she doesn't.

"I know she's a little weird. With her religion, and all. *We* sure don't get along. But that's different. We've *never* gotten along. Grandma loves you. So does Grandpa. You'll be okay."

No, I won't.

"Until you get more movie roles?" he muttered.

"What? Oh, yeah. A couple leads under Jeff and I'll be able to take good care of you."

"A lead? You mean, like a star?"

"Yeah, a starring role. In a good movie. None of this low budget horror crap."

"Is that what you really want? To star in a movie?"

"Honey, that's what I've been *working* for all these years. I want that more than *anything*. Now eat your dinner."

"I'm not hungry."

"Not hu—this is an expensive dinner," she snapped. "Now *eat.*"

He stared at the plate silently for a while.

"I have to go to the bathroom," he lied.

"Okay. But when you come back, you'll eat, right?"

He nodded, then left the table and crossed the restaurant. As he rounded the tables and chairs, he thought of a scene from one of the movies he had watched at Mr. Moser's. *Prime Cut.* Lee Marvin played a gangster who was sent to Kansas City to find and punish Gene Hackman. Not only had Hackman broken a few promises to old friends and business partners and cheated them out of a lot of money, but he had killed some of them—he even had one ground up into hot dogs at his meat packing plant. When Marvin was through with him, Hackman ended up full of bullets and fed to some pigs.

Brett had liked the movie. A lot. It had given him a deep feeling of satisfaction.

Some people simply deserved to be punished.

On the other hand, some deserved to be rewarded, like Luke, the Princess, Han, and Chewbacca at the end of *Star Wars*.

Brett thought about rewards and punishments as he walked toward the RESTROOMS sign in the back and passed by the men's room. He went to a bank of payphones and fished in his pocket for some change.

———————————

Mom tapped her fingernails on the steering wheel as she drove out of St. Helena.

"You're just upset with me, that's all," she said stiffly. "I wanted us to have a nice evening together, but..." She shook her head and sighed.

Brett gazed straight ahead, barely hearing her. His mind was intentionally blank, his body relaxed. Somehow, he had managed to get the walls working again.

"I'm just tired," he said quietly.

"Then why don't you let me take you home instead of to your friend's house?"

"I have to pick up something I left there. Then I'll go home."

She sighed again. "I came a long way to see you, you know. And my friend *paid* for it. What's he going to think when I tell him you didn't even want to be *with* me?"

He pressed his lips together over the sharp reply that came to mind.

Brett watched the road ahead for several minutes, then said, "Turn here, by the mailbox."

When the car started down the bumpy dirt road, Mom said, "Jesus, this is a rented car, you know!"

Lighted windows at the end of the road drew nearer.

"Is this the house?"

Brett nodded.

She stopped in the drive and Brett said, "Come in. He'd like to meet you."

Mom sighed but turned off the engine and got out, following him to the door.

"Aren't you going to *knock*?" she asked when Brett walked into the house.

"He doesn't mind." He let her in and closed the door. "He said he was —" He swallowed a dry knot in his throat. "— was going to do some laundry tonight. He's probably in the laundry room."

Brett led her to the end of the hall, opened the door—he would not allow his hands to tremble—and stepped aside so she could go ahead.

The light beyond the door was so dim that the room seemed bathed in gray, like a black-and-white movie. As soon as Mom stepped down into the room, her heels clicking on the dirty concrete floor, Brett swung the door shut. It slammed with the sound of a gunshot.

"Brett!" she shouted on the other side. "What the hell are you—"

She stopped. There was a scuffle. Then Mom screamed.

Brett stared at the door for a moment, listening to the screaming and the awful, thick hacking noises, the retching and coughing. Then he began to back away, trying to shut the sounds from his ears, realizing that Mom was not the only one screaming.

In the living room, he turned and crossed to the front door. Mom stopped screaming, but Mr. Moser continued. His cries of, "I'm sorry! I'm so sorry! God, I'm sorry, so sorry!" died in the wet sounds of vomiting.

Brett went outside and stood on the porch, thinking of nothing.

———————

It could have been a minute or an hour later when Mr. Moser came out of the house and into the dim yellow glow of the porch light; Brett was not sure.

Mr. Moser held his hands out before him, palms up, fingers clawed, staring at them as if they were not his own. Blood speckled his twisted face and his sleeveless arms were black with it to his elbows. He gulped sobs and his eyes sparkled with tears.

"Dear Jesus," he breathed over and over, "dear Jesus…"

"Did you get it?" Brett asked. "On videotape?"

"I…if I'd known earlier…it was such short notice and I-I-I…I was so upset, so scared…I didn't have time to —"

"You didn't *get* it?" Brett snapped, anger flaring in his head for a moment.

"I-I couldn't, I was too, too—why, Brett? Why did you make me *do* this? *Why*?"

"I thought you enjoyed it," Brett replied flatly, still preoccupied with the fact that his mother's starring role had not been videotaped.

"Not…not like this. What I do…it's different, for different reasons, it's…it's…you wouldn't understand."

"Well, I think it's time you left behind the kid stuff, Mr. Moser." Brett turned and stared silently at his mom's rented car.

Mr. Moser paced behind him, muttering, "Oh, God, oh Jesus God." He stopped abruptly and snapped in a hoarse, pained voice, "And what am I gonna do about the *car*, huh?"

"It's rented."

"*Rented*? Oh, God, that's just…that's…*rented*!"

Brett stepped off the porch.

"If I get caught," Mr. Moser shouted, "you're in just as much trouble as I am, you know! You helped. You're an *accomplice*. Worse than that, you set *up* this whole thing, it was *your* idea."

Brett turned to him and, genuinely worried for a moment, said, "You think anybody'd believe that? I mean, I'm just a *kid*, and...and you killed those boys. I've got the tape." He thought about it for a while, then shook his head, feeling better. "No. I don't think so, Mr. Moser. I really don't." He started across the drive toward the dirt road. "I think I'm gonna walk home. They don't expect me for a while, so I've got time."

"What will you tell them?"

"I don't know. I'll think of something."

"But...what if they notice she doesn't bring you home?"

Grandma. Brett thought of Grandma's stern gaze and the stinging smell of those messy Ben Gay back rubs. He turned to Mr. Moser again and said, "Get rid of the car by tomorrow afternoon. I want to go into San Francisco."

"What? *Why*?"

"There's a movie I want to see. *Bedside Manners*." Then, to himself, Brett muttered, "*You* saw her die. Now I need to."

But Grandma...she was still around to make Brett's life miserable. And Grandpa's.

Mr. Moser bellowed, "Are you out of your—"

"And keep that video camera loaded and ready. In a couple of days, I'm gonna bring my grandma over."

Brett watched as Mr. Moser slowly turned his back, then began to kick the side of his house, pulling his hair and screaming like a toddler throwing a tantrum.

Mr. Moser's screams faded as Brett started down the road, looking forward to getting to know Grandpa.

Punishments

I arrived in Manning the day after I read of Jayne's death in the paper. It was front-page news across the country, the kind of story the press wrings dry.

TEENAGER KILLS CHURCH ORGANIST
IN BIZARRE SEX SLAYING

I wouldn't have read it if I hadn't seen Jayne's picture, her big tortoiseshell glasses perched on her small nose, dull brown hair gathered in the back, her usually timid, fleeting smile opening brightly for the camera. It was a recent picture and she'd changed little in the last ten years.

I immediately arranged to take a day off work, saw that my pet, Clarissa, had plenty of food and water, and left Los Angeles for Manning.

I was raised in Manning, a small Seventh-day Adventist village in the Napa Valley. My parents still lived there, but when I arrived, I went straight to the boy's house. It was easy enough to find; reporters were gathered on the sidewalk waiting for a glimpse of the killer's family. I parked my rented car across the street and stared at the house, wondering what the boy was like, how he'd met her. And if she'd done to him what she'd done to me.

When I was sixteen, I thought of Jayne Potter only as the woman who, each week, placed a square brown cushion on the church organ bench, sat down and played for services. I didn't find her attractive, but at the same time, she was not unattractive. She was simply…there. She had fair skin, dressed plainly, and always wore her hair in a bun or braided. She didn't wear makeup, but because that was against Seventh-day Adventist rules, neither did any of the girls at the Adventist prep school I attended. *They*, however, were the stars of my fantasies; although restricted by dress codes, they somehow managed to dress in ways that accentuated their curves and angles to the fullest. Repression is the mother of stealth.

Miss Potter attended every church function and gave more than her share of time to its causes. At a bake sale or potluck, she was impossible to distract, so great was her concentration on her duties. She seemed driven, as if she *had* to participate in church activities, as if she were repaying an important debt. But in spite of her sizeable contributions to the church, the congregation seemed to ignore her; sometimes I even thought they were *shunning* her. Most people that participated in church activities with any enthusiasm were quite popular socially. Not Miss Potter. She smiled and nodded a lot but spoke little and seldom if ever was spoken to by others.

It wasn't until she came down with a summer cold and my mother sent me to her place with some homemade vegetable soup that our relationship began. I drove there in my mom's car. Miss Potter lived on the north side of town in a mobile home nestled by itself at the foot of a shady hill.

It was a hot summer day, but she came to the door wearing a heavy white terrycloth robe. I didn't expect to be invited in, but she did so immediately. Once inside, with the glare of the sunlight out of my eyes, I could see that she wasn't wearing her glasses and her hair was down, full and wavy on her shoulders and back, and I discovered something. It wasn't an instant discovery; it took a little while to sink in and wasn't fully absorbed until after I'd left her. I discovered that Miss Potter was beautiful.

She didn't seem sick. Her eyes were puffy, but that might have been from crying. I would later realize that she had been. I lost count of the times I found her crying when I came over for my visits. In fact, I lost count of the visits.

Inside, her trailer was dimly lighted; only one small lamp was on by the sofa, but its dark gray shade shed little light. It was sparsely furnished and the walls were bare except for the most hideous portrait of the crucifixion I've ever seen; blood, dark and viscous, poured from Christ's head, hands and feet, and from the gaping hole in his side. His face was a long, cadaverous nightmare.

She thanked me for the soup, took it to the kitchen, then sat on the sofa with a smile, gracefully folding her legs beneath the robe. She patted the cushion beside her and I sat, but there was nothing graceful about *my* movements. I was a clumsy and shy teenager, particularly in the presence of females. Especially females wearing robes. Miss Potter managed to put me at ease, though; we made small talk about school and the upcoming church picnic. As she spoke, she frequently patted my shoulder, hand, and knee—innocuous conversational gestures, but which I had never noticed from her before. She was not the same Miss Potter I knew from church.

After insisting I call her Jayne, she discovered my interest in reptiles and softly said, "Ah, then, I have a book you'll enjoy." She scooted forward and leaned across my lap toward a small bookcase against the wall.

My heart quivered like Jell-O. A shadowed valley plunged between the lapels of her robe and flesh shifted slightly; her skin was white as summer clouds and a faint green-blue vein meandered over the curve of her left breast, disappearing in the shadows. I wanted so badly to follow that vein down into her robe that my fingers actually twitched to reach out and pull the lapel aside. I blushed furiously and stood when she moved, preparing to leave.

At the door, she gave me the book, gently touched a cool hand to the back of my neck and said, "This will give you an excuse to come back and see me." As I stepped out, something brushed my behind; it could have been a shifting wrinkle in my pants or the corner of the end table by the door...or her fingers.

Of course, it *was* her fingers, but I couldn't bring myself to believe it then. I did, however, masturbate my way through variations of that fantasy for the next few nights in the secrecy of my bedroom. Masturbation is, of course, another no-no among Adventists, but I've often attributed any stability I may now possess to my refusal to stop masturbating even after my biology teacher told the class it could cause a nervous breakdown, insanity, and eventual death.

I wanted to talk about this fantasy, as boys do, with my best and, really, my *only* friend, Gary Sigman, but Gary wasn't saying much to anyone that summer. The previous fall, his parents had divorced. Both were teachers at the Adventist grammar school in Manning and had lost their jobs due to the divorce. (The church cannot prevent divorces, but it does punish those involved for allowing their marriages to fail.) Gary became pale and withdrawn. Everyone attributed his subsequent sullenness and weight loss to the upset of the divorce. Everyone but me. I knew something *else* had happened to Gary. He looked older and didn't laugh much anymore. But it was out of my reach, so I decided to let him make the first move to open up. If he had, we might have spent those summer evenings on my back porch whispering about Miss Potter. But he didn't. And we didn't.

When I returned the book three days later, Jayne met me at the door wearing that same robe. I thought that was odd; it was mid-afternoon and surely she was no longer ill. She greeted me pleasantly and led me to the sofa where she presented me with another book. It was huge and full of color photographs of rare and exotic reptiles.

"I don't want to let it out of the house," she said, sitting close to me and opening the book on our laps, "but you're welcome to look at it here if you want. Anytime."

As we paged through the book, her leg rubbed against mine and beneath the book, my crotch began to bulge. I realized I had imagined nothing three days before but didn't know what to do. Dry-mouthed and trembling, I stared blindly at the book, aware only of the burning friction between her leg and mine. When she unexpectedly pulled the book away, I found myself staring down at my erection. Jayne was staring at it, too. Smirking. She slowly reached over and placed her hand on it. Squeezed it slightly, then a little harder. My lungs convulsively sucked in a breath.

"Do you like hot fudge sundaes, Paul?" she whispered. Then she stood and left the room to clatter around in the kitchen a moment. "I do. Would you like one?"

I shook my head.

She returned with a bowl of ice cream, chocolate syrup, nuts and a cherry and said, "*I* would." Placing the bowl on the coffee table, she knelt before me and began to undo my belt.

I was paralyzed. I imagined my mother's horror should she walk in and find us. I remembered Pastor Helmond's recent sermon in which he declared, "Sex is a sweet-tasting poison that will surely *kill your soul!*" I remembered my Bible teacher at school telling the class, "Sex is such a dangerous, unhealthy diversion that, when faced with sexual desires, even married couples should take a cold shower or run around the block instead of giving in to the desire to have intercourse. Unless, of course, it's done for the purpose of reproduction." Long before I even knew what it was, I was told sex was a moral crime, the most treacherous curve on the road to heaven. But when Jayne took me in her hand, I lost all fear of the lake of fire that I had so long been warned about. Placing the bowl on the floor between my legs, she turned off the lamp, spooned ice cream and chocolate syrup onto my cock, sprinkled nuts over it, placed the cherry on the head and hungrily devoured her sundae.

Her sofa converted into a bed, which we put to great use that afternoon. I was clumsy at first, but soon lost my self-consciousness as she covered my body with nibbles and kisses and touched me in ways that were startlingly new. I wanted to see her, touch her, taste her, but when I tugged at her robe, she refused to remove it. I rolled on top of her, but she pushed me away and gasped, "No, no, like *this*," and rolled onto her knees and elbows. I knelt behind her, she guided me in and immediately began to groan. It wasn't a sound of pleasure, it was a *groan*, and I feared I was hurting her somehow. When I started to pull out, she snapped, "No, do it! *Hard!*"

My thrusts were uncertain at first, but I soon lost myself in waves of new sensations. The robe's hem gathered between us, but when I tried to slide it up so I could stroke her back, she quickly pulled it back down and began uttering garbled words between her gasps.

I leaned forward and whispered, "What? What'd you say?" but she spoke into the pillow after that. It would be weeks before those words became clear to me.

I went home on weak knees and said little to my parents on the way to my room. I remained in a stunned silence until the following afternoon when, at her request, I returned to Jayne's trailer like a somnambulist returning to his bed. Once again, she was wearing that robe; once again, she seated me on the sofa. There she stripped me and licked every inch of my body except my cock until I put her hand on it myself and breathed, "Please...please..." She opened the bed and, as before, left her robe on and cried out as we writhed together, her sobbed words buried in the pillow.

There was only silence afterward. Although we exchanged small talk before, we never spoke after. We *never* spoke of what we had just done. As we lay side by side that second time, I tried to stroke her hair, her neck, but she pulled away and curled into a trembling ball. Finally, she whispered hoarsely, "Come back at three tomorrow."

Her strange behavior was lost on me at first because I was too overwhelmed by the fact that I was HAVING SEX. On top of that, it was with an OLDER WOMAN. And I suppose I got a great charge from the fact that my lover was timid Miss Potter, the mousy church organist so ignored by everyone. It was a secret that made me feel somehow superior to everyone around because I knew it and they didn't.

Church became a new experience altogether. Each time I saw Jayne mount that organ bench after carefully putting the cushion in place, I immediately grew hard—right there with Mom and Dad in our usual pew. I covered my erection with my leather-bound monogrammed Revised Standard Version Bible. I watched her throughout the sermon; sometimes her hips squirmed on that cushion, and I wondered if she was thinking of me.

She wasn't.

In the middle of our third week together, Jayne went into the kitchen to make lemonade when I arrived. I spotted her cushion on a chair against the wall and, knowing that her firm, round ass squirmed on that cushion during church services each week, I couldn't resist sitting on it myself. I gulped the cry of pain that came from my mouth as I bounded off the chair. What felt like hundreds of tiny needles had punctured my ass. It was made of heavy brown corduroy and was flat and hard on the bottom. But it was not cushiony.

I carefully touched it, picked it up and examined it. The cushion was stuffed with tacks.

When I heard her coming, I dropped the cushion, spun around and tried to return her smile. She leaned forward to put the tray of lemonade on the coffee table and I stared at her ass, thinking of how she always kept it covered when we fucked, realizing that perhaps it wasn't as smooth and touchable as I'd thought.

For a while, my thoughts were on that cushion and the questions it raised. But as we began to fuck—and that's what we did; I preferred to think at the time, in a naive first-love way, that we were MAKING LOVE, but that simply wasn't the case—she started calling out again and I listened carefully to her words.

"I'm sorry...punish me...I'm so sorry I made you hard...puh-punish me, Daddy, *punish* me!"

I stopped when the words registered, but she reached back and clutched my thigh, dug her nails in, and cried, *"Don't stop!"*

I think she tried to hide her words after that, but I knew what she was saying. I know now—and probably knew then, to some extent, although I didn't admit it to myself—that I should have seen that something was very wrong with quiet, timid Miss Potter and I should have stopped seeing her immediately. But she was my first lover and my first addiction. I never allowed myself to consider ending our relationship; I knew I couldn't. But her cries for punishment—from her *father*!—stayed with me and echoed in my dreams.

Jayne told me to return on Sunday, three days later. It was our longest separation yet and made me see just how attached I had become to our visits. To her.

I fidgeted a lot as I watched her in church that Saturday. After the service, there was a potluck lunch and I went to the car to help Mom carry in the food she'd brought. I asked her what she knew about Miss Potter, but she obviously didn't want to talk about her, so I dropped it. After lunch, as Dad and I were bringing the freshly washed dishes back to the car, he said, "Your mother said you asked about Miss Potter. How come? You hear something?"

I got more nervous than usual. "No," I said. "I just wondered…well, she's so involved in the church but has no friends, no family. Just wondered, that's all."

"Well, I'll tell you. Get in." We got in the front seat and he chewed on a toothpick as he spoke, moving it from side to side with his tongue. "Miss Potter's a good woman. She's devoted to the church but gets no thanks for it. Your mom doesn't like talking about her because…well, she just doesn't think it's right. There's a lot of people in this church could take a lesson from your mom. Anyway, when Miss Potter was a little girl, her father, Hudson Potter, was pastor of this church. One night when she was nine or ten, Jayne left her house, walked to the police station and said her daddy was…molesting her. Sexually." He cocked a brow. "Know what I mean?"

I nodded, feeling a chill coming on.

"There was a big scandal. Pastor Potter was suspended for nearly a year. Stopped coming to church and just stayed in their little house by the grammar school. Nothing was done, really. It was all hushed up. One Sabbath about eighteen months later,

Jayne asked to speak before the congregation. Said she'd made it all up after having an argument with her daddy. The evil had taken hold of her, but now the Holy Spirit was moving her to make amends. Everyone nodded and clicked their tongues like they'd suspected as much all along and offered to return Potter to the pulpit. But by then he'd become a recluse. Most said his daughter had broken him. Ruined him with her cruel lies. He died at home about a year later. Jayne's never been forgiven, even though most of the people here don't even know what happened."

"Do … do you think she was telling the truth?"

He chewed on the toothpick a moment. "That's between her and God, son."

It was another warning I should have heeded but didn't. Five deadly words occurred to me after hearing Dad's story: *Maybe I can help her.*

After sex the next day, when Jayne once again refused to let me touch her, I said, "But I want to. You…you do things to me that feel so *good*, but…you won't let me touch you. I want to make you feel good, too."

"That's what you want?" she whispered, smiling.

"Yes."

"You'll do anything I want?"

I smiled. "Of *course.*"

God, I was such a babe in the woods.

"Then come back on Tuesday at three and you can."

My next warning came Tuesday morning when I went grocery shopping for Mom. As I left the store hugging two brown bags, I saw Gary leaning against the car. He looked horribly pale and thin in the bright sunlight. Before I could greet him, Gary said, "I saw you leaving her place, Paul. Twice."

"What're you—"

"*You* know. Stay away from her. She's sick." He stared at me silently for a long moment, whispered, "She'll make you do bad things," then hurried away, leaving me with my groceries.

It bothered me, yes. I gave it careful thought, yes. But did I do what he said?

No.

Jayne had the bed open when I arrived and immediately began to undress me, whispering, "You promised...anything I ask...anything that will make me feel good." She had me lie on my back, reached under the bed for something, then put it on the bed beside me. Hiking the robe up only slightly, she turned her back to me, straddled me, and sighed as I entered. She moved on me slowly for a moment, then pointed to the object on the bed, rasping, "Take that."

I did. It was a three-foot-long whip with three strips of braided leather sprouting from the handle, each knotted at the end.

"Now, *whip me!*" she hissed.

When I stuttered for a moment, she repeated the order firmly. My first strike was weak and uncertain, and she cried, "Harder!" I brought the whip down again—"*Harder!*"—and again—"*Har*-derrr!"— until it was smacking loudly against the taut terrycloth on her back. "Yes!" she cried, bucking furiously on me. "Punish me! I'm sorry I made you hard, Daddy, sorry I told, sorry, sorry, sorry*sorrySORRY*! *Punish* me!" Her laughter was breathy and high, void of humor but so full of *joy*. I think that's what did it to me, what shattered my initial fear of and disdain for the act: her joy. She loved it.

We were both out of breath afterward and neither of us spoke. As she lay panting on the bed, moaning with each exhalation, I slowly dressed, then left.

At home, I went to my bed in a daze, thinking of everything—my household chores, a phone call I had to make, maybe driving down to Napa tomorrow—except what I had just done.

My visits to Jayne's trailer became a blur after that. The whip always awaited me on the bed. She never removed her robe. We fucked in various positions, and with each blow of the whip she cried out with delight. After a while, so did I. Although I never admitted it to myself then, I came to enjoy those whippings. Part of it was the pleasure she derived from her pain. But there was something else, something I couldn't have identified back then if I'd tried or wanted to, something within me that remained hidden and dormant until I took the whip in my hand. Then it crawled from its lair, suddenly in command, and swelled with pleasure with each strike. While most of those visits are hazy memories, even after only ten years, I vividly remember the day she finally took me to her bedroom.

It was a small trailer, so I assumed she slept on the sofa bed. Not so. Jayne had simply been preparing me for her bedroom.

In the living room, she opened my pants, knelt down and began licking my cock. "This is our secret," she whispered, attacking my erection voraciously with lips, tongue and hands. "I'm sharing it with you because you're...so...good to me." She brought me to the edge quickly and when she saw how I was trembling, she mumbled, "Come. Come on my face." I did and she laughed, rubbing my semen over her face and neck. She stood and kissed me tenderly. I was startled by the realization that it was our first kiss. Staring intensely into my eyes, she breathed, "I...*know*...you'll be so...*good*...to me." Then she led me to the back of the trailer.

Just as a church is a house of God, Jayne's little bedroom was a house of pain. The window was blackened and dim light bled through the red shade of the room's single tiny lamp. It was a garden of chains and straps and pulleys all tediously connected and threaded through eyelets in the walls and ceiling. There in the dark, it made no sense visually. One wall was covered with whips of various lengths and designs. Paddles and manacles and small insect-like clamps hung from hooks. Mounted above them was a long, barbed, harpoon-like object. I wanted to be horrified by it all, and perhaps I pretended to be at first. But as that creature inside me began to awaken, teasingly flicking its black tongue, I shivered with anticipation.

Then I saw the oddest, most incongruous thing of all hanging on the wall just above the head of the bed: A large framed photograph of a man with thick black-and-silver hair, narrow glistening eyes that seemed to bore into my head, and a craggy face as cold as steel. Pastor Hudson Potter, I was certain.

As I began to undress, Jayne dropped her robe and quickly turned off the light. But in that instant, I saw the scars and calluses on her body. All *over* her body.

She lit a candle and took some of the accoutrements from the wall: a short whip, manacles, clamps, spherical weights on thin chains...and that barbed rod. She attached the clamps to her labia, then the weights to the clamps, groaning through clenched teeth. The tender flesh of her pussy hung impossibly low, like the flabby, sinking skin of a very old woman. Climbing onto the bed, she put the manacles on her wrists and ankles and had me attach them to the chains hanging from the ceiling. At her request, I turned the crank on the wall and she slowly rose a few feet above the bed, weights dangling from her rubbery labia. I was trembling as I flipped the latch that locked the crank.

"Now," she whispered, "whip me. Punish me."

I started slowly, like the first time, whipping her legs and sides as I knelt on the bed.

"No, *no*! My cunt! Whip my filthy, sinful, evil *cunt*!"

"Juh-Jayne, I can't—"

"*Do it!*"

I did.

She writhed and laughed and cried obscene apologies, her head hanging back so she could look at her father's icy face. The weights bobbed and she began to bleed as the teeth of the clamps bit into her flesh.

That was when I began to laugh and whip her harder. My cock was rigid and I began to stroke it with my free hand, breathing faster.

"Now, Paul, *now*! Put it in me!"

I stopped, confused. "What—"

"The *rod*!" she growled. "Stick it in me. All the way in. *Fuck me* with it. Punish me."

I hesitantly lifted the pointed rod from the bed. Barbs curved like small evil grins. Something happened to me then. A clean bright light inside me went out and a ragged hot flame spat up in its place. I think I smiled as I slid the rod into Jayne.

"Fuck me with it Daddy Daddy I'm sorry fuck me—"

A bit deeper.

"—Daddy sorry I told sorry I made you hard sorry Daddy punish me *fuck meee*!"

Until the first barb was touching her vagina. I think it was the blood that stopped me. One of the weights plopped onto the bed taking a piece of flesh with it and I caught some blood on my face. I realized what I was about to do and gasped, pulled out the rod, dropped it and ran to the bathroom to vomit. It wasn't because I was horrified or disgusted by what I was doing, but because I suddenly knew how badly I wanted to do it.

Jayne screamed obscenities at me as I lowered her to the bed, unhooked the manacles, then dressed. As I left her for the last time, I heard her crying, "I'm sorry, Daddy, so sorry. I need to be punished. Punished."

Gary Sigman committed suicide two years later. Had Jayne done that long before, things would have been very different for us all, especially for the boy who finally did what she wanted. But suicide, of course, is an unpardonable sin.

Despite my parents' disapproval, I drifted away from the church. Instead of attending an Adventist college, as they wanted, I went to UCLA. There I met Roz, a beautiful business major. One night while we were making love, I began to pound the mattress with my fist, lost in passion. When I finally heard her screams, I realized it wasn't the mattress I was pounding. I expected her to press charges, but she didn't. I paid her dental bill and never saw her again.

I tried prostitutes for a while, but they weren't safe. One night I left a motel room in Hollywood and met the girl's pimp in the parking lot. When he saw the blood on my hand and shirt, he beat me senseless. When he hurried in to check on his girl, I limped to my car and left, certain he would kill me if I didn't.

I remained parked before the boy's house in Manning for two hours, watching the reporters surrounding the front yard.

I considered visiting my parents, but they would want me to stay a while and I couldn't. I had to get back to my pet, Clarissa. Sometimes, if left alone too long, she stops eating, just out of spite. Sometimes I have to force feed her.

I found her on Sunset Boulevard. In the right light, she even looks a bit like Jayne. She's about seventeen or so and says she has no family. I keep her in a box in the spare bedroom.

I finally started the car, drove away from the house, and left Manning.

About the Author

Ray Garton has been writing novels, novellas, short stories, and essays for more than 30 years. His work spans the genres of horror, crime, suspense, and even comedy. *Live Girls* was nominated for the Bram Stoker Award in 1988, and Garton received the Grand Master of Horror Award at the 2006 World Horror Convention. He lives in northern California with his wife Dawn, where he is at work on a new novel.

BIBLIOGRAPHY

NOVELS AND NOVELLAS
411
Bestial
Biofire
Crawlers
Crucifax
Dark Channel

Darklings
Live Girls
Lot Lizards
Loveless
Night Life
Meds
Murder Was My Alibi
Ravenous
Scissors
Seductions
Serpent Girl
Sex and Violence in Hollywood
Shackled
The Folks
The Folks 2
The Loveliest Dead
The Man in the Palace Theater
The New Neighbor
Trade Secrets
Trailer Park Noir
Vortex
Zombie Love

COLLECTIONS
Methods of Madness
'Nids And Other Stories
Pieces of Hate
Slivers of Bone
The Disappeared and Other Stories
The Girl in the Basement and Other Stories
Wailing and Gnashing of Teeth

Curious about other Crossroad Press books? Stop by our website: http://crossroadpress.com
We offer quality writing
in digital, audio, and print formats.

Subscribe to our newsletter on the website homepage and receive a free eBook.

www.ingramcontent.com/pod-product-compliance
Lightning Source LLC
Chambersburg PA
CBHW021439240626
47153CB00001B/213